A THOUSAND AUTUMNS

PART OF THE DE OPPRESSO LIBER SERIES

BY
C.C. SOUTHERLAND JR.

Books by C. Southerland

De Oppresso Liber
A Thousand Autumns

ISBN: 1-4392-3651-8
ISBN-13: 9781439236512

Visit www.booksurge.com to order additional copies.

Table of Contents: A THOUSAND AUTUMNS

Dedication:

Special thanks to those individuals who have encouraged and supported me in the 30 year process of bringing this book to print. To beloved wife, Suzanne Southerland, for her tireless encouragement over the many long years spent writing these novels. To Retired Special Forces officer Major LaBarge, for reading, reviewing and believing in this book, and for being the first to actually order a hard copy. To Colonel Bud Dent, for reminding me that Claymores "bark". To English Teacher Nancy Fowler, who picked on my grammer until I just about got it right. To FBI Special Agent Joe Frechette for appreciating a good gun fight, and to FBI Special Agent-Bishop Mike McPheeters, who let me rappel through life with him. To Mr. Roger Cox, for flying a high profile in my life and for teaching me to fly in more ways than one. To Dr. Chet Evans, Dr. Mark Feldman and Dr. Terrance Barry all of whom, somehow, believed in this project from the start. To Dr. Charles Rivera, who shared with me his Montagnard past while fighting his own fatal battle with cancer. To Doctor Caroline Smith for sending me her dogtags. To all those people over the years, whose names I can hardly remember, but whose images are stamped in my heart, for their encouragement and boundless enthusiasm, I dedicate this book.

COMBAT MEDICAL BADGE: Awarded to members of the Army Medical Department, Naval Medical Department, Air Force Medical Service or Special Forces Medical Sergeant who are in the grade of Colonel or below while assigned or attached to a medical unit of company or smaller size organic to an infantry/special forces unit during any period the unit was engaged in active ground combat subsequent to 6 December 1941. Only one award is authorized for service in Vietnam, Laos, the Dominican Republic, Korea (subsequent to 4 January 1969), El Salvador, Grenada, Panama, Southwest Asia and Somalia... Specific eligibility requirements by geographic area are listed in Army Regulation 600-8-22.

(Taken from "Army StudyGuide.com")

From the dedicatory monument located in Arlington National cemetery respecting those lost during the "Secret War in Laos, 1961-1973"

In Memory of Legions Lost and the Soldiers of the Secret War in Laos.

We stand in tribute of forgotten men...for their sacrifice, courage valor and honor. We honor them by this living memorial...starkly beautiful in its simplicity, for it stands defiantly alone, as did those soldiers in their seasons of death. It will serve as a poignant reminder of our battlefield allies, and is a tribute long overdue to proud Human endeavor... courage and valor in a long war lost in the unfulfilled hopes for Southeast Asia.

As the fallen leaves of Autumn
in unregimented ranks,
Countless unremembered soldiers
rest...eternally.
Let us now praise forgotten men...
and some there be,
Which have no memorial;
Who have perished, as though
They had never been.
But they served, they died;
for cause and by happenstance...
Expended in the hopes for Southeast Asia,
and will forever be remembered,
Mourned for their sacrifice.
If by weeping I could change
the course of events,
My tears would pour down ceaselessly
for a thousand Autumns.

Preface

What if?

"Of all sad words by tongue or pen, the saddest are these, it might have been...(John Greenleaf Whittier)" A great many historical novelists of the late 20th century have entertained readers with "what if" notions. What if this decision had been made instead of that one to affect the course of human events? In looking back on the Vietnam era, it seems that most of the "what ifs?" have focused on... "What if we had not reacted the way we did in the Gulf of Tonkin," or "What if we had withdrawn from Vietnam when it became clear that electoral and democratic process were being trampled by dictatorships...?" History is left to detail the true events of that time, for better or worse.

Among those who served in Special Forces during the Vietnam era, it has been my observation that when most are posed with the question "what if", the answers almost always have something to do with Montagnards. Montagnard is a French word, which is most literally interpreted in English, *"Highlander"*. Montagnards were the aboriginal highlanders of Central Southeast Asia. Although they were officially considered to be Vietnamese citizens by the US government, neither the Vietnamese, nor the Montagnards themselves accepted the affiliation. Neither their cultural nor their geographic boundaries coincided with "Lowlander" Vietnamese ethic. During the Arab-Israeli War of 1967, America watched the little nation of Israel carve out for herself a significant piece of geography from neighboring giants Egypt, Syria and

Jordan. Among those who could view this happenstance from a world perspective, there were some who pondered over Southeast Asia and posed the question "What if?" What if the fiercely independent, faultlessly loyal Montagnard people could carve out their own homeland from the midst of raging dowagers locked in that bloodletting struggle between North and South Vietnam? How might it survive as an independent, newborn nation? What would it look like? Certainly, it would have occupied most of II Corps and perhaps a big piece of I Corps as well. But, in examining the core convictions of the Montagnard People, their lands were indeed the highlands and much of those highlands were in Southern Laos. So, it is not proper to gauge our musings in terms of Vietnamese boundaries. By the early 70's, there were in fact a number of U.S. military think tanks that had considered the idea, some even seriously. "What if a dedicated effort had been made by US policymakers to secure an independent homeland for the Montagnard People? What if?"

*"It is not the critic who counts, not the one who points out how the strong man stumbled or where the doer of deeds could have done them better. The credit belongs to the man who is actually in the arena; whose faith is marred by dust and sweat and blood; who strives valiantly; who errs and comes short again and again; who knows the great enthusiasms, the great devotions, and spends himself in a worthy cause; who, at the best, knows the triumph of high achievement; and who, at the worst, if he fails, at least fails while **daring greatly**, so that his place will never be with those cold and timid souls who know neither victory nor defeat."*

President Theodore Roosevelt

Prologue:

In the Spring of 1971, the United States Army, acting on recommendations from a highly classified, distinguished advisory panel, inserted one, single Special Forces A Team, designated Team A-321, into a very remote area of Southern Laos. This campaign was initieated during the throes of a graduated withdrawal from Vietnam by conventional ground units, pursuant to reluctant directives from the Nixon administration and on the heels of a defeatist bill, enacted into law by the United States Congress on January 5, 1971. It was titled the "Cooper Church Amendment". This amendement was of particular historical significance because it was the first time in history, that a United States Congress had restricted deployment of troops during a war against the wishes of a popularly elected President (although similar bills had been attempted in virtually every prior war engaged by the United States). As the Nixon administration predicted, this amendment had the profound effect of harming U.S. military efforts in Southeast Asia and essentially rendered United States negotiators impotent at subsequent Paris peace talks.

Although the U.S. military was in essence "winning" in Southeast Asia, as evidenced by victories in the Tet Offensive and in every other major engagement of the conflict, the United States was faced with an extraordinary conundrum in that the very political structure, which determined to commit our military to much sacrifice and bloodshed, decided to betray the original designs of U.S. involvement in Vietnam. This occurred not so much because of military prowess on the part of the enemy; rather from conflicts within the U.S., although some will argue, this was motivated by a persistent Viet Cong enemy. However, in the end, it was not the unconventional Viet Cong who conquered, rather, conventional enemy ground forces, which in absolute violation of avowed treaty agreements, stormed in to Saigon in 1975 and commenced a systematic program of genocide and retaliatory extermination. If one includes all the innocent dead of Cambodia, Laos and Vietnam following the U.S. retreat, total killed rivaled in atrocity, the numbers of innocent Jews exterminated by Hitler during World War II. Although we know the deaths of innocent people in Southeast Asia reached well up into the millions, we cannot be entirely certain of the magnitude of this tragedy because, unlike post World War II Germany, journalistic opinion mongers of Western media were not permitted direct access to the killing fields which they had themselves, in large measure, facilitated.

Of many errors history ascribed to U.S. strategy during the Vietnam era, clearly, failure to take into account the nature of unconventional warfare stands out as a major contributor. Of the 4 geographic sectors or "Corps" into which U.S. strategists divided Vietnam, the first and perhaps only Corp to ever be completely "pacified" was II Corp, largely composing the Central Highlands. Most of the combat engagements in this section of Vietnam were carried out by Special Forces operatives, who successfully trained and worked with aboriginal highlanders or "Montagnard" cultures of the Central Highlands. These gallant, courageous people struggled, not only against a cruel, determined Communist presence on their borders, but a relentless, age old prejudice from all Ethnic Vietnamese, both Northern and Southern. Rear echelon U.S. policy makers found it convenient to lump the Montagnards into a leaky bucket of all Vietnamese citizens, though neither Ethnic Vietnamese nor Montagnards considered themselves to be part of the same nation.

After nearly 10 years of advisorship in Southeast Asia, there developed a strong advocacy for the Montagnards in U.S. military circles. Anticipating a disastrous outcome upon retirement of the United States from South Vietnam, concerned military strategists attempted to offer some form of resolution for the Montagnards. One solution was to propose an independent Montargnard nation or province within boundaries of Vietnam and Laos in which Montagnards and their near cousins, Meo-Hmong tribesmen, lived. Accordingly, a very select group of U.S. advisors were sought out to serve as a nidus for this ambition. They initiated a project called "Operation Fisherman" in which a Lima Site was established in a very remote area of Southern Laos, dubbed "Swordfish Lair". The intention was to reproduce the *"Buon Enao"* experiment which had been very successfully carried out 8 years earlier, with the added intention of producing an independent nation state (something that almost happened *unintentionally* during the *Buon Enao* era, when the Montagnards united and developed an independent, secesstionist front called FULRO). Historians who analyzed the successes of *Buon Enao* placed great emhais on the embedment of well equipped, talented medics, who brought with them liberation from disease, injury and pestilence, which seemed to be even more valued by most Montagnards than liberation from communism. A-Sites in the Central highlands became, in essence, fortified medical dispensaries with the added sideline of gathering, equipping and training local militias.

The Saga of Swordfish Lair is told primarily through recollections of a Junior team medic, Sergeant Gabriel McCarthy, one of twelve Special Forces operatives tasked with fulfilling the objectives of Operation Fisherman. Sergeant McCarthy, along with the Senior team medic, Sergeant First Class Micheal Glickman, are sent to be healers or *"Bac Si's"* to the people. They are accompanied by two officers, team commander Captain Ronald Fernstead and exective officer 1st Lieutenant Ronald Erickson; two Operations and Intelligence non-commissioned officers, Master sergeant Carmen Briant and SFC Daniel Johnston; two Weapons specialists, SFC Arnold Estrada and Sgt. Kirk Brooksly; two Engineers, SSG Philip Volkert and Sgt. Kip Haskell; and two Communications specialists, SSG Thomas Gowen and Sgt. Ronald Winkle. These twelve men are tasked with facilitating the birth of a new nation from a tiny piece of remote mountaintop real estate, in a highly classified mission. They have been provided with extraordinary high tech assets for the time. However, they are very limited in their rules of engagement largely dictated by legal constraints of the Cooper Church amendment. This is their story and it begins here with a recollection from the advent of the deployment:

Swordfish Lair, Laos, Late May, 1971

Special Forces Medical Sergeant Gabriel McCarthy watched amusedly as weapons specialist SFC Arnold Estrada sat in the center of a circle of Montagnards. Each man in the circle had placed in front of him a spare loincloth, measuring about 18 inches by 48 inches in rectangular dimension. Estrada was instructing the Yards on how to field strip their rifles, consisting largely of Korean era surplus M-2 .30 caliber Carbines, a tried and true Montagnard weapon. SFC Arnoldo Estrada looked very much the part of a bull, surrounded by petite matadors. He was emphasizing through an interpreter the importance of keeping every piece of the weapon in sequence as it is field stripped. *"Lay every part out from left to right in order just as you will put it back,"* he was saying via interpreter. Of course, most of the Yards present for this little ritual were at least as familiar with the reliable, compact weapon as Estrada was. Being uncertain of just exactly what the minimum level of expertise was, Estrada was teaching this by the somewhat boring numbers, just as he had many times during the 60's among Montagnard villages not nearly as familiar with weaponry as so many of these present Yards were.

Instead of focusing on the lesson in field stripping an M-2 carbine, the gregarious Montagnards were intent on playing with their gargantuan, newfound Mexican-American friend. As Arnie turned his back on one set of Yards, they would surreptitiously switch parts between their loincloths so that when Estrada turned around, to his horror, he would observe two receiver groups on the same loincloth and two stock assemblies on the other. As he chastised the afflicted Yards who flashed back the most apologetic looks, those now situated to his rear, would switch the same pieces, leading the gruff old NCO to suspect that perhaps he had somehow mistakenly instructed them collectively in a way that led to their confusion. They continued antagonizing him in this way until all broke out in unrestrained laughter wherein, to the unbridled chagrin of Estrada, they all fieldstripped and reassembled the weapons before them in record time. Gabriel could not help but be impressed with the wit and humor of these Lilliputian people.

Team A-321 had been infiltrated on to this "L-Site" or "Lima Site", located high up in a remote area of the Chaine Annamitique mountains for approximately a month. During those first few days following insertion, the Americans had spent a great deal of time receiving shipments from Huey or Chinook air shuttles, constantly cycling back and forth between their L-Site, dubbed Swordfish Lair, and air bases east at Da Nang or from Plieku, southeast of their camp. The big twin rotored Chinooks would not land, but simply lowered large crated parcels suspended from beneath their airframes down onto the campsite. This process had continued day after day, amassing a huge stockpile of stores and equipment. In the process of organizing resources, Gabriel found that he had much to learn about this strange, new people and place. His 22 year old female Montagnard translator, Ca Rangh, was a patient teacher.

"You listen, Sergeant Makarlty. It be very important for you understand how our people live. Most important in Montagnard society is family, then household which contain many families, all part of same family, how you say... ," at this, Ca wrinkled her brow as if mentally reviewing a series of words, then brightened up as she found the correct bit of data. "...Relatives! Yes?" Gabriel nodded in appreciation for the mental aptitude of this bright young woman. He considered, not for the first time, how far she might go in an academic community that could properly exploit the candid intellect she displayed so unpretentiously. "Next, relatives or clan is most important and then on top of all is village. There be no single peoples in Montagnard village. All work together. If no work, no eat. Man is part of family, strong in body. Woman is part of family, strong in heart. Man cut tree, fish, hunt, build house, bury dead, strike gong and make *numpai*. Woman bring water, make fire, cook, make clothes, care for children. Woman control entrance to *bhok-gah* which is front door to long house. Only family enter in back door all others may only enter front door by permission of wife. Man work for woman. Woman is owner of family possessions. Man must honor mother of wife above all other women. Man must live with and care for family of his wife."

"So, then Ca, do the women run the village? Do they have the authority to make all the important decisions?"

"No, no, Sargent Makarlty, man have authority to make final decision. But man is not permitted to own property. It is our way. Women own property, man … manage… property with permission from woman."

"But, what if man and woman do not agree on some issue? Suppose man want to sell property?" Gabriel found himself inadvertently dropping pronouns and adverbs, matching Ca's melodious language patterns.

"Man cannot sell property without permission of owner. Wife is owner."

"What happens if husband and wife disagree?"

"Husband and wife do not disagree, family no let this happen. Older members of family help young men from be stupid. Young men often stupid, sometimes young women be stupid too, but not so much as young men. Young men and women work together and in time, after baby come, not be so stupid. It is the way of life. You have baby, Sargent Makarlty?"

"No Ca, I've never been married. I suppose that makes me still a bit stupid, yes?" He replied with a bit of a grin.

"Ohhhhh nooooo, Sargent Makhalty," she responded revealing another of her magnificent blushes, "we understand your ways different from our ways. I no wish to offend," she bowed her head as she said this. Gabriel reached over and placed his index finger under her chin, gently raising her contrite continence to meet his eyes.

"We must be clear about something right now, Ca. I will never be offended by anything you do or say unless you want me to be offended. We must learn to trust each other and not let little misunderstandings pass between us that might become big misunderstandings without good reason. I am a stranger here. You have accepted me as a guest. It is *your* customs that I must learn and honor. If ever I do anything to offend you or anyone else, it will most likely be because I do not know. I must depend on you to tell me and to teach me what is the proper way. Do you understand what I mean in this?"

She had been looking at him with a neutral expression which transitioned ever so slightly, into a gentle, warm smile. He expressed himself with so much sincerity and effort that she could not help but find herself growing very fond of him. She'd been warned. *Do not become too attached to the Americans.* Other Yards who knew and worked with Americans during the previous decade had counseled the people about their peculiar habits and customs. The older tribesmen had particularly warned the women not to become involved, nor to develop any "husbandly" relationships. The Americans would not stay. Everyone knew this. In the past, these tall, round eyed, foreign men had never remained in one place for more than half a year. There had been women left behind to bear the shame of half-breed children, children who would be shunned by their own and whom the communists would later punish for nothing but appearance, if given the chance. During their briefing in Tan Son Nhut, Gowen and the younger NCO's had particularly been counseled about this point, '*do not have sex with the Montagnard women.*' In enlisted parlance this was translated "if you can't keep your dick in your pants, you have no business on this mission". A-321 had been advised that if any American in their group had doubts about his ability to adhere to that maxim, they would be relieved and replaced prior to insertion. Each man had been interviewed by a military shrink on the issue; particularly the unmarried

Junior NCO's and, of course, Gowen who was divorced. They had all committed to a hands off policy, but Gabriel was realizing at this moment how easy it would be to find himself drawn to this intelligent, attractive young woman, and she found herself struggling with the same notions.

"I understand you, Sargent Makarlty. And you must promise me that you always speak from heart to tell me if what I do is correct thing. From this day forward, we be friends. Friends for thousand autumns."

"A Thousand Autumns?" he replied with a question mark look.

"Yes," she replied, "it is our way of saying 'for the longest time'... what you would say... forever, yes?"

He smiled back again and replied, "well, forever I understand, but why do you use a thousand autumns to describe forever?"

"Because a thousand autumns is beyond memory of family ancestors. No one can remember names of family ancestors for thousand autumns."

"Hmmm," he mused, "I'd have to say that would be a very impressive genealogy, to know your ancestors going back a thousand years."

"Not thousand *years*, Bac Si, thousand *autumns*. You remain with us long enough, you understand difference."

With this simple, sincere exchange, a wistful something once again passed between them.

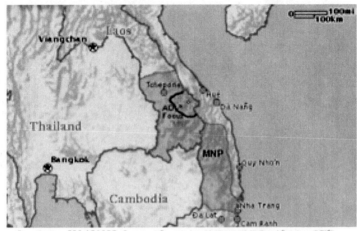

Classification: TOP SECRET - Proposed Boundaries; Montagnard National Province (MNP)

Chapter 1 – First Patrol

June, 1971

June 1st, 1971

As junior medic, Sergeant Gabriel McCarthy intended to awaken early that morning, despite an arduous evening in the dispensary. There had been two labor and deliveries the night before. In the aftermath of smiles and maternal bonding, Gabe had only intended about 3 hour's worth of sleep before arising to secure his gear and start out on this first patrol at dawn. The senior medic, Sergeant First Class Michael Glickman did not retire at all. He remained awake following the last delivery, writing an operative note and making up patient charts. Afterward, he assembled for young Sgt. McCarthy an M-5 Aidbag, which SFC Glickman organized in such a way as to mount on McCarthy's rucksack frame. Glickman started by taking ladder shaped bendable wire frames used to make up splints. He formed this around the inside periphery of the aidbag, stiffening the loose canvas bag into a square configuration. In addition, he took two 4x18 inch wooden plywood splints and taped them side by side into the bottom of the bag. This lent rigidity to the otherwise floppy canvas as well as provided utilitarian splints if needed. Inside the zippered lid flap there were four ¼ liter sized cylindrical pouches sewn in for IV canisters. He inserted into these two 250-cc bottles of serum albumin with cutter sets and 18 gauge IV butterfly needles. In the remaining two bottle pouches, he placed small 250 cc IV bottles filled with Dextrose 5% in half normal saline. Inside the bag, which was compartmentalized, he organized two canvas bound field instrument sets, one for dental, the other for minor surgical instruments. In addition, he placed a disinfectant filled wide mouthed plastic bottle with screw on lid. This could be used as a cold instrument sterilizer. One entire section of the bag was dedicated to field battle dressings ranging from the simple 2x4 inch packets each soldier normally carries on individual web gear, to the larger, highly compressed kits that would open into big dressings sufficient to cover an entire torso.

Overlying seams between compartments, Glickman placed a series of plastic, screw capped casings which he had brought from the states in the team box. They were available in most hardware stores for organizing various sizes of nuts and bolts. They consisted of cylindrical plastic cups with threaded outer screw margins on the open side and inner screw margins just beneath a segmented bottom. This permitted each cup to screw into another with only a single lid on one end. In this manner, it was possible to screw each cup-like segment together, forming a tube of compartments, each of which contained pills. Glickman used ½ inch cloth adhesive tape to make up labels for each plastic canister. He included Chloriquine-Primaquine (CP tabs), Griesiofulvin, Benadryl, Dimetapp, Lomotil, Flagyl, Mintezol and the Army pill solution to all woes, APC's (tablets containing Aspirin, Phenacetin, and Caffiene). In another tube section, he placed Cepacol Throat lozenges, Penicillan VK (fortunately, it was still effective against most bacteria in this part of the world), Erythromycin, Tetracycline, Valium, Dexedrine, Tylenol #3 (containing 30 mg. of Codiene), solution disinfecting tablets and ammonia inhalant ampules.

Next, he took some empty cardboard grenade canisters and filled them with injectables, labeled and tape reinforced so as not to break glass ampules in which most injectable medications were contained. The canisters he also labeled. They contained injectable adrenaline (Epinephrine) carefully differentiated by labeling either 1:10,000 or 1:1,000 concentrations. In addition, he placed ampules of Nor-Epinephrine, Sodium Bicarbonate, Mannitol, Solu-cortef, Narcan, Thorazine, Compazine, Atropine, injectable Benadryl, Streptomycin, Chloramphenicol, Crystalline Penicillin, Scopalomine, Sodium Pentathol, 2% Xylocaine and a bunch of Morphine Sulfate syrettes. He used a small, "mini"grenade canister also to make up an eye kit including a small squirt bottle of sterile solution, eye patches and Corticosteroid ointments along with Timoptic, optical topical anesthetic and anti-biotic agents. Each of six canisters he placed so that lid halves of the canisters faced upward, revealing listed contents on tape labeled lids. Inserted in between the canisters, he disbursed 3, 5, 10 and 20 cc plastic, disposable syringes. In a small, plastic, tackle box case for fly fishing lures, he assembled various gauge sterile needles, Butterfly IV starters and Angiocaths. This fit into a recess on one side. In a flat canvas valise which rested on top of everything else, he placed suture material, small, disposable sterile towels with 7½ size sterile glove sets, steri-strips, flat packets of Merthiolate, Betadine, moleskin, tongue depressors, one half and one inch roles of medical adhesive tape. In one of the three outer pockets on Gabriel's rucksack, he stuffed cravats, ACE wraps, a tin case of various sized band aids, topical antibiotic ointment and cream, tubes of Sulfamylon, topical Hydrocortisone, Tinactin Tolnaftate, Kwell cream, and a large plastic bottle of Multi-Vitamins.

Into other pockets sewn onto the outside of the M-5 aidkit, Glickman placed inflatable leg and arm splints (a new innovation for the military at that time) as well as a stethoscope and percussion hammer. The bulky blood pressure cuff was placed into one of the other rucksack pouches. Glickman also placed into one of Gabe's tiger-stripe fatigue leg pockets a mini otoscope/opthalmascope kit and a tiny, box shaped microscope unit. Laced into his web belt, which was already laced through his trouser waist loops, was a black nylon pouch containing paired hemostats, a small flashlight and heavy duty "penny cutter" bandage scissors (also new to the US Army inventory at the time).

While Gabriel slept, Glickman went on to collect a number of personal equipment items reflecting all the benefits of his years of experience in the field. In the end, he constructed a versatile rucksack medical aid resource, which was designed to "travel light, but travel right", optimizing utilitarian equipment while minimizing weight. He turned off McCarthys little wind up, case folded alarm clock, and let the junior medic get that extra hour of sleep which would make so much difference on this first day of patrol. When the time came, at 0600, the Senior Medic awakened his young ward. Sgt. McCarthy started with the sudden shock of drawing up from deep sleep. On checking his wristwatch, Gabe started to panic, before Glickman showed him all the packed gear.

"Better get a quick shower, kid. It'll be your last for a while. I'll take care of everything here."

As Gabe hustled off to the field shower, little more than a fenestrated bucket suspended over wooden frameworks, he considered what Glickman had done for him. He also realized that verbal thanks would be inappropriate. Gabriel returned 8 minutes later, still goosebumply from his refreshing wet sprinkle, to find tigerstripped fatigues and personal gear all laid out. Again, Gabe dressed without comment, unable to contain an appreciative glance or two that Glickman went out of his way to ignore. McCarthy had drawn for weapons a Car-15 along with a match barrel .45 caliber colt sidearm and holster. A Navy survival knife in sheath with wetstone was taped upside down onto the left side chest strap of his LBE web gear and a sewing kit with extra buttons stitched into the tails of his field blouse. Glickman advised against wearing socks while marching in jungle boots, but had used a couple pairs of socks for soundproofing such things as the canteen cup.

"Those jungle boots will dry out a lot faster without socks and once you break them in, they won't cause blisters." That had been good counsel provided during those first days in the field. By now, the boots were comfortable enough without wearing socks and with little fear of blister formation. In addition, socks would retain moisture in and about the feet leading to immersion foot. That was a significant consideration at this time of the year. June is normally when Monsoon Season begins in Laos. The Americans expected to start this patrol dry and end it wet.

With a sublte tapping of sunlight on their left shoulders the patrol of 6 Americans and 18 Montagnards filed out through the perimeter, into downward sloping bush, thickening with lowering elevations to the south and east. They hiked steadily up and down the verdant mountains, thankful for some occasional rest stops, increasingly aware of rising humidity under an ambient sun. They marched most of that day, about 35 klicks, before coming to a small village at the extreme southern boundary of their area of operations, codenamed "AO Focus". The name of the village was *Loc Phieu*. It was situated in a small valley between terraced mountain ridges wet with shallow irrigation and newly replanted rice shoots. The team executive officer, 1ˢᵗ Lieutenant Ronald Erickson, led the patrol. SSG Phillip Volkert, SFC Gabriel Johnston, SSG Thomas Gowen, SFC Arnoldo Estrada and SGT Gabriel McCarthy, represented the American contingent and trudged along with a hardy little group of about 15 Montagnards, with the balance on flank and point security. As the Yards grew in proficiency at field craft, they would take more command initiative and there would be fewer Americans in single patrol elements like this one. The whole point of their mission here in Laos, dubbed "Operation Fisherman" was to provide self-sufficiency among the Montagnard people of Southeast Asia. For these first few patrols, a relatively larger contingent of the group would be Americans. Eventually, there would be only one or two Americans accompanying a given patrol group. However, as time went on, there would be more coinciding patrol elements in the field and 50% of the American team would likely remain on patrol at any given time.

Upon arriving at the village, Lieutenant Erickson and his interpreter parlayed with the village chieftain. As was also customary,

Gabe was introduced to the village medicine man. Almost as soon as preliminary formalities were concluded, Gabe was led to a raised long house. He proceeded to follow the old village *Bac Si* up steps carved into a cut, diagonal tree trunk.

They began coming to him in small groups of two or three at first, mostly parents with children. Many suffered with skin diseases and jungle rot. The more seriously infirm were carried in to him. Several were quite weak with dehydration and had been bound up so as not to spill diarrhea on the floor. There was Malaria and some of the other obscure tropical diseases he had studied back stateside at Fort Sam Houston, Texas; *Dysentary, Dengue Fever, Filariasis, Schistosomiasis...* As Glickman had instructed, it was not wise to offer solutions without involving the local health care authority, and so, Gabe attempted to convey his opinion to the village *Bac Si* and how something might be treated in consultation with the older medicine man. He noticed an unusually high incidence of sores on the lower legs, especially among the very young, or the very old, which in this village meant older then about 40 years of age. Among the children, there was malnutrition and Gabriel gleaned an interesting lesson in development as he compared the bowed legs of apparent vitamin D deficiency in the children to grown ups with bowed legs. Generally, he would select the worst cases and dispense what meager supplies he had, asking the medicine man to follow up with him on outcomes. If things worked, he would arrange for larger quantities of medicines on a future visit. Eventually, it might even be possible to leave certain pharmaceuticals with the locals, but that would take time as past experience had shown that any medicines the Americans left behind were treated like snake oil cure-all's.

SFC Glickman's diverse M-5 aidkit pack seemed to have just about everything. As the evening wore on, the young medic found himself surrounded by villagers astonished at the variety of his ministrations. Most of the older medicine man's solutions were quite simple by comparison. Wary of their increasing awe, Gabriel attempted with every patient to show respect and proper regard to the village medicine man, instructing the people to follow up with their well known shaman, to assure the recipes being distributed would indeed work. "These things certainly will not work unless accompanied by the direction and prayers of your *Bac Si*", he told them via his field interpreter, a robust young Montagnard warrior named Tope Rangh, Brother of Ca Rangh.

Before Gabe realized it, the sun was long down under western mountain peaks, and he was working by light of torch flames. Estrada passed by later that evening.

"Doc, I'm headed out with a few Yards to set up ambushes on trails leading into this village. The comunistas have been sending patrols around here lately to mess with these people. We've spoken with the chief, and none of his villagers are planning on being out tonight. Be sure your patients know not to take any walks away from the village, OK?"

Gabe nodded his acknowledgment and continued treating patients on into the night. They came to him until after midnight, asking him to check and re-check their families, their relatives, wondering if they needed more pills or salves. Later in the evening, they brought into him the hopeless cases; old men and women, very young children, dying of sickness and diseases too far gone. Blackwater fever, terminal malria, end stage parasitc diseases. He used up all of his D_5W ½NS intravenous sets attempting to rehydrate some of the worst cases among the children. He had to withhold the Serum Albumin, knowing it would draw fluids from intracellular spaces and possibly upset electrolyte physiology. As the night wore on, Gabriel realized that one old man had died while waiting to see him. When Gabriel discovered him, the old man was just sitting back against a post, staring up into the ceiling. Gabe had seen death while working in United States Army Hospitals, but there, death was always surrounded by some formality of institutional health care. He approached the old man attempting to take vital signs for a single sheet record he had begun at the foot of each patient bedroll. In reaching for the old man's wrist, the first thing was the coldness. A missing sense of vibration and warmth, which Gabe suddenly realized one just takes for granted in the living. He did not notice any stiffness setting in, but knew that would follow. He gazed into the eyes, realizing now, how empty and glassy they appeared, certainly not a mirror of any remaining soul. Much to Gabriel's own surprise, emotions started welling up within, emotions over which he had little control, and he wept for this nameless old man. As he did so, the old medicine man observed him from aside. Relatives were summoned by a series of silent hand signals. Young men and women familiar with this part of the circle of life came to the young American and patted him gently on the shoulder. They attempted to convey their thanks for his efforts in behalf of their departed father, grandfather, uncle, brother; whatever title fit in to the surreal theater of this world so far removed from everything Gabriel McCarthy had known before. And yet, they were the same titles for relatives used round the world. It was the same process of living and dying, of familial joy and sorrow. The realization of it meant all the more and he could not contain a tremulous empathy as he went on rounding other patients, glimpsing over his shoulder as they bore away the body of the old man. Sometime just after 0230, Gabe finally leaned back, sitting cross-legged, against a columnar supporting beam in the longhouse, surrendering to overwhelming fatigue. The older Montagnard *Bac Si* gently lowered him onto a woven mat and all were quiet so as not to disturb their new attendant young American *Bac Si*.

During his sound slumber, Gabe startled once, briefly, to a sound of distant gunfire. Automatic weapons punctuated the night far removed from this longhouse. He looked at the inside of his wrist, lifting back the coverflap over his watchface. It was just after 4:00 AM. From the sounds of the firefight, there were mostly Car-15 and M-2 Carbine shots with a very few answering AK-47's, these accompanied by a couple of loud bangs, apparently from concussion grenades. It lasted just a few seconds and all was silent again. The old medicine man had been sitting alongside. Gabe was uncertain what to do. He started to rise, but the old man gently palmed him on the shoulder, shaking his head. With knowing eyes, the old *Bac Si* seemed to be explaining, *"This does not concern us. There are others attending to this thing which is happening out there in the jungle. You must go back to sleep and pretend that it is simply a dream..."*. Gabe understood the captioned expression and settled back down lapsing shortly into a less deep sleep, sensing from within fitful dreams that his weapons were close by.

He was awakened by stirrings within the longhouse, just before sunrise. Montagnard inhabitants were rising to the new day. He blinked awake and sat up. Estrada was back in the longhouse, along with Volkert and Johnston. All three had been out on Ambush sites last night. Erickson was entering the longhouse which, unbeknownst to Gabe, seemed to have become designated quarters for the visiting Americans at one end, and a semi-hospital ward on the other. Gabe looked up at the XO as Erickson came over to him:

"So Doc, did you get caught up on your beauty sleep?"

"I suppose so, sir. Did I miss something last night?"

"Well, Estrada tripped an ambush off to the west of the Village. He took down a squad of about 8 gooks with his 5 Yards. They look like Khmer Rouge. That's a bit of a surprise this far north. We think there may have been one or two who survived because there were blood trails going off into the bush at first light when we went back to check out the kill zone. If so, the villagers can expect some company, later on today or tonight."

"Do you think maybe we got these people into something here sir?"

"Well, nothing we did not expect. This time of year, the communists send around conscription and tax collection squads to intimidate the villagers. These people are fed up with it. They asked if we could help them discourage the confiscation of their rice harvest. It was probably just coincidence that we would trip a goon squad on the first night out. We'll stay with this village for the next couple of days, or however long it takes to goad Charlie's reserve element into coming back. When he does, we should have a bit of a surprise for him."

The Americans were offered breakfast of rice and fish heads, which they accepted while exchanging bits of C-Rations and re-hydrated LRP's with their Montagnard hosts. There was also a small quantity of very hot, cabbage like vegetable which Volkert and Johnston explained was sort of like a Montagnard version of Korean Kem Chi. At certain times of the year, it was the only source of vitamins in their diet. When they were deprived of it, or as was more commonly the case, when it was in short supply, they suffered from Vitamin C deficiency. For that reason, offering to share the precious piquant vegetables was a sign of growing respect the village people were beginning to have for these strange looking Americans.

High up overhead, an F-109 Wild Weasel was circling the area. In the RIO seat, an electronics officer (EO) scanned a new reconnaissance device, called a thermal signature imaging system. It had come, along with several other gadgets, out of Fort Hood, Texas from the MAASTER project. It provided a means to pick up thermal signatures of people at various resolutions below. When combined with image enhancement and magnification, it offered remarkable detail in varying degrees of color signifying matched temperatures of things below. The EO understood very well that because mammals are warm-blooded animals, their heat signatures are quite distinct. By characterizing these heat sig-natures and then magnifying in on the source, it was possible to visualize a semblance of human forms moving under vegetation of less heat intensity. Information was being passed down to an American ground advisory force about movement in the woods to their west and jungle to their east. Erickson had arranged with the village chieftain, not to have any friendlies go anywhere out-side the village except into highly visible areas of rice paddies off to the immediate north and south.

As McCarthy opened up his field clinic again that morning, bits of intelligence were being fed to Lieutenant Erickson who recorded information onto a large circular aiming board he was using to track movement of human heat signatures toward the village. Erickson had been advised of a mid sized group of about 30 human type heat signatures moving eastward to slightly north-easterly about 15 kilometers away. They were passing through densely overgrown bush in a ravine between two mountain bases. Along their present azimuth and rate of movement, if they were indeed headed to this village, they were moving very slowly and would likely arrive in about 8-12 hours, given the heavy undergrowth they were traveling through, apparently avoiding trails. Erickson had wondered how well this new system would work in an actual combat environment. His concerns were mollified when the RIO/EO described signs of blood trails, one leading off to what was very likely a dead body and another heading in the general direction of the group in the ravine. "Whew, this system really bares the enemy's rear end to us", Erickson thought out loud. "If they cannot move undetected, we really do *'know all'*."

As the day wore on, F-109 Weasels were replaced in shifts by other, similar aircraft with the same equipment. They were slated to go in continuous shifts around the clock. Erickson was increasingly impressed by this confirmation of the operation plan. He had to admit, when Major Scadlock had first told them about the level of aerial support they would be receiving, he had not believed it to be entirely plausible.

Over the balance of that morning, after clinic, Gabe worked with village elders to enact better field sanitation practices, attempting to explain such nuances as fecal - oral routes of infection, and the necessary chain of malarial vectors - infected human, mosquito, blood, stagnant water to lay eggs, larvae, mosquito, uninfected human.... They set about locating standing water around the camp and either channeled it out, or poured a flammable liquid meniscus on top. Gabe tactfully suggested some ideas for field latrines and waste disposal. He explained that the Montagnards had many enemies. The Communists and Vietnamese were only one type of enemy. There were other, far more dangerous enemies, living right in their midst. He had brought with him a compact field microscope. This very clever, microsized unit, was especially designed for Special Forces use. It fit in a trouser leg pocket, and could potentially magnify to the limit of any standard light microscope, albeit with a smaller field of view.

Under its magnification, he showed a drop of water from one of many small standing puddles on fringes of the camp. It stank of urine and excrement. It contained collected run off from higher rice paddies. He put a drop of this under his microscope and invited the village people to look through the objective. They were unanimously astonished at the tiny reticule world of wriggling forms seen through the eyepiece. At first, they saw no correlation between his magic viewing box and any life threatening enemies. It took re-iteration and great patience with a steady, quick witted interpreter- Ca's brother, Tope Rangh, to begin to convey these concepts. By that time, it was getting late into the day, and many of the villagers started leaving for evening meal preparation. The village was situated in a rather unusual agricultural water table. More often, rice paddies would lie on flatlands, irrigated by gravity flow off from higher elevations. Because of the nature of these highlands, there would have been very little land in which to seed within the valley between north and south saddle contours. Accordingly, some previous generation of Montagnards had terraced the north and south elevations. They'd set up a rather clever irrigation system, which would stem runoff from higher mountains to the west. The result was a village situated at an elevation between rice paddies above to the north and south, and eastern jungles below. Malaria breeding *Culex* and *Anophyles* mosquitoes could easily make their way into standing water pools within saturated rice fields surrounding the village. It was a breeding ground for disease. Epidemiologists might have designated the location to be an interesting symbiotic environment of bountiful soils collected by runoff from the mountains. This runoff fed the population of hardy mountain people who were constant hosts to some of the most dangerous bacterial and parasitic life-forms on the planet.

Unbeknownst to Gabe, as he went through day long nuances of field sanitation with the village people, Lieutenant Erickson had been receiving updates on movement of threatening *human* life forms represented as thermal signatures. The one wounded patroller that had crawled off from the ambush on the night previous, intercepted a larger force at the near mouth of the ravine. The group had paused and apparently taken chow for a while, building a small cooking fire. Thereafter, they began to move out again, clearly following an azimuth toward the village. By about 1645 that afternoon, they broke down into three elements, two of which were circling around terraced hills to the north and south, clearly intending to form a pincer apex from the east. The single remaining element had sent scouts forward to observe the village. By 1735, flanking elements were about halfway around north and south ridges above the village.

Enemy observation scouts were also located on fringes of the western bush, evidently attempting to secure information on number and armament of forces, which had ambushed the previous night's probing squad. At 1745, Erickson mounted the top of a small platform, erected in the center of the village as a sort of meeting place and speaking pulpit. Next to him, Gowen held the plotboard and wore a headset with boom microphone mounted over his left cheek. Erickson took his M-79 and fired a flout shot in the general direction of about where one of the enemy observers was located on the plotboard.

On board the modified Wild Weasel, call-signed "Bugeyes 8", the RIO/EO immediately recognized the thermal signature of a 40 mm shell explosion. He keyed his mike.

"Minnow 3 this is Bugeyes 8, You are off to the southwest by about 25 meters." Gowen conveyed this to Lt. Erickson.

Erickson again took aim, amazed by this new technology. He adjusted his sights slightly, allowing for the flout shot arcing slightly northward and not quite so far westward. Thwunk!! The big round went off again.

"You were well within killing radius on that one sir," came the radio return via Gowen.

Erickson repeated this process for each of three enemy scouts identified by the Weasel as being located on the village periphery. The RIO/EO reported that one had crawled away from the blast area, clearly leaking something warm, heading in the general direction of a larger base element. By this time, the redball Sun was dipping down into Western peaks. All Montagnard villagers had returned from their fields and Bugeyes reported enemy flanking elements forming diagonal skirmish lines off to the northwest and southwest.

"Looks like it's time to call in Spectre, sir" Gowen ventured, looking down at the plotboard.

"Go ahead, Tom, you've probably had more experience at this than I have."

"Yes sir." Gowen advised the Weasel pilot that he was going to an alternative frequency. Upon dialing it, an AC-130A Spectre gun ship came on line. The big bird had been called in earlier that afternoon and was monitoring on multiple net frequencies.

"Fire Breather one, this is minnow three, over."

"Minnow three, this is Fire Breather one at angels 3 on clockwise racetrack. We have enemy signatures."

"Very well, Firebreather, engage, I say again, engage."

"This is Firebreather, engaging at this time, wilco."

A blanket of lights and sound came down from the sky, raining into areas west and east of the village. In the ebbing light of dusk, as the sun sank on irregular contours westward, one could see sections of Jungle to the east and west chop up like a huge sweeping Damocletian scythe, passing over the area. It lasted for about 45 seconds, then all went silent. Several minutes passed, and finally:

"Minnow, this is Firebreather, your signatures are dropping to ambient temperature, over"

"Firebreather, this is minnow, thanks for now. How much longer will you be on station, over"

"This is Firebreather, between our relief wings, we can remain on station all night at your discretion, over"

"This is Minnow, thanks again Firebreather, break, switching back over to bugeyes, over."

With that, he switched back over to the Weasel, which also had been monitoring the "Puff" net. In their planning, they determined to make separate nets for each delivery element. While anyone on the net could of course transmit, each element had its own communications protocol and, unless there was a dire emergency or need for coordination, only the designated delivery element would normally transmit on a given net. The system seemed to work quite well.

Erickson directed several of the Yards to check out locations he had bracketed with the M-79 to see if they could find any dead or wounded enemy scouts. They went cautiously off into the bush, returning after dark about 25 minutes later, with two bodies and weapons. Tomorrow, they would collect the rest.

No ambushes were sent out that night. Each of the Americans took a two-hour watch with 2 Yards. They monitored the radio, checking in hourly with the overlooking Weasel. There was no further enemy activity to report.

The next morning, just after sunrise, several of the villagers accompanied a sweeping patrol to assess the effect of last evening's action. Clearly, no communists had bothered them that night. This being late Spring harvest season, they had come to expect regular NVA/Pathet Lao patrols passing by to collect rice tribute and conscription levies. Many villagers had been quite fearful after the Americans had brought in victims from the first ambush. Few understood the "fire rain" of last evening, but over that night had been explained this was a powerful new weapon used by the Americans to protect the village. When bodies of over 30 dead enemy soldiers were brought in from various points about the village, many villagers recognized the characteristic red waistbands of Khmer Rouge thugs who had brutalized and bullied them these last few weeks. There was a grim celebration among relatives and previously silent plaintiffs to the atrocities committed by these now dead quasi-soldiers. For some, it was justice long overdue. While a few of the villagers worried about retribution, most felt that they had to take a stand with one side or the other. Montagnard people in this valley had always been fiercely independent and during the last great war (WW-II) some old timers had been part of a Mon-Khmer resistance cell against the incessantly cruel Japanese. Although these tribal people lived in an area considered to be Laos, they were not technically Laotian by someone else's reckoning. They didn't really care about others labeling them Laotian, it's just that they did not consider themselves Vietnamese either. They certainly were not communists. They were Montagnard, Katu tribesmen of this land and they had never known anything but intimidation and brutality from arbiters of the so-called "great cause of the people's liberation", whether Cambodian, Vietnamese or Pathet Lao. These Americans came here only after asking permission to visit through intermediaries of other villages in the area. When they arrived, they provided service to sick and infirmed members of the village, something the communists never even vaguely offered to do. In fact, some of the maim and halt of this village were physically mutilated victims of the communists, intended to be conspicuous reminders of a firm communist will over them.

As the village chieftan and elders met with Erickson in the main Longhouse to discuss the concept of operation Fisherman, Sgt. Gabriel McCarthy mounted onto the same raised dais, which Erickson had used the evening prior as a launching platform. Alongside Gabe, the old medicine man stood in resolute support. Via the medium of Tope Rangh acting as translator, Gabriel addressed the assembled villagers, pausing every sentence to let Tope translate.

"Last night, you saw what seemed like magic coming down from the sky and destroying our enemies... That was a necessary thing... If we had not destroyed them, they would likely have destroyed us, and gone on hurting you... We all know that it is better not to kill, but sometimes, it is a necessary thing... There is another war that is hurting this village... It is a battle with the enemy of disease... Disease has killed many more of your people than the communists have.... It prevents you from growing old with honor and dignity.... So many of you are sick so much of the time that you cannot make the rice fields give up all they have to give.... Many of your children die very young... and the few old people you have suffer very much....I know you do not want this to happen.... Many of you think, 'so, it is what happens in life. People live for as long as they are lucky enough to live. If the communists do not kill us, sickness in time will do so'... I see your sickness..... You have many fevers among you..... Your children have swollen bellies and bent legs.... sometimes, your bowels spill on the ground, without your control... We have come to tell you that you can fight against these bad things, just as together, we fought against the communists last night .... If we work together, you can live much better. Your children will not die so much...... Your old people will get older..... If you will let us work together with your *Bac Si*, we can help you realize these things. .... I see some of you shaking your heads.... But, it is not so hard as you think..... It is much like raining death out of the sky... Your bodies are like the village..... The enemy is disease.... You have powers to reach out like fire from the sky above and kill this enemy called disease.... Some of you saw my device yesterday, my microscope.... Those of you who did not, come to me later, and I will show you the enemy..... It is very small, but very many..... too many to kill all, but also, so many that it is not so hard to kill most with the right weapons.... The things you must do will seem ridiculous and simple.... Perhaps you would rather take a large knife and cut your enemy.... But, large knives will not hurt this enemy.... I will show you what will hurt this enemy...."

With that, Gabe leaned over and picked up a basin of water, holding it out to SFC Daniel Johnston. Johnston was an absolute Nubian wonder to these people. They all saw him as an authoritative dark prince among the American soldiers. Some of the children had been scolded by their parents for attempting to rub his skin, looking to see if the color would come off. Few parents would admit thinking to do the same themselves. But most all would later check the children's hands to see if there was any dark paint or stain. With exaggerated movements, Johnston reached into the basin, dramatically taking out a bar of soap that he held up high for all to see. He then wet his hands in the basin and lathered his hands up with the soap, again holding them high up in the air. Thereafter, he rinsed and wiped his hands on an olive drab towel from his own field pack.

Gabe turned back to the audience.

"That is how you kill this enemy.... It may not seem so bold as bringing in the dead bodies of your tormentors.... but it will save many more of you than our bullets or bombs can.....If you let us, we will show you how to fight both enemies...."

Gabe then turned to the village medicine man, bowing as he did so, attempting to give the impression that he had offered this speech at the old man's bidding. The old *Bac Si* nodded and stepped up to address the people himself. Gabe stepped back and sat back down against a railing, inclining his head toward Tope Rangh to receive the translation.

"Old *Bac Si* say you young to be Bac Si, but you speak truth.... That he has known many people die from this village over many years.... Most not die from communists.... Most die from sickness....He say that he is probably *Bac Si* only because he live longer than most.....That in his life, he see many things.... but he now sees new things that make him realize old things which he has never say out loud.... He say that he offer prayers over every baby in this village for long enough that his prayers brought most of these people into living.... He want all of these people to live longer than he will, because he love this people very much..... He say, if work together with Americans, maybe it help everyone more."

With that, the old man stepped back and descended from the platform. He was greeted below by his people who came up to him to touch his shoulder, bowing their heads as they did so. As each villager passed in succession, the old man's eyes became moist, and eventually tears began to run down his cheeks.

June 5ᵗʰ, 1971

Regimental Field Commander Muc Bo Thau was reading his daily situation reports. His attention was drawn right away to missing patrols. He noted a platoon sized patrol unaccounted for. It had failed to return from reconnoitering in the area of *Loc Phieu*, an insignificant little village up in the mountains. Five days had passed, now, with no news from them. The patrol was largely made up of Khmer Rouge from Captain Phut Phnom's Cambodians. Commander Thau mused, *"I give them a simple, little, Laotian Montagnard village to conduct enforcement over, and they disappear. Probably all drunk on numpai or fighting each other over booty."* Now, the patrol was at least 3 days overdue. It might be nothing more than a malfunctioning radio, something quite common to the people's army. However, he would have to keep an eye on this situation over the next few days. Spring rice harvest was in and he expected as usual, that local people would hoard their stores. He had directed punishment to this Little Village, and many like it, on several occasions just over the last few months. By this time, the people should know better than to resist his iron will. Should he discover that the villagers had in some way delayed these patrols, they would have to be chastised.

Another concern centered on some unconfirmed reports about an American Special Forces detachment, supposedly operating on the Laotian side of Mount Aterat. This was, in his opinion, highly unlikely. There had been numerous spurious reports on clandestine enemy activity since the American 5th Special Forces completed its withdrawal last February. It remained a puzzle to him why the Americans had withdrawn the most successful facet of American intervention in Southeast Asia, at least in terms of winning over the barbaric Mountain people. The departure of the Green Berets was, in his opinion as well as many others, a sure omen that the North would prevail. Of course, the Montagnards were still very independent, not easily convinced of the people's great cause. But, the mountain savages had always been troublesome. When his own people were finally victorious, when he took his place in the politburo of this new dominion, when he had power to administer force unopposed by the Americans, he would help eliminate their noisome culture.

Aside from a few, predictable, ground reconnaissance efforts, and the abortive Lam Son 719 incursion by the South Vietnamese, the Americans had done very little in this sector for over a year, now. He was almost bored and voraciously conspired for an opportunity to distinguish himself.

Early June in the Village of Loc Phieu, Laos

"Such a peeing place!!" exclaimed the village chieftain in his sing song, clucking language. A large group of villagers had gathered around the amazing urinal, more correctly termed *"urinoil"*. Late that afternoon, a Huey C slick had delivered several bundles of supplies, including inventory replacements for Gabe's M-5 Med-kit, and a 55 gallon drum just a bit over 1/2 filled with used oil. They had previously dug a circular hole in the ground, down to bedrock, about 2-3 feet deep. Into this hole, they placed the oil drum over a tar paper covering. Protruding out of the bottom of the drum, well down into the bedrock, was a 1 1/2 inch pipe securely soldered into the drum, suspended within a 3 inch pipe. The 3 inch pipe was cap welded with a 1 inch vent sticking up out of the cap all the way up to the rim of the drum. Running up from this vent was a large, circular funnel into which male members of the village could easily urinate. After back-filling the excavation, they had placed about 12 inches of water in the bottom, then poured 32 gallons of waste oil on top. The result was an oil seal layer that prevented urine odor and could be installed in the middle of the camp without producing a stinking latrine. . Fecal-oral transmission of disease was perhaps the greatest plague that these villagers would face on a regular basis. In this part of the world, there were in 1971, relatively few urine borne tropical diseases. Gabe was well aware that *Schistosomiasis hematobium* , a urine borne form of *Schistosomiasis,* was largely limited to Africa. Occasionally, certain forms of *Filariasis* could be transmitted in the urine, however, for the most part, urine comes out of the body effectively filtered within the kidneys. The fundamental reason for this urinal was to train the Montagnards to control their body wastes and by so doing to prevent diseases in general. More importantly, it would prevent contamination of the water table and lessen the much more prevalent fecal oral route transmission of disease. If a people are careful about where they urinate, generally, they will be more careful about their defecation habits. Because the women seemed just as interested in trying out the new urinal gadget, planking was arranged about the funnel to allow for squatting. An unnecessary privacy screen and adjacent defecation pits with half cut burn out drums made the system complete.

For alternative waste disposal, straddle trenches had been dug around edges of the village, also with privacy screens. Youngsters had been assigned to refill 5 gallon tip can pairs on a daily basis, one can being filled with soapy water, the other with clear, rinse water. All the villagers were instructed on washing of hands whenever they relieved themselves. They took to this gleefully after an animated lecture from the village jester. In addition, they went about eliminating puddles of free standing water from around the village periphery. They were issued mosquito repellant, which most would only use in the deep bush. Food preparation was supplemented by Vitamins and balanced to include indigenous vegetables and meat along with the usual bounty of rice and freshwater fish head sauce. Finally, every villager was immunized against Tetanus, Diptheria and Pertusis.

By the time a week had passed, most reasonable field sanitation and personal hygiene measures were in place. Hand soap had been given to every villager, and they faithfully embraced a new paradigm of washing themselves from head to toe at least once per week.

Over the next 3 months, incidence of skin diseases would drop precipitously. There would be less sick and ill members of the village due to gastrointestinal disease and therefore more who could work the fields, providing bounty back to the village. The children were more energetic and just seemed happier. All in all, nearly everyone in the village would agree that they had never been better off, health wise, than since the Americans arrived.

Over that week, Lieutenant Erickson agreed with the chief to leave a rotating group of strike force Montagnards there in the village of *Loc Phieu*. Seismographic sensors were placed into the western ravine and the strikers were taught how to use the sensors to detect movement. Daily air support would continue to dispense intelligence about biological heat signatures moving in to the area. The chief agreed to move his village into *Swordfish Lair* if he was informed of any threat, and offered to send young men to *Swordfish Lair* for militia training. Unlike communist conscriptions, these young men would return to the village at the end of their training. One week after their arrival, the American led patrol departed *Loc Phieu* and moved on to another village called *Anh tna Gau*, 13 kilometers away and two valleys over.

Lieutenant Erickson's patrol was not received with great courtesy at *Anh tna Gau*. The people there had been punished by NVA regulars several weeks back. Some of their community resisted a roving communist recruitment patrol, which had taken a large store of rice and announced the impressment of several young men. With cross bows and a couple of old World War II vintage Japanese Arisaka type 38 rifles, the village elders, several of whose sons were being conscripted, attempted to drive off the communists. Though spirited, the villagers were not much of a force to be reckoned with against automatic weapons. An even dozen were buried by mourning villagers and ever since, they had relented with silent animosity to all communist demands. When the Americans arrived, the people of *Anh tna Gau* viewed them as just another occupation force. The people were reserved, somewhat condescending, and generally impassive. When Erickson communicated with them, via his interpreter, the locals made it clear that they did not want these Americans in their village, but they would not resist them. Lt. Erickson advised the leaders that if they ever needed help, to let someone in *Loc Phieu* know, and the Americans would come to them if possible. The patrol left before sundown, Gabe having seen several people who timidly approached him with dire health concerns. Evidently, they heard that he was a powerful *Bac Si* through local word of mouth communications network via distant relatives in *Loc Phieu*. He left them some handsoaps, Lomotil, a powerful anti-diarrheal, and parcels of antibiotics among several people with serious infections. It seemed quite clear that the people of *Anh tna Gau* would have quite willingly let him stay on alone, but feared to entertain an entire American/Montagnard military presence in their village.

Over the next 2 and a half weeks, this cycle was pretty much repeated. Some villages would receive them with warm courtesy while others let it be known that they would prefer not to get involved. In all, Erickson's patrol visited 7 different Montagnard communities, stretching out over several hundred square kilometers from southernmost to northernmost boundaries of the eastern periphery of AO Focus. Always, the Americans would attempt to coordinate with whomsoever received them, leaving in peaceful courtesy those who would not. As time went on, they found their receptions in various locales more anticipated. Always, there was plenty for Gabe to do. Even in those villages reticent to accept American patrols, there were always people anxious to petition for medical assistance. Through some basic means of bush communication by word of mouth, the presence of an American *Bac Si* was somehow forecast in advance. On advice from Johnston and Estrada, Erickson started to avoid a predictable route, leaving one location in a particular direction, and then following a more circuitous route to their next destination. They would be resupplied from time to time by pre-arranged heliborne deliveries that kept Gabe amply provided with medical items and sanitation materials.

About 5 days after the Americans left that first village, *Loc Phieu*, sensors placed in the ravine which commanded westward passage into the valley, picked up repetitive ground movements. Air support was requested by a communications trained Montagnard striker via radio dispatch with Sgt. Ron Winkle at Swordfish Lair. A flyover picked up another platoon sized troop activity and after confirming that there were no friendlies known to be in that area, a Spectre was called in which decimated the enemy ground force. There were no further incursions from the west into that particular valley for the balance of June. At every other village which received them, the Americans left similar resources for communication and air support. They were reinforced by a growing contingent of new recruits from acquiescent villages, willing to volunteer their young men for a four week training cycle at *Swordfish Lair*. Afterwards, these recruits would return to proximity locations nearby their own village wherein they would become citizen soldiers, participating in regular village commerce while providing support to one or two full time Montagnard strikers with radio skills. It was truly amazing to the Americans how quickly the network grew.

Just over three weeks after departing *Swordfish Lair*, the first monsoons hit. Erickson's team arrived, dripping wet, at the last village on their patrol route, the village of *Lo Dao*. This was another hamlet in which the locals had been recently visited and intimidated by communists to a point that they were hesitant to receive the American patrol. Though courteous, the village elders simply asked that unless something was to be demanded, would the Americans please leave. *Lo Dao* was their last stop before ending a month long patrol sojourn. Throughout the patrol, Erickson's group had been blanketed by air reconnaissance and support. They had regular intelligence on movement in, around, or near their position. It was particularly difficult at times, especially in those villages that did not receive them cordially, to distinguish friend from foe. As was typical with encounters which seemed taciturn, the Americans left *Lo Dao* before sundown and headed out into the bush for several klicks. They then set up a soggy Rest Over Night position (RON) and placed out ambush elements on various trails or points of access toward the RON. Aside from that first ambush at *Loc Phieu* they had not made direct enemy contact since the first week of the patrol.

Just as they started setting out their security measures for the RON, some of the outlying Yards on perimeter security brought into camp a Montagnard who identified himself as a citizen of *Lo Dao*. He carried in his arms, a Montagnard child, a little girl of about 3 or 4 years. She was only semi conscious and had been seriously injured on her left leg. Through an interpreter, the visitor explained that a group of children had been playing out to the south of their village. Apparently, they set off a land mine, and several had been injured, including this little girl. They were asking for the American patrol to return with their *Bac Si* and render assistance. Erickson summoned Sgt. Gabriel McCarthy who had been setting out a claymore mine on the perimeter. Upon hearing of the land mine incident, he entreated the Lieutenant to return to the village. Lieutenant Erickson seemed quite willing to do so. Volkert, Estrada, Johnston and Gowen were less enthusiastic. It was the typically quiet Volkert who spoke up first:

"Look, sir, we are out about 5 klicks from that village. In the dark, if we take good security precautions, it may take us 4 to 5 hours gettin back. Tomorrow morning, we can make the trek in one or two. Why don't we wait until tomorrow morning and secure this RON for tonight? Doc can work on this little girl right here".

The other three vets agreed. Clearly, Erickson was not convinced. He invited McCarthy's opinion.

"Well, it's true, I can work on the little girl right here, but I don't know how seriously the other victims have been injured and supposedly, they're all kids. With kids, you can't wait too long to render aid if they've been badly hurt. They fail to thrive like adults. The more time that passes, it's possible I can do less to help." McCarthy ventured as discretely as possible, not wanting to countermand the older members of the detachment, but tempering this with his concerns over child casualties back at the village.

Lieutenant Erickson pondered things for a few moments. It was already dark. The terrain they were in was low mountain woods, not really jungle, and therefore providing a much more extended field of view in daylight. Around the village, there were denser areas with watersource runoffs from Mountains to the west. He reviewed mentally his primary mission on this patrol, which was to establish contact with the villages in this area and if possible to win them over. Certainly, a civic action mission such as this was just the sort of thing to accomplish his directive.

The visitor was standing by, attempting to convey his urging for haste to the interpreters. He let the little girl, limp in his arms, be taken and placed down where Gabe could minister to her. He continued to implore that the Americans return to his village. To Estrada, who was watching quietly from off to one side, it seemed as though the adult was far more concerned about the team returning to his village, than he was about the little girl being treated by the American medic. Estrada had witnessed many so called "civic action encounters" in his 3 tours. Most often, parents stayed glued to their children when medical aid was being rendered. This man had not represented himself as a parent. Having kids of their own, Estrada could certainly empathize with injured children. However, it was just bad policy to go back into a denied village, and he voiced this opinion to Lt. Erickson.

"My decision", stated Erickson with a determined emphasis, "we go back, tonight. Johnston, Estrada, round 'em up and let's start a night file back to the village."

Johnston and Estrada said nothing more. If they had reservations, they kept it to themselves like the professionals that they were. They simply conveyed back to each of their respective squad elements what the intent was. Several of the Yards were rather vocal in expressing their doubts about the night movement, but stirred on by the Americans, they harnessed up and prepared to move back out the way they had come.

As the group headed back, Erickson chose to follow an Azimuth, instead of trails, along which the villager tried to lead them, claiming that these would be faster routes of return. In this, the Lieutenant attempted to mollify somewhat the concerns of Johnston and the others. However, Erickson realized also that as they approached the village, they would encounter increasingly dense bush, eventually passing through outright jungle during the last kilometer or so of the trek. They would have to use trails for that final segment of the return route.

Lt. Erickson set out flanks while still in the wooded area. A quarter moon offered some dim illumination. The date window on his Seiko military chronometer indicated that it was the 29th day of June, 1971. They traveled overland for about 3 klicks slowly, carefully, with point security forming a three point fan out ahead. This took about 2 ½ hours. As they approached more dense, lower lying country closer to the village, it was necessary to tighten up their ranks somewhat in order to keep sight of each other in the dark. Estrada approached Gabe from the side, whispering to him.

"Listen, Doc, we realize you just doin what you think is best for these kids. It was the LT's decision to take the bait on this. But, listen, Doc, we got a bad feelin bout this, and we been round long enough to trust these feelings. If we step into deep shit, you listen for me to yell, and you get into the middle o' whatever direction the shooting is coming from, comprende amigo? You've got to get into the middle of em, even though all you gonna wanna do is hunker down. You do that, and you be dead. This is no shit Doc. When you get into the middle of them, shoot low, cause they gonna be lyin down, and we all gonna be standin up, those of us that still be among the living. Try not to hit any of our own people, try to shoot only at flashes coming from the ground, not from waist high or above. You shoot with your weapon up, high on your chest, just like I showed you back at

Bragg. We make it through t'night doc, and you'll learn a thing or two, hey compadre?"

For the first time, it dawned on Gabriel just how dangerous a situation they were in. Up to this point, all he had focused on was concern over injured children. He suddenly realized the tactical folly of being led back to some village at night by a single villager. He only hoped he had not influenced his team into a nightmare. Still, he had a genuinely injured child with him. Gabe had bound the wound himself, had started an IV on her, administered antibiotics and set her on a collapsible litter, upon which she was being transported as a whimpering little bundle beside him in the middle of the patrol movement. *"Surely, the people of Lo Dao would not let the communists use one of their own children like this?"* he thought. The little girl was wrapped from the waist down in a characteristic black sarong, typical of the Montagnard females. Lower portions of the sarong were shredded and burned from blast energy. Both of her legs were burned and her left leg was badly shattered below the knee. She arrived with a tourniquet in place. He had loosened the tourniquet and clamped what bleeders he could see in the glow of a flashlight. He had also given her a small titration of morphine, but she really did not seem to need it. She was conscious, but would not talk, nor answer any of the questions posed by his interpreter, Tope Rangh. Gabriel could not fathom such a deception, nor, it seemed, could Lieutenant Erickson. However, Estrada and the others had been over here for a long time. They were more used to what went on. What if they were right? Gabe had practiced IA drills many times. He had also practiced ambush tactics. He was keenly aware of the devastation that could be inflicted during those first 5 life or death seconds. He knew in his mind that the only way to survive a near ambush was to charge the ambush, to get into the middle of it so that the enemy's massed firepower is compromised. Even that, however, only left the ambushees with slightly better than even odds given that, once in the middle, a standing individual could move quicker than an enemy rifleman in a prone position.

It was still a one on one slugfest until units could be reassembled in order to concentrate firepower. What about the little girl on the litter? She would be dropped right into the kill zone. *"Surely, they could not do that,"* he thought, *"Didn't Ho's little red book say something about caring for the peasants"?*

Lieutenant Erickson was having some of these same misgivings. However, he had made a command decision, and for better or worse, his job now was to see it through. He leaned heavily on whatever suggestions Johnston, Gowen, Volkert and Estrada offered en route. While keeping as much of an interval as possible in the dark, he let Johnston set up a two tiered patrol formation and carry out the tactics of movement. They used a sort of "bounding overwatch" patrolling tactic. This was a new patrol strategy, which had become popular at the behest of General John Cushman, one of the rising generation of savvy veteran generals to come out of Vietnam. While it served well in this wooded area, they would be back to a large file formation on the final trail in to the village. Erickson had Gowen call in a sitrep to base camp prior to striking out, and the reply had urged him to use his own discretion in situ. He was silently praying that his discretion was lucky tonight. Just prior to entering the dripping, humid jungle, Erickson had Bugeyes 2 up above offer a thermal signature observation. During the wet season, gross human signatures showed up even better because vegetation in the area was cooled down. However, the cooling of uniforms and weapons by wet weather also served to reduce resolution between signatures. The pilot reported several linear arrays of horizontal human signatures, in and around the village. These might have been sleeping formations within village longhouses, or any one of them could have been a linear ambush formation. Bugeyes could not be more specific than that.

The patrol formation thinned even more as it approached the final trail into thickets and dense jungle around the village. Their villager guide seemed to want to lead them down the trail. He encouraged them to hurry. He emphasized the urgency with which the children needed treatment. Interpreters where not even translating his comments. Everyone was totally focused on the dark envelope into which they now ventured. Volkert was up toward point. As they passed about 300 meters down the trail, he noticed the villager escort passing them, whispering loudly to go on. He saw the guide pass on to the front, beyond the forward point element, and rushing headlong into the night. If it was going to happen, it would happen soon. He only hoped the others could feel the tension as well, and respond quickly when the time came. He slipped his weapon off safety and onto semi-automatic.

Gabe was in the middle of the formation alongside his small patient on the taut litter. He was carrying a small 250 ml IV bottle of Normal Saline in his left hand, his weapon in his right, pointing to the left, over the litter. Lt. Erickson was about one fourth of the way back from the front of the file directly behind pace counter and compass keeper. Gowen was, as usual, close by Erickson with the radio. Estrada was about 10 meters behind Gabe McCarthy, and Daniel Johnston was about one fourth forward from the rear end of the file. The yards had been trained to walk at night with weapons facing back and forth along a trail. In other words, as though every other man were left handed with his muzzle pointed to the right. Except for an occasional insect buzz around the ears, which no one dared to swat at, and the drip, drip drip of monsoon season, there was absolutely no sound from the jungle.

The communist Lieutenant had set his ambush platoon up about 2 meters from trail's edge. Any farther away, and no one could possibly see what they were shooting at. He had set them up so that they would be in line to the right side of their enemy marching in file back toward the village. This was because most Americans were right handed and preferred to point their weapons toward the left. The Judas agent, as one such was called by American Intelligence, had just passed the center of the kill zone and would pass beyond unmolested per arrangement. He would go on to the village and wait for them, claiming his just share of bounty from dead after the kill. When the American patrol point men were beyond his own position toward the upper middle third of the line. The communist officer would initiate his ambush by opening fire. Several times during the early evening, he had walked up and down the trail to make absolutely certain that his men were totally concealed. He had severely reprimanded one man for coughing, striking him across the face with a shell casing tipped stick he carried for effect. He was certain it had drawn blood, but the man did not make another sound thereafter.

The NVA officer was almost surprised when he finally realized that the Americans were moving past his own position. They were moving soundlessly in the dripping jungle, making no sloshing sounds at all on impacted earthen trail. They were almost invisible against the jungle in their tiger fatigues. He flipped down his weapon select and opened fire on a dark figure 2 meters away from him. The response startled him enough that he paused for a moment.

The reaction of the American strike force patrol was instantaneous. They had practiced this many times, and most were expecting it. Those with weapons pointing to the right returned fire before most of the communists had even followed up on their lieutenant's initial volley. As left pointing members of the patrol swung around, leveling their weapons also to the right, the ambushee's fire was intensified over a 1-2 second interval. By that time, those few communists who had been asleep were startled awake, pulling their triggers without really aiming, or even taking their weapons off safe. To those standing members of the American Patrol, every muzzle flash from waist down was a priority target. Gabe dropped the IV bottle onto the litter which was in process of being dropped by litter bearers swinging their own weapons, suspended from slings over their shoulders, up and over to their right. The little girl could not be a priority now. If they failed to break this ambush, she would not have a chance anyway. Gabe fought an enormous urge to drop down and seek low ground cover. He plunged forward into the jungle to his right firing on semi-automatic, in a 60 degree arc as he had been taught. To his left, he saw a muzzle flash, low to the ground. He leveled on that and fired several shots, hearing a low moan and gurgle. Without stopping, he plunged forward, seeking out other low muzzle flashes, aware of higher muzzle flashes to his right and left, slightly to his rear. They spooked him, causing him to want to swivel onto them, but an inner quicktime voice reminded him that he must trust the level of the flashes. He looked off to his right and saw a dark figure rising from the ground, firing a "clack clack" Kalishnakov sounding weapon on full automatic, another indication that this was the enemy. Gabe leveled his own weapon in that direction firing repeatedly into the form as it went down, the AK sounding gun silenced. Off to the right, he heard an animal like roar. It was a sound almost inhuman, accompanied by a stumping and swishing of plant life. Gabriel paused to change magazines and followed the sound in the bush, parallel to the trail back in the direction from which they had just come. Somehow, he knew it was Estrada. Above all else he knew, as certainly the enemy knew, that insane roar was the sound of invincible death. Estrada swept back down the trail relentlessly, mercilessly kicking and shooting in sweeps before him. Gabe stumbled over something terrified that he might fall to the ground and be mistaken for the recumbent enemy. He stepped repeatedly in wet, semi soft contours. Once, he saw a figure running away, off to the left. In his enhanced night vision, he caught a pit helmet over black pajamas. He leveled and fired several times, certain that he was hitting, but unable to stop the plunging form.

And suddenly, it was over. Not 45 seconds had passed from first to last shot. However, the jungle was not restored to silence. In place of the violent crescendo of gunfire, various melodies of human screams and moans filled the night. Gabe stopped for a moment, aware for the first time that he could actually see in the dark. He felt light on his feet and sensed that he could move with a speed and grace he had never known before. The first thing to pierce his haze of heightened sense was cognizance of the little girl in a fallen litter back on the trail. He turned to his right, plunging several yards back to the trail, then turning again to the right, racing uptrail to the destitute litter. There, lying on the ground was the pathetic child, huddled into a fetal position, her bandaged left leg lying unnoticed under an edge of the litter. He rushed to her, gathering her up into his arms, catching up the fallen IV bottle with cutter line, now dark with bloody backflow up into the tubing. She clung to him like a little chimpanzee, attempting to wrap the bloody, bandaged stump of her left leg around him as she curled her burned right leg also about his waist. Off to his right, he heard Estrada growling and yelling, chopping and cutting with his pack machete as if he were clearing a trail. As he moved further down the trail, away from Gabe's position, moans and screams fell silent. Gabe suddenly grasped what the fearsome weapons sergeant was doing, and for a moment, he had a vision of Estrada spitting out the nose of that young hoodlum back at Raleigh Durham.

Off to the south, up trail from his center position, there remained groaning and moaning. Occasionally, there would be a shot, silencing some particular human resonance. Gabe realized that the Yards were systematically killing wounded enemy and hoped that Erickson would put a stop to it, if for no other reason than to have a prisoner who might explain how they could launch such an exceptionally cruel ruse as to use a child for bait. Gabriel hung the IV bottle from a hinged wire suspension loop band on the base of the bottle. This he gripped in his teeth and walked forward, up the trail toward the village. The yards were bringing several wounded comrades back onto the trail. One came over to take the little girl so as to free up the medic to tend adult wounded. Reluctantly, Gabriel gave up the terrified child. In the dark, he found four injured Yards. It seemed as if he could be everywhere at once. His night vision was crystal clear, illuminating the jungle around him. He had never had such a rush of clear thought and movement. He knew without looking where the familiar appliances were in his M-5 aid bag. He rushed from injured to injured, building a mental document on each, keenly aware of what had just been done, and what he had yet to do. Dressings, irrigation, ligature, morphine, start an IV, splint an extremity; everything rushed by as though it were being viewed from roving camera. He bound up each man, mostly leg or lower extremity wounds, with one lower abdominal graze being tended by comrades with battle dressings. Gabe felt like he had never been able to think so clearly nor so fast in all his life. In the midst of this, he was brought to Lieutenant Erickson who had taken a round in the right flank, just above the gluteal fold. The seat of his trousers was awash with blood.

"Serves me right, Doc," Erickson grimaced between clenched teeth, "getting shot in the ass as a lesson for not listening to the old farts." He winced as Gabe cut away the seat of his pants to reveal a slashing furrow of bloody red meat.

"Can you move your leg backward, sir?"

Erickson painfully attempted to extend his thigh, succeeding in moving it about 20 degrees covering 10 to 12 inches of space. "Awwwoh! Hurts like hell, Doc."

"I know, sir, but the good news is, if you can move it, you probably still have a sciatic nerve. The muscle will heal." He placed a large battle dressing over the area, and plunged a morphine syrette into Erickson's thigh.

"This will have to do for now, sir, I have to see some of the others."

"Go on Doc. Let me know when you have a count." Erickson winced back through gritted teeth.

One of the Yards came up to him "*Bac Si*! Come now! Tope Rangh, he hurt!!"

Gabe rushed back down-trail. As he approached the litter, still splayed across the trail, he came upon Tope Rangh. Evidently, Gabe passed by him previously, before they had brought the injured interpreter out of the bush. Gabriel realized that Tope must have gone down right next to him a few feet into the bush. Tope's lower left leg was a mess. Clearly, a 7.62 AK round had passed through, striking from left front, drilling across the leg just in front of the fibula, hitting the tibia full force, shattering columnar bone and in the process, fracturing the strutlike fibula as well. Tope's leg was flaccid below the wound located about halfway between the Tibial Tubercle, below the knee, and the Malleoli of the ankle. The leg hung from a thick island of tissue connected to lower leg on the lateral posterior aspect, and a thin peninsula of tissue medially. Gabe placed a tourniquet around his distal thigh, stemming the gush of blood, which had formed a pool in which Tope was lying. Battle dressings were gathered around the leg and a pneumatic splint slipped on carefully over these dressings. It was then inflated over the moans of Tope. They released the tourniquet just a bit, only to see a cloud of dark fluid form within the clear plastic tube despite compression directly over the wound. Johnston had come up to help and started to tighten the tourniquet up again, but Gabe stopped him:

"Wait, I think it's mostly venous backflow pressure. Loosen the tourniquet completely and let's see what happens."

Daniel Johnston was not at all clear what the young medic was saying, but did as advised. Sure enough, bleeding slowed and stopped within the clear plastic cocoon.

"Guess you know your stuff, doc." He said.

"Not enough to keep my mouth shut about coming back to this jinxed village."

"Doc, you advised what you thought was right. It was the LT's call, and we all went along with it. As it is, looks like we came out all right."

Looking around him at the wounded, Gabe failed to see how everything was all right. Big Daniel Johnston seemed to read his mind.

"I know it looks bad from here, Doc, but we wiped out most of a whole platoon, and didn't lose one single man. And WE were the ones being ambushed! In the laws of jungle parlance, that means 'we done all right' ".

Gabe nodded looking for recognition into the familiar dark features of his more senior NCO Assistant Team Sergeant. As he gazed over at Johnston, a peculiar thing started to happen. Gabe's night vision started to blur and he could no longer see more than just a few inches away. His legs felt wobbly and weak, and he found himself settling down onto his haunches. He felt a sudden urge to urinate and noticed blurry others urinating off into the bushes, some onto places where the bodies of their enemies lay. His head started to spin and he looked over again at Johnston, pitching forward onto the big black man's shoulder for a moment.

"That's all right Doc, you done good. Don't you worry, it's just the adrenaline washing back out of your system. It'll pass."

As Gabe hung there, suspended for a moment on the broad shoulder of SFC Johnston, he had a vague recollection that this must be a parasympathetic response, but his mind could not focus, and for a few seconds he passed out, coming to in graded stages. Daniel Johnston was slapping him lightly on the cheeks.

"Come on back, now Doc, we be needing you too much right now for you to go out on us."

Gabe started upright, gathering in his aid bag and weapon. He arose and stepped off to the other side of the trail, away from where the enemy dead were strewn about, emptying the rest of his bladder opposite where the little girl's litter still lay diagonally across the trail.

Well before sunrise, Erickson's patrol entered the village, first sending security on ahead, then toting their wounded into *Lo Dao*. Johnston and Volkert sought out the village chief who made a blinky-eyed appearance, visibly shaking off the deep sleep of early morning. His cognizance heightened quickly as he saw wounded members of the American patrol. He'd stirred earlier at the sounds of shots nearby the village, but by the time he had awakened to them, they were pretty much over. He had figured that one side or the other would conquer for the moment, then all would fade into obscurity as the biology of the jungle once again took over. His job as Chief was to manage his people as best he could within this troubled land. Now he realized that he would need to deal with the victors. He would discover what sort of vengeance these Americans were capable of, for although he knew his village was not the instigator of this firefight, the conquerors would almost certainly hold the villagers responsible. Indeed, last night, shortly after the Americans had left, the communists showed up demanding to know what sort of intercourse the Americans had with this village. When the villagers unanimously insisted that the Americans had simply left when asked to do so, the communists were incredulous. They searched the village, and found a circular piece of chocolate wrapped in tin foil from an American C-Ration in possession of one of their children. They confiscated the chocolate and the child, departing on the trail of the Americans northward, much to the travails of desperate parents. The old chieftain had to forcefully restrain the parents and could only hope that the communists would bring the child back intact. If not, ... well ... better one child than the whole village. If these communists decided to turn their wrath in force upon them, it might indeed cost the whole village.

Actually, the chief was almost pleasantly surprised to see the Americans with their Montagnard strike force emerging from jungle to the north. It meant that somehow, an encounter had taken place in which two forces of approximately equal size concluded a firefight with the Americans victorious. Or else, the communists had run off to the Northwest. In any event, the Chief had to deal with the Americans at this moment, and they seemed quite grim. Through an interpreter, he heard words that began to sow real fear into his heart.

"Chief, assemble your people."

"Why must my people assemble? It is yet very early and most remain asleep. Cannot this wait until the light of morning?"

"No, chief, it cannot. Assemble your people, now!"

The chief observed members of the American Patrol taking up circumferential positions about the village, clearly blocking any possible escape. With trembling hands, he walked over to a huge, horizontal bamboo trunk, cut with grooves to cause a loud drum-like resonance. He raised a weighted club and began beating on the bamboo. Many of the villagers had heard shots earlier and were awake, peeking out of long-houses. Village fires were stoked in order to raise some illumination in the epicenter of the village. As the old chief gazed about the increasing luminance, he observed one of the Americans holding onto the little girl who had been taken earlier. At least she was still alive. However, she was bandaged and it looked as though her left leg was gone below the knee. Had the Americans done this thing? He wondered.

As villagers assembled the parents of the missing girl rushed forward upon seeing her, and took her from the arms of an American. He held a bottle connected to her by a line which seemed to be sticking in her arm. Without fear or hesitation, the mother jerked the connecting line out of her daughter, causing the girl to start crying. She looked with cold eyes at the American who had momentarily attempted to stop her. With her lost babe in arms, she was ready to die before letting anyone take her child away again. The American did not force the issue, much to the old Chief's relief. The leader of the Americans was wounded. He conversed with the big, black Nubian who then addressed the Chief through a Montagnard interpreter:

"Chief. If someone steals in your village, what is done?"

This seemed like a prelude to some form of public punishment. The Chieftan was careful about his next answer.

"It would depend upon the nature of the theft."

"Suppose someone stole one of your children and hurt that child for an evil purpose?"

Now, this seemed strange. Certainly, this village had not stolen one of its own children. Were they playing some clever allegory in order to wreak vengeance with some sort of object lesson?

"But, one of our children was stolen by the communists! Surely you can understand that we have suffered over the loss of her. Why do you wish to punish us more?"

As the interpreter conveyed this back to the American, the black man shook his head while expressing misunderstanding with his large, ebony eyebrows.

"No, No, we are not here to punish you. We are here to support you in seeking justice for the kidnapping of one of your children. She was brought to us earlier by someone representing himself as her father or guardian. We were told she was one of many children injured by a land mine, and that you had summoned us back to this village in order to help."

As the interpretation proceeded, nearly all the village people broke out simultaneously exclaiming that this was a lie and in fact the child had been abducted by the communists just last evening. The little girl's mother stood silent, but with growing confusion.

"You see, chief, we believe there is one among you who led this kidnapping; the same one who came to us last night representing himself as one of you. This bad man, this cruel, very bad man, showed us your little girl with her terrible injury. How could we resist her suffering in our hearts? Many of us have little ones of our own. How could we say 'no' to returning if we could help in some way?"

"But, it was not us!" the chief insisted, still wary that they were going to somehow hurt his people for this travesty. "When she left us, she was whole. They must have maimed her before they found you." Even as he said it, he felt a distant rage beginning to well up within him, intensified by all the years of obliging, of paying homage to his much-hated communist viceroys. He turned and looked over the village population assembled around him. It was the girl's mother who first pointed out the Judas agent.

"Here! Here! He is not one of us." She said pointing to a man who stood in their midst. The man replied back at her.

"Why, shut up old mother. You know that I have been here many years. You are just angry over the price of my pigs. Surely that is not reason to betray me to these strangers!"

Johnston had the conversation translated to him and directed that his Yards bring the man forward. Realizing resistance was futile, the man stepped forward boldly. He was clad in a loincloth, similar to most the rest of the villagers. He certainly bore a resemblance to the man who had come into their camp last night, but that man had on a black shirt, and in the dark, one could not be absolutely certain. The accused man insisted that this was a matter of personal disagreement with this one woman. He maintained that he had been a member of the village for many years. He turned around, clearly seeking to engage the stares of all the villagers. Was there intimidation in his countenance? SFC Daniel Johnston turned to the old Chieftan.

"You decide chief. Is this man a part of your village? If he is, we will leave him alone. If not, our justice will be swift and discrete. No trace of him will ever be found."

The old chief looked at the accused man. Clearly, he was not a member of the village. He had Montagnard like features, certainly, but he did not belong to this caste. The Judas agent glared at the chief. In his eyes, the message was clear, *'If you do not protect me from these round eyes, my people will seek vengeance upon you.'* The chief saw the intonation broadcast loud and clear. He also saw cruelty and dark sadism, which could disfigure that beautiful little girl without conscience. If the chief spoke to liberate this man, the communists would reward him. But, he would lose his people, for surely, though they would stand behind his decision, none would respect his leadership if he let this travesty go unpunished. The chief looked over at the child's mother. She had already condemned herself by identifying the man. Nothing could be done to save her if this man reported back to his communist cadre. On the other hand, if the Americans were to render judgment on the Judas agent, it would fill the village with a sense of conciliation. Were the Americans really strong enough to execute this man and prevent the story from being told among their own Montagnards? It was a terrible dilemma. The old Chief had to make up his mind, for hesitance made an impression of its own. In the end, it was his love for his own people that motivated his reply.

"This man, I do not know. I believe he was with the communist patrol that came through last night and abducted our little girl after you left us."

The man lunged forward at the old Montagnard chieftain as the mother of the girl shouted in her language,

"Yes, yes! He is the one who hurt my baby!!"

Occupying a place in space between Judas agent and old chief, there was an ominous presence that up until this point had stood silently off to one side of the old chief. As the communist infiltrator lunged forward, Estrada stepped between. The charging man ran head on into Estrada, striking him midsection, then falling backward as if running into a solid wall. Looking up into glowering eyes of the Latin toro, the communist agent saw death. He fumbled under his loincloth, pulling a grenade from his crotch. As he did so, Estrada raised a huge right boot which came stomping down on the man's right hand, crushing it against the ground as the left hand went for the grenade pin. Estrada leaned over and caught the left hand, picking the man up while his right hand was still pinned under the boot, pulling his enemy's arm up , raising the man's midsection off the ground and straining the arms directly up and down. As pressure mounted on his right hand, the Judas agent could not continue to grasp the grenade and it fell from his fingers. It was quickly snatched up by one of the strike force Montagnards.

In one, fluid movement, Estrada released his boot grip of the man, continuing to raise the left arm with his right hand, raising the man up and off the ground. Arnie then grabbed the man's hair, which was long enough to offer a great handful. In quick movements, which seemed almost graceful for someone so imposing, Estrada let go of the left arm. He grabbed his K-bar knife suspended upside down from the left chest strap of load bearing equipment, and cut the man's throat. He did so with no trace of masochism or satisfaction. Rather, like a kosher butcher, attempting to administer as humane and decisive an end to this despot as possible. Those villagers who observed noted that the communists never killed publicly like this. In their public executions, they were always just as cruel and pain lingering as imaginable. By contrast, this big American lowered the corpse, almost respectfully, to the ground and directed several of his strikers to remove the body with as little fanfare as possible. Johnston attempted to draw people's attention away by addressing them again through the interpreter.

"You have suffered from the communists for so long. Surely, there must come a time when you decide to take a stand against them. When you are ready, please, let us know."

Even in this, the people were amazed; no demands or threats, no ultimatums. For the balance of that day, the villagers offered of their meager means to the visiting American Patrol, treating them like welcomed guests. Though collectively, the village was not entirely ready to accept an affiliation treatise, they certainly wanted to express a form of thanks for returning their lost child. Via an interpreter, Gabe explained to the mother that if she would bring the little girl to *Swordfish Lair*, they could reconstruct the stump under anesthesia, then possibly even arrange for a prosthesis. The mother seemed genuinely willing to comply. Later, the parents explained how the girl had been selected from among all the other children by the C Ration chocolate disc. With the disclosure, Gabe castigated himself severely, for he was the one who had left the incriminating chocolate treat with her. He recognized that in some distant, convoluted way, he had played a role in the mutilation of this little girl. For that, he felt beholding to her. Her parents perceived this somehow and cordially permitted him to develop a passing relationship with their crippled child. As time went on, over days, months and years to follow, he found himself praying for her often. In so doing, he beseechingly expressed the fervent invocation that as she grew in understanding and knowledge that comes of age, she would not subscribe the same degree of tormented conviction, which he would ever ascribe to himself, in her behalf.

DISTRIBUTION OF *BRUGIA MALAYI*

FIGURE VII.42. Distribution of filariasis malayi. (Courtesy of Dr. J. F. B. Edeson in the Bulletin of the World Health Organization, 1962.)

Chapter 2 – Friendship & Retribution

July, 1971

On the day after the execution of the Judas Agent at *Lo Dao*, what was left of Lieutenant Erickson's patrol departed, leaving behind a sterile ambush site. After confiscating weapons and intelligence, bodies of the enemy dead were moved and posed in a different location far removed from *Lo Dao* so as to confuse and lead off any communist investigation into the incident. This left the appearance of an American Long Range Patrol (LRP) having tangled with them. Johnston had advised Erickson on this just prior to Lieutenant Erickson being med-evaced out. As yet, the people of *Lo Dao* remained uncommitted in their loyalties to either side and the Americans did not want to leave any strong communist inclination to punish the village. *Lo Dao*, as well as any other villages in the area would appear to have been innocent bystanders. No trace of the Judas Agent would ever be found. Nobody on the patrol would ever mention his person or his demise.

Sgt. Gabriel McCarthy evacuated his wounded casualties out on the day of the ambush. An extemporaneous LZ was set up northeast of the village. A casualty report was communicated by radio with Glickman who would see to triage and disposition from the L-Site. Under command of SFC Johnston, the entire patrol returned to Swordfish lair toward the end of that week hiking all of about 48 kilometers back. Taken as a whole, their efforts were considered quite successful. Out of 7 villages visited, they recruited 3 and pretty much left one, *Lo Dao*, a strong candidate for future affiliation. They had accumulated 51 confirmed enemy KIA (Killed in Action). Their own losses included 1 US WIA (Wounded in Action) –Lieutenant Erickson- and 5 CIDG WIA. Of these, the most critical was Tope Rangh.

When medevacs took out the wounded, SFC Glickman strongly lobbied that the Montagnards be returned to the L-Site dispensary rather than evacuated to an ARVN facility. Although he was quite capable of managing wound care on 4 of the 5, if Tope's leg was to be saved, the hardy little interpreter would have to be evacuated to a skilled surgical limb salvage team. Therefore, both Tope Rangh and Lieutenant Erickson were taken out on the same medevac, bound for South Vietnam. Erickson was sent on to a US field hospital at Pleiku wherein he was taken to Surgery at a field MAST unit and the damage to his derriere repaired. They performed a debridement and delayed primary closure that would keep him down (bottomside up) for about 4 weeks. On the same helicopter which took Erickson to the US MAST at Pleiku, Tope Rangh was taken to a Vietnamese Military Hospital in keeping with theater wide mandates that ARVN care for their own indigenous wounded. SFC Glickman had done everything possible to keep Tope within the American system, but once out of Area Focus, Special Operations command did not have as much influence, and bureaucracy reigned supreme.

Upon returning to the L-Site Saturday, July 3rd, 1971; Gabe attended, along with the remaining patrol members, to a debriefing session, during which they presented a detailed after action report of their month long patrol. Much to the surprise of everyone who had been away, there were Vietnamese LLDB present at the debriefing. The Viets came into the teamhouse conference room without being invited, and remained in a state of subliminal tension evident to everyone. Later, Briant gathered the Americans together to give them an update on this unexpected turn of events. The LLDB team had arrived on the day after the wounded were delivered to Pleiku. They had evidently been alerted by Tope Rangh's admission into an ARVN hospital, that there was still a Special Forces operational detachment mission running within the MACV theater. They had not realized it was actually in Laos. Vietnamese military insistence on disclosure regarding the Special Forces site location was met with either denial or reticence from U.S. MACV liaisons. Catching scent of a very sensitive, and therefore likely, very expensive operation, Captain Nguyen Van Nuong, designated ferret for General Duong An Minh, proceeded to interpose his own influence into the operation. Acting on a breaking opportunity, Captain Nuong demanded that his LLDB team be transported back to the L-Site by the same Medevac helicopter that had delivered Tope Rangh. Somehow, the Viets managed to get lower echelon approval (with the tacit influence of Big Minh and President Thieu) for an airlift back to the medevac site and showed up 2 days later demanding accommodation by U.S. forces present. Captain Fernstead had little opportunity to determine what to do with them and so offered temporary quarters in the U.S. team bunker until he could get things straightened out. This added close quarters to the unwelcome relationship, further straining things.

Traditionally, the LLDB would assume counterpart roles parallel to American Special Forces A-teams. On the same day as their arrival, the Viets assigned their own communications NCO's to the commo bunker. When Gowen refused to let them use the equipment, they protested to Captain Fernstead who sustained the decision to deny them radio access and so they simply sat in the bunker and observed. The radio equipment used in operation Fisherman was newer and different from what the Viets were used to. Very long range, Amplitude Modulated communications went beyond their expertise. Also, the Nebo code encryption was entirely unfamiliar to the LLDB. Gowen and Winkle had no idea whether or not the Viets could speak any English. They were certainly part of some intelligence gathering effort on the part of ARVN to find out more about this operation. The Vietnamese

Weapons and Engineer NCO's were sent to work on camp defense network construction, but they considered labor in common with Montagnards to be beneath them. Therefore, they demanded assignment to supervisory positions in which they would supposedly oversee manual labor on construction of defenses. It did not take them long to become tyrannical in this. Their presence was very different from the Americans who would actually work, sweat and labor side by side with the Yards. There were also two LLDB medics. However, their training was limited to litter bearing and bandaging. They could offer no expertise in the dispensary, and refused to participate in mundane nursing duties such as changing sheets, emptying bedpans, drawing blood or rounding on patients. Glickman caught them nosing round the narcotics locker and had to make certain it was secured. Just after arriving, the Vietnamese executive contingent formed a coalition in which their team *Dai'Uy* addressed Captain Fernstead in broken English with audience support from Viet Executive Officer and two Senior NCO's. The team Captain, *Dai'Uy* Van Nuong, seated himself directly in front of Fernstead, across from an OD field desk and folding chair. Three other Vietnamese stood in a semi circle around their officer, looking down on Fernstead.

"But Dai'Uy Flnsed", you must see, this our country and we must better coordinate with you on any operation. If needed, I have authority take control here. You are guests in my country."

"*Dai'Uy* Nuong, I have not been advised of any such authority on your part. In fact, I was not advised that you even had clearance to be a part of this operation." Fernstead carried on the conversation as the lone American in his own command day room, somewhat irritated by the massed presence of this Vietnamese delegation.

"But under ARVN, MACV and CIDG conventions, Luc Luong Dac Biet have such authority." At this, the retinue of Vietnamese cadre nodded their heads solemnly, attesting to some familiarity with English.

"Sir, you are quite aware that those conventions ceased to be in force when the CIDG program ended in December of 1970." As he said this, all the Vietnamese soldiers shook their heads.

"But you here, in Vietnam, these Vietnamese citizens. We have authority over Vietnamese citizens." Again, the four Viets nodded in support. Fernstead was having trouble keeping his temper.

"Technically, sir, this is not Vietnam, therefore, you would have no such authority even if the CIDG directives were still in force, which they are not."

"What you mean, this not Vietnam? Where are we? Laos?..." at that he began chattering away in Vietnamese with his Lieutenant and NCO's who were all speaking at once. Finally, He turned back to Fernstead.

"Dai' Uy Flnsed I must insist, we use radio, talk to my superiors for instructions. Our radios no work in these mountains, must use yours." He spoke as if issuing an aside on his way to accomplishing an accepted directive. Fernstead remained seated behind his field desk.

Dai'Uy Nuong, our radio net is classified and I have no authority to let you use our equipment, which your communications people would probably not be familiar with anyway. However, if you would like, I can arrange for transportation of you and your entire team back to Pleiku."

At that, all the Vietnamese LLDB again began shaking their heads vigorously.

"No, No, Capn Flnsed, we have orders; stay here and make communication. You must comply!" The Vietnamese Captain rolled his voice in such a way as to intone sincerity mixed with righteous indignation.

"*Dai'Uy* Nuong, you understand how classified operations work. I have no authority to grant your people use of our radios. You have only one option here, I will arrange for you and your team to be taken back to your area command. You can resolve the issue with your superiors there."

The Vietnamese officer was clearly flummoxed. He realized that once he was removed from this site, he would no longer have any decision making influence over the situation. Under Vietnamese regulations, he would have to be on site for at least thirty days in order for his presence to be considered a Permanent Change of Station (PCS). If he were to be returned to Pleiku, he might not be provided an opportunity to come back. Captain Nuong had scoped out the camp and realized that great power was being exercised over this operation. Where there was great power, there was much money. So long as he was present, *Dai'Uy* Nuong knew that he had a chance to slice out a piece of the resource pie. Once gone, he would surely be separated from this potentially profitable opportunity. He would also be cut off from the epicenter of intelligence that General Minh had tasked him to accomplish. In any case, all the Viets knew that presence was 9/10's of profit. Although somewhat intimidated by the idea that they might be in Laos, they were not about to be willingly displaced. However, the Vietnamese officer also understood that he had a dire need to communicate with General Minh regarding the location and circumstances of this L-Site. Dai'Uy Nuong's demeanor changed to placating and patronizing.

"Dai' Uy, we stay here with you, our American counterparts. This where we belong. We serve these people and help you. I know you only not let us make communication because you young and not familiar with policy here. We want help you. We stay. Meantime, you explain superiors that we be here. Tell them talk to our superiors. This all get straighten out." This commentary also proceeded to the accompaniment of nodding heads.

Fernstead figured his alternatives. Like unwanted in-laws on a honeymoon, they were here. There seemed no way he could force them to leave short of bearing arms against them, something he clearly did not want to do. To be certain that they understood he was not agreeing with their position, he replied in slowly measured tones.

"I will convey the situation to our superiors who will then coordinate with yours. In the meantime, if you insist on remaining here, you must respect all confidential aspects of this location. That means you may not use our radios unless I am personally there to oversee any transmissions. Your people would be most welcome in assisting our construction crews and medical facility. I expect your team to make daily musters with our own and you, sir, to be accountable for the actions of all your men while in this location. Is that clear?"

The LLDB captain hardened his features a bit.

"I tolerate you talk like that only because you young and not understand nature of our two countries' relationship. Vietnamese Captains must be longer experience before promote to Captain, therefore, you not know. But, I accept your offer and make this clear, my men under my control. One other thing must be clear also, I only take orders from my command chain, not American. I must speak directly to my superiors for change orders, you understand this"

In truth, Vietnamese rank advancements were not largely based on merit. Every 3 or 4 years, Vietnamese authorities would issue an ARVN directive that all first lieutenants in grade over 7 years be promoted to Captain. Unless a Vietnamese junior officer had family or political connections, it could indeed take a very long time to advance to senior field grade rank. Often, those becoming Captains had spent much of their executive training in the rear, well removed from forward field commands. Although Fernstead knew nothing of Captain Nuong's background, the American officer had himself spent 3 tours in Vietnam and during that time, had undergone many exchanges with LLDB. This Long Low Dirty Bastard was not unlike most of the rest with whom he had worked during mid to late 60's. One of the things that had so endeared Captain Fernstead to the idea of operation Fisherman was that he would act under a single command and control structure, delivered from meddling LLDB. The present circumstance posed a major diplomatic as well as practical conundrum. He could only play host for now, and so acknowledged.

Dai'Uy Nuong considered this exchange to be a great victory in terms of "face". He knew that his own command authorities, under General Minh, would insist on knowing more about what was going on before issuing orders for the LLDB team to withdraw. In the meantime, his Vietnamese team could become entrenched and start to siphon off some of the riches here for the taking. *Dai'Uy* Nuong would have to figure out some way to send back a portion of gleaned profits to his own superiors, but one of the great things about being isolated like this was that his debit ledger was not open to scrutiny from above. So long as he got something back to them, at least in principle if not substance, they would keep him here. He could become a wealthy man.

For Ca Rangh, the presence of LLDB in her village was like a nightmare revisited. Five years prior, she was living in a small Katu village in Thula Thien province. At the time, her husband had been missing for over a year. He had last been seen when conscripted, much against his will, by a communist propaganda squad. Frantic after a year of no word from him, she had sought out the South Vietnamese for help, naively believing that because her husband was taken by communists, anti-communist Ethnic Vietnamese would come to her aid in attempting to find him. She sent a letter off to the local province chief. Being impressed with a Katu Montagnard who could actually write in good Vietnamese, the province chief replied to her correspondence, informing her by letter that her village fell under the auspices of a Vietnamese LLDB team at *Kham Duc* in Quang Tin province. Ca determined to go to *Kham Duc*. On arriving in *Kham Duc*, she sought directions from an old Montagnard man she passed by at the entrance to the village. He was carrying a huge sheaf of similarly sized sticks on his back, balanced in a manner that suggested he had carried such loads for many years. On hearing her inquiry, he eye'd her warily, recognizing her quaint mountain accent. He answered her in the Katu dialect:

"Be careful, little sister, the *Luc Luong* do not care much for our people."

She replied earnestly

"But old grandfather, they are the enemies of our enemies, and it is said that the enemy of my enemy is my friend."

He replied with a wistful shrug of his encumbered shoulders as he passed her, breathing out a final epithet from under the large bundle: "In this case, child, you may find that the enemy of our enemy are one and the same. Again, be careful little sister."

That day was the first time Ca had ever seen Americans. She dared not approach any of them, although she spoke their language, having been tutored in French and English as a child by French missionaries. They seemed so strange; large and foreign. Some of them had eyes the color of the sky, like the French citizens she'd known as a child. They all seemed to be busy doing something. Their English accents were also peculiar to her recollection of the proper English she had been taught. One or two of them seemed to notice her, apparently recognizing her unusual, homespun Katu Montagnard clothing. She dared not make eye contact with any of them, for they were aliens in this land.

Kham Duc was certainly not a large community when compared to *Da Nang*, or even *Plieku*. However, it was the largest community Ca had ever been in. As a girl of not quite 18 at the time, she took upon herself a great risk in deciding to travel alone searching for her husband. She felt that this quest should be hers and hers alone. As if to signify that because she had a husband now she was an adult, she felt that seeking out her husband was fundamentally her responsibility. Of course, had her family known of her intentions, they would have either accompanied her or forbidden her to go all together. For that reason, she struck out on her own, taking a small, rolled haversack filled with rice and fish heads along with a few personal items. It had taken her about a week to make her way eastward toward a city called *Quang Nam*. On the outskirts of *Quang Nam*, she passed through a Jeh Montagnard village seeking proper directions to *Kham Duc*.

She was directed to a trail of sorts, which supposedly led to *Kham Duc*. On her second night after leaving the Jeh village, she had been awakened, within the pitched branches of an overnight hootch she constructed off the trail. Her sleep was disturbed by staccato sounds of gunfire. This sound was not new to her, but it was much closer than she had ever heard it before. After laying awake sleepless for the rest of the night, she struck out at first light. About a kilometer down the trail, she came across the remains of six Asian men, all dressed in black pajamas, strewn across the trail. They were horribly mutilated, apparently by grenades and small arms fire. Some were missing legs. After witnessing the horror, Ca had rushed headlong into the jungle, away from the abhorrent scene. She realized that travelling by trail was perhaps even more dangerous than the jungle itself. And so, she took to travelling parallel with the trail in a direction, as best she could determine to be, south by west. Four days later, she found *Kham Duc*. In the interim, she had indeed left behind any semblance of adolescence and became a creature of survival. After entering into *Kham Duc* and speaking with the old man, Ca Rangh eventually made her way to the LLDB command post.

Her first impression of the LLDB was a mix of rash haughtiness and slothfulness. Wherever the LLDB went, they seemed to expect Montagnards to know their place. That place was evidently far beneath any form of acknowledgement that Montagnards were anything like fellow human beings. In her first observed encounter between a Montagnard and an LLDB enlisted man, she observed the garishly uniformed South Vietnamese soldier grab a Montagnard child about 7 years old playing alongside a muddy walkway. The Viet proceeded to throw the child in front of him, into an unusually deep puddle, and used the child to step on as he passed over the puddle. She heard him comment to another LLDB soldier, as they both stepped onto and over the child, that they did not want to upset their *"Spit Shine"*, laughing and pointing to their boots. She had no idea what a "Spit Shine" was, observing that both the LLDB soldier's boots were quite filthy with mud anyway. The poor child was pressed down into the depths of the puddle such that his face and torso were completely submerged. After the LLDB soldiers passed, the little boy came up spluttering and crying. Ca came to his aid, tenderly lifting him out of the puddle and wiping him dry with her haversack, in the process soiling her own clothing. She was interrupted in the act of doing so by another LLDB soldier, this one an officer, though she did not understand the rank insignia. He spoke, however, with an air of control and assertion, which told her instinctively that he was a man in charge of others.

"You there, keep your child away from this area. He has just been taught a valuable lesson to stay away from places he does not belong!" The officer gestured pointing back to the LLDB bunker behind him.

"Please sir," she replied in the Vietnamese tongue, "he is not my son, I am just helping him." She stood up straight, as the little boy whimpered, burying himself within the folds of her skirt. For a moment, she had an unkind thought that she also wished the child would go away so that she could discuss the issue of her husband with this Vietnamese officer who seemed to exert some kind of authority. As she attempted to gently nudge him away, the child seemed all the more determined to cling to her thigh and dress.

"Actually, sir, I have come to ask for your help, about my husband."

The Vietnamese looked her over. Beneath the traditional homespun trappings, he perceived the body of a strong, healthy young woman, uncommonly attractive for a Montagnard.

"Your husband? What, is he beating you? I cannot interfere!"

"Oh, no sir, he is a very honorable man, very kind and tender. He has been taken away by the communists and I know he is being held against his will. There are patrols. They come to our village, take things from us, rice and our young men. They do this with guns and much rudeness. Perhaps I can help you to intercept them in the mountains. Perhaps if you do so, they will tell you about my husband, where we can find him?"

The LLDB officer snorted, in derision, "What, do you think me stupid? For all I know, you may be a VC, come to lead us into an ambush!"

At that, the vision returned to her mind of those dead men, lying alongside the trail. Certainly, they were not members of this army, therefore, probably communists. However, she could easily understand this officer's hesitation. He went on as she began shaking her head attempting to earnestly explain that she was not a communist. The Vietnamese officer leered at her:

"*MOI DO CHO DE* !"

She recoiled at the profane, acrimonious insult, not understanding what she had done to deserve such verbal abuse. The Vietnamese officer continued:

"You come here to deceive our brave men to going into those barren, worthless mountains just so that you can die gloriously leading us to our deaths so that the Communists can claim another propaganda victory!"

The more he spoke, clearly the more infuriated he was becoming. She stopped shaking her head, transfixed by the transformation of this Vietnamese soldier into some kind of maniacal creature.

"That would suit you just fine wouldn't it? And you would surely die just for the privilege of claiming our blood no doubt!"

As he spoke, he started advancing toward her. She would have backed away but for the clinging child which caused her to stumble back toward the puddle. The LLDB officer stepped forward quickly, grabbing her by the lapels, slapping her senselessly across the face. For a moment she was dazed and shaken as lights seemed to dance before her eyes. She had just started to recover when the Viet backhanded her again, knocking her down and the child with her. As she fell to the ground, the LLDB officer reached down, grabbing her hair and pulling her back up, ignoring the sobbing child, again lying in the mud..

"*DO CHO DE!* I will teach you to come here and pretend to invite us up into your filthy mountains!" With that, he pivoted on his heel, dragging her into the bunker. In the way of her people, she continued to resist in as polite a manner as she could, believing that so long as she did not fight, the soldier would not punish her any more. Ca was aware of a damp earthen parterre as she was dragged roughly into a dark, foreboding, sandbagged corner, wherein he threw her down at the same time unbuckling his trousers. She realized instantly what was about to happen and immediately began to scream for help. This only invited a kick in the abdomen from her tormentor as he shouted down at her.

"Go ahead and yell, you little VC tramp! See what your screaming will bring you!"

As he spoke, two or three other Vietnamese, similarly attired with red berets, entered into the bunker and watched tacitly as their officer stripped Ca of her wrap around sarong, kicking her as she clung to the folds, attempting to prevent him from unwinding her out of the garment. Realizing that kicking her in the ribs was having little effect, he took to kicking her in the head, which further dazed and disassociated her. For a moment, she blacked out, and as she did so, her grip lessened, enabling the Viet to jerk up forcibly, rolling her out of her clothing and onto the floor, mostly naked. She forcibly pressed her knees together, and as her consciousness seemed to return, she fought back in earnest, kicking and flailing her arms, but to no avail. The other LLDB joined in the fracas now, pinning her to the musty floor, forcing her legs apart.

Each of them took a turn with her and when they were finished the officer, who was the first, came over to her. He picked up her hardy fabric sarong and flung it over her head, leaving her bottom uncovered. She clawed her way out of the broadcloth garment, wrapping it around her in a pitiful, instinctive attempt to cover her shame. Sensing this, the officer shouted:

"Now, you can just go back to your VC friends and tell them what happens to stupid little Montagnard girls who come here and try to deceive us! Get out! Get out! Get out!" With that he commenced kicking her in the direction of the bunker entrance, but not so hard that she was unable to come to her hands and knees. She crawled out, disheveled, bleeding and wet receiving a final kick to her bare rectum as she cleared the doorway.

Once through the doorway, Ca attempted to stand up, but stumbled and tripped over her clothing, falling face forward into the same mud puddle she had rescued the little boy from about 20 minutes earlier. The child was still there, looking at her in shock as she lay face down in the puddle. He came forward, attempting to help her, as she had helped him. Still disoriented, she flinched from the little hands which reached around her matted hair and lifted her head out of the muddy mire. When she recognized the little boy, she looked at him and for the first time in the entire ordeal, she began to weep. The little boy pulled on her hand, tugging her away from the scene. She tacitly followed him, wrapping her sarong around herself as she did so.

The little Montagnard boy took her haversack and lead Ca Rangh through the streets of *Kham Duc* like a guide dog leading someone blind. She could only look down at the ground, thankful that her long hair hid her bruised and swollen face from those around who would surely know what had happened from her screams inside the bunker. They walked on together for what seemed like a very long time. As she looked down at the ground, haloed within the fall of her hair, she perceived that they were passing through some sort of gated complex. Eventually, the little boy lead her to a tarmac bunker, also sandbagged. Instinctively, she quivered as she viewed jungle boots again on the ground next to her within the periphery of her veiled hair. She winced on hearing the strange, but understood, sound of English. It was the Americans.

"Good Lord, Ma'am! What hap..." the interrogatory was cut off by the little boy who shook his head vigorously, apparently also understanding the English and doing everything within his seven year old power to implore the American Green Beret not to ask. Evidently, the American did understand and instead, started to put his arm around Ca from which she shrank away. She heard him call out to someone:

"*Mommason*! Come on over here! Houdgie," the American addressed the little boy as though they were on very familiar terms, "Tell Sergeant Packer and Captain Doorman to come over as soon as possible."

Ca again felt a presence near her and somehow knew it to be maternal. For the first time since leaving the LLDB bunker, she raised her eyes, to behold the face of an old Montagnard woman. The old one looked upon her with the eyes of a grandmother who understands. This old woman, they called "Mommason", led Ca into an American bunker. Ca noticed a large white circle with a red cross in it, painted on one side of the structure as she entered. It was very unlike the Vietnamese bunker. The flooring was wooden and everything was clean, dry, well lighted. It had a strange, pungent odor about it and although she had never smelled disinfectant before, she knew somehow that it was an odor of cleanness. The old woman spoke to Ca softly, and when he returned, little Houdgie took hold of her hand again. Gently, reassuringly, Mommason explained to Ca that she must let the American examine her. This American was a very good *Bac Si* and would know how to make her better. Ca wondered if anything could ever make her better again, but submitted to an examination.

The American draped her lower body with a clean, white sheet, obviously attempting to show some modesty in her behalf. He then instructed Ca through Mommason to lie back. Although she understood his English quite well, Ca preferred to let Mommason translate the statement in her even more remote Jeh dialect. Reluctantly, Ca did as she was instructed. The American had instruments and bandages nearby. More gently than she could have imagined any man capable of being, the American washed and cleaned her. Eventually, he asked her several questions, intimate, embarrassing questions she had never discussed with a man before.

"Ma'am, you seem to be bleeding down here a bit".... pause for the translation.... "there are several tears that I can see, and perhaps some deeper ones... but I think maybe that is not the only reason... Ma'am, is this by any chance the time of your full moon?"

Ca, looked away toward the wall next to the bed in which she was lying, before the old woman even translated the question, Ca gave a short nod, acknowledging that, indeed, she was two days into her menstrual cycle. She had worn a little thatch of woven palmlike leaves as was the custom of her people during this time of month. It had been held in place by cloth strips forming a sort of corset that had been summarily torn off by the LLDB during her rape. At one point during the ordeal, she'd hoped that perhaps when the soldiers realized this was her time of month, they would be repulsed enough to give up on the violation, but they seemed not to notice in the least. The American, evidently sensing her response to his English language, spoke again, slower, more distinctly as though giving her a chance to understand him.

"Well, ma'am, it might be just as well. At least you can be sure that there will not be one more thing to remind you of this bad day." Again, Ca nodded, understanding him, and subliminally surprised that he would know this intimate thing that she thought only her mother and sisters knew, that a woman cannot conceive during the time of her full moon.

Ca felt something cold and metallic being gently inserted within her and started to close her legs, but the old woman explained that this would not hurt her. Ca felt a tepid liquid flushing into her, evidently washing out the residue of her tormentors. Finally, a soft pad was placed over her and she was at last able to close and lower her legs, thereafter drifting off to sleep.

Ca spent several weeks in the American A Camp. She helped Mommason prepare food in the field mess kitchen, afraid to leave the safety of the American compound for fear of seeing the LLDB out in the city. On one occasion, she was terrified all over again when she caught sight of that same LLDB officer, the one they called "Lootenant", coming into camp, escorted by the American commander, Captain Doorman. Ca managed to hide herself from the Vietnamese presence throughout her time with the Americans. Eventually, her skills as a translator became evident and she was often called to help with translating between Vietnamese, English, French and any one of several Montagnard dialects, but never for the LLDB. She came to realize with time that the Americans had little respect for the Vietnamese "advisors" and did everything possible to keep the Viets out of their compound. This usually meant placating the LLDB by permitting a degree of supervised extortion over Montagnards outside the camp. Little Houdgie lived also in the American camp. His own parents had been killed by the VC and he occasionally helped the Americans by discretely hanging around the LLDB bunker site in *Kham Duc*, later relating to the Americans what he overheard.

Ca Rangh finally left the American A Camp at *Kham Duc* and returned to her home village. She had since, on a number of occasions between the years of 1966 and 1970, offered encouragement to the people of her province in supporting the American Green Berets. However, she herself never remained with any of the American A-Camps because of the presence of LLDB once the camps were established and relatively secured. One day, about a year prior, she had been approached by one of McClary's wives. Ca was asked to join with them up in the Laotian mountains for the purpose of rallying Montagnards to autonomy without Vietnamese involvement. McClary's wife talked Ca's entire family into making the move. During all these months here at Swordfish Lair, Ca had pretty much forgotten all about the horror at *Kham Duc*. Then, one day while *Bac Si* McCarthy was away on patrol, she'd heard the same voice directed against one of the other women in Swordfish lair, a vocal ingram that would remain forever scorched within her most terrible memories.

"*MOI DO CHO DE*! Make way for your superiors!"

It was the same voice, the same female directed profanity from *Kham Duc*, the very same Vietnamese officer who had orchestrated her rape. He had just pushed aside another Montagnard woman as he entered the dispensary. The Vietnamese officer was accompanied by five other LLDB soldiers. To her added trepidation, Ca identified two more of them as having participated in her rape five years prior. The group of them marched in to the Dispensary, taking in the facility and all of its resources. One of the LLDB enlisted men started to open a supply cabinet when SFC Glickman came out of the operatory wearing a scrub green top with spatters of blood from having just sewn up a leg laceration on one of the Montagnard perimeter workers. He took in the scene and understood immediately, who they were.

"HEY!"

It was all Glickman had to say. Everyone in the confined space turned to the glaring American NCO, reduced by his withering stare. Without a word, the LLDB gathered and departed, following their officer.

Over the next few days, Ca was to learn that the Vietnamese leader was now a Captain or "*Dai Uy*". She had never known his name before, never wanted to. But, she was informed along with the rest of the Montagnards when *Dai Uy* Nuong announced his presence in the camp. She recognized also three of his enlisted men as individuals who had participated in her rape. One of the rapists was now the LLDB team sergeant. The other two were both communications NCO's. Over the next few days, as they became fixtures within the camp, she had inevitably crossed one or more of their paths, involuntarily trembling as she did so. It took her about a week to realize that none of them recognized her in the slightest. She had nonetheless done whatever possible to discretely avoid them during the short balance of time that *Bac Si* McCarthy was gone on patrol.

The first thing Sgt. Gabriel McCarthy wanted to do after the debriefing was seek out Ca in order to explain what had happened to her brother, Tope. Gabe was well aware that she had admonished Tope to watch out for the young American medic, prior to the patrol disembarking. Gabriel now added to a growing list of self-recriminations that, while Tope had done his sister's bidding, Gabe had not accompanied Ca Rangh's brother back whole. She'd visited with Tope briefly before Glickman evacuated him after the initial evaluation at Swordfish lair. The Senior Medic had summoned a Medevac from *Pleiku* upon determining he did not have the necessary resources to save Tope Rangh's leg at the L-Site. Ca discussed the circumstances of the ambush with her brother. Tope explained how bravely *Bac Si* McCarthy comported himself. How the young American medic boldly attacked the ambush and shot an enemy soldier who would surely have killed Tope Rangh otherwise. That Tope had been wounded on the initial volley of gunfire was simply a consequence of having been in harms way, something they all understood by virtue of being aboriginal Montagnards in this hostile land. Gabe's earnest entreaties on presenting himself after the patrol were considered quite touching to Ca and her parents. They counted themselves, and their son, lucky to have such a friend. They were pleased to acknowledge a growing reputation among the regional tribes for this young *Bac Si*. He was rapidly transitioning from reputation to Legend among the Katu and Jeh Montagnard people of that region.

Tope's parents still remained quite concerned, about what had happened to Tope since he'd been evacuated from Swordfish lair. The Rangh family plead with Glickman to mend their son locally. When the Senior American Medic explained that the only chance for saving Tope's leg was a better facility, they reluctantly agreed. The Rangh family had heard nothing over the last several days other than a curt acknowledgment from one of the LLDB sergeants that a Montagnard from this village had indeed been admitted to an ARVN hospital in Pleiku prior to the LLDB team arriving at this L-Site.

Upon their return from the grueling month long patrol, Fernstead offered each American a 3 day pass to go east and recuperate. Gabe took the occasion to fly back to Pleiku with the daily slick evolutions. He took along a grocery list of material needs as well as a firm commitment to find Tope and report back on his progress. Sgt. Gabriel McCarthy also took along a requisition authority document that precluded the need to ferret out and confiscate or 'procure' supplies as so many Special Forces Medics had to do during the 60's. Despite that, the young Green Beret Sgt. was eye'd suspiciously at every facility staffed with personnel old enough to recall the exploits of Special Forces scrounger medics from the past. Among other things he needed to accomplish during the 3 day furlough, Gabe was on a vital hunt for knowledge. He spent every spare moment studying; on the Helicopter, in military ground transportation conveyances, waiting in line.... He'd secured a copy of "*A Manual of Tropical Medicine*" by Hunter, Frye and Swartzwelder. It accompanied him everywhere as he found himself discovering more precise definition for so many of the things he had seen in country.

After arriving at *Pleiku*, with requisition authority in hand, he obtained a Jeep. As part of his cover, he simply explained that he was arranging this for a visiting command grade officer. He found this made it much easier to move about with a Green Beret as an enlisted man. He wore a JUWTF/SOCLANT advisory flash. Command Grade officers were pretty much expected to be involved with anything high-level. It was assumed that Gabe's requisition authority was being used at the behest of some command grade officer who had sent him off to do errands. In this way, he was able to move about and accomplish his plans while in *Pleiku*. His first stop was the 327th ARVN Evac. hospital closest to primary Med-Evac landing strips on the south end of the Airfield. Even with his pass, he was prevented from entering the hospital. At the reception desk, he inquired of several Vietnamese medical personnel after Tope Rangh. Most expressed the opinion that there had been no Montagnards in this hospital since the U.S. 5th Group left. Others simply directed him to look into other hospitals around *Pleiku*. He did so over the next couple days. No place Gabe visited had any record of a Katu Montagnard on their patient list. He also made several visits to Lieutenant Ron Erickson, in recovery at the American Field Hospital. Erickson had been still under the influence of morphine when he arrived from the field and had no idea where Tope might have been taken. Toward the end of the third day, frustrated in his search for Tope Rangh, Gabe went back to the airfield and found the Med-Evac crew who had brought in both Lt. Ron Erickson and Tope Rangh. The U.S. crew recalled only a reticent Vietnamese litter team taking their time to transport the Montagnard off in the direction of the 327th.

Sgt. Gabriel McCarthy decided to alter his search pattern. He secured a white lab coat and blue scrubs from the American Evac hospital. At the American facility, complete scrubs could only be worn inside or immediately around the Operating Rooms area. Gabe had noticed at the Vietnamese medical facilities, many people wandering around hospital wards in the more comfortable scrub blues. Blues had come into vogue as they did not contrast so harshly with blood as did scrub whites of the early to mid 60's. Late in the day on Wednesday, July 7th, 1971, Gabe returned to the 327th and found a cleaning room in which he changed into white lab coat and blue scrubs. He then introduced himself to the Vietnamese Medical Officer on duty who spoke very good English, having spent time at Walter Reed Army Hospital in the United States.

McCarthy introduced himself as a visiting American physician doing a Fellowship in tropical diseases. He struck up a conversation with the Vietnamese physician duty officer, A Dr. Thuong, who seemed genuinely happy to have an American with whom to discuss medicine. As the conversation became more cordial, Gabriel offered the Viet a gift, a fifth of Bacardi Rum from which they both took a few shots. Eventually, Gabe was invited to make rounds and see the hospital. It was filthy by U.S. standards. However, the American went out of his way to emphasize what an excellent opportunity this place offered him to study tropical medicine. They stopped by the laboratory, and Gabriel was invited to look at several stool specimen slides, through which he readily identified the capped ova of *Trichostrongylus Orientalis*, as well as the more circular *Ascaris Lumbricoides* and the bipolar *Trichuris Trichiura*, all parasites endemic to this area of the world. Gabriel also looked at several blood smears of *Plasmodium Malariae* with the pathopneumonic *trophozoite - schizont* infested red cells along with adult ameboid trophozoites mixed in among cellular remains of young erythrocytes. He was able to discuss in some depth the differences between *Falciprium, Ovalie* and *Vivax* life cycles as well as morphologies. He even caught a mislabeled slide. The Vietnamese physician was delighted. He was so used to working with poorly trained support technicians; Dr. Thuong flattered himself a superdoc due to his American training and prided himself in being able to keep pace mentally with the young American visiting physician. At last, Gabriel launched his ploy:

"You know, Doctor Thuong, one thing I am particularly interested in is Filariasis, especially the form *Burgia Malayi*. We see a lot of *Wuchereria Bancrofti* left over from World War two veterens of the Phillipines, but *Burgia* is a rare genus for us. Do you presently have any patients who might be infected?"

"Hmmm," the Vietnamese physician furrowed his brow in thought. "We used to see more when we had Montagnards coming through here a couple of years back. Not many now since the American Special Forces people have left. Those mountain people are a filthy, infectious race. They carry all manner of diseases. We do not see *Burgia* so much in the lowland coastal areas. However," He suddenly brightened, as if recalling a lost penny, "We just may have someone for you! Follow me."

They left the medical wing of the hospital walking together toward the surgical wards. The Viet Doc seemed to show off his American colleague as they walked together, giving the impression of a cordial and long standing affiliation. It brought Dr. Thuong much face.

Finally, they arrived at a long tented extension of the outer southwestern hospital superstructure. It was filled with olive drab nylon cots on which various wounded were reclining. As they stepped down onto the lower, ground level concrete slab that served as triage area flooring, the Vietnamese physician explained:

"This is a temporary holding ward into which we receive our wounded and then process them either directly to surgery or to the recovery wards. There is a patient over toward the back, which we may find rather interesting."

It was a GP Large, military tent, staked into concrete slab flooring. Lower edges of the bottomless tent fluttered about the margins. Large, wooden uprights supported the structure with canvas patches in various places on the ceiling. Lighting was provided by rolling up the walls, or from carbon streaked Coleman Lanterns hanging on cords suspended from overhead rafters. The floor was black with dried blood, grit and grime. It appeared as if no one had ever cleaned the area with anything more than a very occasional broom. There was a high stacked pile of debris, swept into one corner. Nearby that corner, there was a single figure, lying on the ground. As they approached, the Vietnamese physician started to explain:

"Here, we have one of your average Montagnard savages. You will notice, he prefers to sleep on the floor rather than a much cleaner cot..."

Gabe noticed with a brief glance around that there were no unoccupied cots anywhere nearby. He became transfixed on the reclining figure as they approached, his heart pounding loud enough that he was certain it would betray him. Before the two white coat clad "physicians", lay Tope Rangh, still wearing the same battle dressings placed on his leg over a week before. Someone had removed the inflated plastic splint that Gabe applied in the field and the leg, now putrid with foul smell and pus, lay dangling loosely on the floor next to his other leg. It appeared as if Tope had not been changed or bathed since he had been there. About him on the floor were scraps of food that had apparently been tossed in his direction, or perhaps in the general direction of the trash heap that he lay nearby. The Viet wrinkled his nose as he looked down at the helpless Montagnard.

"He has refused any treatment, of course. He demands his own *Bac Si*. Although that is our own Vietnamese word for doctor, the Montagnards use it also to refer to their primitive tribal witch doctors. I am certain he must be infected with *Burgia Malayi,* as you can see even under his trousers, swelling in the Inguinal lymph nodes."

Gabe rushed to his prostrate friend. He recalled a mental image of Tope Rangh walking beside the little girl on a dark, foreboding trail that fateful night, shielding her with his own body as the ambush ignited. And later, of Tope's courageous restraint as they bound his wound before the morphine could take effect. In the view of the Vietnamese physician, it seemed a rather extraordinary sight to observe this bright, young American Physician crouching down over that stinking savage. Gabe realized his friend was dying. He called out softly...

"Tope... Tope... speak to me..."

Tope Rangh's mouth was moving in soundless repetitions of the same movement. The lips would purse, then open up as the back of the tongue touched the roof of his mouth. He would then clench his teeth and give a little whistle as he exhaled. Gabe shook him gently, which seemed to cause some stirring. As some unknown reserve of energy rose up within Tope's failing consciousness, the silent pronunciations began to take on a bare whisper of sound:

"*Bac... Si*"

"*Bac...Si*"

"*Bac...Si*"

Gabe began to weep. As he did so, he reached under his friend's body and lifted him up, noticing how much lighter Tope was in his arms. The Vietnamese Doctor found this most amazing; he attempted to intervene:

"But, Doctor! You do not need to lift him up. I can call an orderly and we can take his blood where he lies for our research!"

Sergeant Gabriel McCarthy swung his friend up into his chest, overwhelmed with emotion. He could hardly hear the continued protests of what seemed a poor excuse for a Vietnamese physician. Gabe started to walk out of the ward. As he passed by the cots of others patients, most pinched their noses and turned their heads in grimaces of disgust over the foul odor of the Montagnard animal this lunatic American Doctor was carrying around. Finally, the Viet physician interposed himself in front of Gabe and the entrance to the rest of the hospital.

"But, Doctor! You cannot take him into other parts of the hospital! He is infectious and there are recovering Vietnamese patients who might be at risk!!!"

Gabriel kicked upward with all the force of leg muscles made hard from long marches in mountain country. He caught the Viet physician squarely on the right kneecap with the tip of his jungle boot, smashing the knee joint backwards beyond its limit of natural extension. There was a terrible scream which turned heads throughout the hospital as white coated Dr. Thuong went down onto the filthy floor. Gabriel retraced his own steps down one long corridor to the North Wing, then back east to the front entrance. Several personnel attempted to stop him, but were turned back from the foul odor and putrid leg of the bundled Montagnard in the arms of this determined, crazy American Doctor, only recently introduced by Dr. Thuong.

Upon exiting the hospital building, Gabe hastened to the jeep, setting Tope down as gently as possible into the front passenger seat. The young American then rushed around to the Driver's side and stomped the starter into life as he simultaneously pounced down on the clutch. At first, the jeep engine coughed, then seemed to find its rhythm and finally settled into a high revved, four-cylinder whine. Gabe engaged the clutch and lurched off toward the airstrip. He went directly to the American Medevac crew that had previously brought Lt. Erickson and Tope Rangh into *Pleiku*. Through some merciful providence, they were also one of the standby crews for today. He drove up to them, screeching to a halt scant yards short of the rotor radius, shouting "Start your engines! Start your engines!!" They were, needless to say, a bit puzzled at the sight of this shrieking American in Scrub blue top and White Officer's Lab coat approaching them this way. Gabe reached under the seat, into a kit he had hidden with some personal items. He withdrew a .45 automatic, which he fired up into the air.

"Start your engines, NOW dammit!"

This broke the reverie. Not daring to argue with a man in scrubs and white coat, waving a pistol, they moved to flight positions within their bird and began a rapid ignition sequence. At the same time, Gabe went round and lifted Tope Rangh out of the passenger seat, carrying him to the Medevac slick and laying him down on a long, red nylon seat, set against the engine compartment toward the back. One of the pilots looked back from his seat, wrinkling his nose as he did so, catching a whiff of the putrid leg. He shook his head, pointing off in the direction of the Evacuation Hospitals. Gabe responded by raising the pistol, pointing it at the pilot and projecting his thumb upward. The pilot swayed away from the pistol, then beginning to realize the situation, shouted over the sound of spinning up engines:

"Where to Doc?"

"Area Focus, a Special Forces L-Site over on the Laotian side. You know where it is, you were there earlier this week."

That caused both pilots to swivel around in their seats. They simultaneously caught a faint recognition of the same E-5 Green Beret who had come to them earlier asking about some Montagnard. Yes, this was the same one, very much out of uniform. And the patient, it was that same Montagnard they had delivered last week. It looked as though the patient had not changed clothes or dressings since they had last seen him. While neither pilot was particularly enthused about going back in to Laos, they sensed a life and death urgency here. Gabe turned to the crew chief who was also a medic, asking if there were medical supplies on board. The crew chief opened up one of two mounted M-5 bags on either side of the fusilage. Gabe motioned to some sterile dressings, a bandage scissors and a liter bottle of Sterile Saline. He directed the medic to use scissors and pry off the tin lid-cap of the Saline, then instructed him to cut away the pus soaked, crusty bandages, which were tossed out of the chopper bay, onto the tarmac. Superficially, the wound looked awful. It was crusted with dried pus and there were even maggots milling about. As it was, the maggots were what saved Tope Rangh's life. They had consumed much of the necrotic tissue that grew bacteria thriving in the nutrient rich environment of the wound, lowering the bacterial wound load. Never surrendering his .45 incentive, Gabe prodded the Medic to irrigate the wound copiously as the helicopter finished its wind up checklist. As the sound of the engines made voice communications difficult, the medic crew chief pointed to a headset suspended from a hook behind one of the pilot's seats. As Gabe donned the headset, the Pilot keyed his mike.

"Look, Doc, or whoever you are, we have to get authority to leave this airfield. We'll be forced down otherwise, even if you shoot us."

Gabe found the mike key and spoke back into the boom mouthpiece, which he pressed up against his lips.

"You tell them authority 2 Charlie Foxtrot - Fisherman. Then tell them to broadcast that Saint is inbound with urgent cargo."

The pilot considered this for a moment, then switched his radio to tower frequency and transmitted the code phrase. The tower controller replied:

"Wait one"; just short of a minute later, the controller came back:

"Dalmation three you are cleared for immediate departure. All other air traffic will hold until you clear the area. Your flight plan has been filed and when you return, go directly to *Da Nang* for debriefing. Do not, repeat, Do not return to *Pleiku*. Do you copy, over?"

"Copy, out."

Again, the astonished co- pilot looked back into the bay of his Huey C model medevac. *"Who was this guy?"* This was the third time in a week they had been tasked to go out to that spooky Laotian Special Forces Camp. What was going on here? About that same time, an ARVN MP jeep roared from around the edge of a building, over toward the 327th, at the far end of the airstrip. The pilot realized intuitively that the ARVN's were hell bent for his bird. He was not quite wound up to normal hoverlift RPM, but knew his aircraft well, and sensed the need for speed. He raised the cyclic and felt his skids lift lightly off the tarmac. He kicked left rudder and pivoted his helicopter slightly to the left, swinging the spinning tail rotor toward the oncoming ARVN jeep. This caused the jeep to swerve slightly so as to come up parallel with the helicopter. An ARVN officer was waving at the pilot, apparently shouting for him to land. Instead, as the co-pilot waved back, the pilot increased his pull on the collective and tilted the cyclic forward, causing his helicopter to lean forward and rush off, away from the Viets. Less then two minutes later, they were up to 3500 feet, headed North and slightly West.

Gabe started an IV on Tope Rangh. The Med-Evac Crewchief hung a bottle of D_5W with ½ Normal Saline. As the lifegiving fluid started to fill his veins, Tope's tough Montagnard body began stirring within the cradling arms of Gabriel McCarthy. Tope opened his eyes, looking up into the stern face of his American friend. With parched voice only just barely audible in the open bay, he spoke with his lips close to Gabe's left ear.

"*Bac Si*, I knew you would come."

This started another flood of emotion in Gabe. He leaned down, shouting back into Tope's right ear.

"I should have come sooner. I am sorry my friend."

Tope shook his head weakly.

"No, you come for me. I know you would come for me."

Gabe buried his face in the tussled hair of his little Montagnard charge and wept again as the helicopter rushed back to their home in the Mountains.

SFC Glickman was waiting for them on the landing pad when they finally arrived. It became apparent as soon as they received the *Saint* alert from Winkle what was going on. How Gabe could have gotten Tope out of the Viet hospital, SFC Michael Glickman had no idea, but clearly, ARVN had not treated the patient well. Already, Glickman was vowing that he would never send another Montagnard to an ARVN facility, no matter what. His convictions on this were confirmed again when he saw McCarthy coming off the Medevac Slick, carrying Tope Rangh while the Medevac Crew chief walked alongside holding an IV bottle up high. A litter team was prepared and in less than 10 meters from the outer circumference of the rotor blades, they had Tope resting on a litter with IV bottle suspension rod. Gabe turned and attempted to shout thanks to the Crew Chief, who nodded understandingly, voices not heard over the sound of the helicopter engine. The crew chief gave him an OK and thumbs up sign, turning to re-board his bird with many questions left unanswered. The Medevac crew would return to *Da Nang* as directed wherein they would undergo a lengthy debriefing conducted by a Light Colonel without a nametag. Most of their questions would be answered and more importantly, they would all feel that they had accomplished something of value in returning the little Montagnard to his home. As they were the only Medevac crew in the Republic of Viet Nam who had transported wounded from and to AO Focus, they were taken from their assignment at *Pleiku* and permanently assigned to the air wing of operation Fisherman in *Da Nang*. Among other things, this would close one more avenue to the ARVN's for potential interference.

Back at the L-Site, Glickman and McCarthy took Tope Rangh directly to the Operating Room. A thorough examination of the leg revealed a fulminent purulence below the knee with localized necrotizing fascitis arrested below the knee joint thanks to the maggots and the wound having been left open. On Tope's right thigh, there was another wound which neither McCarthy nor Glickman had realized until they undressed him on the operating room table. It was a very superficial scrape measuring about 5 centimeters by 25 centimeters in rectangular area. Evidently, the Viets had harvested a superficial split thickness skin graft from his uninjured right thigh to place on some needy injured ARVN soldier. The senselessness of this act registered so high on a stupidity scale that both medics were amazed even the ARVN's were so dense as to think a homogenous allograft would take between two separate individuals without tissue rejection. The medics could not know that a new test, called tissue phenotyping had been introduced into the 327th just that week. Eager to see if they could predict tissue compatibilities, Vietnamese surgeons had harvested a split thickness skin graft from Tope's leg. There was no need to waste any local anesthesia on this primitive Montagnard, and he never cried out as they ran a straight razor like Wecke dermatome over his right thigh while he lay there, quietly, on that filthy floor.

Glickman and McCarthy performed the amputation that evening. They placed long clamps on each of the remaining muscle groups, without even knowing the names of all the muscles. Because there was more healthy tissue on the back side, they created a flap from the calf, which they were able to rotate forward and up over cut bone ends, sealed with bone wax. In the process of cutting each muscle, they found three large vessels, one behind and below the knee, just in front of what they knew to be the Gastrocnemius muscle group at its widest girth below the knee. Another they found in front of the leg, coming into the leg through a little window between the two leg bones, and a third, which they traced back up to the first, coming down parallel to the fibula on the lateral aspect. Each vessel they tied off with black silk ligature. There were also a couple of large veins to ligate with simple chromic gut suture. They found nerves paralleling the first artery as well as two nerves that wrapped around the leg from laterally. These, they sliced cleanly and buried into muscle bellies to discourage phantom pains. Glickman had heard about this technique called "neuromyotomy", while back in the States last time, visiting Womack. He hoped to at least lessen the chances of a common complication from leg amputations. After securing vessels and nerves, they rotated muscle flaps and skin from behind, forward, suturing the flap with a forward facing incision line. In the end, the stump was clean and up high enough away from the primary wound that there was little chance of contamination. It was about as high as a Below Knee (BK) amputation could be performed while still preserving motion at the knee joint. This would facilitate Tope much better in later life than an Above Knee (AK) amputation. Tope would be followed with 20,000,000 units of Crystalline Penicillin G 3 times per day as well as 3 grams daily of a new antibiotic drug called Streptomycin. Over the next few months, his stump would heal well. When Gabriel attempted to send him to *Da Nang* to be fitted for a prosthesis, Tope preferred instead to have one of the local Montagnard craftsmen carve out a wooden peg leg. With some trial and error, it fit quite well. They mounted into an extended foot post on the prosthesis, a tube capped M-79 grenade launcher muzzle with which Tope could launch 40 mm shells from bandoleers he could carry in hollow recesses higher up on the mahogany prosthesis. Gabe had to admit, it was very unlike anything Tope could have ever obtained, at any "civilized" prosthetic facility; a high tech. leg prosthesis with one hell of a kick.

On the day after performing Tope's amputation, Gabriel offered his debriefing to Fernstead and Briant. As had become usual, the LLDB insisted that one of their English speaking senior team sergeants be present. He took copious notes. Their presence everywhere was like a growing cancer in the camp. There had been several incidents of Vietnamese beating very young or very old Montagnards, although never in the presence of any armed U.S. member of the camp. When Captain Fernstead would confront *Dai'Uy* Nuong over such issues, it always seemed as if the *Dai'Uy* expected some sort of quid pro quo in exchange for bringing his men under control. If there was a particular decision from Fernstead, or any American, which the Viets did not like, they would take it out on the Yards. Women were insulted, children bullied and there were increasingly querulous incidents which adult male Montagnards would want to avenge for some Viet insult or another. *Dai'Uy* Nuong kept insisting that if he could just use the radio, he was certain the comfort of contact with ARVN superiors would calm his men, and intimidation of the Yards would cease. Fernstead had contacted higher command who'd advised him to let the status quo stand. "No contact between Vietnamese and their higher Chain of Command from L-Site communications resources. Continue to encourage the LLDB team to leave peacefully and report back in person to their own headquarters." In the meantime, Fernstead's orders remained quite clear. *Leave the Vietnamese alone at all costs. Do not provoke any incidents.*

The LLDB commenced a tax levy on the Montagnards. The Americans provided indigenous remuneration in the form of material goods for the Yards. In the Central Highlands, rice harvests where readily convertible into Piastres as food was plentifully supplied by the Americans. The LLDB often confiscated rice and goods on the premise that these might be Viet Cong contraband. This had all been a farce. Even prior to the Tet offensive in 1967, for all intents, Vietcong activity was shut down in the Central Highlands. After the Tet Offensive, Vietcong activity throughout most of the rest of South Vietnam was curtailed. By the 1970's, Communist incursions into either Laos or South Vietnam were NVA regulars or political indoctrination squads. Here, in Swordfish Lair, the Vietnamese LLDB had no black market available within which to fence confiscated rice levies. They set about working out the practical problem of converting resources, which they could take away from the Montagnards, into personal profit for themselves.

Upon hearing of Montagnard property confiscation, a ritual of process ensued, during which Briant or Johnston would approach the LLDB *Dai'Uy* in his hootch, formerly the American enlisted bunk house. Most of the Americans had taken to sleeping elsewhere and so the LLDB pretty much inhabited that part of the American team bunker. Personal items belonging to the Americans had started disappearing. Such incidents were unknown during the theft free era prior to LLDB occupation. Careful to hide any substantive evidence, there was never quite enough to make a case against the Viets. Even if there were, the LLDB would claim that it had just been a misunderstanding, or in the case of the Americans, that some item had been given freely, than reported stolen.

Things went on this way throughout most the month of July. There came a day in late July, on Sunday the 27th, when Gabe opened his dispensary to the usual morning sick call. Two LLDB medics took up positions at the head of a small path leading to the Dispensary, turning away some people, letting others pass. Ca came in after a small scuffle with one of them, and went about her work, setting up the dispensary and pulling patient records.

"Ca, what's going on out there?"

"LLDB say we must pay for medical services. Must pay them, and they will pay you. We ask, 'What *Bac Si* say about this?' They say, *"Bac Si* have no say about this, it is ad-min-strative level", she paused to slowly pronounce the multi-syllable word. "They say, *Bac Si* have orders, do what they tell him so they can pay for medical supplies, which must be purchase with Piastres. They say without medical supplies, *Bac Si* has no power to heal. They say anybody with medical supplies can heal. LLDB say if we have medicine from you and want trade your medicine for their medicine, they sell your medicine and let us have your service. They say medicine same, just American medicine have more value cause come all the way from America."

Gabriel put his temper on slow boil as he walked out to the two Vietnamese medics stopping people in front of the dispensary. He brought with him a table and was followed by Ca who carried his aid bag and records. Gabe passed up the Viet medics who eyed him suspiciously. He walked out to the middle of the camp and used Ca to make an announcement.

"Listen people of this place... Medical service here is paid for by your labors in behalf of this camp... You have already earned these services and do not need to pay anybody for them... You need only be genuinely sick and Sergeant Glickman or I will see you... If we give you medicine, it is NOT the same as what the LLDB give. You should not exchange it. .." We will hold sick call here, in the center of camp where there are no paths to be blocked."

With that, he started to examine an old woman whom he had been treating for amoebic dysentary. He heard a scuffle behind him and turned to find Ca down on the ground with a furious look on her face. As she arose, she looked furtively at Gabe, and back at one of the LLDB medics who was standing off to the side with a "what me worry?" look. Clearly, he had just knocked her down for processing the next patient. The Viet stood taller than Ca and now towered over her. Gabe walked over to the LLDB, towering over him by at least six inches.

"HEY! You are relieved here. Leave! Now!"

The LLDB could not meet the American's fierce scowl and so looked away while saying.

"You no relieve me. Only *Dai'Uy* Nuong relieve me."

With that, Gabriel grabbed the man by the scruff of his neck, spun him around and placed a size eleven panama soled jungle boot squarely up his rear end. This sent the man sprawling, following which, Gabe grabbed his surprised partner and proceeded with the same maneuver. It caused them both to lose face tremendously in front of all the patients present, and both LLDB medics scurried dejectedly off to the team bunker. Gabe proceeded with his morning sick call. About 15 minutes later, *Dai'Uy* Nuong, accompanied by his Executive Officer and Team Sergeant came into the area. Ca shrank back from the appearance of two of these men whom she knew had participated in raping her many years ago. They interposed themselves between the patients and the examining station as though they were to be seen next. After finishing with collecting a parasite specimen from a 3 year old using tongue depressor and scotch tape, Gabe gave the child a lollipop and sent him off with his mother. Mother and son left by a circuitous route, avoiding the simmering tempest, which was clearly brewing.

"*Dai'Uy*, line forms to the rear. You will have to wait your turn like all the rest."

"You call me Sir! *Dai'Uy* sir!"

"I will call you *Dai'Uy* jackass and if you want me to demonstrate just like on your medics, you keep blocking that line."

With that, the *Dai'Uy's* eyes opened wide with indignation. He motioned to his executive officer with a gesture of his left arm pointing in one rapid movement from the Vietnamese Lieutenant to Sgt. Gabriel McCarthy, like sicing a dog. The Lieutenant advanced on McCarthy who was seated, starting to rise. As he did so, the Lieutenant swung a pointed crop with shell casing fastened into the end. He had used it often on Yards around the camp when he felt they needed motivation. The stick swung round in a wide arc, striking Gabe just below his left eye almost instantly raising a welt. Without stopping, the Lieutenant advanced pushing the American Medic back into his seat, and raising the stick to strike again. On falling back into the seat, Gabe swung his right leg in a sweeping arc in front of the chair. This caught the Lieutenant on his left leg, just as it was swinging forward to advance a step. With his leg swept out from under him the Vietnamese Lieutenant fell hard onto his left side, voicing an audible "Umph" as he hit the dirt. At the same moment, Gabriel rose up to his full height, which was at least 5 inches above the tallest LLDB. The Senior NCO Viet Team Sergeant attempted to rush forward and push McCarthy back down into the chair, or on the ground. As he did so, Gabe grabbed his neck and pirouetted with him, turning the smaller Vietnamese in a nearly complete circle, like an unruly child with his head held down, facing the ground. As the circle completed about 270 degrees, the Viet NCO stumbled over the rising Lieutenant at which time, Gabe let him go. Momentum from the LLDB Team Sergeant carried him forward, knocking the Lieutenant down again, and causing the Sergeant to stumble forward into the *Dai'Uy*.

The whole thing choreographed out much like an indignant parent disciplining unruly children. It was a massive loss of face

for the LLDB. To the *Dai'Uy*, that could not be. He must maintain face in the company of these primitive people. He could
not permit a junior NCO, even an American, to be so grossly in-
subordinate. He drew out his 9 mm browning automatic pistol,
which he always carried in a highly polished black leather holster on his right side. *Dai'Uy* Nuong aimed intentionally at the
young American's outer left shoulder. He shot a grazing round
that passed through superficial portions of the left Deltoid muscle
on Sgt. Gabriel McCarthy. As it did so, the bullet passed beyond,
striking the old woman dysentary patient who was standing to
the rear. Gabe felt a searing pain at the same time he heard the
muted gasp of the old Lady. He grabbed his left shoulder with
his right hand as he spun to look at the old woman falling to
the ground behind him. He rushed to her as she fell with the
full metal jacketed bullet passing cleanly through her right lung,
piercing a pliant, bare breast which had nursed a family of 7 children during her relatively long lifetime of 43 years. She fell forward against the young medic wheezing a thin mist of red spray
from both front and back sides of her chest, coughing a frothy red
sputum from the side of her mouth. One of her daughters, standing behind the *Dai'Uy,* began to scream "NYA, NYA..." no!
no! as she rushed around the Viets to her mother's side. The old
woman slumped down Gabriel McCarthy's front with wide eyes,
still surprised and uncomprehending of exactly what had happened. Gabe attempted to hold her, but instead felt her wrenched
back away by her 21 year old 4th daughter who clutched the old
woman's head to her own bare breast, wailing lamentations in her
native tongue for a dying mother. All the Montagnards standing behind the LLDB delegation rushed around them to come to
the aid of the old woman, along with her daughter. The voice of
Dai'Uy Nuong shrieked out loudly from behind Gabriel.

"You in big trouble! You under arrest. I see you in jail many
year for what you do!!"

It was as if the LLDB Captain was entirely unaware of the old
woman, still fixated on restoring his own face with the American.

The sight of the old woman lying in her daughter's arms loosed a tempest within Sgt. Gabriel McCarthy. As with all the Americans, Gabriel carried his weapon on his person always. He kept a loaded Car-15 slung diagonally across his back with the sling suspended forward from upper left to lower right across his chest. Just as with the ambush, he felt again a rush of rage and clarity. In seeming slow motion, he pivoted back to his right, facing the *Dai'Uy*. As Gabe did so, his right hand swung down to his right side and around to his back. His left hand grasped the sling at his lower right chest swinging it in a spinning motion around his body, causing the weapon's grip to come down into his right hand which reached back, grabbing the handle and at the same time, flipping the selector switch off safe. The maneuver happened so fast, it was as if the weapon stayed in one position as his body spun around into it. He leveled his Car 15 on the *Dai'Uy,* instinctively aware that none of the Montagnards were located on that side of the amphitheater like camp epicenter. His thumb moved so hard in coming down on the selector switch, that it clicked beyond semi automatic to full automatic just as his index finger closed the trigger. The burst stitched across the *Dai'Uy* from his lower right to his upper left, patterning off just over his left collarbone. Both other LLDB Viets were going for their own weapons, but as Gabriel stopped the upward kick of his weapon, he immediately slapped his left hand down over the handguard, bringing the weapon down in a merciless arc onto both LLDB Lieutenant and Team Sergeant. They took 13 rounds between them, both with at least one to the head. This abruptly stopped any attempt at counterattack. In a blind rage, Gabriel spent his entire magazine into the three bodies at his feet. After doing so, he turned his attentions toward the team bunker to where he walked in quick, surrealistic cadence, dropping his empty magazine and reloading from a spare, always carried on the inner pocket of his left pantleg thigh pouch. His thumb flipped the safety switch back to semi-auto and he leveled his weapon on the first of two armed LLDB uniformed NCO's (the two weapons specialists) exiting the bunker. He fired three rounds into each, stepping over their fallen bodies into the opening behind, where the two medics had secured their own M-2 carbines and started to fire on full automatic in his direction. Neither of them bothered to aim. Their shots went wild, striking sandbags as Gabe returned fire. He placed three rounds into each, shooting with great accuracy into wide-eyed staring faces, silencing both opposing weapons almost simultaneously.

Outside the now bloody team bunker, Montagnards on the perimeter had come in at hearing the initial shots despite cuffings and cursings from LLDB engineer site bosses. The Americans also gathered in from various places about camp. Volkert was setting up wiring on a foo gas incendiary. Fernstead was typing up a monthly report with Johnston. Gowen, as usual, was in the commo bunker monitoring patrol and command frequencies. Estrada was setting up fields of fire for the new 81 mm mortar pits. Briant, Brookbush , Glickman, Winkle and Haskell were out on Patrol. Volkert was first to arrive and realized immediately what had happened, but with no idea by whom. The remaining Viets came along last. As they did, the Montagnards turned on them, striking three more of them down with shovels and pick axes. Dying shouts from the LLDB work details caused both communications NCO's, ever intent on watching Gowen, to come dashing out of the commo bunker. They were met by Ca Rangh. She had taken up the fallen LLDB team sergeant's M-16 and interdicted the two remaining LLDB soldiers. She cut them down with a full, 30 round magazine. Gowen had no idea what was happening and for a moment wondered if their camp was being sapped by infiltrators. He cautiously peeked out of the bunker with his own weapon locked and cocked. Encountering first the dead Viets at the entrance to the bunker, he cautiously advanced beyond them to discover Ca poised over the two bullet-ridden ARVN, looking down with a blank stare, weapon hanging in both hands, listlessly at arms length. She stood there trembling, as though a child reliving some awful nightmare, her right index finger repeatedly squeezing the trigger of the empty weapon in her hands. Gingerly, Gowen approached her, tenderly putting his arm around her shoulders and delicately prying the weapon away while leading her back to the infirmary.

Chapter 3 – Mentors

July-August, 1971

Captain Fernstead sat at his field desk, alone now for the first time in nearly a month. Up until today, one of the LLDB officers or Senior NCO's had been present to intrude on his thoughts, actions and discussions. They had often been asked to excuse themselves when Fernstead intended some private interview with various human components of Swordfish lair. Typically, however, they would move a few steps away, and look in another direction as if not listening in. When Fernstead would insist that they leave his space, the Viet(s) would step around the corner of the bunker maze door entrance and simply eavesdrop. There was no finesse about it. They had been rude, disruptive, and contrary to every notion of good order or discipline. Personally, Fernstead was nearly delighted that they were gone, if only their demise had not been the wage of relief. Repeatedly, he'd exhorted them to return to their own command, and repeatedly they had demurred, realizing that once gone they would not be permitted to return. Actually, it was better that they were not going back, possibly to offer a lot of information that would almost certainly compromise the L-Site. Captain Fernstead realized, while what had happened was terrible in its outcome, it was probably best for the security of Operation Fisherman. But what was he, as commander of this L-site, to do now? Before him, on his typewriter, mounted within the platen roller, was a sheet of paper. Centered on top of the page was a letterhead title:

Classified - Secret Document, COVERSHEET REQUIRED
Dispatch # <u>138</u>
From: <u>Ronald A. Fernstead, Cpt. Commanding</u>
L Site-321 HQ Area Focus
Code Name: Fisherman
Monday-29-July-1971.
SUBJECT: Disposition of extemporaneous LLDB team to L Site 321 base camp
TO: MACV-SOG II Corps, Operation Fisherman COC
I. GENERAL:
   A. Operations:

Fernstead had been looking at this much of the typed sheet for about 20 minutes. He noticed again that the 's, m, and t' characters were slightly askew in the old Royal manual typewriter he'd used for years. He had brought it along with other team equipment, carried over in the team box for this mission. Even on this well funded mission, it was difficult getting military supply to come up with manual field typewriters, and besides, this one was like an old friend. Fernstead only wished it could tell him what to write at such a moment. How could he explain this awful thing, which had happened on his watch? He tried to conceive of a report that would be truthful and yet somehow convey the necessity of that final, bloody consequence. He wished again for input from the ever-omniscient team sergeant, Carmen Briant, who always seemed to know how to deal with crises involving discrimination between shades of gray. The LLDB team were all dead, their bodies piled in body bags along with weapons and gear, out by the landing pad. Not surprisingly, the rest of the camp was back to "pre LLDB" normal.

Captain Fernstead wondered whether or not Sergeant McCarthy, the medic, could get through this thing. . The maturing young medic was profoundly grieved over the death of that old Montagnard woman, killed by a ricochet, which had winged McCarthy's own left arm. Of course, every one of the Viets were armed and after all, the American Medic had been shot first. There were plenty of witnesses that supported his action, certainly in shooting the Captain, Lieutenant, and Team Sergeant. McCarthy's assault on the others, might suggest an inappropriate initiative, which some distant board of inquiry, could easily misunderstand. How could anyone outside this theater of operation really understand? The LLDB were condemned by their own avarice, by staying on within the camp. It had always been that way with the Vietnamese and the Montagnards. Certainly, any solutions to "The Vietnam Problem" could not be found in forcing the two cultures together.

Of all the things Captain Fernstead had been impressed by when it came to actual outcomes in this sad era, he found himself more and more impressed by the medics. It was the medics who were making this operation work. They were bringing together the tribes and unifying the people toward American proposals of independence and self-determination. Without any aspirations to do so, Glickman and McCarthy were rising to the status of sainthood among the Yards. If McCarthy were pulled from this operation in order to face a board of inquiry, it could ruin the entire mission. The Viets would insist on disclosures that might well shut down the camp and leave the Montagnards victim to communist reprisals for everything accomplished up to this point. In the end, Captain Ronald Fernstead typed a full and detailed disclosure, explaining the entire incident, along with his own assessment that the conflict had been inexorably forced by the LLDB.

The next day, Briant, Winkle, Glickman, Haskell, and Volkert arrived back from their wet patrol circuit, emerging from down below the monsoon clouds blanketed around Swordfish lair summit. Capt. Fernstead felt he had better brief all the Americans in person on the incident. Prior to conducting the patrol after action debriefing, Fernstead brought MSG Carmen Briant back into his hootch and explained the entire matter. Briant seemed almost to have expected it. With staid, expressionless eyes, focused intently on his commander's narrative, Briant waited until the Captain was entirely finished before offering comment:

"Sir, it was inevitable. From the first day, when they refused to leave, they were marked men. Frankly, I would have been surprised to arrive back and find them still alive. So what's the take on this from higher up?"

In response, Fernstead handed Briant a Flash Report received just that morning. It read:

BODIES OF LLDB TEAM RETURNED TO ARVN COM-MAND TUESDAY, 30 JULY, 1971. U.S. SPECIAL FORCES LONG-RANGE RECONNAISSANCE TEAM RE-PORTS VIETNAMESE TEAM DISCOVERED AMBUSHED WITH BODIES MUTILATED, EVIDENTLY WHILE PATROLLING IN SPECIAL OPS AREA FOCUS. CLASSIFIED NATURE OF OPERATION PRECLUDES FURTHER DISCLOSURE ON EXACT LOCATION AND TIME OF FATAL ACTION. FURTHER REPORTS FROM LOCATION TEAM INDICATE EVIDENCE OF VALIANT RESISTANCE ON THE PART OF VIETNAMESE LLDB UNIT AT AMBUSH SITE. RECOMMEND POSTHUMUS CITATION ISSUED TO COMMANDER OF LLDB CON-TINGENT FOR GALLANT ACTION IN SERVICE TO THE REPUBLIC OF VIETNAM.

There were cc copies listed to ARVN, MACV, and I Corps command from headquarters MACV-SOG, C&C North. Briant sniffed out loud:

"So, that's the way it is! They're going to sweep this under the latrine, which frankly sir is where it belongs. This way the Viets died heros, and a credit to their Corps. Their deaths will also serve to dissuade any further peek-a-boos from other left over LLDB teams out this way. From what I figure, after Lam Son 719, ARVN will be needing all the manpower they can find to re-plenish 1st and 2nd Divisions. That's another good reason for them not to spend counterpart teams on classified incursions like this."

Briant paused while they both mused a few moments in silence. Then the team sergeant posed a final interrogatory.

"So, what effect has this had on the camp, sir?"

Fernstead looked away from his team sergeant, searching in vain for a window into a more serene world. He found only acetate overlay maps.

"Top, I'm almost ashamed to say, it seems to have had zero effect on anyone, perhaps except myself. It is as if everything were exactly the same way it was the day before the LLDB team arrived. It bothers me, though. I feel like we have lost something of the soul of this place. Perhaps it's young McCarthy. He was so full of conscience and idealism. He's changed. Oh, he still is totally committed to the mission, and the team. If anything, he demonstrates even greater determination to fulfill his role here. More possessive, more... well, you know, more Montagnard. But, he is changed. The innocence is gone, and with it something of youth and virtue that I think we will all miss. You know, he'll make a great physician someday, I just wonder if he will be more or less of one because of what has happened here."

Briant stood facing his commanding officer silently, silhouetted against a dim light reflecting off the entrance, into the bunker. There was nothing he could say. He had seen it before, and believed he would see it again. Young, pedigree pups coming of age, how they change when they taste first blood. Perhaps it was because Gabriel McCarthy was a Medic, his purpose more noble, more... more untainted. His was, after all, the only job description on the team whose express purpose in training was not so much to kill the enemy as it was to heal and mend. Briant remembered a distant young Sergeant Michael Glickman back in June of 65 at *Duc Co*, going through the same thing. It was a dichotomy so like the insanity of this war that these medics, both dedicated to healing, would become almost as efficient at killing. Briant had been told that McCarthy single-handedly killed seven men, half the LLDB team, all armed, and after having been shot in the arm himself. Perhaps in some circles, it would be something to admire, but here, it instilled something closer to pity in the mind and heart of Carmen Briant. As he had done so often when struggling with the pains of this land, he thought of Roxanne and found solace. This prompted MSG Briant to excuse himself from his brooding Captain. He went off to finish writing the progressive letter he had started on patrol. To the top sergeant, this ritual of writing home was essential so that Carmen Briant, husband and father, could find comfort in personal communication with his wife; betraying nothing in his script to her about the realities of Master Sergeant Briant, soldier and warrior.

To SFC Glickman, it seemed as though the camp was better off, morale wise, than at any time since before the unwelcome LLDB in-laws had arrived. He understood what his junior apprentice was going through. In an oft-repeated behavioral complexity among Special Forces medics dealing with intensity, McCarthy had immersed himself back into the work. No one discussed anything out loud about the incident. If the time came when Gabe wanted to talk it out, Glickman would be there for him, always someone who could understand, which was the best therapy for this sort of ailment.

In early summer of 1965, Buck Sergeant Michael Glickman had himself been a young medic at an A-Camp located West of Pleiku in the Central Highlands, nearby a Jarai Montagnard village. He also had been absorbed with the wonder of engaging miracles in modern medicine among a humble, courageous people. Their camp came under siege that mid summer of 65. It was the first time North Vietnamese Regulars had mixed forces with Viet Cong and a few Red Chinese advisors. In this same area, over a decade before, French Groupment Mobile 100 had taken a terrible beating July of 1954. Attempting to repeat history, the NVA politburo figured that if they could split South Vietnam by driving a wedge from Cambodia to the South China Sea, they would send the Americans packing, just as they had the French before them. By July of 1965, an entire regiment of North Vietnamese army regulars was laying siege to the Special Forces camp at *Duc Co*. Acting alone, Viet Cong units had been unsuccessful in over running the A-Site. They had been repulsed several times by fierce resistance from the Montagnards, a course which smacked of a sort of reverse Viet Minh call to arms. Not wanting to permit any seeds of counter-revolution sown among the Montagnards, Hanoi sent NVA regulars in to big brother the VC. The ensuing siege lasted nearly 4 months until finally, mid November, 1965, Battalion sized elements from the U.S. 7th and 5th Cavalries came riding to the rescue at the Battle of Ia Drang. During those months under seige, many precedents were set in Vietnam war lore. The first use of B-52 strategic bombers was brought to bear, as well as heliborne reinforcements of troops and close air support.

At *Duc Co*, Glickman had apportioned himself to many duties, from calling in napalm to sustaining casualty lists which at one point had risen up over 107 wounded, with 11 critically injured. Whomsoever *Duc Co* camp defenders had gotten to him alive, Sgt. Michael Glickman kept alive until evacuation could be arranged. On one occasion, a CH-3C "Jolly Green Giant" helicopter was shot down during extraction with 4 of his criticals aboard. He'd mourned over them most of the ensuing week. At another point in the conflict, camp defenders began bringing enemy wounded to his infirmary. After being thoroughly searched for weapons or grenades, injured enemy troops were given beds alongside friendly casualties. Glickman ministered to them with the same mind and heart. Some devout communists resolutely refused to accept medical aid. Those few would refuse medication, rip off dressings, pull out IV's, even yank out inflated Foley catheters. As there were not enough resources to spend a great deal of effort on restraining the most aggressive communists, Glickman offered the wounded ones an option of staying or leaving disarmed. Officers would of course be detained and questioned, but most of the hard core communist officers were not at the front. The majority of captured enemy were simple infantry grunts who had no idea exactly why they were where they were. At the battlefield level there was no such thing as any real prisoner exchange in Vietnam. Later in the war, when it became politically advantageous, the communists would take officers, particularly fliers, into POW containment camps. Occasionally, if U.S. ground forces could be taken alive, they would be held as propaganda instruments. But for the most part, wounded U.S. advisors encountered by the communists were shot in the head almost as a matter of policy. In conventional U.S. ground units, wounded enemy who did not fall victims to renegade battlefield vendettas came under indigenous purview. The South Vietnamese found American empathy for their enemy almost as confusing as Vietnamese Communists did. Except in the case of a wounded POW, which might prove beneficial to intelligence, the South Vietnamese did little to expend resources on captured wounded. Although somewhat less inclined to shoot wounded communists in the head, enemy wounded morbidity processed through ARVN ran very high. MACV had its own stunningly efficient U.S. Medical Evacuation system. It was carefully restricted to U.S. personnel, except for an occasional ARVN V.I.P. . Only in the Special Forces dispensaries and field hospitals did blood from U.S. and Asian, friend and foe, run together on the same operating room floors. The Montagnards were ferocious warriors, who elicited also a strong sense of the warrior's code. Montagnard retribution against acts of communist cruelty was unflinching and unmerciful. However during plain engagements, often Montagnards lent more respect to mud infantry soldiers from the North than among South Vietnamese ARVN troops. In the case of a wounded communist soldier who clearly was not part of some bullying indoctrination cadre or political propaganda regime, the Yards tolerated battlefield courtesies. Enemy wounded brought into Special Forces medical facilities were cared for with resources disconcerting and foreign in every way to the communists. Wounded enemy POW's were well fed and treated with a modicum of respect. Frequently among the Viet Cong, and occasionally, even among North Vietnamese Regulars, wounded enemy in Special Forces camps would *"Chu Hoi"*, or offer to change sides. Of course, the Americans were keenly aware that this could be a route for placement of double agents, and so precautions were taken not to entrust weapons or intelligence until the sincerity of a *Chu Hoi* could be tested under many different circumstances. There were a number of *Chu Hoi's* exposed as double agents. Within thousands of personality and circumstantial permutations evolving around the *Chu Hoi* program, there were occasionally those who did manage to rise up and occupy sensitive positions, only to later betray their trustees. However, a surprising number of enemy wounded *Chu Hoi's* within Special Forces camps of mid to late 60's became genuine devotees to the Montagnards and their American advisors.

Glickman had been hesitant to evacuate enemy wounded during the siege at *Duc Co*, knowing that they would likely be routed to ARVN facilities. And so, even in 1965, he did the best he could for them on site. It was very, very difficult for the communists to counter this force of ministered recovery from their U.S. enemy. Medical resources within the northern communist theater were not even meager compared to the south, U.S. or ARVN. Many of what few, very good, medicines were available to the communist North, had been manufactured in the evil United States. There were even NVA propaganda cadres devoted to switching labels on U.S. medicines purchased through other third world countries. Frequently, when labels could not be switched, medicines came in boxes marked, "Captured American Medical Supplies".

The result of all this was a genuine blow to communist propaganda in Southeast Asia. A concerned North Vietnamese Political cadre directed that greater efforts be made to drag communist wounded off the battlefield rather than have them fall into potentially merciful hands of U.S. advisors. Medics were generally designated as priority targets among U.S. Army personnel and particularly among Special Forces advisors. For that reason, in Vietnam, unlike most other U.S. armed conflicts of the twentieth century, Medics did not wear white arm-bands with red crosses to identify them as such. Medical Aid Bags were similarly not identified by colors that would set them apart. Early on, 5th

Group command had recognized the urgency of keeping Special Forces Medics in the field. One big problem with this was that it normally took about 3 times longer to train a medic than the other enlisted combat specialists. When a Medic was killed or incapacitated, it would take considerable effort to replace him. The medics were more than simply part of an American advisory force. They became integral to the community in which they served. For this reason, by 1967, 5th Group command had taken to establishing a reserve of 'temporary replacement' medics. These B team reserves would go into the camps and temporarily replace wounded or KIA A-Team medics. They would fill slots without establishing deeper roots of a genuine *Bac Si*, until such time as an entire replacement team could be obtained with two fully trained medics from the extended training system. Because any given A-Team was normally rotated every six months, it did not make sense to bring in new medics, scarce to begin with, to serve out a short term tour then start all over when a new team cycle began. As it would usually take about three months just to really ingrain a medic into an A Site community, their maximum practical and moral effectiveness was during the last half of a given tour. There were many reservations expressed about the wisdom of rotating out successful A-Teams in just 6 months and particularly, a *Bac Si* that had become endeared to the Montagnards. However, as Special Forces Medics became more popular in a given province, the propaganda price on their heads increased proportionately and so six months remained the tour de force. Staff Sergeant. Barry Sadler, composer of the famous *"Ballad of the Green Berets"*, was a B team medic. Among other B-team level support tasks, his job was to fill in for dead medics until a new team could be assigned with permanent medics. He was recovering at Da Nang from a leg wound incurred on patrol by a punji stake when he composed his celebrated medley.

Glickman received a Distinguished Service Cross for his role at *Duc Co*. He re-enlisted twice thereafter with assurances that he would be able to continue his tour of duty in Vietnam. He continued in Southeast Asia from 1965 until Late 1969, after which he returned to Fort Bragg wherein he became an instructor at the Special Forces Advanced Medical Training School and Dog Lab. By 1971, he was hungry again for action and field service, much like other veterans selected for the team by the oversight committee of Operation Fisherman.

August 1ˢᵗ, 1971

Sgt. McCarthy and SFC Glickman were performing their first field Cesarean Section together, this on the granddaughter of old Duc So Lim, one of the village Elders. The girl's husband had been impressed into a communist goon squad about 8 months back. He was reported shortly thereafter as having been killed in "dedicated action for the glorious cause of the people". She doubted that very much, as he'd never wanted anything to do with other people aside from those of his own village and new wife. More likely, she was certain, he had been killed trying to escape the communists and make his way back to his village. He had been about 17 years old. She had just turned fifteen. She was left, now, carrying his child. This was a baby she very much wanted, as it represented in essence the most powerful emotion she'd ever felt toward another human being; not, perhaps, after the fashion of melodramatic romances more familiar to Western cultures. They were simply two Montagnard children from the same village who had grown up together, distantly related, 4ᵗʰ or 5ᵗʰ cousins. They had known each other throughout their upbringing and as they each grew into the respective flowers of male and female pubescence, they had realized about one another a special friendship. This friendship, kindled with mutually growing awareness of sensuality and passion, had flowered into a relationship that made the families of both boy and girl very happy. The couple had exchanged what could be called vows in the presence of village chieftain, village priest and most of the rest of the local populous. While people who knew and loved them most celebrated the union and all of its promise with a traditional feast, the young couple had separated themselves to a quiet, private place and consummated their relationship. Both were virgins and could not imagine being anything but, as youthful promiscuity outside of marriage was not a part of their credo.

When it had become clear during her labor that she was not big enough to deliver this baby, she tried to anently assure her father that she could imagine no better way to be called back to the gods than with the baby of her late husband. For the medics, this cephalopelvic disproportion was an opportunity not only to save both mother and baby, but also to raise U.S. advisory stature and influence among the locals.

After 26 hours of prima-para labor, Glickman realized that she would not dilate more then the 5 centimeters she had arrived at about 12 hours prior. Her contractions had become almost constant by this point and the Senior Medic finally made the call to go ahead with an expedient Cesarean section. If she were to survive this labor, they would have to do the Cesarean right there, in the field hospital at Swordfish lair. The first step after getting her onto their bunkered OR table was to ease her pain. Both medics had spent some time during her labor reading up on whatever they could find about the effects of anesthetic agents on a fetus. All they really had for general anesthesia was Diethyl Ether and nothing they could find in their available reading material seemed to support the use of Ether on a pregnant woman. Of course, it had once been good enough for the Queen of England, but neither of the medics were privy to that information as they searched in vain for some commendation of Ether as an obstetrical agent. Both knew that spinal blocks were often used in the United States to provide anesthesia to women in labor. Both had rotated through OB-GYN during their OJT externships and saw anesthesiologists administer spinal anesthesia at some point during labor. The result had most often been a successful merger of pain relief with continued capacity to push. Both Glickman and McCarthy had been taught to give Pudendal blocks, but that was nearly useless in a C-section. Glickman knew that if the spinal block was given high enough, they could eliminate her pain sufficient for her to endure a low abdominal incsion. However, he also knew that the higher and deeper the spinal anesthetic, the more influence it had on motor control. At some point, it might even interfere with respiration.

Gabe had seen four spinal inducements during his training. As his recollection was the most recent, Glickman decided to have Gabe perform the procedure. The senior medic would supervise by reading the process out loud from a medical text while offering oversight. With the help of Ca Rangh and the girl's mother, they rolled the pear shaped patient over onto her right side and curled her into as much of a fetal position as she could manage against her obtunded belly. Glickman scrubbed her back with Phisohex, then painted the groove of her mid spine with Zephrin as Gabe donned sterile gloves. They then prepared a hypodermic with a few drops of saline and heparin, used to coat the plunger portion of a glass syringe prior to inserting plunger into barrel. Prior to prepping her back, Gichrist had palpated for the curve of her upper pelvis, the iliac crests. From the point at which they joined with her tailbone, or sacrum, he counted spinal column vertebral segment "bumps" up the back. After counting up about 4 spinal processes, he drove his thumbnail deeply into the notch between numbers 5 and 6 up from her sacrum, or about somewhere between what he could determine to be vertebrae T-12 and L-1. The nail imprint was still clearly indented on her skin after prepping the area. Into its center, Gabe injected a small wheal of local anesthetic from a disposable 3 cc syringe. She did not wince in the slightest at this as she was doing everything possible to prevent involuntary movement from cycles of contractions that now wracked her with spasmodic pain. After waiting for a lull, Gabe inserted a long spinal needle on glass syringe steadily into the thumbnail indent, advancing the barrel with delicate movement, which was as slow as he could allow for the intervals between contractions. At one point during advancement, the glass plunger began to magically inject without any external pressure. Gabe stopped advancing at that moment and the glass syringe with solution just seemed to inject itself into the girl's taunt back.

After injecting half of the 20 cc syringe with her lying on the right side, they rolled her over onto the left side and injected the remaining 10 cc. Glickman read out loud something about a vacuum space between the two outer layers of meninges lining the spinal chord, which caused the solution to inject itself. It seemed to the observing Montagnards in the room as if a magic, invisible hand was there to mercifully plunge this strange instrument at just the crucial moment.

"Let me give you a little tip on Local Anesthetics, kid." Glickman offered one of his regular medical gem side bars. "On these OB-GYN cases, you can run through a lot of Lidocaine, or Prilocaine if you have it. At *Duc Co*, we ran out of locals about three weeks into the siege. I read once that Bendaryl could be infiltrated as a local anesthetic in a pinch. We used it at *Duc Co*, particularly for intercostal blocks in chest injuries. When it took, Benadryl would hold the block for a long, long time, sometimes weeks. In a pinch, you might want to keep that in mind."

It was typical of Glickman to offer these little asides as they went about various procedures together. Gabe savored these sessions with SFC Glickman as he felt that more could be learned in situations like this than under any other circumstance. Book learning took ten times more effort and lacked the visual reinforcement of laying on hands.

After the Epidural blockade, both medics then proceeded to wash their patient's belly and paint her with Povidone-Iodine. Had the anxious villagers been made aware of what was to proceed without being so impressed by the spinal block, they might have attempted to intercede and stop the process. However, being firmly convinced that invisible hands were aiding the tall, confident Americans, tribal observers held back away from the sterile field and stood on tiptoes trying to watch from an outer periphery of the field operating room. At the first stroke of the scalpel on her obtund belly, the observers collectively winced. She was without feeling at that point, but it seemed an incredible thing to the others that she could bear the horrible incision into her abdomen without so much as a grimace, especially while still conscious. Eventually, Ca and Duc So Lim insisted that only immediate family be permitted to stay in the hospital. These few remaining souls spoke to her, as far away from the sterile field as possible; to comfort and reassure the girl until Ca asked them to be silent so the medics could concentrate.

As Gabe placed the incision, Glickman again broke scrub, leaving Ca to retract. The Senior Medic read verbatim from a textbook of surgery, obstetrics and gynecology, supervising and explaining as they went along. The junior medic found the confident, reassuring voice of SFC Glickman to be like a calming balm in this turbulent mix of emotion as he incised, uncertain of exactly what he was doing, certain only that it was better than letting both mother and child die by doing nothing. The enormous realization that he was blindly cutting into living flesh of two lives bore down on him immensely. Prior to each layer, Glickman would explain carefully what to expect, and what to do next. Gabe had by this time realized a natural sense of oneness with the scalpel. It was as if the tips of his fingers extended onto the ultimate edge of the blade. He instinctively held the instrument gently. He let the blade work and was careful to dissect as cleanly as possible, intentionally resisting the urge to "trace" with the blade tip, preferring instead to make clean, continuous strokes. Glickman had emphasized this to him over and over again, "The way you open up is the way you have to close. Think about that as you dissect down and ignore the temptation to think only of getting in. If you do, panic takes over and all you'll be able to fixate on is the quickest way out."

The initial incision was placed between belly button and mons pubis in parallel with her navel and the hairless vertical line of her vagina below. As dissection proceeded through outer fascial layers, they began to encounter portions of muscle belly and end membranes encompassing the tight abdominal musculature.

Following instructions in the textbook, as related by Glickman, Gabe formed a linear incision so as to divide a muscle called *rectus abdominis* neatly down the center. Ca positioned Army-Navy retractors to separate the split, segmented muscles on either side. Deep to this, they encountered peritoneum that was also carefully divided and tagged with suture for closure later. As the marvel of female anatomy opened up before them Gabe identified the bladder, deflated and continuous with a foley catheter exiting out from her body below. This had been done just prior to prepping the belly. Glickman had to show both Ca and Gabe how to identify the tiny urethra for placement of the catheter. Ca was rather amazed that the wizened Senior Medic should know such intimate things about a woman's body. At the same time, she was rather bemused with the realization that she had never herself seen or understood how or from exactly where her own body urinated.

Above the diminutive bladder, a tense, glistening Uterus occupied most of the field of view. It was somewhat muscular in appearance and had two little twiglike structures located on the upper end, which Glickman identified as the Fallopian Tubes with ovaries. In making an incision into the uterus, the idea was to place it down low, in the less expansile portion of the structure. This would avoid scar tissue on the inflated upper limbus that might someday bear more children. A longitudinal scar would have the protracted effect of attempting to blow up a balloon with a piece of electrical tape stuck to it during subsequent pregnancies. In addition, the baby was inside the upper portion of the uterine sack. Gabe felt for the head, pressed far down against the lower end. He palpated a soft, circumferential area down below the head and it was here that he placed his smile shaped incision.

Fluid and blood surged out onto the field. At the same time, first evidence of a partite human within was revealed in the form of short, wet black hair on a cheesy mat of life form. All about, tangles of umbilicus were apparent as Gabe reached in with two fingers and gently popped the head out of the incision line. Fortunately, the length was just right and so he was able to avoid ripping either end of the uterine incision. Once the head was through, tiny, hunched shoulders followed and then the rest. Finally, only the umbilicus remained streaming from the incision and attached to an area within which they understood to be the placenta. They could see it within, already red and bleeding, clearly separating from the opposite wall of the uterus.

An amazing metamorphosis occurred as chord was clamped and airway aspirated with a glass asepto on rubber bulb syringe. The bluish white life form that they held upside down began to change color from blue to pink. In the process, there was a shudder and gasp, followed by a tiny, high-pitched cry that brought smiles to everyone in the room. They cut the umbilicus between two clamps and handed a male newborn up to his mother. She gathered her infant into her arms. In a natural rhythm of grace and movement, she presented her newborn babe to breast.

After delivering the placenta through the uterus, and checking for bleeding pieces of tissue, called cotyledons, on the uterine wall, Gabe closed each layer in sequence with deep absorbable sutures and large, Vertical Mattress, Black Silk sutures on the abdomen. They used two centimeter cut sections from a Foley catheter to form buttresses that would take tension off near skin edges and prevent skin sutures from tearing through. Everyone remained awake most the rest of the night cherishing this amazing miracle of new life, savoring this side of the cycle of life and death. It added somewhat to the general sentiment also that this baby was a nephew to the old woman who had been killed by the LLDB ricochet.

They permitted the exhausted mother to remain on the Operating Room Table, turning the wriggling newborn temporarily over to a relative who could also wet nurse the baby. Little by little, the villagers filed out of the dispensary, leaving for their longhouse homes west of the central promontory. Finally, only Ca, Glickman, Gabe and the patient remained. After all the relatives left, Ca had taken the baby into her arms and sat down next to a wall, leaning back against the sandbagged surface. Gabe watched her there with that baby, so calm, so natural. She had washed her hands carefully, then inserted her right little finger into the baby's lips with the tuft of her pinky pointed upward into the roof of the baby's gummy mouth. This instigated a suckling reflex that caused the newborn to settle into a steady rhythm of sucking on her finger until falling asleep. Gabe candidly watched Ca as she rocked the sleeping babe in her arms. He also went over and checked on the mother, assuring that her abdominal wound was not seeping. He realized while doing so, how completely captivated everyone, including himself, had become by this new life. He looked about, basking in the closest thing to total satisfaction he had ever known. Glickman broke into the reverie as though reading Gabriel's thoughts.

"This is what it's all about, kid. There's not another place in the world right now where some pimple nose adolescent fresh out of high school is gonna do something like you did here tonight. It's why I had to come back. There's no way to describe the rush. Guys like us with just a year of heavy duty cramming come over here and do stuff that would take most other people on this planet six to eight years to learn. We give whatever our knowledge and experience can offer to these people, because they have no one else. While our teammates look at the enemy through gun sights, we view the real enemy with a microscope. I suppose we should both be thankful in a strange sort of way. Thankful that Charlie scares off the egg head MD's whose net worth to the Army is so high that they won't let military MD's out here to risk their precious titled asses on a bunch of munchkins. "

"So, you have thought of them as munchkins too. Funny, first time I saw them when we arrived here, I thought the same thing" Gabe replied, grateful for the camaraderie to genuinely appreciate what he was feeling right now.

"They are munchkins, kid, and this is the land of Oz, for you and me. We get to come here and realize the fulfillment of dreams that we never even knew we had; heart, brains and courage, wasn't that what they wanted in the fairy tale? Isn't that what we get here?"

"I suppose it is. Course, now I wish I could cram in some more brains. There was so much to learn back at Fort Sam. Every day here, I wish I had learned more."

"Yea, I know kid. It's like you wake up every morning with a hard on that points to San Antonio. The problem is, in order to go back there, to the world, you would have to leave here. It's good back there, don't get me wrong. Teaching is great. You get to relearn this stuff and learn more besides. Of course, there's a wife and family, you'll find out about that too, when the time comes. I love my own wife and kids more than anything else in this world. But, the Yards come so close that sometimes, it's hard to separate them from my own. They feel like my own. Of course, they can be pretty tough kids. When you lose one, it hurts real bad, but you get over it. They help you get over it."

Gabe reflected on this. He had experienced a terrible loss when the old woman died and he still pined over the little girl in *Lo Dao* maimed by the communists because of a candy bar he had left her. He grieved along with their families over the tragic side of the cycle of life. But in this place, mourning the dead, grieving over the wounded, these things could only be a transient pastime. The Yards just filled up his life with other things, as though they knew that was what he needed most. In this place, grief was replaced, for example, with the happiness of this new life. Not as though they had a low opinion of life. They valued living, as all people do. But, they just seemed to understand the rhythm of life and death better than the culture Gabriel had grown up with. No, perhaps they understood how to lay emphasis on the most important part of the cycle ...*life*, death, *life*.

"It's been great being here with you, Sergeant Glickman. You're the real *Bac Si*. I can't imagine anyone I would ever want to share an OR with, anywhere, anytime. You're what makes it happen. You're the Wizard of Oz. You're the one I come to for brains, for heart, for courage."

"Look, kid, don't go canonizing me. I'm Jewish, remember? The only Saint we've got on this team is Briant and he's enough for us all. Believe me, it means a lot to have your trust, but don't go making me into something I'm not. That way I don't fall so far or so hard when I screw up. And believe me, we all screw up from time to time. You remember that when it's *your* turn to be Pope."

"I hope the day never comes. I like it just fine walking in your shadow, *Bac Si* Glickman."

"Careful kid, only the Montagnards have a right to ordain someone *Bac Si*. Now, let's get some sleep. We'll both need it while you're gone on patrol, and with the monsoons, it may be a while before you get many dry winks"

The next morning, Sgt. Gabriel McCartly went back on patrol, along with Fernstead and Gowen. They descended from Swordfish lair, back down into the misty, wet world below, accompanied by 25 Montagnard Strikers. The strike force training school was growing in size daily, but every new recruit had to be put through some sort of training cycle before going out into the field. Fernstead and Briant had figured that by the end of the summer, they would be able to patrol in disbursed, company sized elements, divided up so as not to move in one large group. By fielding in several Platoon sized elements like this, they could link up quickly to form a company sized rapid reaction force if needed. The plan was working even better than expected. McClary was out there in the bush, visiting different villages, working his recruiting magic via his vast family assets. Young Montagnard recruits were coming in on their own once they knew they would not be forced. They took to training like the natural warriors that they were. They did this fundamentally because they would not tolerate being intimidated by the communists and because they believed in what the Medics were doing. They saw genuine, measurable outcomes. Not so many women died in childbirth. Not so many elderly were sick all the time. Not so many children died of diseases like Diphtheria, Tetanus or Pertussis, things that had been common before. The communists spoke of liberating people from political oppression. The Americans were actually liberating this people from sickness and disease. Perhaps that was the ultimate liberation. After all, communism, capitalism, imperial colonialism, they were all just political ideas. There were no real Bourgeois or Proletariats here, just a society of people struggling against political and natural enemies. For hundreds of years, this people had fought, and most often won, against the former a great many more times then the latter.

Washington DC, August 2nd, 1971

He was a third term Congressman from New England and quite convinced that the solution to the Vietnam problem was really quite simple. Congressman Riley Hathoway sat on the powerful house Ways and Means committee. He would likely become chairman someday, so long as his own party retained a majority in Congress. Never having served in the military himself, he had not been considered a viable candidate for any of the defense committees that directly controlled the purse strings to Vietnam. Congressman Hathoway stood solidly behind the Cooper-Church Amendment. In his opinion, it finally put a firm stop to that madman, Nixon, who actually thought there was a military solution possible in Southeast Asia. It was so simple from Congressman Hathoway's viewpoint as a politician. Cut funding and the whole thing would go away. Over time, Hathoway had learned to play this game. He knew very well what his constituents wanted to hear and he could promise pie in the sky along with the best of them. The basis for his continuing popularity within his own constituency was in raising money for special interest projects. Hathoway had been a firm disciple of President Johnson's "Great Society", and saw no reason why any American, or really, anyone in the world, should have to suffer from unemployment, hunger or lack of health care. In looking at the vast sums of money being expended on the Vietnam conflict, he could not help but consider how many other worthy projects that money would fund given his own oversight. The Congressman found himself becoming more and more aligned with anti-war movements. These seemed to further support his own ambition of taking as much as possible from the common fund and giving as much as possible to the people who put him in office. Of course, Vietnam had served his party well as a pretense for raiding funds from the Social Security Administration to pay for the war effort, something a staid World War II majority generation was only begrudgingly likely to accept. In his own mind, the ultimate ambition of any good politician should be to milk as much money out of the citizenry as possible in order to buy as many votes as possible. At that moment in history, the biggest cash cow outside of U.S. taxpayers was the Vietnam war chest and he wanted a bigger piece of it. Toward that end, he had taken steps to become more involved. Seated together with him in a congressional briefing room, were members of his staff, discussing plans for an upcoming visit to South Vietnam. His executive secretary, Marion Schiller, was addressing him at the moment.

"You are scheduled to arrive, sir, on the first of September. The itinerary calls for three days visiting various bases and meeting with dignitaries of the South Vietnamese government."

Congressman Hathoway replied with the deep, cantilevered voice of a professional orator, the same that had served him so well as a civil attorney in his home district for over ten years prior to becoming a professional politician.

"Very well, Marion. I want to be certain that first on the agenda is a visit with the South Vietnamese President, Nguyen Van Thieu. No better way to eat the snake than by starting with the head of the snake."

"Yes sir, as I understand it, President Thieu is always very courteous toward U.S. Congressional emissaries. He will make time to see you whenever you prefer."

"I'll bet he damn well is courteous. The man knows who butters his bread. I represent the American People who bring most of whatever economy he has into his country right now."

Marion nodded, suppressing a silent retort that, while the office of a U.S. congressional representative is certainly officious, it hardly represents ALL of the American people. However, she had learned long ago that the key to keeping her powerful boss happy was to convince him that he was on the fast track to the White House and that everyone around him felt that way. She smiled demurely, realizing the true nature of this visit to Vietnam as a fuel gathering expedition. She answered in the manner she knew he enjoyed most.

"I'm sure you're right, Congressman Hathoway."

Not far from Aloui, Laos, August 2nd, 1971

Muc Bo Thau surveyed the Russian advisor sitting across from him. Accompanying this Moscavite, in every conversation there was, of necessity, an interpreter. Regimental Commander Thau had never learned Russian, nor English. He did speak fluent French and several Southeast Asian indigenous dialects. Although the Russian had some rudimentary skills in French, it was not sufficient to carry on a delicate conversation. It bothered Commander Thau that such highly sensitive matters must pass through an interpreter. One could never be certain that just the correct intonation was being communicated. There was also the problem of the interpreter being a security risk. This particular interpreter was a middle-aged woman named Thanh Diem. She had come up to North Vietnam from the South in the mid 60's when an American Pacification program resulted in the burning of her village. The capitalists had offered to relocate her people into an "agroville", or strategic hamlet. All it accomplished was to demonstrate to the Vietnamese peasant how well off the arrogant Vietnamese upper class was and how brutal the Viet Cong could be. The Americans were somewhere in the middle, connecting bipolar miseries for Vietnamese peasants. After aligning herself with Communism and embracing the "people's cause" Thanh Diem had been assigned to study languages in Hanoi during the late 60's. She proved adept at learning both English and

Russian. Since her assignment to this command, Thanh seemed to be doing a competent job and so Commander Muc Bo Thau tolerated her. But just the same, he also arranged for one of his agents to check out her personal life and ascertain that she had no possible contacts outside of her Russian Advisor assignee. Thanh Diem proceeded with interpreting the conversation in behalf of Regimental Field Commander Muc Bo Thau:

"But, Komrade Brietlovich Markov, we specifically asked for a Doctor of Medicine. Perhaps you do not understand our situation. There is an American insurgency camp somewhere in the mountains of Laos, east of here. They have with them doctors who are winning over the hearts of Montagnard people in that area. We have neither the medical expertise nor resources to counter this clever propaganda ploy and therefore requested of your Komisar a medical Advisor."

There was a pause as the interpreter finished her translation. This repeated pause with each translation added to a growing irritation on the part of Commander Muc Bo Thau. It did not begin to irritate him, however, as much as the supercilious attitude of "Komrade" Markov. The Russian looked back with confident, smirking, almost belittling eyes. The interpreter began translating from Russian back into Vietnamese.

"But, comrade Thau.... I am much better than Medical Doctor for this situation... I assure you... I am military microbiologist... My expertise is in bacteriological warfare."

"But, I thought we did not use Chemical, Bacteriological nor Nuclear weapons as a matter of convention."

"Comrade,... you must realize,... as they say in the West, ... all is fair in love and war. ... So long as we can deny it, ...we can do it. ... Bacteriological warfare has already been used against the Americans ... with considerable success."

"Really? How so? I have heard of no such weapons!" Muc Bo Thau considered himself quite well informed and was certain that such a ploy would come to his attention.

"Of course not, ... Comrade Thau. ... All such deployments are classified. ... But, ... given that you have a very high security level, ... I shall give you an example of one such operation. ... For many years, ... venereal diseases have been readily treated by Penicillin, ... a powerful antibiotic. Through various research methods, ... we have discovered a resistant form of Gonorrhea. ... One that will not respond... to conventional doses of Penicillin. Just four years ago, the Americans successfully treated Gonorrhea... with only 1.2 million units of Procaine Penicillin. ... Now... they are having to up the dose almost every 6 months over the last 3 years. They presently treat ... with two injections of 4.8 million units. In the end, ... they will only enhance our resistant strain ... of *Nisseria*, ... that is the genus name of the bacteria ... which causes the disease you see. ... Our weapon strain will survive despite antibiotics ... and propagate in the host who will then become a carrier. ... They take it back to the United States and spread it within their promiscuous Capitalist homeland. ... They are already beginning to report cases of resistant strains ... of Gonorrhea in their medical literature. ... It was such an easy thing! ... All we had to do was infect a few prostitutes who mixed with the American Troops."

Regimental Field Commander Muc Bo Thau sat back astonished. Now this was a weapon worth considering! One deployed by the enemy's own vices. But there was a big drawback.

"But, Komrade Markov, if the Americans do not know that we are doing this to them, what propaganda value does it have?"

"The propaganda value, ... my little comrade, ... is demoralization of the enemy. ... Their decadence becomes an indictment ... against their depraved war with your valiant homeland. ... Their gullible, liberal, stupid youth ... are assisting to spread it along with their war protests. They justify their self-gratification ... for youthful, undisciplined sex ... with ridiculous slogans such as ... 'Free Love' and 'Flower Power'. They actually wave banners ... at their war rallies which say these things. ... This is what gave us the idea. ... Most of our own communist peoples ... do not even suspect ... we are punishing the Americans ... on their own soil ... through their own vices. Propagation of this disease among capitalist societies... permits all Communist peoples in the world ... to reveal lurid, intimate weaknesses in Western Democratic principles. ... It is even rumored among American troops that there is an American hospital ship ... in the Gulf of Tonkin which quarantines cases ... of what they call 'Black Syph'. ... They say the patients on this ship, ... never get to go home because of their incurable venereal diseases. ... Of course, that is probably just a myth. ... We have only altered Gram Negative, Intracellular, Diplococcal Bacteria, ... no *Treponemes*, the organisms that cause Syphilis, but you see the propaganda benefit is the same. ... Rumors persist which demoralize ... the average American soldier ... and if the American Military Command attempts ... to deny these rumors out loud, ... their overly eager American Press ... will jump on the allegation and make it ... into a matter of believable hysteria, ... It is really quite brilliant, Comrade Thau, ... but perhaps just a bit too sophisticated for an old infantryman eh?"

The interpreter was almost embarrassed to translate this last sentence. *'You arrogant, patronizing ass!'* Muc Bo Thau thought, being careful not to betray his thoughts in word or expression. He merely blinked away his rage and continued.

"I fail to see how a venereal disease will resolve our own situation Komrade Markov. Perhaps someday, we will have to eliminate the Montagnard people. But for now, we must keep them from falling to decadent American philanthropy. We can hardly afford to have one more local enemy."

The big Russian nodded as he received this interpretation. "Yes, comrade Thau. ... However, if a few of the Montagnard people are eliminated as, how shall we say... 'collateral damage', would it cause you any difficulties?"

"None whatsoever, I am quite in agreement with my Southern Vietnamese countrymen about this one thing. The Montagnards are little more than a barbaric, sub-human species that occupy our highlands because we will not tolerate them in any civilized area. They are cultural flotsam, but one which can cause us problems if we do not handle them carefully."

"Very well, comrade Thau. ... Then, I have a plan which should eliminate your noxious American doctors... ... We shall summon an enemy against them ... which they do not expect. A sort of biological, ..., how would you say,... 'ambush' ... yes?"

Chapter 4 – Second Assault

August and September, 1971

The weather consisted of intermittent, drenching monsoon showers alternating with a blurry summer sun, making the trek oppressively hot and humid. Muc Bo Thau accompanied this particular patrol. It was made up of a company sized field element. While uncommon for a Regimental Field Commander to venture so close to any possible hostilities, he wanted to see first hand how this new weapon would be deployed. Breathing heavily with the Laotian mountain trek, Captain Breitlovich Markov wheezed along dressed in Russian Spetznatz camouflage. Clearly, the Russian was not at all qualified as a Spetznatz soldier. By his own admission, he had never even been parachute qualified. Evidently, he took some pride from the uniform of his elite countrymen. He wore also a pith helmet, similar to other officers in the group. Muc Bo Thau had himself presented the headgear to Markov on the premise that it was a gift, representing the bond between their two nations. This was actually true, but it also mattered that they were all quite concerned the tall, arrogant Russian microbiologist, might suffer a sunstroke during one of those times when the blazing summer sun burned through dusky, leaden rain clouds They were proceeding toward the little village of *Loc Phieu* wherein two entire platoon sized elements had simply vanished a few months back. Although this concerned Commander Thau, he felt quite confident traveling with a company of hardened NVA veterans, all savvy to risks in this part of the world. They proceeded as far as the upper edge of a ravine that led down into the fruitful valley of *Loc Phieu* below.

The female translator, Thanh Diem, approached Commander Thau, bearing an interrogatory from the Russian.

"Most Honorable Commander Thau, Komrade Markov wishes to know if this is the stream which feeds into the village of *Loc Phieu?*"

"Yes it is. The stream is quite small here, but enlarges from other feeder streams as it goes down hill. Eventually, it disburses around the village providing irrigation for their rice paddies. These are the headwaters."

She went back to communicate this to the Russian, at which point there, in undergrowth alongside the stream, the Russian called a halt to their march. As the seasoned troops deployed automatically to set up a defensive perimeter, Markov collected several enclosed metallic cages from the packs of soldier bearers designated to carry them. Each of the cages were solid metallic boxes, spotted with small, fine mesh screens, which permitted air to circulate in and through the cage. One soldier was assigned to each cage bearer with the seemingly ridiculous task of fanning the cages in order to prevent them from overheating.

Overlooking the affront of not being asked to order this halt, Muc Bo Thau watched in growing curiosity as the Russian began to don a contamination suit over his cloth uniform. In the sticky, humid summer heat, it seemed a rather absurd, thing to do.

"Commander Thau... Komrade Markov advises that you should recall your men from down stream ... and tell them to move back uphill of this ravine. ... They should be removed by at least fifty meters from this place."

Muc Bo Thau gave the orders to make it so. He then asked again, via Thanh Diem, for the Russian to outline exactly what was about to happen. Markov paused to lift up a small cage marked with black electrical tape.

"This, comrade Thau, is the first assault force. ... Inside these cages, ... there are male and female rats which are infested ...

with fleas carrying a bacterium called *Pasteurella pestis*. ... Pasturella grows well at temperatures between 30 and 37 degrees centigrade, or between about 85 and 99 degrees Fahrenheit, the temperature scale used by the Americans. ... The rats are domestic rodents that will naturally follow this stream ... down to the village in search of a ... murine domicile. The bacteria which these rats carry via fleas will flourish along this streamside ... microclimate of humid coolness, leading down to the village. ... These rodents belong to the genus ... *R. rattus* . ... They are quite common in the tropics, and cannot be traced back to us. ... Most of them should make it down to the village wherein they will circulate among the villagers, ... leaving their fleas that we have especially prepared, ... a marvelous insect called ... *Xenopsylla cheopis*. ... The fleas will find their human hosts ... and infect them.... by biting human skin as they regurgitate bacteria from an ... anatomic insect structure called the ... proventriculus. This all happens while they feed, you see."

Again, the Russian seemed to enjoy using scientific terms which, obviously, nobody but himself understood.

"But, Komrade Markov. What kind of disease will these fleas cause?" The question had not been asked before. Muc Bo Thau was almost reticent to pose the question as he considered this a rather ignoble method of defeating an enemy. He understood only that they were employing bacteria and that Bacterial Warfare could kill by disease transmission. Markov looked around at the troops, then at the translator. His reply in Russian caused the translator to pause. Thanh Diem formed an alarmed, astonished look of her own, betraying her nature as something other than a mechanical translation device.

"Well, what does Komrade Markov say? Tell me NOW!"

"Komrad Markov says that these fleas cause Plague, Black Death."

On the instant the phrase was translated, those within hearing could not help but pause in their activities, casting furtive looks at the gathering of cages and officers. Many started to edge back away from the horrid menace, moving upstream, distancing themselves as much as discipline would allow. Muc Bo Thau widened his own eyes at the translation.

"But, how can you be certain that it will be contained to this area? Such a disease could wipe out half of my own command!"

"Well, in this, dear comrade Thau, we must trust the Americans. They are well trained and educated. They should recognize the disease very quickly and, if they do so, they will quarantine the area. You have lost many men attempting to enter this valley, yes? Well, you will not need to send in any more men for a long time now."

"But, the Americans have medicines to treat this disease! We are not so well supplied!"

"All the more reason for you to remove your men from the area right away."

There were so many reservations forming in his mind, Muc Bo Thau could not begin to verbalize a coherent reply for translation. He took several seconds to compose himself, then addressed the translator.

"But, if the Americans treat and cure this disease, they will be heros! How does this serve our cause comrade Markov?"

As the translator posed the question, the Russian was just preparing to don a hood. Pausing, he placed the yellow hood under his left arm for a moment as he looked back at Muc Bo Thau with a triumphant smirk.

"Ahhh, my friend! Behold, the coup de gras!" He held up a second cage with red tape on it.

"Within this cage, my friends, is the second assault force. We shall return in two weeks to deliver it. This cage contains another type of rodent called *Clethrionymus glariolus*. It is also carrying an insect. However, the insect infesting this rodent is a tick called *Haemaphysalis spinigera*. This is the second assault. It bears a unique signature. In my own native country of Russia, Americans introduced a fur bearing muskrat, *Ondatra*, in the 1930's. These large North American rodent species flourished in my Fatherland about the area of Omsk and Novosibibirsk in Western Siberia. They supported ticks that introduced several epidemics of a terrible disease called Hemorrhagic fever. It is a virus and has no direct cure. Many of the early symptoms are identical to Plague. Most Americans are vaccinated against Plague before they come to Southeast Asia. In dealing with the epidemic, they will likely spread insecticides to deal with the rats and fleas. Although the insecticides in high enough quantities can kill these ticks, they are not as vulnerable as fleas. Also, the insecticides will actually make the ticks more aggressive toward finding a mammalian host, especially after their rodenticides wind up killing my rats, which will be the delivery vehicles for these ticks. A well-conducted quarantine campaign on the part of the American physicians, along with prophylactic antibiotics will likely protect the Americans from Plague. However, no American serviceman has ever been vaccinated against Russian Hemorrhagic fever. While treating the Plague, they will become infected by this second disease that will kill all the Americans... as well as many Montagnards surviving the Plague. You see, my friends, when the Montagnards realize that the Americans cannot even save themselves from dying a horrible death by disease, they will most certainly lose faith in American medicine."

Muc Bo Thau had been passing his gaze back and forth between the Russian and the cages with different colored tapes. The logic here seemed so twisted. What was needed was a clear and resounding defeat of this American insurgency among the Montagnard people. Without a public example, the people would not learn. Killing the Americans was important, but doing it with brutal force would make it count for something. This methodology of insects and bacteria and viruses, held a universal evil that could work both ways. Sort of like trying to use snakes to kill the enemy. Often, the snake killed the handler. Muc Bo Thau had serious doubts about this whole business, but was not quite ready to raise any verbal objections just yet. Instead, he rallied his men to march back uphill. Captain Brietlovich Markov remained behind, donning his hood, and then opening each of the cages in the black tape color sequence. As he expected, the rats scurried about the immediate vicinity of the stream, then moved in rapid starts and stops in the general direction of downstream. Several hours later, the first assault wave of his bacteriological weapon would encounter a group of Montagnard children playing nearby one of the shallow streams running alongside the south end of the village. Growing up in a botanical universe, none of the children were particularly intimidated by scurrying rats as they emerged from the treeline, bound for the village. Several of the older children even practiced their own natural hunting skills by stalking the emerging rats as they passed.

From high above, movements in the form of thermal heat signatures had been monitored by a Bugeyes F-109. A Hercules AC-130 Spectre had been alerted and was en route to intercept the company sized element moving into this valley. When the enemy column halted, then turned around, the strike was placed on hold. Eventually, it was called off. The F-109 E/O observed one final human signature remain behind, manipulating what appeared to be a series of tiny signatures, which moved off rapidly, losing recognition within cooler thermoclines alongside some streambed. "I wonder what you're up to, Charlie old boy? " pondered the E/O. A call was placed down to Swordfish lair, advising them to beware the water supply for *Loc Phieu*, as the enemy may have tampered with it.

MSG Carmen Briant's July and September patrols followed a reverse trail to the one Lieutenant Erickson had taken that previous June. They started up toward the north in *Lo Dao*, then worked their way south. During the previous month, as the July patrol passed through each village, Glickman offered to vaccinate adults and children as part of a Civic Action Project (CAP). They were cycling through the same route, about half way through their patrol, toward the middle of September, when they received an intelligence report by radio that something may have been put into the water supply of *Loc Phieu*. Briant's team arrived two days later. At the time, the villagers were starting to show signs of endemic sickness. SFC Glickman recognized the epidemic almost immediately. He radioed Swordfish lair, conferring with the Junior Medic, Sgt. Gabriel McCarthy, and detailing instructions for McCarthy to join them at *Loc Phieu*. Sgt. McCarthy arrived the following day, transported by a chopper filled with medical supplies that included IV fluids, cutter sets with needles and all their stores of Streptomycin, Aureomycin, Oxytetracycline and Chloramphenicol. He also brought Parathion and Diazinon as well as, Powdered Warfarin and Fumarin the former two insecticides, the latter two rodenticides. By day three, Glickman had worked together with the village *Bac Si* and Chieftan to quarantine two longhouses, connected by a log corridor at the downstream, south side of the village. As soon as supplies arrived, Glickman and McCarthy proceeded to spread mixed powders along every seam and corner in the quarantined long houses. Several of the other Americans were shown how to operate gasoline powered disbursement blowers. These were used to spread insecticides and rodenticides liberally about the village, especially near streams. Water had to be flown in and children were necessarily restricted to a single longhouse about which a bare minimum of chemical was disbursed. Inside the downhill quarantine longhouses, Glickman had already enlisted the aid of several family members who would not be separated from the immediate presence of sick kindred. They gingerly followed a daily ritual to scrub and lysol floors, walls and ceiling beams, carefully watching out for any fleas per Glickman's instruction.

Bamboo sleeping mats were laid out with alternating head to foot sleeping postures. Alongside each was a bucket into which patients could relieve themselves. The two medics went about setting up Input/Output I&O sheets as well as Medicine Administration Records (MAR), and Vital Signs charting. At first, the Americans had to do almost everything themselves. By the fourth day, with the help of the old village *Bac Si*, they had trained an indigenous nursing staff on the rudiments of patient care, leaving mostly chart work that could not be done by illiterate Montagnards. Briant insisted on being within quarantine from the start. Volkert and Winkle remained outside to enforce the quarantine, controlling access into and out of the area, as well as coordinating things with Base Camp. It was nearly 36 hours after arriving before McCarthy found time to pause for a bite to eat and grab a few hours' rest. Prior to retiring, Gabe opened a box of A-1 unit C Rations for his first meal in a day and a half. Glickman joined him to discuss various patient profiles, while Briant directed the Yards who were providing essential services in sanitation and hygiene as well as helping to feed those too sick to help themselves. Gabe chatted with Glickman as they ate:

"So, this is Plague. It's just like the book says; sudden onset of high fever with lymphadenitis and toxemia. Then, they get those bubos. How many have we lost so far?"

Glickman looked up from his paper work and paused a moment to finish chewing one of his canned peaches before answering.

"So far, we have eighteen dead, mostly very old or very young. The first case was a child, nine years old. The antibiotics seem to be breaking through this prodromal phase. We have about 56 still very sick and it looks like we may lose about ten of those in the next 24 hours, mostly kids. Just be thankful that this outbreak appears to be limited to murine plague and that we caught it before converting to pneumonic plague."

"Have you ever dealt with a Plague outbreak before, Mike?"

"Oh yeah kid, back in 68, in a little village between *Ban Me Thout* and *Dak Nam*. It actually happened during the Tet Offensive in late January. Surprisingly, everything in the mountains was pretty quiet during that time. All the bad guys were in the big cities. Of course, we had major problems getting supplies once Tet started. Lost 63 Yards in that one. Whenever I smell burning flesh, I think of that time. You'll think the same of this one before we're finished, kid. We have to burn the dead. It's the best way to assure we've sterilized this quarantine. The bacilli remain viable for prolonged periods in dead bodies. Burying them is no good."

Gabe had smelled the distinct odor already. It stayed with him now all the time, the only variance being that sometimes it was more pungent than others.

"Only a day and a half here, and I feel like I've known this disease my whole life," Gabe mused.

"You have known this disease your whole life, kid. At one time, Plague killed over 2/3rd of the world's human population. Those who survived did so because they had some genetic predisposition for avoidance. It's in our genes to know this disease. It's part of our culture."

Gabe looked awry at his older mentor. "But, it's virtually unknown in the United States!"

"Not at all. In fact, it was one of the first diseases you learned about when you were a child."

Gabe responded skeptically, "How do you figure?"

Glickman looked at him with that old sage expression. "Do you remember learning a nursery rhyme when you were an adolescent that begins with 'Ring Around the Rosy?"

"Yea, sure:

'Ring Around the Rosy
Pockets Full of Posies
Ashes, Ashes,
We All Fall Down'

But, what does that have to do with Plague?"

Glickman queried again, "Do you remember who taught you that rhyme , kid?"

"Hmmm, no I don't. Just picked it up when I was little."

"How about when you learned it?"

"Nope, I don't remember when. But, now that you mention it, I think it was probably one of the first rhymes that I ever learned."

"It is for most children. It's a common rhyme in all English speaking countries around the world. There are similar children's rhymes in most languages. The children of this village have such a rhyme in their own dialect."

"Well, I suppose it makes sense that all children sing rhymes. But, I still don't see what that has to do with Plague."

"Not just rhymes, kid, *this* rhyme. It's almost the same in every language on the earth. Now, consider what those bubos look like. Describe one to me."

"Well, they are pink or rose colored bumps about the size of a tennis ball in an adult, a golf ball in a child. They have concentric rings about them."

"Ring around the rosy, Now where are the bubos."

Gabe was momentarily taken aback as he began to comprehend what Glickman was conceptualizing. He went on.

"In the Inguinal and Axillary lymph nodes."

"Yea, kid, right close by where most clothing has pockets. Suppose one of these kids were wearing pants and put his hands inside his pants pocket. What do you think he would feel?"

Gabe responded with increasing awe in his voice "Pockets full of Posies! But, I though posies were flowers."

"Not in this case, kid, posies are the old English name for inguinal bubos. About 75 percent of bubos are inguinal, or posies. Now, smell the air and you'll understand the next line."

"Ashes, Ashes; of course!"

"Now, look around this long house. Most of these people were healthy and working in the fields yesterday. Today, they can't even stand up to pee. What was the last sentence of the rhyme?"

"We all fall down!"

"Remember that when I tell you to take your Sulfadiazine tabs every 4 hours for prophylaxis. We may have been immunized prior to coming over, but that only provides us with an antibody titer that can be quickly overwhelmed in a very virulent episode. This bug reproduces a lot faster than our body can manufacture antibodies. That's what makes it such a quick killer. We'll do these people no good if we get sick ourselves.

Gabriel nodded, consciensously downing a 2.0 gram tablet of Sulfadiazene. Afterwards, he got about 4 hours sleep before being awakened for the next 4-hour watch. This cycle went on day after day. The long houses filled steadily for the first week after Gabe's arrival. To the young medic, time began to blur as he continued the seemingly endless cycle of rounding on sick and dying patients, most very young or very old. At each bedside, he would check vital signs, palpate lymph nodes and in new admissions, aspirate the bubos to confirm a microscopic appearance of bipolar, pleomorphic bacilli on Gram's stain. He was constantly restarting IV's and/or preparing antibiotic mixes for the IV's. Several times each day, they would pile up the dead on one of the outside raised porches or *Bhok gah's* of the longhouses. Early on, they had used body bags, but these quickly ran out. In the late afternoon of each day, Volkert would pour gasoline into a rut cut uphill from a fire pit located downhill to the south of the longhouses. Adult bodies piled on the upper ramps would be placed into this pit by tossing them in a "One, two, three, HEAVE" off the upper platform. In the event they missed landing in the fire pit, located about 5 meters downhill, someone, usually Briant, would have to climb down and place the bodies properly into the pit. The fire pits were located just far enough away from the longhouses not to pose a threat of setting fire to their wooden structures.

Each pit was surrounded by six tiers of two holed CBS cement building blocks. The blocks had been stuffed with animal hair and feathers repeatedly doused with water, plentiful from the monsoons. Once all dead human and any discovered rat bodies were inside the pit, one of the Montagnards (out of respect for the villagers, none of the Americans actually fired the pyres) would toss a flaming torch into the pit. As heat in the pit grew, the hollowed cement blocks would give off steam that rose directly up into the air, forming a heavy condensation ring about the pit. This lessened smoke dissipation. From time to time, a block would crack with a loud pop, to be replaced the next mid day after the pit had cooled down. Although they were very light, none of the medical team could bring themselves to toss any adolescent bodies into the pit. Each little body was wrapped in some way and carried over to the edge, wherein it was carefully laid on the top tier of bricks, then gently nudged over the side. The death and burning of these children was especially hard to bear. Often, weeping parents, separated by the quarantine from their children would have to be restrained from crossing quarantine lines to hold their dead offspring. Sometimes, they would break through well- intended restraints and cross anyway. In which case, after being pried from the small corpses, they would be called upon to substitute their grief for work and service within the quarantined longhouse wards.

All this visibly shook up the Americans, even SFC Michael Glickman. In his seeming cold professionalism, he could not separate the agony of these parents from memories of his own children back in the States. He could not fathom being deprived of their lives like this. With Briant, it was the same. Gabe, of course, was also emotionally affected by the tragedy of it all, but realized that there was some unique, deeper emotion, titillated by a parent's agony, which perhaps only another parent could fully empathize with.

By the 9th day following that first case, admissions started to taper off, and by the 12th day after opening the quarantine, the number of incoming slowed to less than the number of dead outgoing. As a growing population of Montagnards recovering from the illness were able to pitch in, the shift work became less burdensome, permitting Glickman and McCarthy to spend more time between shifts to sleep and recover from their own accumulated fatigue.

On the morning of the 14th day of the quarantine, exactly two weeks after bugeyes had reported activity about the headwaters, SSG Phillip Volkert, the senior engineering NCO, called for Briant. They carried on their conversation from across the quarantine perimeter, having to shout back and forth. All the other Americans and translators could hear the gist of their conversation.

"Top, we got a sitrep from Bugeyes about 5 minutes ago. Looks like there's another group of warm bodies coming up to the headwaters of that stream. Upstairs, they're thinking Charlie may be up to some more dirty tricks."

Briant was quick to respond. "Form a strike force and head out to intercept them. Call in some close air support *now*, see if we can get some rotary wing gun ships and standby an AC-130 Spectre. We're going to have to capture some live bodies to confirm what they've done here. This is a major break with the Geneva Convention, not to mention an international human rights violation. We need to gather evidence on this thing very carefully." He turned back into the long house. "Doc, are you able to break quarantine?"

Glickman responded eagerly, "Sure, I've been through a Plague epidemic before. I've got a stronger immunity as a result. You two should stay in quarantine another day or so beyond the apogee of the epidemic. Besides, I need to get up there and look'em square in the face, see if they have any idea what they've done here."

With that, Glickman jumped down from the upper platform of the Longhouse. The usual cut log steps had been removed to prevent people from entering or leaving undetected. On landing below, he bounded after SSG Phillip Volkert who was calling out to his Yards to form up a quick reaction force. They were all ready and only had to wait for Glickman who accepted a borrowed LBE, an M-79 launcher, and a Browning 9 millimeter pistol. He quickly donned a bandoleer of mixed High Explosive (HE), Buckshot (double ott) and White Phosphorus (WP) 40 mm rounds for the M-79. The patrol of ten Yards and 3 Americans moved out about 15 minutes later, heading up stream toward headwaters of the ravine that fed into this valley. Volkert kept Winkle alongside with a PRC-77 radiotelephone to his ear as information was exchanged with Bugeyes. Glickman took point. He wanted to be the first to encounter whatever someone might be putting into the water. *"Had to be infected rats."* He was certain of it. If it was rats, then someone had to stop the rats before they made contact again with the village. A more appropriate weapon would probably have been a flame-thrower but, even if they'd had one, here in the thick bush it would be useless. Glickman moved briskly up the hill, driven by adrenaline and a keen sense of urgency. Volkert followed close on his heels, calling out distances from the enemy in a low voice from an interval of 5 meters behind the point man. About 45 minutes from the time they set out, they paused some 250 meters from the headwaters where a few advance human heat signatures were being tracked by Bugeyes. The majority of the enemy unit was apparently further back up over the ridgeline. Volkert instructed Winkle to call in the AC-130 Spectre to take out whatever enemy troops they could get at on the higher veldt leading into this ravine. Less than ten minutes later, the comforting drone of an approaching heavy, propeller driven aircraft filled the air around them. Bugeyes radioed down that the helicopter gunships were about 8 minutes behind. Volkert was also advised that the same, or very similar, pattern of tiny heat signatures was being observed, as had been seen during the previous observation. From his position on point, Glickman crouched down and started creeping forward along the stream. From behind, in muted whispers, Volkert tried to dissuade him. But, whatever they were doing up ahead, SFC Michael Glickman was determined that he would have to see it in order to better understand the threat they faced. He edged up to within 50 meters of the headwaters, to a point in which he could just see figures ahead, dressed in yellow, rubber moon suits. They were surrounded by open and closed cages, which had evidently been taken off backpacks. These were set down off to one side. Headed downstream, Glickman could see the vanguard of two large, dark rats. They were unlike any he had seen before. They were huge, with shorter ears and darker in color. They had long, naked tails that swished loudly alongside the streambed as they moved in starts and stops downstream toward Glickman's position. He had only a few moments to formulate a plan. The three moon suited figures ahead were quite preoccupied with their work. Plastic visors of their moon suits limited their field of vision considerably. There were three AK-47's resting alongside the backpacks. These were at least several seconds away from their owners. Michael Glickman figured his first priority must be to stop those rats. It would be necessary to sterilize this streambed. He finally decided on the White Phosphorus 40 mm rounds, thinking that he could fire a glancing shot off an edge of the streambed and hopefully get the disbursement pattern to scatter upstream.

This time, Captain Markov had brought along extra contamination suits. He'd dressed up two volunteers whom he was training to understand bacteriological warfare. They had carried the cages marked with red tape. One of those remaining with him was the translator, Thanh Diem. Commander Muc Bo Thau returned back to his base camp earlier in the week after the first contagion release. The Viet regimental commander had seen quite enough of Bacterial warfare. *"Ahhh, these orientals,"* Markov thought. *"So superstitious. How could they ever make good communists?"* Between the three of them, Markov's group opened about four cages containing two or three rats each. Inside of his suit, Markov could not hear particularly well. He had to put his hood right up against the others in order to communicate. Somewhere outside his hood, he heard a distinctive "Thump" off to his left rear. As he turned to look, the male Viet assistant, who was an NCO accustomed to quicker reactions in a combat environment, went automatically for his weapon. Instinctively, Thanh Diem followed his lead, trusting in his veteran instincts. As the Russian adjusted his vision to look downstream, a second "Thump" went off, and for the first time Markov realized that there were bright stars scattered along the streambed and in the thick forest around them. Some of these were starting fires, even in the dampened vegetation around the streambed. At first, Markov had the impression that it was like standing up too fast after lying down for a time. Irregular lights that he thought were coming from within his own eye sockets dazzled him. He arched up and down to view around an area of condensation forming on his visor as he heard a third "Thump" and saw an oblong blur hurdling through the air in his general direction. It fell short of his position and exploded, breaking into an uneven circle of bright white fragments, some of which struck his legs, burning through his plastic moon suit and embedding into his legs and thighs. He felt immediate, horrible pain, prompting him to reach down and grab at his legs. As he did so, his hands started burning through his rubber gloves and he screamed within his hood. Falling down to his right, on an incline sloping down toward the stream, Markov landed in several of the bright white phosphors which burned through his right side into his right rib cage and back. He screamed repeatedly as burning fragments clung to him, sinking deeper and deeper into his body. He realized momentarily that the shot had been intended for the cages stacked around him and, indeed most of the round had been expended into the area of piled cages slightly downhill from the backpacks. He was now rolling amidst the bulk of scattered burning phosphorus. Off in the distance, he heard a fourth "Thump" and screamed in realization that another hellish projectile was being shot in this direction.

As the NVA male noncom and female translator reached their weapons, they both pulled off their hoods first thing. Each in succession attempted to engage the safety switches and triggers of their weapons, but found the gloves to be too bulky. They had to momentarily pause for what seemed an eternity as they tore off their gloves and gathered up their weapons into familiar handholds, quickly thumbing down the levered selector switch to automatic as they returned fire back into the forest. By that time, a fifth "Thump" had sounded leaving a trail of white phosphorus fragments along the stream, leading back to the grenadier. They both opened fire at once charging into the bush toward their concealed enemy.

Glickman took the first round in the right shoulder, the second grazed his neck. He felt a thud, which knocked him down. He could vaguely make out two forms skirmishing toward him through the bush. His right arm would not work. He had been in the act of breaking the M-79, intending to load another shell when he was hit. He now reached up for another WP round and charged it into the barrel. Snapping up the tubed weapon single handed from the butt, he flipped it shut on the hinge and left handed, aimed again upstream in an attempt to cover the other side. He was intent on sterilizing as much of the area as possible. Those dead kids, they were his first and foremost priority as he sensed the bush around him chopping up to a chorus of AK-47 rounds. The sound of that sixth "Thwunk" directed the NVA directly to his position. They were able to make him out laying on his side, single handedly buttstroking his weapon down on something close to him alongside the stream. Within their peripheral vision, they could see another burst of White Phosphorus, largely ignored as they bore down on their antagonist. They both expended the balance of their magazines into this "grenadier" whom they now recognized, with some fascination, to be a caucasian, almost certainly American. As they both started patting within their suits for fresh magazines, one took up a security position as the other bent over the riddled American to examine his body and weapons. In the process, the examiner noticed a dead rat that had apparently been butt stroked by the American. Of far more interest, however, was the holstered Browning 9 millimeter handgun under his recumbent right hip. It would make a most impressive war prize and indisputable proof of having actually killed an American. In reaching down to loosen the American's handgun from its bloody holster, the NVA could not see one of several ticks that had been scurrying off the dead rat and onto the warmth of the larger, fallen mammal, now wet with blood. Another mammalian appendage moved just close enough for one tick to instinctively cling to the moving hand. As it did so, the tick crawled up onto a wrist, somehow unnoticed within layered folds of a heavy, plastic, sleeve. The tick traveled a ways up onto the soft, underside of an arm and, finding the body temperature and host conditions optimal, bit down into the skin, injecting a small dose of anesthetic saliva as it did so. The tick then proceeded to secure itself by a pincer like *hypostome*, surrounding its mouth. It cut into the skin with tiny dorsal cutting organs called *chelicerae* and began feasting on the oxygen rich blood rising up through capillary loops, which spilled into an area of paired palpi lateral to a chitinous ring lying at the base of the tick's mouth. The tick did not perceive movement of the arm, only a very primitive ecstatic response to finding this new host. This initiated a reproductive sequence from deep within the tick's physiology. At the same time, viral laden insect saliva mixed with sub papillary venous loop circulation of the host.

Volkert had been on the horn with Bugeyes when he heard the first, distinctive M-79 "Thumps" up ahead. The E/O officer monitoring the situation on board the F-109 circling high above, lifted his head up and away from the hooded screen as the entire area of observation lit up with the intense heat of the white phosphorus spread. This rendered the immediate area unobservable. Quickly, SSgt Phillip Volkert organized a skirmish line of Yards and started up the ravine. At the same time, he called up the AC-130 Spectre to commence fire on as many of the company sized farther removed elements as possible. They heard the high pitched whine of raining Spectre munitions dealing death off in the distance as Volkert's skirmishers came upon two NVA in bright yellow plastic suits with AK-47's. One was standing point security and started to level his weapon on the advancing skirmish line. He was quickly cut down by return fire. The other, who was bent over the fallen American had set a weapon down alongside Glickman and could not retrieve it in time to even have a chance of getting off a shot. Helplessly, Thanh Diem raised her hands, high over her head. Volkert had two Yard strikers secure the female enemy soldier as he rushed to the side of his fallen friend. Glickman was shot in several places about his abdomen and torso. Aside from a grazing neck wound, none of the shots had hit him in the head. Volkert gathered him up into his arms calling "Mike! Mike! Oh, Why! Why'd you do it *Bac Si*? Another two minutes and we'd have assaulted them all together! You know better! Why *Bac Si?*"

Glickman opened his eyes and from far away whispered something. Volkert put his ear next to the medic's bloody lips and heard a gurgled whisper.

"Tell McCarthy..... Big Rats... Ticks....no more... dead kids..."

At that moment, Winkle came up to Volkert. "Grit! AC-130 Spectre has flushed them out, they're headed back this way! The phosphorus has blinded Bugeyes and most of a company sized element of NVA regulars is coming this way! We have Cobras at the mouth of the Ravine. What d'ya wannna do?"

Grit (Phillip) Volkert rose up quickly gently letting down his friend as he did so. Through some miracle of timing and location, Volkert just missed offering his own arms as a blood meal to ticks crawling down around the dead Medic's right side waist. Most of the insects were clustered nearby a side arm holster from which the NVA interpreter had taken the pistol that she was now being relieved of by her captors. Volkert grabbed up the radio, contacting the Cobra gunship leader on a common net frequency.

"Cobra leader, this is Minnow Two, say your location and strength, over."

"Minnow Two this is Serpent Flight Leader. We are a full flight wing. You should know what that means, over."

"Serpent Flight Leader, I don't have time to dick around here! We're about to be assaulted by what's left of a very pissed off NVA company coming over that ridge top and down into this ravine. Can you see us at all, over?"

"Minnow Two, the brush is too thick. We cannot tell good guys from bad guys. We see some movement on this side of the ravine along with some bright yellow uniforms, over"

Volkert thought quickly. He reached into Winkle's backpack and brought out a rolled, bright magenta colored landing panel, which the team always carried during field operations in order to coordinate expedient Landing Zones. Each of the corners of this panel had grommeted eyelets and from each of these, parachute chord was tied so as to have tie downs for staking the panel to the ground when rotor downwash would blow over the landing zone. Glickman quickly tied two of these corners together, forming a loop at one short side end of the long rectangular panel. He then dropped the loop over his head, letting the panel fall down his back . It cascaded down from his shoulders falling onto the ground behind, forming a sort of veil train extending back onto the ground about 2 to 3 feet out behind.

"Serpent leader! Do you see the landing panel, over?"

"Minnow two, that is affirmative. We see a bright, reddish colored landing panel that's being held up vertically and is visible through the bush, over."

"Great! Now on my word, you tell your flight wing to open fire and keep firing 10 meters in front of this landing panel."

"Say again Minnow Two? That's shaving it a bit close buckaroo, over!"

"In a minute SIR, the enemy's going to be shaving our asses a bit close! We're outgunned more than five to one. DO YOU ROGER THAT?"

The Cobra commander, a captain out of *Pleiku*, smiled a bit at this pugnacious American NCO. He shook his head slightly, as he took a grease pencil from his left sleeve and made a mark on the inside plexiglass dome of his cockpit. This would be his aiming point. He knew the other pilots were placing similar marks on their inner cockpits. With a rueful sigh, he keyed the battle net and spoke quickly:

"Roger, Minnow Two, wilco, break, Serpent Flight, you heard the man, come on line and form a parallel phalanx of fire 10 meters ahead of the bright red spot. Await ground force initiation."

Grit Volkert formed his skirmish line into a sort of wide, shallow V by extending out his arms to either side and slightly behind him. He kept Winkle off to his right side with the radio, placing the two of them at the apex of the flattened V formation made up of their remaining 12 man element. The fearless yards lined up, five off to either side of Volkert and Winkle. They had to be admonished repeatedly to keep a reverse V formation and resist coming up on line with the spearhead. He could hear movement sounds of the NVA coming from the other side of the ridgeline as he started moving forward with his strikers.

The NVA officers raced their men toward the ravine, away from the open ground in which they had been attacked by the AC-130 Spectre. As they topped the ridgeline, they looked down a slight grade toward the American/Montagnard skirmish line and heard as well as saw fragments of four helicopters over the dense forest beyond. Quickly surmising the situation, the NVA officers shouted a familiar command back to their men.

Bat ziu! Bat ziu! "By the Belt! By the Belt" This battle cry was used frequently by the NVA when in close combat with air supported American troops. It meant simply, get in close and grab them by the throat, mix in with them so that they cannot use their superior air power. This was clearly on the mind of every one of the 62 remaining NVA soldiers whose company sized element had just encountered Puff the Magic Dragon's big brother. As the two elements closed, Volkert spoke into the radio one last time.

"Now, Now, Now!!!"

The four in line Cobra gunships began firing just ahead of the bright red panel now moving toward the ridgeline. Pilots could not make out uniforms under the foliage. All they could really see was the advancing red panel and so they set up an impenetrable curtain of projected firepower right ahead and to either side of the petulant red dot. Volkert and Winkle could feel a violent turbulence in the air over their heads. It almost created a vacuum that took their breath away. As they moved forward, the enemy line disintegrated before them. Striker yards on the far ends commenced picking off flank elements to either side as the enemy became visible. A few of the NVA attempted to return fire, but their line was not well formed, and some wound up shooting their own comrades in the back. Within 12 seconds of commencement, the assault had been headed, turned and transitioned into a rout. Volkert kept moving forward, faster now, much to the consternation of the pilots who were in dire, genuine fear of immolating their red dot aiming point. As the NVA took to their heels, uphill toward less dense vegetation, Volkert again grabbed the radio.

"Sir! Send two of your birds around to the other side of the ridge and catch them as they come out into open terrain over the ridgeline."

"Roger that Minnow Two. Serpents One and Four break, up and over the top. Take them as they come out and for the love of Buddah, try not to shoot our own guys. Minnow, hold up on the ridgeline, otherwise, you may take fire from the enfilade."

"Roger that, Serpent Leader. Waste em, waste em all! They put a plague into that village back there!"

The Cobra commander was caught up in the rush of this action, Volkert's additional bit of admonition did not really sink in. The pilot thought that the word "plague" was used figuratively and took it to mean that this enemy unit had terrorized the village. It was enough for him, however. Through the trees, which thinned toward higher elevations, he could not see the enemy dropping their rifles as they ran away from those horrible, grasshopper like warbirds. The two flanking helicopters came up over the ridgeline and formed crisscrossing fields of fire angled diagonally away from the American spearhead, in parallel with the leading edge of the advancing V skirmish line. As enemy soldiers emerged from under the thinning canopy, their black pajamas became all too apparent, and they were mowed down relentlessly. Some fell to the ground intending to play dead, not realizing that from the air, it is hard to discern if a body has fallen to the ground wounded, or to take up a stationary, prone aiming position. Gunship helicopter pilots routinely fired into a prone body until it burst open, which was one sure way of knowing a black clad enemy, was dead from a distance. Volkert advanced up to the ridgeline with his assault force. As the Montagnard strikers advanced, they also placed security shots into fallen bodies of the enemy, making certain that none would shoot them from behind the skirmish line as it moved forward. On the ridgeline, each of the skirmishers picked off any standing targets until finally, less than 3 minutes after it had begun, it was over. Incredibly, none of the Montagnards or Americans, other than Glickman, had been killed or wounded. All about them lay the bodies of fallen enemy dead. Unlike most battlefields wherein there is at least some movement among wounded, none of the black, pajama-clad forms were moving at all. From the lay of the land, it was impossible for any one to have escaped unseen. From beyond the ridgeline, Bugeyes could sweep the area of higher elevation west of the Laotian striker patrol. To the Bugeyes E/O observer, the balance of all horizontal thermal signatures in the uphill area were gradually cooling to ambient temperature.

Volkert sat down on a fallen log. He took the radio handset again.

"Serpent Flight, this is Minnow Two. Thanks. You all know that we can't begin to…"

The Cobra flight wing leader cut him off by clicking his microphone repeatedly in mid sentence. He then broke through with his own transmission."

"Minnow Two, it has been a privilege to go into action with you, SIR! We are close to bingo and must pigeon on back to base. Any time you need a scratch itched, just give us a call. This is Serpent Flight Leader forming up on echelon right, returning to base."

Volkert watched rubber legged as the four cobras formed up into a lopsided "V" wing formation and headed off to the southeast. All around, his men were leaning against tree trunks, sitting down or urinating. Volkert keyed his mike again:

"Bugeyes, thank you again for covering our six." He was rewarded for this salutation with a "click click" from the E/O on Bugeyes above. Volkert checked for one more player on the combat net:

"Top, are you monitoring?"

MSG Briant had been listening to every move, itching to get in on the action, almost regretting his decision to be here in the longhouses with the sick. He didn't have to ponder too hard to know where he had done more good this week. He keyed back :

"Yea, Grit. Casualties?"

"Only one, they got Doc."

"WHAT! Glickman? How?"

"He just went up ahead along the ravine and began engaging the enemy with the thumper, punching willie pete projectiles uphill. Imagine that! After all his years in the field, he would take on the enemy point element with an M-79. I can't figure out what got into him."

"Glickman wasn't dumb. He knew better than to play John Wayne like that. There had to be a good reason for his doing what he did. Do you have any clue?"

"Well, he whispered something to me before he checked out. Something like tell McCarthy about rats, big rats and ticks and ...well, he said something about... no more dead kids."

Gabriel McCarthy was close by Top Briant as the conversation went on. He let out a breath on hearing that Glickman was dead. It couldn't be! Not *Bac Si* Glickman! He was the Wizard of Oz! How could he die? In this moment of staggering grief, he almost missed the last epitaph, *big rats... ticks... dead kids*? There was something wrong with that. Big rats... but the rats that had infested this camp were small rats, belonging to a common tropical genus and species called *R. Ratus*. Ticks???... but it was *fleas* which normally carried plague, ticks carried a host of other diseases. *Dead kids, no more dead kids*, what did that mean? It could mean that this second attempt on the village was a different kind of bacteriological assault. Something other than plague, but what? Typhus? Tularensis? He suddenly grabbed up the radio from Briant.

"Volkert! Don't let anyone touch Glickman's body until I get there, you understand? No one touches the body... and stay away from the area that he was incinerating!"

"Well, Doc, I've touched the body already, so has the only NVA POW we have. Who, buy the way, is a female interpreter and speaks English. Oh, and she's dressed in a bright yellow moon suit."

"Bring her down in that suit and quarantine her away from those we have who are presently sick. And, another thing, that whole area has to be sterilized. We should call in napalm on the entire ravine."

"Y'know, doc, come to think of it, that's probably what Glickman was trying to do with the WP. He was shooting it all around the stream. Looked like he wasn't even aiming at the gooks."

Gabe violated his quarantine, leaving Briant to make arrangements via Fernstead for a napalm strike into the ravine. The young medic trekked uphill, taking along rubber gloves, an Operating Room gown and blue filter mask. He wondered all the way up if he could manage to keep it together when he saw Glickman. But, he knew that he had to. It was Glickman's last wish. *"No more dead kids. Come on up here and figure it out, kid."* That's what he was saying. Trekking up the ravine, McCarthy passed several Yards leading down the POW, still clad in yellow plastic contamination suit per instructions. They had duct taped her hands behind her back as well as her mouth. He viewed her in retrospect as they passed. She was taller than most of the Yards, slim figured within her yellow suit. She had shoulder length hair, and a trace of defiance on her duct taped continence. The hike up to the headwaters took about three-quarters of an hour. When he arrived, Gabe found Volkert still there surrounded by about 6 yards. The rest had returned to the village with the prisoner. In the distance, there were enemy dead strewn about all the way up to and over the ridgeline.

"Did you find any rats?"

"What?" Volkert replied, rather surprised that would be the first thing out of the wizening young medic's mouth.

"Rats? Did you find any rats, alive or dead?"

"Oh yeah, a bunch," Volkert replied, "in fact, there was one big, dead rat over by Mike. Looks like he butt stroked the critter. I hadn't noticed before, but on coming back, it stuck out given, you know, what he said."

"Where's the rat?" Volkert led Gabe around the body, showing a large, brownish black dead rat with small ears and a long tail. There were also several ticks crawling over the body of Michael Glickman.

"Careful of those ticks, Grit. They carry something. I don't know what yet, but it's something at least as bad as what we've been dealing with this last week."

"Bad as Plague? What could be worse than Plague?"

"Believe me, there are worse things. They just kill more selectively. Are there any other rats?"

Volkert let out a sigh. "Well, there are a bunch of burned out carcasses and some cages up at the headwaters."

Gabe accompanied Grit Volkert up to the headwaters, finding one bullet ridden, dead NVA in a hoodless, gloveless yellow plastic suit. There was also a caucasian in another yellow suit, probably Russian from the looks of his cloth uniform, visible through burn holes in the yellow moon suit. He was horribly burned with white phosphorus all over his body. He had clearly died screaming, and rolled down grade into this small streamlet which formed the headwaters feeding the irrigation fields of *Loc Phieu*. The Russian was fully clad with hood and gloves except for areas in which the suit had burned through. It was still smoldering within the swelling corpse. All the cages were empty and most were burned. The heat generated by burning Phosphorus easily dissolves metal. All around the stream, leading up to this area, there had been smoldering pieces of rat carcass, about an even dozen.

"Grit, go up on the ridge and take off your shirt. I need to check you for ticks."

"Now Doc? Are you serious?"

"Grit, this could mean your life or death. I'm serious."

Shaking his head, Volkert complied. Gabe checked him from head to toe, even insisting that he drop his trousers. Finding no evidence of ticks, or tick bites, Gabriel breathed a little easier. "Did you say that NVA POW touched Glickman?"

"Yea, Doc. She was checking over Glickman's body when we found her. She took Mike's 9 millimeter, but we took it back."

Much to the distress of all the Americans, Gabriel convinced them to leave Glickman where he lay. Gabe took Mike's dogtags after donning protective gear and in the process, very carefully, flicked off a tick from his gloved finger that had risen up from under Glickman's tunic. With one last glance, Sergeant Gabriel McCarthy bid adieu to his mentor and friend as he followed Volkert and the last of the Yards down the ravine, toward the village. Later that night, A-7's from the aircraft carrier U.S.S. *Independence* off the coast of South Vietnam flew in and dropped several hundred pounds of napalm into the ravine, sterilizing the area and incinerating the mortal remains of SFC Michael Glickman.

Back in *Loc Phieu*, the captured female NVA was placed in a 2x2 meter containment cubicle. It was made up of a bamboo cage with thatched roof and set off from the rest of the compound in an area of separate quarantine. As a military interpreter, Thanh Diem had been trained in interrogation techniques. She anticipated a very different treatment than she was receiving. After cutting loose her bindings, they gave her food and water, but from a distance. They let her lie down within her open air cell and rest, instead of being forced to stay awake. At first, she attributed this to naiveté with POW interrogation, on the part of her captors. Perhaps she was being held for some higher authority that would process her at another facility. On the day after her arrival, the tall American whom she had passed while coming downhill from the headwaters visited her. He had a tired, bedraggled look on his face and sat down just outside her cage. Two older women, both of whom gazed upon her with unconcealed contempt, accompanied him.

"You understand English, I am told."

"Yes, I speak your language."

"There are some things which I have to ask you. But first, I must ask that you take off all of your clothing. I promise that you will not be molested. I apologize that we can not provide you a more private place to do this. I can only offer that these women will remain present as witnesses."

"Witnesses? What extraordinary courtesy this American was pretending!" Of course, she had expected to be strip searched for weapons. Frankly, she was surprised that it had not been done when she first arrived. She had only been patted down in a brief body search when they first apprehended her. Again, she attributed this to poor interrogation technique.

"I will undress myself; you do not have to make them come in here." She was certain the venomous, primitive Montagnard women would be rough with her.

"They will remain on this side as witnesses to assure that you are not molested."

Interpreter Diem undressed. She had already removed the heavy rubber moon suit as it was unbearably hot. That remained piled up on one side of her cage. She had used it as a pillow the night before. She removed tops and bottoms of a black pajama field uniform that she'd worn in company with her male counterparts. She followed by removing her underwear until she stood naked before the American. Rather than give him the satisfaction of observing her attempting to cover herself, she stood upright, with her chin up, forming an expression on her face to suggest that she had no compunction at all about standing naked before her enemy. The American asked her to turn and face away from him, which she did. He then directed her to back up closer to the bamboo bars. She could feel his gaze upon her from behind, but he did not touch her at all. Instead, he instructed her to raise up her arms and slowly turn around. She did so, keenly aware of him closely examining her body surfaces, wondering if he was taking some sort of perverse pleasure from the process. Abruptly, he instructed her to stop as she rotated her right side toward him.

"There, on your forearm, just below your elbow." She followed his gaze down to a spot on her bare arm, on the soft, inner side of her forearm. There, to her growing horror was an engorged tick. She lost all reserve in front of her captors and started to scream while holding her arm out away from her body, as if it were a separate entity.

"Please, put your arm through these bamboo bars and permit me to remove that tick."

She did so without hesitation. The American took a matchstick and lit it up, letting it burn out quickly. He then touched the still glowing tip to the backside of the fat tick which stirred and moved in place. As it did so, he gently lifted it up with a pair of tweezers and placed it into a petrie dish handed him by one of the Montagnard women. In its place on her arm, there was a tiny welt with a central puncture that bled slightly as the insect was removed.

"Now that you know what we are looking for, please check the rest of your body, between your toes and as much of your private parts as you can see. We will help you with the rest."

She did this, anxiously examining every part of her body that was visible to her. She relied on the others to examine the rest, cooperating by spreading her buttocks and running through her own scalp with a comb. There were no other ticks on her person.

They provided her with a change of clothing. A simple Montagnard sarong, but it was clean and the cloth was soft and comfortable next to her skin. All of the clothing she had previously worn was collected and burned.

"Please, can you tell me, am I going to get sick?"

The American answered:

"We are going to do the best we can to find out what sort of disease this tick may be carrying. It would help if you could tell us as much as you know about where it came from."

"I think it might have come from the Russian, Comrade Markov. Not from his person, but from some rats that he was turning loose at the stream. He said that they came from Russia, that they carried some kind of fever."

"What kind of fever? There are many diseases that cause fever. Do you remember him saying what kind of fever these ticks could cause?"

"Bleeding fevers. He said bleeding fevers." Her voice was quivering now. There was no reserve between captive and captor. She knew that the Americans had great expertise in medicine and realized that her only hope to avoid a terrible, uncertain, death was to cooperate in every way possible.

"Bleeding fevers?... Do you mean Hemorrhagic fevers?"

"Yes, yes, the translation, it is the same... Bleeding, hemorrhagic, it means the same, yes?"

"Yes, it does." The American was very grim faced now.

"Do you have medicines? Can you prevent this disease?"

"Most hemorrhagic fevers are caused by viruses. Unlike Plague, which can be treated with antibiotics, viruses can only be treated by making up serum antibodies from an infected host."

"What does that mean? I do not understand what you say. Please, can you give me medicine?"

She was trembling now, clearly terrified by the prospect of what might result from this tick-bite. Gabriel decided that it would serve no purpose to frighten her.

"We will give you what we have."

This calmed her somewhat. The American seemed sincere and she had heard stories, as most field soldiers had, about the peculiar kindness the Americans sometimes displayed toward captured enemy soldiers. Communist propaganda mills interpreted this as an attempt to decadently buy captured prisoners away from communism, but for whatever reason, if the Americans would help deliver her from this terrible threat, she would willingly accept their oblations.

Later that day, she was given a shot of gamma globulin and several placebo pills, which was about all Gabriel could offer. The medic also instructed a work detail to dig a twelve by twelve-inch deep and wide trench about the quarantine cell. This was filled with white powders, insecticides and rodenticides, forming a visible barrier nobody but the American would cross over.

When she had first arrived, the Yards generally exhibited toward her all the animosity and bitterness of a villainess who offered them countenance for what had happened to their village. By the third day after her arrival, community vituperation started giving way to a sort of loathing pity. She began on the evening of the second day with a fever and headache. Her eyes became red and sore. She felt lethargic and found it exceedingly painful even to rise up enough to relieve herself. On the morning of the third day following her first interview with the American, her gums and nose began to bleed. From that time onward, none in the camp would come close to her bamboo cell, except the American medic. On the afternoon of that third day, he crossed over the barrier trench and actually cut open the cell door. He entered, wearing rubber gloves and a mask. He brought with him a clean bedroll, soap, and water, which he used to bathe her. After covering the bedroll with a poncho, he gently eased her onto the softer surface. Already, she was starting to bruise over elbows, heels and buttocks. Throughout that evening, and for the next few days, he stayed with her, there in that cage, while MSG Briant brought daily food and supplies up to the white trench. Gabriel could do little more than provide her with morphine and decent nursing care. By day five following her tick borne inoculation, she started passing blood in both stool and urine. During sober moments, she would talk with Sgt. McCarthy, whom she now referred to as *Bac Si*, just as she had heard the villagers do. She started by relating to him memories of her childhood and upbringing. As time passed, she began telling him about her defection to North Vietnam and the reason that she had become a communist. She disclosed this latter information almost apologetically. He did what he could to comfort her. Sometime around the third day of their joint isolation, six days following inoculation, she began to disclose information about her mission as an interpreter there in

Loc Phieu. This information was not petitioned, but she offered it up willingly, as though seeking absolution with its disclosure. She told Gabriel about Regimental Field Commander Muc Bo Thau and the decisions he had made regarding this province. She explained her association with the Russian and all that she could recall about their conversations and deployment of bacteriologic weapons. She recalled that he had referred to Plague infested rats as the "first assault" and intended to follow with this second breed of rats as a second assault. She revealed various things that the Russian had discussed about venereal diseases and bacteriological warfare. She had been with Commander Thau long enough to know he was a cruel man and that he had imposed many atrocities on the Montagnards in this region. MSG Carmen Briant listened in on some of this and started taking notes.

On the eighth day after releasing the second assault rats, Thanh Diem began coughing up blood. In the early morning hours on the day thereafter, she died. Gabriel was at her side, holding her bruised, quivering right hand through two layers of latex gloves. For five days, he had remained in the cage with her, bathing and feeding her, talking with her, taking brief naps with her. During those five days, he lived closer to death than he had ever known. Every time he injected her with morphine, every time he was spattered with blood or body fluids, he faced the visage of death. He took every precaution possible and remained with her, realizing that beyond her veil of torment, he would very likely never see another human being physically suffer quite so much. He continued to accommodate her death grip, long after it turned stiff and cool, until twilight on the morning of her death. When Briant came shortly after sunrise, Gabe arose and exited from the cell. He took off his gloves, mask and surgeons gown, tossing them into the cell to lie alongside the withered, mutilated carcass of what had been just the week before, a vibrant, intelligent, attractive, young woman. Briant went and retrieved others who piled dried kindling around the cage, then doused the area liberally with gasoline. Carmen Briant offered to let Gabe toss the pyre. He did so, being gradually forced back as the burgeoning inferno leapt up, beyond the margins of the white, powder filled trench. Finally, he turned and walked away from the place, shuffling, trance-like, toward the quarantine longhouse. By now it had become nearly emptied of Plague patients. He approached the lower pylons and sank to shadowed earth on the west side. Briant followed the young medic, along with a gathering host of Montagnards and the other Americans. The ordeal had clearly changed Sgt. Gabriel McCarthy.. They all looked down upon him as he lay there in deep slumber, mid shadows cast from the rising sun, surrounded by people who loved him dearly. They could not help but notice the change. His face was worn and aged. He was obviously thinner than before the epidemic had begun. Perhaps most noticeable, where once his scalp had been topped with a solid tone of deep reddish brown hair, a startling transition had proceeded over the last few days. The cowlick which stood up like a small, clipped Chinese fan over his right eye had transmogrified into a startling white plume, blending backward toward a distinctly faded reddish brown mane of irregular, salt and pepper colored, crew cut hair. In the space of one week, his hair had transmogrified, leaving him a smattering of crew cut grey hair.

Travis Air Force Base Easter Perimeter

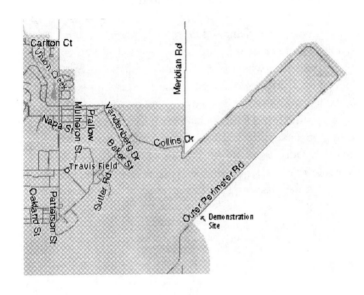

Chapter 5 – Ambush, Influence and Mixed Emotions

August thru Early November 1971

Over time, the A-Team formed its own ecosystem within the verve of AO Focus. Data began to assimilate in the form of experience and insight. The officers of Team A-321 started to grasp what it was that genuinely made progress toward accomplishing their prime objective of self-sufficiency among the Montagnard and Hmong people. It was the medics who seemed to have the greatest impact on ameliorating the lives of the villagers, and in winning over hearts as well as minds. What the medics did was good. There was no way to misconstrue this despite confusing edicts of propaganda from all sides.

However, in the violence that permeated this part of Southeast Asia, there was the very genuine problem of a determined communist will on surrounding villages and on virtually all people within the Area of Operations. Frequently, in order to make a point, the communists would employ cruelty or even horror. This was perhaps most clearly demonstrated during the aftermath of one CAP project in *Lo Dao*, the Katu Montagnard village located at the extreme northeast sector of Area Focus.

Over that summer, the American medics had been tasked with initiating a vaccination program among tribal children. This was, of course, done in conjunction with local medicine men who had been impressed by the growing reputation of the American medics to enhance the prestige of native apothecaries while working together to deliver their people from physical malady. A vaccination project had begun mid to late summer. It was during that time, in September, that MSG Carmen Briant led a patrol from north to south through the AO. His patrol would eventually end up at *Loc Phieu* to deal with the Plague epidemic. SFC Michael Glickman and SSG Philip Volkert accompanied Carmen Briant on this patrol. The three American advisors traveled with a growing contingent of about 30 field savy Montagnards. Early on his final patrol, prior to encountering the Plague epidemic down south, SFC Glickman had passed through and met with the village *Bac Si* of *Lo Dao*. After formal courtesies were exchanged between patrol leader Briant and village chieftain, SFC Glickman sought out the company of the local healer. Inquiries were made about the little girl who had been mutilated by the communists that prior June. She was well and growing strong. Without mentioning anything about the Judas Agent who had been executed by the Americans, the old native *Bac Si* asked about the other, Junior American *Bac Si*. His people had been most impressed with the young American's caring and demeanor. "The young American seemed genuinely concerned about our people, as also the present *Bac Si* is" (referring to Glickman ,this added as a polite after-tone to the conversation). Characteristically, SFC Michael Glickman had begun the introductions by complimenting the grizzled old medicine man on how well he cared for his people and how generally clean and informed they were about supporting a "good feeling of the body. This clearly pleased the old medico.

SFC Glickman explained that, much like teaching children to avoid certain insects and snakes, it would be very good to teach them to avoid things that make sickness. Because children could not always be expected to understand good advice, there was a special potion that would help them to avoid some of these problems. Could the Americans help the medicine man provide this for the children? It was agreed that volunteers would be called for from among the village parents. If they were willing to let their children be immunized and if neither children nor parents had any problems later, very likely more would want to do so. Accordingly, a call was issued via the appropriate vehicles of both village chieftain and medicine man. Several families timidly consented to permit their children to take the peppermint flavored Salk Polio Vaccine as well as to receive a combined series of Rubella, Roseola, Typhoid and Tetanus toxoid injections. The village overall remained hesitant to accept these Americans, however, and therefore again refused Briant's offer to have some people remain behind with a radio. About a week after the Americans left, an NVA political indoctrination patrol passed through the same village unseen by Bugeyes, which was at that time monitoring what was happening in *Loc Phieu*, down in the extreme southern province of AO Focus.

They were a hard-core North Vietnamese communist goon squad. Their express mission was to bully and intimidate. Having had quite enough of bacteriological warfare, Commander Muc Bo Thau, accompanied this particular indoctrination patrol into the northern province of *Lo Dao*. He would occasionally risk exposure of his high rank on such a patrol in order to demonstrate his courage as well as assure that the proper message was being conveyed to the common people. After being informed of the immunizations by a few intimidated villagers, he issued orders to herd the village people together. Commander Thau then personally announced that they had submitted to a very bad thing when they permitted the Americans to do this to the children. To emphasize his edict, every child that had been immunized was singled out. They segregated the children by pointing out perceived immunization sites on their arms. Actually, by that time, these tiny injection marks were pretty much invisible and a number of children, including many who had not been vaccinated, were collectively herded up for exhibition.

Preempting an emotional uprising by parents, the children were removed en masse on the guise of being tended while parents were retained at an indoctrination meeting to explain the evils of American Imperialism. After the meeting was over, late in the evening, the communists left the village. The next morning, at first light, frantic parents went searching for their missing offspring. Juvenile remains were found in the jungle. Every little arm which, in the opinion of the communists, may have been vaccinated had been hacked off. The children had apparently been bound and gagged prior to being dismembered so as to prevent any sounds of screaming disrupting the political meeting. After being thus mutilated, the children were left to exsanguinate in the humid jungle. All the arms had been collected and hung on cords from trees, forming a sort of pathway to the small bodies. This horror was meant to subdue the people. As is often the case with such extreme cruelty, it backfired on the perpetrators, launching a generalized uprising from every Montagnard village in the area. Most all of the Katu in AO focus, and many Northern Jeh Montagnard tribes as well united against this terrible act. The Americans were asked to help in seeking retribution and, more importantly, in preventing such a thing from happening again.

It was decided that the best way to prevent any more atrocities was to eliminate extended communist squad movement in the area. Mountains to the west and north pretty much hindered overland movements into the AO from that direction. The southern region of the AO was at much lower altitudes. It was invested with areas of double and triple canopy jungle merging sharply into mountains on the north and west. In the southern area, there were any number of trails, which could provide patrol routes in to and out of AO Focus. The communists had long since learned, daytime patrols out in the open were foolish when conducted against an enemy that owned the skies and possessed the vision perspective of a hungry raptor. Therefore, most communist patrols were carried out at night.

Nighttime movement apart from trails through the jungle was essentially impossible. Therefore, nightly patrols by the communists took place along jungle trails. These were virtually the only access into or out of AO Focus. While the communists could be chased during the day by American patrols, nighttime pursuit was more difficult. Accordingly, Captain Fernstead came up with a sort of "hammer and anvil" plan to stop the communists by using his roving patrol unit as the hammer, and special ambush teams as the anvil.

It was decided that these ambushes would best be conducted at dawn, when enemy patrols were returning back toward Laotian base camps east, toward Ho Chi Minh Trail complexes. There were a number of advantages to this approach. By setting only outbound ambushes there was a "psyops" (psychological operations) aspect to the mission plan. The enemy would develop a much more primitive, instinctive fear of entering the AO if they believed that they could go in, but they could not get back out again. Deployment of an ambushing element is much more effective if it can be done in small groups. These make less noise and do not need to move on trails that can be easily observed or counter ambushed. This means daytime, off trail small squad movement and nighttime deployment. To ambush inbound enemy patrols would require the opposite. In addition, by ambushing only those groups returning back west at dawn, ambush teams could be certain that they were indeed interdicting the enemy and not eastbound *Sin Loi's* or other civilians.

At the north end of the AO, mountains formed a natural infiltration barrier to ground elements. In order to hike up to *Lo Dao*, communist indoctrination squads would have to pass through the southern end of AO Focus. Accordingly, the team's two weapons NCO's were tasked with organizing ambush teams capable of striking out from deployment sites on expedient LZ's located within a few klicks of essential, jungle shrouded access trails into or out of the southern hemisphere of AO Focus. Unbeknownst to NVA patrols, when a layered, canopy jungle is viewed above, from a helicopter, trails cut into the bush at ground level form a sort of dull, linear glyphic, as observed from directly above. This is because matted trails absorb more warmth during the day than the surrounding jungle. Virtually every trail into the area was thus mapped out and enemy foot patrol routes could be observed during regular reconnaissance overflights by Bugeyes. Most of these trails merged into three or four primary trail segments as they passed deeper into western Laos toward the Ho Chi Minh trail. It was here that returning foot patrols, fleeing a potential daytime encounter with Fernstead's "hammer" patrols, could most predictably be interdicted.

Beginning late July, on at least a weekly basis, the weapons NCO's deployed dawn ambush teams. As time went on, the Montagnards were capable of fielding their own ambush elements, but they had to be properly trained in this dangerous, rather technical skill. Initially, it had been decided that both Brooksly and Estrada would alternate training sorties. However, as time went on, it became quite clear that SFC Arnoldo Estrada's talents lay in planning and coordination, whereas Sgt. Kirk Brooksly's talents were in stealthy fieldcraft. That is not to say Estrada was weak in fieldcraft. Nor was Brooksly particularly weak in developing an operations plan. It was the Montagnards themselves who decided that they would rather have Estrada plan the ambushes, to pick the time and place, whereas, they would rather have Brooksly training teams in the field. Estrada just always seemed to know when and where. In the maze of pathways leading back to the west, picking an ambush site based on projected data from Bugeyes and hitting on nearly every mission took some real *"chutzpah"*, as Glickman had once put it. Estrada had such chutzpah. However, in the bush, Arnie Estrada was just as massive and aggressive as in any other situation. Although any of the Yards would have wanted him on their side in a frontal assault, for a stealthy near ambush, they much preferred Brooksly. This did not lead to any hard feelings between the two American weapons specialists, merely an understanding of how respective talents and manpower resources for the unit could be most effectively deployed in training the Yards and carrying out mission directives.

The Junior weapons NCO, Sgt. Kirk Brooksly (he would develop the nickname "Ambush Brooksly", pronounced by the Yards in jest, 'amboos blookboos') would depart from base camp with one or two green Montagnard recruits, along with a core group of hand picked strikers. These were a seasoned cadre of Yards who evolved extraordinary bush skills in movement, concealment and most importantly, patience. Brooksly was himself lean, lithe and graceful although somewhat tall at six foot one, a decided disadvantage for most jungle predators. He managed, however, to use his height as an expediency in directing and overseeing the little Montagnards with whom he would work and train. About once per week at varied times so as not to establish any predictable pattern, a Huey C slick would lift off from Swordfish lair carrying Brooksly and 6-8 Yards aboard. They would overfly the jungle to some open area just large enough for a transient LZ, located within a 2-5 kilometer radius from some essential venous trail leading out of AO Focus, feeding indirectly back to the Ho Chi Minh trail.

After being infiltrated into a designated area, the team would move a short distance in some random direction into the jungle and then go to ground. This was a difficult time for the newer recruits. It called for intense concentration on the part of every team member to become a stationary human sensory element. During that time, each would go through a sort of *"Chi"* with the jungle. While remaining as humanly motionless as possible, each man would posture into a shape that allowed stillness, and relative comfort but not conducive to drowsiness; no concentrated pressure points, no crossed extremities. Weapons and vision fields faced outward from a perimeter of human concentration. Every body settled into a topography of wet, dripping earth and vegetation along with other invisible life forms. Gradually, the unit would become sort of mind melded into a cohesive thing, which could move as close to being one as is possible. Brooksly would lead his squad off through the bush in a general direction toward the target. They would move with slow, bizarre, almost comical, mime-like movements. This resulted in very short distances per day through dense jungle. Extra efforts were made not to break plant limbs or tramp foliage. Always, they had to be alert for snakes and other potentially poisonous or dangerous jungle life. When possible, the rear guard would cover tracks occasionally left in any exposed soil. Meals were always taken without any fire and with very little discernible noise, heating rehydrated LRP (Long Range Patrol) rations by warming the moisture added packets on their bellies. Most of any C ration entrees were generally left behind except for favored fruits and deserts, essential perks in which to take some respite from the grueling ordeal of extremely disciplined movement. Brooksly had managed to procure special bonuses for his men in the form of small bottles of Tobasco sauce, which the Yards dearly treasured.

It could take two or three days to move just 3-4 kilometers at this pace. During the nights, there could be no movement. Just before sundown, when the jungle became a cascading filter of odd colored lights, on hand signal from Brooksly, they would go into a Rest Over Night (RON) position mid jungle. This RON formed a human circle with heads toward the center and feet extended outward like spokes of a wheel. Through a prearranged choreography, certain members of the team would set out 4 claymore mines forming a sort of swastika like pattern surrounding the team so that, if detonated, the swath cutting claymores would sweep a 360 ° circumference around the RON. It would produce a circular kill zone without injuring the nuclear omphalos in repose. The last physical act of waning dayglow would be for each man to write in ink on the palm of his hand the 10 digit coordinates of their RON. This would be erased next morning. Throughout the night, each man would take a two-hour watch. At the end of two hours, he would gently awaken the man sleeping clockwise, to his right.

Located at the hub of the circle was an AN PRC-77 radio with new battery and erect, long whip antennae. Each man assigned sequentially to watch would sit upright in pitch-darkness.

He would hold the radio transmitter/receiver to his shoulder with fingers from one hand resting gently upon the transmit button. In the other hand would be a V shaped, plastic grip handspring "clacker" or detonator for the claymores, with safety on. Car-15, also with safety on, rested in his lap whilst ears strained to read night sounds of the jungle. There is a normality of jungle sound as with most things in nature. Movement of human bipeds through ink black jungle at night without light can only be accomplished with much rustling and bumbling and irregular noise. Occasionally, a large, animal predator might pass somewhere near the RON, but these also had a normalcy of sound which, to the practiced ear, could be readily identified. Rainy season in the jungles of Laos begins around the end of June and lasts until Mid- October. Often, these "anvil" ambush teams would co-habit a dripping, sauna-like jungle. This could make sleeping soundly a real challenge. It was useless to set up any sort of shelter and too hot to sleep under ponchos. Therefore, each man learned to doze by lowering his boonie hat enough to shield most of the face from heavy droplets of jungle condensation dripping down throughout the night. The greatest challenge of all was insects. By 1970, a nearly odorless insect repellant had been developed by the U.S. military for use in the jungles. It discouraged bites, but did not repel arthropods from crawling onto the human body. Learning not to scratch was perhaps the hardest thing of all. Selection, training and experience virtually eliminated snoring from the group, and each man slept quietly with only the occasional stirrings essential to any barest definition of human sleep.

Just before dawn, when they were most vulnerable, during the last watch, always Brooksly, awoke every other member of the group. They collectively would rise up to a sitting position, weapons facing outward. If they were to be attacked en masse, it could only be done at dawn by surrounding pincer elements that were far enough removed to avoid being heard during the night. For this reason, as the sun began sending its first vestige of illumination into the jungle from the east, the entire team was once again at maximum sensory reception with every weapon trained outward. In the event the team was attacked, the radiotelephone operator (RTO) would announce a call sign followed by 10 digit grid coordinates. On call artillery support, mostly 4.2 mortars or, if close enough, 81 mm mortars from the A-Site would then proceed to drop rounds into the jungle all around the broadcast grid coordinates. This of course required a certain precision which, if off just a bit, could easily result in laying rounds onto the RON position itself.

Well into the morning, after the sun had risen sufficient to lend its more usual dull, amber glow to the steamy jungle floor, they would collect their claymores and switch back to flexible jungle whip antennas in reverse cadence from the night before. Thereafter, the group would once again move out at their slow, deliberate pace. Finally, on the 2nd or 3rd day following insertion, they would come upon the trail. This was another very dangerous time for them as trails were likely to be occupied during the day by civilians or villagers in commerce. If the team was spotted, the mission would be compromised.

Upon intersecting the trail, Brooksly would conduct a very careful reconnoiter, then blend back into the jungle and gather his group to review sand table position assignments until after sundown. Then, under poncho and red handlight filter, each man would rehearse his role. Weapons would be checked and all gear secured. About two hours before dawn, returning along carefully rehearsed movement paths, they would form a linear near ambush position parallel to the trail. Each man would be separated by about 1.5 meters from his fellows, covering a distance of 15 to 20 linear meters of trailside. In the event they happened to be near a bend on the trail, Brooksly would take up a flank right angle "bloody nose" position to the rest at the uptrail side of the ambush line. They would position about 3 meters from the trail path. Each man would set up a 120° sweep to his immediate front except for the flanks who would set up 60° sweeps into the kill zone. This created cris-crossing fields of fire, always at knee level, using the automatic weapons as hewing devices to sickle down anything bipedal.

Typically, as dawn approached, returning enemy patrols would come down the trails bone tired, wet and reduced to a sort of noctambulation that diminishes wariness to its lowest level. If the enemy were going eastward, or into the AO, they would pass without incident, but their number and assets were carefully observed for later intelligence reporting to the hammer element. If the enemy group was larger than 15 to 18 men (they rarely were), they would pass unmolested as the size of the ambush team could not cover a sufficiently long enough kill zone to sweep the entire prey unit. If they were a closely clumped together 15, or just about any kind of element less than 10, they would qualify for activating the kill zone. Always, it was up to Brooksly to initiate the ambush. Every man would be ready; weapons locked and cocked, thumbs on selector switches.

At the first shot from Brooksly, every man would fire from a prone position at knee level, sweeping in one direction from right to left on full auto. This would swing their weapons in unison, moving away from rightward brass ejection. At the end of the first arc, thumbs would simultaneously press down on selector switches and swing back weapons in an arc from left to right on semi-automatic. At that point, team numbers 2, 4 and 6 would pull lanyards attached to pins on concussion grenades laid out along a shielded edge of trail shoulder closest to them. At the same moment, first and last flank numbers continued to sweep the kill zone on semi automatic until expending all ammunition in one magazine. By that time, team members 2, 4 and 6 would be sweeping the zone again after recovering from popping the grenades. During those few seconds, the flanks would change magazines.

Between 1st and 2nd magazines, team members 2, 4 and 6 would carefully toss a second concussion grenade each into the melee. After everyone had expended 2 magazines, or 60 rounds per man, and 4 -6 concussion grenades into one 18-meter kill zone, flanks would secure the trail ends while the rest of the team moved forward to assess a body count. Typically, the initial sweep at full auto would strike legs and bring down whatever erect figures were in the kill zone on the first arc. The return arc on semiauto was more deliberate and would actually be sort of aimed at anything still erect, always at knee level, bringing the upper body down to the ground by chopping or sweeping out the lower body.

The first round of concussion grenades would stun anything still left standing. Because of such close proximity, fragmentation grenades could not be used. However, by the time that second wave of 3 concussion grenades landed amidst close quarters of downed men, the effect was to blow the clustered bodies to pieces. As a result, there was little more than raw carnage and debris left inside the kill zone by the time it was all over, usually about 30-45 seconds after the initiating shot. While flank security was maintained, the middle members would collect weapons, documents and anything that might be of any apparent intelligence value, into plastic bags. The entire team would then move very quickly overland to an exfiltration LZ, usually no more then a kilometer away.

Movement during exfiltration was very different from the slow, purposeful trek of the inbound stalk, but unless the enemy had anticipated the ambush, which was unlikely, there was insufficient time to form a reaction force against the ambush team, especially with daylight coming on and air support inbound. During these harried minutes, Ambush Brooksly would be radioing in a prearranged call sign causing Estrada in a standby Huey at basecamp to fire up and take off toward whichever transient LZ coincided with the call sign. As the helicopter came inbound, Brooksly would pop colored smoke that the helicopter pilot would identify over the radio. With color confirmation, the warbird would swoop down and retrieve the clambering patrol.

Between July and October of 1971, 43 of these ambushes were carried out successfully, by Brooksly and other ambush teams he had trained. The body count, measured in weapons collected from the enemy, amounted to 481 rifles along with invaluable paper intelligence articles. More significantly, the psychological impact on the enemy was profound. Katu drafted Viet Cong inducted from villages in the area actually deserted their units and returned to their home villages, confident that hard liner communists from the north would not likely follow them. They also brought valuable human intelligence, information on the enemy. Most importantly, Montagnard and Hmong tribes-people of that area realized for the first time in their cultural history, that they could exact retribution for atrocities committed against them by the communists. During those three months, not one single American or indigenous combatant was killed or wounded on hammer/anvil ops. Making every effort to avoid sitting on his scarifying tush, Lieutenant Erickson rejoined the team at Swordfish Lair in mid August. Had it not been for the loss of SFC Glickman in late August, the entire American team would have been intact and fully functioning.

Regimental Field Commander Muc Bo Thau was beyond furious. Over that summer to fall monsoon season, many Katu and Jeh Montagnard provinces within his immediate area command had crumbled to the American corrupters. That abortive attempt of the Russian "advisor" to use bacteriological warfare had resulted in the loss of an entire company of NVA regular troops. Had he remained with them down south at *Loc Phieu*, instead of participating in the political action at *Lo Dao* up north, he might well have become a casualty himself! In addition, the bungling Russian microbiologist had possibly contaminated an entire sector of his command theater. Against the risk of contamination, Commander Thau would no longer send units into the *Loc Phieu* area, and so, it had effectively been denied him. His report to higher command was somewhat flowered down but the numbers, even moderated, where an indictment of his failure to secure that region.

Fortunately, U.S. backed Cambodian military actions against the Khmer Rouge down south distracted politburo higher command from looking at Commander Thau's area command with any fine scrutiny. Hopefully, with a little more support, Commander Thau could turn things around again at the end of monsoon season. Clearly, the clever, deceptive, humanitarian appearing acts of the Americans in rendering health care to the peasants were having a profound effect on local support. His patrols no longer had free transit of the area. It seemed as though the Montagnards and Hmong living in the area actually had the audacity to provide intelligence to the Americans, so much so that his patrols were severely hindered. His own public demonstration in punishing the villagers of *Lo Dao* by sacrificing a few of their children had clearly backfired. When he was younger, he had always considered the sophisticated medical system of the Americans a sign of their weakness and self-indulgence. When soldiers were injured, they had to be tough and exemplary so as to inspire the uninjured to fight harder. Seriously wounded men were better off dead than living a half-life of charitable aid and dependency. He had never understood what value it served to spend so much time and effort on caring for the weak, the sick and injured. He was now beginning to rethink his youthful naiveté. Clearly, more than any other influence, improved health care was doing something to rally the people living under his command. They had some sort of foolish belief that they were living better just because some American *Bac Si's* passed out soap and pills and had the temerity to immunize their children. Well, perhaps he could not "kill them with kindness" as the Americans were. However, he might conjure up something to do about the American ambushes.

November 3rd, 1971 Sgt. Kirk Brooksly was leading in another ambush squad. He had aged considerably over that summer and early fall. The constant regimen of highly disciplined movement, laced with regular adrenaline surges near seminal killing events repeated month after month, were exacting a toll on his humanity. Kirk had become hard and carnivorous. Fernstead and Estrada both monitored him carefully to assure that he would not

burn out. Quite the contrary, as time went on, he and his pro-
liferating ambush teams got better and better at their conjoined
predatory aptitude. They would spend no more than one or two
days between missions, then slink back into the seductive jungle,
ever waiting to embrace them. They understood that it was the
jungle which made them strong, which joined them in a primitive kinship far more endearing than even their inherited clan
structures.

Monsoon season ceased with the coming of cooler temperatures around late October. This also usually marked an increase
in foot patrols on the part of the enemy. A mission had been
pegged by SFC Estrada along a trail they called highway 101 in
the central extremity of AO Focus. It would be the first "dry"
anvil mission since the hammer and anvil project had begun last
summer. Highway 101 ran perpendicular to the Ho Chi Minh
trail, merging with its numerous conduits to the west. As usual,
the basecamp Huey C slick overflew their target site from high
above. This permitted each man to visualize the serpentine nature of the trail and conceptualize best points of ambush. The
pilot then began searching for an acceptable LZ somewhere in a
2 to 5 klick radius from the trail. The term "transient LZ" was
used to describe any space large enough to permit a vertical hover
descent without considerable risk of striking the rotors. On this
particular morning, the LZ was a small, open berm. It was essentially bare of any tall vegetation, but carpeted with a verdant
spread of waist high elephant grass. As the chopper descended,
the copilot was first to see movement in the grass to their right
front. It appeared to be a sleeping man within a semi-spherical
foxhole. He had just been startled awake. Characteristic black pajamas and conical straw woven hat belied the more sinister nature
of an AK-47 resting on the ground beside him.

Corporal Dau Vo Tien had been one of those members of the
squad, which mutilated the children of *Lo Dao*. Not surprisingly, he would often think about the incident. When he did,
he recalled being ordered to bind and gag the children. This he

had done professionally, and with discipline befitting a soldier assigned to that special political squad of the Regional Commander. He recalled a momentary hesitation when the order was given, thinking that this was work unworthy of a true soldier. However, clearly, this was a lesson the villagers would never forget and, after all, it was the Americans who were really doing this to the children, not themselves. They were simply exacting necessary retribution for such forbidden collaboration with the enemy. He was in a strange way proud of these children who seemed willing to make themselves sacrifices so as to steel the will of the people. According to his leaders, what they had done was necessary, not unlike some similar things he had done before "for the good of the people".

This present assignment was boring duty for Corporal Dau Vo Tien. The area commander had sent out orders that distributed his best soldiers in the district among these silly open spaces. Commander Muc Bo Thau had studied the American ambush strategy. He realized that he could not interdict ambush teams at random ambush sites as he could not predict where the ambushes would be along many kilometers of trail traveled by reconnaissance and roving political indoctrination patrols. However, there were only so many places in which a helicopter could land around fringes of jungle. Accordingly, he decided to place single sentries at each of these locations. They would go in on one disseminating patrol. They would have to be trained to read maps and understand where they would be going. They would also have to take along provisions for they might be staying on site over long periods of time. Muc Bo Thau figured that if he could interdict helicopters at landing sites, he could stop the ambush patrols. So it was that Corporal Tien had been assigned to this little clearing in the jungle about 5 days ago. He stayed in the area, alone all that time. He dug a four-foot spherical concavity into the earth on a hillside incline from which he would wait and listen. It was possible to feel helicopter vibrations within one of these listening domes long before one could even hear the helicopters themselves.

The weather was rather pleasant, now that rainy season was over. His instructions were to watch for any American helicopters. If one of them attempted to land, he would wait until it was well into the clearing, when maneuverability was most difficult within the diminutive landing space. Then, he would shoot into the pilot's compartment, which would bring down the helicopter. Corporal Dau Vo Tien prided himself on being a vigilant soldier. However, in the end, it was boredom that spelled his demise. Five days of inactivity had dulled his senses. He explored as much of the area around his little habitat as he could, to the limits of his orders, which were not to move so far into the jungle as to be out of sight of the open space. He picked out several good spots from which to shoot down a helicopter and had fantasized numerous times over what it would be like to ambush an American Helicopter full of screaming American soldiers.

He would return to his company a hero. He would collect souvenirs from the aircraft. Perhaps make a bracelet out of the little chain which twirled the rear rotor. His friends had told him about that. He would take the flat plates with names that the Americans wore around their necks or in their bootlaces. What did they call them? Dogtags...yes that was it, how appropriate; for they were all dogs, these Americans. He would.... What was that vibration? What was that cold shiver, calling him back to reality from his mid morning nap? As he startled awake, he had trouble discerning if the moronic shape of the big bird was part of his dream. It took a few more seconds for him to separate dream from stark reality. He reached down for his weapon, placed in a familiar posture at his side with the handle almost under his palm. The AK-47 has a long plate slide on its side that serves as selector switch to make it safe, semi or full automatic. He thumb clicked it to full automatic as he swung it around in an arc, seemingly in slow motion, as the big bird of prey appeared to draw him into a predator's hypnotic trance. He began shouting in slow motion and swinging, willing his finger to pull the trigger as the gun was still only one half a subtended arc's distance to its target. Once his finger pulled, the kick of the weapon carried it on and up to the left with a slight climb as it kicked and pulled on full auto.

At the same instant, the pilot was working to counter an involuntary left rudder kick from his co-pilot who was reacting to the swinging rifle. Through many missions and consummate discipline, the senior pilot knew that the real enemy was not so much a bullet as it was anything that interfered with the swinging rotors above. He loudly yelled over the intercom "MINE!" which sent an immediate, preemptory order to the co-pilot who went limp and turned over control of the airframe to the left seat. The first rounds sounded like "Pop Pop Pop's" on the underside of the vehicle. One round did travel up into the underside, lodging in heavy armor plate under the co-pilot's seat.

This C model Huey was essentially a slick, with no door gunners so as to make more room for delivery of the squad and its gear. Brooksly had been standing up on starboard side skids getting ready to clear the landing. He saw the awakening communist sleeping within his round dugout at about the same time as the co-pilot. Fortunately, the helicopter had approached from an angle outside the listening conus of the dugout. Otherwise, the occupant might have been alerted sooner. Kirk was in the act of standing up on the skid and twisting to his left toward the front of the aircraft. Suddenly, he felt a powerful baseball bat strike his right knee. The bullet entered from the antero-medial aspect and blew outward from the posterior lateral aspect. Fortunately, his left hand was tightly gripped to a handhold just inside the starboard side forward door. Otherwise, he would have been knocked off the airframe by the impact of the high velocity round. His right hand was gripping a Car-15. His thumb flipped the safety down, causing the selector to stand straight up on semi-automatic. Through a growing fog of pain from his right leg, he screamed into the co-pilot's helmet "Get me turned toward him!". The pilot heard this through the intercom, which the co-pilot had left on voice activation. As the bird began to pivot left, the pilot fought to prevent sideslipping into surrounding vegetation.

This exposed Brooksly to the enemy who was firing his AK-47 in an upward directed arc that by now had cleared the cockpit and passed through the rotorpath.

In unhurried, calculated moves, totally oblivious to the knee, Sgt. Kirk Brooksly levelled his Car-15 on the enemy soldier. He lined the rear reticle up with alleluia tangs straddling the front post. When they formed a straight line of sight with the enemy soldier's chest, Brooksly pulled the trigger. He followed with a controlled series of squeezes blending man and weapon. Holding the retracted buttstock steady against fleshy parts of his extended forearm, he repeatedly squeezed the trigger in a controlled, short sequence ..."Tat Tat Tat Tat Tat Tat Tat Tat Tat Tat Tat Tat ...". Most of the shots struck home. Each shot caused a puff of dust on the black pajama blouse. Corporal Dau Vo Tien fell over backwards into his cupola like foxhole, under a relentless stream of tiny, high velocity projectiles vectoring into his chest.

Brooksly could see that their tormentor was down and most certainly dead. He pulled himself back toward the central floor panel of the helicopter as the pilot now pulled more collective, keeping the cyclic balanced for vertical lift. Once they cleared the tops of the trees, he tilted the cyclic forward, raising the tail. Like an accelerating cartoon character, the helicopter shot forward and upward away from the compromised LZ.

Brooksly was aware that he had no control of his right leg below the knee. The floor grate of the helicopter was now wet with warm, red blood pooling around his leg. One of the Montagnards closest to him bit open a battlefield dressing to cover the wound, while another worked to help Brooksly stretch out on the floor in front of the canvas seats. A third was applying a makeshift, gunsling tourniquet about the American's thigh. Instead of flying back to Swordfish Lair, the pilot flew due east, passing north of Hien, flying directly over Ba Na and just south of An Ngai. He landed at Da Nang less then 35 minutes later, having radioed ahead for an awaiting Cracker Box ambulance and Triage team. An evac team of 3 medics charged up to the open bay just as the skids touched down and helped to slide the wounded American onto a taut stretcher held perpendicular to the aircraft. From there, he was carried over to the Cracker Box, which drove off with considerable dispatch to a U.S. MASH unit.

At the triage station, a nurse in OD's was first to examine his knee and tourniquet. She plunged a syrette of Morphine into Brooksly's right bicep while another nurse began cutting off his tiger pattern camouflage fatigues. An MP came forward, gently wresting away his weapon and load bearing equipment, still festooned with banana clips and grenades. Someone, probably one of the nurses, started an IV and someone else started to unwind the tourniquet slightly which loosed a torrent of blood quickly stemmed by again tightening up the K-Bar knife handle being used as a windlass.

Brooksly was taken into an inflatable operating theatre close by. It was surprisingly cool compared to the contrasting heat outside. An anesthesiologist assured Kirk that he would be comfortable in just a few more seconds.

The next conscious moment for Ambush Brooksly occurred on board a C-141 Starlifter jet transport bound for home. Bleeding had been controlled, and the tourniquet was gone, but the wound had necessarily been left open. His entire leg was incorporated in a Keller-Blake half-ring splint, secured around white folded, triangular cravats stretched across parallel telescoping struts on either side of the leg. There was a rubberized half circle of padded tubing following the curve of his buttock at one end. The frame was bound to his foot with a figure of eight cravat at a right angle. His leg was held straight out with the knee encompassed about by loose layers of gauze and muslin. From time to time, a gentle, plain looking nurse would pass by and check his IV drip chamber as well as manually take his pulse and respirations. Although she could not discern an accurate, audible blood pressure due to tremor and noise inside the aircraft, she did record a palpable systolic pressure and noted that it was stable around 105 mm on the cuff manometer. The patient had lost a fair amount of blood, but surgeons in Da Nang felt he was stable enough not to require any whole blood or plasma expanders for the ride back to the States. Because the leg was nearly disarticulated at the knee, there was little benefit to keeping him in country. He drifted in and out of consciousness several times during the 18-hour flight to Travis Air Force Base in central California.

Over the last 250 miles or so prior to landing, he had begun to feel intense pain. When he asked the nurse for something, she explained that they would be landing soon and the doctors at Travis may need to examine him in a sentient state. So he would have to endure a bit longer. By the time the plane touched down and taxied into a receiving area around the northeast end of Travis AFB tarmac, he was in absolute agony. The kneecap had been comminuted and both peri-patellar as well as subsartorial plexi, with their abundant distribution of sensory nerves, were causing reflex arcs of spasm into the quadriceps of his thigh. Finally, he was carried by the same stretcher he had been loaded onto from the helicopter off the back ramp of the airplane toward an awaiting Cadillac station wagon type ambulance.

On the other side of a not so distant fence, topped with rolled concertina barbed wire, gathered a group of about 20, long haired war protesters. Leading this group was a thin young man with long, stringy hair and blue tinted spectacle granny glasses. His name was Jerry. He had a peachfuzz beard and sideburns. He wore a loud, flower print shirt and a vest embroidered with large peace symbol on the back. Jerry came from an upper middle class family in a posh Chicago suburb. He had done reasonably well in high school thanks largely to his mother's convincing a divorce court judge that Jerry's lecherous father should foot the bill from a good private school for their only son. Upon graduating from High School in 1969, Jerry had insisted that he wanted to go to College at the University of California - Berkley. Again, his mother demanded that if the boy could get accepted to such a good name school, the father must ante up for tuition, board, vehicle and spending allowance.

Jerry realized shortly after arriving at Berkley, that in this academic society he was far more significant than the average Joe Shmoe American. He gravitated to the arts and decided during a social studies class toward the end of his first semester, that he would major in Political Science and minor in Journalism. His professors preached persuasively about McCarthyism and the Vietnam war. Whenever a peace rally was held, Jerry took the opportunity to skip his more boring classes in favor of mingling with a fraternity of liberal academic elite. He had, of course, sampled drugs such as marijuana and hard liquor in High School. During his first semester in College, he also experimented with LSD. He found the experience to be at least as mind expanding as college in general. Jerry had shared a hashish pipe with one of his professors, and felt very much the role of significant entity among these people he considered to be admirable peers. At the end of his freshman year, Jerry turned 18 and was required to register for the draft. He ignored the law on this initially, but later went down and registered specifically so that he could publicly burn his draft card as a confirmation of his opinion on the war in Vietnam. Perhaps much more importantly, it served as a public, poignant statement in the life of a somewhat insecure young man, something that drew attention to him. It made him feel important in a narrow society that applauded civil disobedience against a government willing to tolerate it.

By the end of his sophomore year, Jerry had risen within the ranks of groupie compatriots, to a point that he was being recognized for his leadership in organizing people and events. Younger freshman looked up to him as an intellectually enlightened person. There were, in fact, relatively few upperclassmen for him to compete against as many of the people with whom he had started at Berkley, did not bother to maintain their grade point average and were academically suspended during their first or second years. Many of them insisted that they had to flee to Canada, away from the persecuting arm of Evil Uncle Sam who would otherwise force march them into an immoral war after torturing them with human rights deprivations in the form of military basic training.

Jerry managed to commit himself enough to pre-requisite studies that he maintained a mid-range 2.75 GPA. His discovery of amphetamines during freshman year had contributed considerably to this. It also helped immensely that his draft lottery number was up there in the high 200's and likely would not be called up, which was less stress for him. Jerry was also convinced that his own personal protest movement was causing the war to wind down. With growing communal contentment in self and academic gemien, he grew less and less tolerant of authority, unless it was flattering to him personally. He resented that any designated authority should have any say whatsoever about his personal choices and decisions. He esteemed rebellious musical ditties of the time, such as Arlo Guthrie's *"Alice's Restaurant"* and the Beatle's *"Give Peace A Chance."* He believed in personal rights, which he had never really done anything to earn, but which were his by virtue of being a member of this community of enlightened beings who theoretically endorsed love of all humankind as a credo. Of course, he did not really love everyone. In fact, he had a seething resentment for anything to do with the U.S. military, any form of police officer and especially, politicians in suits and ties.

So it was that on this day, November 6th, 1971, Jerry was leading a group of protesters outside the northeast perimeter fence of Travis Air Force Base southwest of Sacramento, just east of Fairfield, California. Within his group, there were several people from UC Davis, Berkley, Stanford and some of the smaller junior colleges, which always seemed to supply ample groupies who looked up to true leaders from the hallowed stanchions of western pseudo-ivy league campuses.

Jerry had arrived the previous evening in his '64 Volkswagen Mini Van filled with flower power youngsters. They approached the long airstrip from Meridian Road, then followed the Outer Perimeter Road around to a relatively primitive spot on the northeast side of the airbase, parallel to the long runways. Jerry had spent the rest of the night on a raised cushion over the engine housing in back of his VW van, sleeping with one of the little girls in the group. She had insisted that she was a freshman at Davis. Someone confided to him that she was most likely a local high school teeny-bopper. Jerry really didn't care so long as she sensuously embraced the cause and his own libertarian persona. They had all been stoned on some excellent Mexican Red and only with some considerable difficulty were rustled from various vehicular nooks to rally their protest this morning.

The subject of their animosity would be the daily arrival of the so-called "Band Aid Clipper," which they knew would be landing with wounded soldiers directly from Vietnam. How better to reach out and really let America know how resentful the intelligent youth of this country were about an immoral war than to use visible, "non-violent" protest as a means of coercion. In actuality, very few were up to violent protest as, aside from being inebriated most of the time, none of these youths had done much to encourage any kind of physical conditioning beyond a high hepatic tolerance to toxic substances.

The military pigs where there. A Jeep with two armed Air Force security types was parked between the fence and the big jet airplane to assure that no one tried to cut any precious gate wire. The Air Force MP's had long since learned to tune out verbal abuse during these protests. News people who used to show up quite a bit in the late Sixties didn't come out much any more, and in Jerry's opinion, were really showing no stamina in the cause. For now, he would have to do something really outrageous to get people's attention, and that was after all, what he really wanted most. He had brought devices to achieve this end.

Using old bicycle inner tubes, Jerry and some of his cohorts had conducted "rotten vegetable artillery practice" in yonder fields the week before. They had become quite good at hoisting rotten vegetables 50-70 yards which was plenty far enough to reach rear entry tail ramps of big airplanes parked on this side of the runway. It had not been done before and he was very much hoping that it would bring out the 6:00 o'clock news people. As the huge tail ramp lowered, he lined up his elastic battery, placing stinking tomatoes or badly bruised mangos into makeshift pouches on rubber bicycle inner tube slingshots. Each of the ends of two folded tubes had been sewn into a loop and there was a longhaired accomplice on each leading end to hoist the stretch. On command, as the first few litters started emerging on to concrete at the bottom of the ramp, Jerry and his accomplices let fly with a volley of about half dozen rotten vegetables.

Sgt. Kirk Brooksly was defining the limits of human misery. The knee was screaming with pain and he was biting hard into a rolled piece of gauze to keep from crying out. The swing and sway of the litter added to his agony. Just as he reached the tarmac, one of the enlisted medics on the leading end of the litter, caught a peripheral glimpse of several red projectiles hurtling their way from that obnoxious hippie group on the other side of the fence. A red headed, freckle faced medic, whose name was PFC Donald MacKenzie had himself returned with a serious infection, along with other wounded from Vietnam, only 3 months ago. He was presently assigned to garrison support duty while awaiting reassignment now that he was physically recovered from a "toe popper" ballistic wound that had blown off some of the third and fourth toes of his left foot. The wound had suppurated into a nasty infection that eventually resolved. Still unresolved were occasional flashbacks he would experience from time to time. Seeing a grenade-sized object hurtling in his direction, he instinctively went to ground, dropping the litter as he did so. One of the stinking tomatoes arced gracefully from its apogee directly down onto the loosely bandaged knee of Kirk Brooksly. The knee had already started to hemorrhage on striking the ground as Kirk fell from the litter behind MacKenzie. The impact of the tomato projectile happened about a second later. It was a large tomato, even for a rotten one. It struck in total mass onto saturated dressings, just off center of the exit wound caused by the AK-47 round, on the posterior -lateral side of his knee.

Sergeant Brooksly could hold his agony no longer. Biting through the rolled gauze, he arched his head and neck back while screaming through clenched teeth, then finally, mercifully, passed out. The medic who had dropped the litter looked back in horror, realizing that he had not only dropped his charge, but also failed to shield a wounded comrade from the stinking barrage. PFC MacKenzie looked over at the group of hecklers who were now hooting and cajoling in celebration of their success at striking home with their first volley. In his overwrought mind, he could not tell whether they were wearing enemy uniforms or civilian clothing. What was clear, they were the enemy. During those few seconds that condense rage into unthinking action, MacKenzie stood up and raced toward the fence.

Standing next to a Jeep between the C-141 Starlifter and the perimeter fence were two air force security enlisted types, both bearing M-16's mounted with sheathed bayonets. They each had a magazine, which only contained 5 rounds and was more for show than go. As PFC MacKenzie's rage propelled him forward, he realized that he would pass close by one of the Air Force Security guards en route to the fence. He saw a weapon for the taking. Air Force recruits were never considered to be real soldiers by the likes of combatants in the Army or Marines. Air Force Security guard MP's, or AirSecs, always seemed to be protected, starched and spit shined. They also wore blue berets and blue dickeys that gave them a bit of a garish look to the more prevailing uniform codes of infantrymen. AirSecs were generally considered by members of the combat arms to be at the bottom of a male chain of bravado, and commanders who realized this, permitted the rakish uniform enhancement to lend a bit of pride and esteem. All MacKenzie saw was a non-combatant with an accessible weapon.

Both Airmen were focused on the protestors, wondering just how to deal with the slinging situation. Neither saw MacKenzie rushing up from behind, nor heard him over the hoots and cat-calls of the civilians behind the fence. MacKenzie ran to the nearest Airman. The M-16 was still right shouldered and hung loosely by a sling drapped over his right arm. MacKenzie wrenched the weapon off the Air Force Security Guard's shoulder, stunning him momentarily. As the medic continued his adrenaline rush toward the fence, the other Air Sec yelled at both his fellow Airman and the enraged Army medic. Seeing the weapon wrested from his compatriot airman, unthinking gestures moved the other, armed Security guard to unsling his own M-16 forward and down off his shoulder. In the same moment, MacKenzie pulled back the charging handle on the M-16 now in his possession. This seated a live round into the chamber.

As MacKenzie slapdashed toward the hooting crowd, a few of the less stoned youths began to form cognizant, instinctive conclusions of what might happen when an enraged man with a gun leveled his fury on them for what some were beginning to realize was a profound violation. Some of the girls began to scream, which only barely distracted the more intoxicated male leaders of the group. MacKenzie approached the fence close enough for the sun to cast cris crossing shadows over his enraged features. He aimed into the thickest part of the group and opened fire. There were only 5 rounds in the magazine, and only 2 of these struck home. One hit a sixteen-year old girl playing high school hookie on the pretense of having stayed over with a girlfriend classmate the evening before. This was the same girl who had slept with Jerry. She was hit in the right forearm that she had raised instinctively to ward off this terrible evil. The round passed through, blowing off most of her arm, then grazing her right cheek and nipping off a bit of her right earlobe, pulling off a sheaf of hair as it whistled close by her shrieking cranium. The second scoring round struck the hippie leader, Jerry, diagonally in the front left side of his chest. It passed through the inferior apex of the heart, blowing out most of the left lung as it formed a gaping exit wound postero-laterally fringed with fabric edges of a peace symbol wrapping round on the backside of his vest.

In the meantime, the Air Force Security guard who was still armed had leveled his own weapon on PFC MacKenzie while continuously shouting for the out of control Army medic to HALT!, STOP!!, HALT!!! As MacKenzie opened fire on the hippie protestor group, the Airman opened fire on MacKenzie, striking home from the left rear with three rounds, center of mass. This caused the redheaded 19 year-old to plunge forward, striking the fence with his upper body and then catapult back onto the tarmac as his finger instinctively squeezed off a last round, which went up harmlessly into the air. One of the Airman's rounds passed through MacKenzie's body and struck another protester in the right hip, tossing the screaming, long haired youth backward, onto close cropped scrub grass and trampled sage lining the other side of the fence.

The terror of this scene impacted most on those more sober members of the protest group. This was real blood and horror. It was unlike anything they could have been prepared for by movies, or press coverage or enlightened philosophy. A brutal realization settled over adolescent civilians on the other side of the fence. Stark, horrible reality engulfed the pitiable flower children, now in various degrees of shock and hysteria.

As the disarmed Airman raced over to MacKenzie's supine, recumbent body, the other airman grabbed for a Jeep mounted radiotelephone and reported to the Sergeant of the Guard. Pilots on the Starlifter who had seen part of the tragedy unfold, were also reporting to the tower. In less then 5 minutes, a caravan of vehicles and staff officers arrived on scene. It would take local news media about 15 minutes longer to show up. By that time, both civilian and military casualties were being secured, and areas on both sides of the fence were being roped off by increasing numbers of Air Force security personnel. Left to mark the scene most in the memory of those who would recall the incident was a poignant recollection of two pools of blood. One streamlet flowed downhill from the raised tarmac perimeter on the airbase side of the fence. The other flowed from Jerry's dead body, staining trampled ground outside the fence, pooling down toward the fenceposts. Both flows mingled and pooled together under the fence line into a sort of yin-yang swirl of shared regrets.

When Brooksly was shot in the right knee while in Laos, the wound had almost immediately been covered by a dry, sterile, battle dressing. There was relatively little contamination. The area was copiously irrigated in Da Nang and he received 20 million units of Crystalline Penicillin as well as 3 grams of Streptomycin, a powerful antibiotic. This was standard war wound therapy and worked well, most of the time, to prevent massive infections. In keeping with proper war wound theory, the massive injury was left open to heal by second intent, thus minimizing the risk of bacteria taking hold in a closed wound, anaerobic environment. It would have worked too, except that the rotten tomato ballistic that struck Brooksly carried an unusual form of fungus called Coccidiomycosis, from the place where it had been harvested and over ripened in the San Joaquin Valley, South of Travis AFB. Surgeons were delayed in recognizing the non-bacterial cause of the contamination. In a very disheartening decision to save his life, surgeons at Letterman Army Hospital in the Presidio of San Francisco, wherein he was eventually transferred, ultimately decided to amputate Sgt. Kirk Brooksly's right leg above the knee.

Following a long hospitlatization at the Presidio, Ambush Brooksly was subsequently discharged from active duty. He returned to his hometown in Idaho. Eventually, he would marry a good woman who could see beyond his physical handicap to the courage and honor beneath. Over the ensuing months after returning home, he would bear an immense burden on his young, athletic, one-legged frame. For many years, he suffered from terrible memories of pitch-black nights and bloody trails at dawn. Failing the best efforts of several excellent VA psychiatrists, it was ultimately his wife who, while holding him to her during myriad tortured nightmares over several years, would eventually heal the emotional wounds, which cut off so much more than a leg. They would have 4 children together. He would become a much-revered high school shop teacher and track coach. It would be several years before he would see any of his brothers in arms from Team A-321 again.

Chapter 6 – Rejoinder

November – December, 1971

November 6th, 1971; Saigon, South Vietnam

About the same moment Kirk Brooksly was being conveyed away from a bloody tarmac at Travis Air Force Base, Congressman Riley Hathoway stepped off the bottom panel of a mobile aircraft reception stairway, onto an unrolled strip of red carpet. Although well aware that this sort of thing was a canned reception ceremony designed for many visiting dignitaries, he allowed himself the conceit of believing that the carpet was new and that his own footsteps would be the first to tread its' unsoiled length. Hathoway was greeted by a U.S. Major General (two stars) and two Brigadier (one star) U.S. Generals, as well as General Duong An Minh of the Army of the Republic of Vietnam. The arrogant Congressman considered himself slighted by the absence of General Creighton W. Abrams, U.S. Military Commander in Chief of South Vietnam at that time.

It was early evening in Vietnam. While Congressman Hathoway was fretting over what he considered to be his lack luster reception, General Abrams was involved in a crucial strategy assessment session based on late breaking intelligence concerning the disastrous outcome of operation *Chenla II*. *Chenla II* was a military operation conceived and conducted by Cambodia's nationalist military force, the *Forces Armees Nationales Khmeres*, or FANK. After several unsuccessful forays beginning late Summer of 1971, FANK had finally developed a military superstructure that was scoring some big gains against elements of the communist Cambodian Khmer Rouge. This led the haphazard Khmer Rouge to rally their scattered forces around NVA leadership and supply. The partnership led to Cambodian Communists laying siege around a city called Kompong Thom, North of Phnom Penh. As FANK had commenced to effectively whittle away their Khmer Rouge adversaries over the previous summer, it became clear to the NVA that if FANK broke this siege at Kompong Thom, pro U.S. forces could effectively sever the Ho Chi Minh Trail as it ran south through Cambodia. Accordingly, the NVA 9th Division arrived in October, combining with Khmer Rouge 205th and 207th regiments to help ambush a FANK advance on Route 6 between Kompong Thmar and Tang Kauk, both cities southeast of Kompong Thom. The result of this was a shattering defeat for FANK. Ten to twenty whole batallions of men and equipment were lost in what some called the single greatest military catastrophe of the war for non-communist forces. On the day of Congressman Hathoway's arrival, General Abrams had just received the first bits of conclusive intelligence on actual outcomes from the disastrous FANK engagement that had taken place ten days prior, on October 27, 1971. To General Abrams, this information sounded the death knell for FANK. Although, in his opinion, the Khmer Rouge lacked effective military leadership of their own, they were nonetheless numerous and with proper coaching from Hanoi could become a powerful force in Cambodia. The outcome of *Chenla II* had in effect reversed the successful outcome of Nixon's *Operation Menu*, the U.S. incursion into Cambodia during April-May of 1970. Although decidedly unpopular in the U.S., *Operation Menu* had done more to lessen pressure on U.S. withdrawal than any other single effort during the war. It also provided Cambodian Nationalist General Lon Nol a decent opportunity to break the communist stranglehold on his country. Unfortunately, Lon Nol demonstrated a painfully familiar Southeast Asian trend toward dictatorship, graft and corruption. In June of 1970, the U.S. Senate repealed the Gulf of Tonkin Resolution by which authority, Nixon had certified the incursion. From that time forward, no U.S. ground forces would be permitted into Cambodia. With increasingly repressive political interference, General Abrams was doing his best to come up with alternatives for both Cambodia and the undisrupted transition of ongoing U.S. troop withdrawals.

Congressman Riley Hathoway could not begin to understand the implications of Cambodian developments within the Southeast Asian theatre, nor did he particularly care to. His only opinion on Cambodia was that the U.S. had no business being involved there. Hathoway was much more concerned about his own diminished prestige in missing the presence of General Abrams at the reception ceremonies. In a show of not so subtle contempt for what Hathoway considered to be an insignificant entourage of three U.S. underling generals, the Congressman informed his itinerary manager that he would be visiting first with President Thieu and General Minh the next morning. This was intended to show deference for several carefully scheduled first day visits with regional U.S. bases and thousands of marshaled U.S. servicemen scheduled for parade formations honoring the arrival of a Congressional V.I.P. General Minh politely responded with assurances that President Thieu would happily receive Congressman Hathoway at any time that was convenient to the U.S. dignitary.

Accordingly, Hathoway arrived just after breakfast the following morning. Minh and Thieu had been up most of the evening profiling the American Congressman. What they discovered in going through extensive public and private information on Hathoway, was an arrogant, New England politician who came from a family of considerable wealth. His stance on the Vietnam war was definitely contra. He had been married for 20 years. He had two children, both in their teens, and a mistress nearly 20 years younger than himself with whom he had maintained an ongoing, barely concealed affair, for over two years. Congressman Hathoway considered the Vietnamese to be an ignorant, hapless people who were incapable of governing themselves and had, therefore, given in to the will of what he considered an absolute dictatorship within their own government. This was the sort of personality which Thieu and Minh delighted in manipulating. Because he underestimated the Asian syllogism, Congressman Hathoway would be particularly vulnerable to certain tools of logic. For one thing, he would be expecting Thieu and Minh to come to him with their palms extended. In this thing, he would be sanctimoniously disappointed and happily surprised at the same time. Both Thieu and Minh knew well enough to whom they should appeal within the U.S. constituency for financial support. Hathoway could be more useful in other ways, as a pawn to advance their own, more circumspect agenda items. To manipulate Congressman Hathoway as an opposition force was a ploy that could be quite useful to the Minh/Thieu dynasty.

"Ahhh, Congressman Hathoway, welcome to South Vietnam! It is a great honor to have you visit the imperial palace of my country."

Congressman Riley Hathoway was suffering from the effects of jet lag, in a big way. Upon retiring in the early afternoon, shortly after arriving, he had slept soundly until about 3:00 AM and was unable to get back to sleep thereafter. Following about an hour's worth of fitful tossing and turning, he finally arose and went over printed briefing materials left for him in preparation of the day's activities. At 0430 local time, Hathoway picked up the telephone in his hotel room and dialed an adjacent room number, expecting to awaken the military liaison assigned to him during this visit. To Hathoway's ire, a young Major on the other end was awake and ready for the phone call. Breakfast was ordered and the Congressman demanded his transient staff assembled to go over the day's agenda. A meeting with President Thieu had been set for 10:00 AM that morning, a standard time for mid morning meetings in Washington DC. In Vietnam, it may as well have been late afternoon. Troops which had been awakened early that morning to prepare uniforms and conduct marching drills would have to stand down if the Congressman was not ready to review them by twelve O'clock, noon. Hathoway would not commit to the proposed agenda one way or the other and simply indicated that it depended on how long the interview with President Thieu lasted. In his opinion, "the troops can wait; President Thieu must run an entire country. A President's time is far more critical."

Following a long repast, grooming and dressing, Congressman Hathoway was transported to the Presidential Palace by military limousine. He instructed his chauffeur to delay until five minutes after the scheduled meeting time. "After all, these people have to understand who the big tamale is here. They wait for me, I do not wait for them." Thieu and Minh both anticipated the delay. When Hathoway was finally presented, they greeted him as though all had been in preparation for his arrival quite some time, which indeed, it had. Few cultures understand better how to play to arrogance than the Vietnamese. Both Thieu and Minh were masters at this.

After exchanging some small talk in which the Vietnamese leaders took every opportunity to aggrandize Congressman Hathoway just short of over-embellishment, they settled down to discuss the war. To Riley Hathoway's surprise, not one word was mentioned about financial aid for Vietnam. Quite the contrary, President Thieu emphasized how much his people wanted self-sufficiency and, in a show of polite indulgence, clearly implied that the Americans had taken control of the government away from the Vietnamese people. This was exactly what Hathoway wanted to hear. It confirmed his position about U.S. intervention in Southeast Asia and softened his feelings considerably toward this leadership. *"After all"*, he thought, *"perhaps we can afford to be more helpful so long as it gets our troops home and gives these people autonomy."* In a show of gentle admonition Congressman Hathoway mentioned the issue of democracy and free elections. To this, Thieu lied convincingly that it was his greatest desire to be confirmed in office by the people of South Vietnam whom he loved dearly. He even managed to shed a tear from his right eye. Big Minh considered it a great artifice of statesmanship.

Congressman Riley Hathoway was completely taken in. By the time he had been in conversation with them for just short of an hour, every conviction which he held about U.S. military occupation was confirmed. Certainly, it was the U.S. military establishment that was dragging this thing out. 'After all, military careers are being made over here, beginning with the delinquent General Creighton Abrams...' *'These poor people just want us to leave them alone with enough of a stockpile to settle their own disputes. All they want is U.S. cooperation, not necessarily U.S. personnel.'*

"Is there anything I can help you with President Thieu?" The interrogatory marked a high point in the discussion, which every politician is inevitably drawn to and which Thieu had carefully prepared for in all the preceding dialogue.

"Well, actually, yes there is Congressman Hathoway."

Had the request involved a plea for money, Hathoway might yet have seen through the ruse, but instead, the very nature of the request played right into Hathoway's own precognition. He listened intently as President Thieu went on.

"You see, Congressman, we have a problem with some of our own people here in Vietnam. They have become quite enamored with certain elements of your military. They are illiterate, ignorant mountain aborigines who have on occasion risen up in open defiance of civilized government. They have been trained and armed by your Special Forces people and despite our best efforts to provide good, sound Vietnamese leadership, they continue to be rebellious and difficult. You see, Congressman, a house divided against itself cannot stand."

Hathoway nodded at the familiar Christian slogan taken from the twelfth chapter of St. Matthew. It was a reference he had used among his own constituents many times and the fact that this Catholic Oriental was familiar with the Good Book seemed to confirm yet another common agenda. That was of course, exactly what Thieu intended. Hathoway responded with a tone of open sincerity.

"What can I do to help you with this, President?"

"Well, sir, we have heard reports of your American Special Forces teams still working with some Montagnards despite assurances to us that there would be no more such intervention among our people."

"You mean the Green Berets? But, I had understood that the Green Berets have been withdrawn back to the States."

"With the exception of direct action missions, that is true, sir. But our sources inform us that there may still be some teams working in Laos, with the Montagnards."

"But, the Cooper-Church amendment specifically forbids U.S. advisors from working with Vietnamese military in Laos! Do you mean to tell me that the U.S. military is acting in direct violation of United States policy and law?"

"It is quite possible, yes."

"Well, I'll certainly have to look into this. If what you say is correct, President Theiu, it will mean the end of whatever high ranking military officers have confirmed this project."

"It may be very difficult to locate the administrative nexus of this project, Congressman. It is very classified. But, I have a suggestion."

"Please, by all means."

"Every military operation depends on funding and resources. We are told that this project is heavily financed and very likely depleting financial resources from our own efforts."

This last was an outright lie on the part of Thieu. His own troops were being generously outfitted and supplied by the United States and every cent of U.S. aid to his government was carefully accounted for implicitly because of a historic trend in South Vietnam to divert money into political pockets. However, it served to satiate an issue that Thieu well knew dwelt in the soul of Congressman Hathoway's political philosophy.

"If you could cut off funding to this project, it would necessarily shut down. It may require some difficult steps to reverse powerful forces at work within your military, but to deny resources to the project will certainly terminate any unrest among the Montagnards."

This suggestion was music to the ears of Congressman Hathoway! If he could do nothing else to aid the war effort here in Vietnam, as a result of their discussion, he would do everything within his power to ferret out and shut down any U.S. Special Forces involvement in Laos.

"I can assure you Mr. President, you will have my absolute cooperation on this."

From there, conversation drifted off to other discussions which again, pandered to the Congressman's *amour propre*. When he finally departed the Presidential Palace after a sumptuous lunch, it was about 1330 hours. The scheduled luncheon and troop review with General Abrams was conspicuously ignored. Congressman Hathoway excused himself from the rest of the day's agenda by claiming, with some veracity, that he was still suffering the effects of jet lag, and felt the need to retire early.

November 16, 1971

Regimental Field Commander Muc Bo Thau was also quite concerned about U.S. advisors. He knew that they were operating in a section of Laos within his own Area Command. By simply plotting out the areas in which communist patrols had disappeared during the last six months, his staff could roughly delineate the limits of AO Focus. After losing the Russian advisor, along with an entire company of men back in September, Commander Thau had specifically forbidden his own units to enter the valley of *Loc Phieu*. He still feared any residual contamination from the abortive attempt at bacteriological warfare. He was also keenly aware of his own pitiful lack of intelligence on a potentially powerful American basecamp somewhere in the area. The entire pass leading into *Loc Phieu* had been sterilized by an

American napalm strike, which said something about how seriously the Americans considered the risk of contamination in the upper mountain pass. Over the last three months, only about one out of every 5 foot patrols that he sent into the area had returned. It was almost spooky, if he were a superstitious man. Were his people getting sick and dying? He had been advised that Plague was a rapid killer. Perhaps there was some lingering disease in the area that was claiming his troops? His own medical people advised him that it seemed unlikely any disease could kill that fast. Of greater credibility, Commander Thau had received reports of numerous, widely disbursed remains from ambushed foot patrols. How could the Americans be so good at interdicting his patrols? A basic tenet of guerilla warfare states that for every actual ambush that is carried out, there are at least half a dozen ambush sites laid and waiting, which never trip the kill zone. Accordingly, there must be a huge U.S. backed force massing in that section of Laos! Perhaps the Americans were planning to do in reverse what had been done to the French in 1952; build up a substantial force in the Laotian mountains, then attack en masse to the west, instead of to the east as the communists had done. Such a move would certainly cut off the Ho Chi Minh trail and potentially be even more destructive to the people's cause than the U.S. Cambodian incursion had been down south. With the recent, stunning triumphs of combined NVA and Khmer Rouge forces against FANK, the Americans may well be considering another approach at cutting the Ho Chi Minh Trail. He needed intelligence on that area and clearly was not getting enough from small foot patrols. It was time to send in a larger unit, at least company sized, with reliable leadership and longer range radios for regular communication. As Commander Thau considered the mission, he looked over a site map. Most of the northern area was high-mountain terrain, much of it impassable by wheeled vehicle and any but the most resolute troops, with adequate gear for scaling mountains if necessary. Areas farther south dropped in elevation to rolling hills invested with verdant jungle. A prudent, conventional military strategist would most likely send in a large, Batallion sized force to sweep up from the south. However, that area was precisely the location in which so many of his smaller patrols had been lost, not to mention a veteran, reinforced company at the Mountain Pass into *Loc Phieu*. In scrutinizing maps of the mountainous area to the north, there was one mountain pass, which ran alongside a small river. Scouts familiar with the sector told Commander Thau that it was one of the only passable routes through the mountains, except during high monsoon season, when mountain runoff into the swollen river made trekking through the area impossible. Precisely because the area was only navigable during certain times of the year, it was not listed on any regular map with roads or trails.

Field Commander Muc Bo Thau fancied himself a clever military strategist. Someone more timid would never have thought to locate a seasonal trail capable of infiltrating troops. Once through the passes, they would have access to more navigable landscape beyond and could easily take control of the entire northern end of that sector. To Muc Bo Thau, it seemed a most clever ploy. It would provide him with command and control forces in a primitive area to supervise Hmong or Montagnard tribes living there. More importantly, by swinging back down south, descending from the mountains, with all the advantages of higher ground, Commander Thau could get what he wanted most, information. What was going on in a region that seemed to swallow up his troops without reason?

November 21st, 1971

Sergeant Kip Jon Haskell lay concealed within a stand of pines mingled among fringes of high jungle vegetation. With the end of monsoon season over a month ago, he had a clear view of the ridgeline and had been patiently observing it over the last 8 hours. Close by, Haskell's Montagnard interpreter was listening to an AN-PRC 77 radio and took the occasion now to inform Haskell that Bugeyes was reporting a large, company sized element moving into the area of the ridge across the chasm from where Sgt. Haskell and his patrol now lay concealed. The ridge-line looked over a ravine sardonically named "Buzzard's Gultch" by Haskell. Just the day before, Kip and his team of seven Yard strikers had entered into the area that they were now observing. While on the other side of the mountainous river chasm, Haskell's team had carefully laid a series of shaped charges constructed to blast outward from "V" shaped gullies that formed switchbacks along an intended kill zone. The trail led around outward curves, alternating in snakelike contours on the opposite ridgeline. On these outer banks, they had set paired Claymore mines. The arc shaped detonation plates were skillfully placed along upper slopes so as to face downward, toward the curves. Having oriented to his craft while yet very young, Haskell had been fine-tuned by his own mentor, Staff Sergeant Philip Volkert. Volkert was almost as gifted with explosives as Kip's own father. Following a detailed academic introduction to explosive materials in Special Forces phase training, Kip had discovered a natural intuition for understanding the physics of unstable compounds. During those first few months at Swordfish Lair, Haskell and Volkert worked together on several demolition projects. With time, Volkert let the younger NCO have his head as natural talent took over and Haskell became more instinctively competent. By fall of 1971, each of the older NCO's had absolute confidence in the ability of their younger American counterparts to exercise individual initiative as leadership and combat instincts "came of age" in the young bucks. As yet, Kip was still feeling the loss of his close friend, Sgt. Kirk Brooksly who had taken a round in the knee earlier that month, diminishing Team A-321 by yet one more American.

Everyone still smarted also over the death of *Bac Si* Michael Glickman back in September. To make matters more compli-cated, due to the sensitive nature of this mission, there would be no military replacements for losses within the American team. The goal of Operation Fisherman had been to prove to a Congressional oversight panel that Montagnards could become independent on their own initiative with very little investment of U.S. lives. As team A-321 had been briefed when the mission was first disclosed, there would be no replacements. McCarthy carried on as *Bac Si* after Glickman and, following an era of mourning, rose to the moment continuing with and serving his mission well. Haskell had grown to respect his compatriot medic very much. McCarthy, Winkle, Haskell and Brooksly had all changed a great deal in the previous six months. Like the other youngsters, Haskell had become more inclined to field operations, leaving Volkert to train and coordinate mission objectives for Combat Engineers (CE's) from base camp. Each sortie, Haskell would take into the field a group of trainees, along with a core of reliable, experienced Montagnards. Accompanying Haskell and his core field troops, they would bring along four or five additional Indigenous docents in various stages of training. For at least one member of the patrolling squad, this would be a first mission. The other Yards would have varying degrees of experience according to a training schedule under the oversight of camp administrators, both American and Montagnard. It was considered a great honor to go on patrol with any American. Those Yards who were assigned to venture out on such missions considered themselves fortunate. In just over six months, a core of strong leadership had formed within the Montagnard community and by this time, fall of 1971, more entire Montagnard field elements were deploying than mixed American/Montagnard. Erickson, Johnson, Briant and Fernstead were still rotating their "Hammer Patrols", made up of two Platoon sized elements of 30 or so well armed men disbursed equidistantly within the AO so as to react to hot spots reported by Bugeyes from time to time. Trail ambush "anvil" elements, such as those led by Brooksly, were tactically distributed along most of the trails leading out of the AO to the south and southwest. Many of these ambush squads were now made up of Montagnard squad leaders trained by Brooksly before his being wounded in action the beginning of November. Estrada was also supervising a four-week training cycle for incoming Yards that included weapons familiarization, chain of command, small unit tactics and military conventions in general. Following this four-week "basic training", Montagnard recruits would be assigned to some element of need within the growing community of area Focus. An essential part of the mission was to build Montagnard and Hmong resources without proportional growth of U.S. personnel. Some Yards would be assigned to medical training under McCarthy, whereas others might provide, clerical or support roles. Such bureaucratic assignments normally went to older men, or women not encumbered with domestic necessities magnified by the drain of males within their communities. Virtually all the young men were assigned to combat arms. This meant either infantry strike forces or combat engineers (CE's), such as Sgt. Haskell's present team was composed of. Kip Haskell was proud of his growing retinue of CE's. They were becoming competent engineers and tacticians. Most importantly, they were highly motivated and quite willing to follow orders. Although personal initiative had been somewhat lacking among the Yards during the early days, Haskell found that as they gained more experience working with the Americans, their confidence grew and so did their inventiveness. With reasonable foundation instruction, they could effectively grasp field tactics and apply these skills to any variety of practical field conditions. As with all good teachers, Haskell found himself learning at least as much from his eager entourage as they were gaining from him. Today would be very instructive for everyone.

Advancing about 500 meters to their left across Buzzard's Gulch, or to the west of their north facing position, Haskell and his CE strikers could just make out point elements of an approaching communist, company sized patrol. Bugeyes had been following the formation for the last couple of days and was presently communicating by radio that at least 125 human thermal signature counts were winding their way along the mountainous trail leading into this northern extremity of AO Focus. This pass was not located on any map because, during monsoon season, it did not exist. Instead, vertical portions of the valley served as a series of runoffs for streams cut into switchbacks along sides of the two abutting mountiains. Down below, at the gulch where the two mountains met, there was a washed out streambed, evidence of the raging deluge occupying much of this pass during monsoon season from late June through mid October.

As Haskell watched the enemy company come into view, he noted a point squad made up of about six scouts. They moved carefully, professionally, clearly aware of their vulnerability in these open faced elevations. The snakelike ravine separated Haskell's observation post from the opposite gullied ridgeline by about 250 meters, adequate range for a sniper but not enough to conduct a far ambush without considerable risk. Several hundred pounds of explosives lay cleverly concealed within that ridgeline opposite to where Haskell now lay concealed. A vinelike network of detcord and wire interconnected all the explosive elements. Several strands of suspended, twisted wires crossed over the ravine far enough to the distant east that its thin black silhouette was invisible to the advancing force. The enemy company mustered just four days prior by command of their regimental field commander, Muc Bo Thau. They had moved in the general direction of Buzzard's Pass which was the only way into Area Focus via a northern central corridor. Only a few old-timer NVA scouts knew the route. However, local Montagnards were very familiar with the area and correctly anticipated enemy troop movement through this ravine. The communist trek by foot to this point over these mountains, took enough time that Haskell, who was patrolling with his Yards in the field two days previously, had sufficient opportunity for transit and meticulous placement of his well camouflaged explosives. Most of the high explosive material was air lifted in by the same Huey C slick air taxis that had become so much a part of their daily existence.

It was not yet mid morning. Haskell's binoculars posed little threat of reflection as he observed his quarry off to the west, approaching the deadly pitfall. Trailing behind six point scouts by about 25 meters came the main body of the company. They were mostly wearing pith helmets, dressed in the characteristic chartreuse and tan uniforms of NVA regulars. Only about every 7th man had his weapon pointed left, toward the steep uphill side of the mountain. The rest were holding their triggers left handed, pointing to the south side of the chasm. Their leaders had correctly assumed that any small weapons ambush would likely be initiated from the south, across the wide ravine from the irregular hills topped with conifers and jungle. If that happened, there would be a quick reaction as this company sized force would return massive small arms fire into whatever telltale gunsmoke or friction flash they would surely observe. Their greatest concern was concealed sniper fire. For that reason, they were carefully scanning the far ridgeline for any sign of muzzle flash.

The column advanced steadily, passing a large granite boulder to the outer, downhill side of the trail shoulder. This represented the westernmost boundary of the kill zone. The eastern limit was marked by a large tree, which appeared to have fallen down from the slope above, blocking the trail to eastward progress. Haskell had sent up a climber on the day prior with 3 sticks of Trinitrotoluene (TNT) to fell the tree that now blocked the trail and marked the eastern extremity of the kill zone. TNT had been tamped into the base of the tree higher up the steep slope. An elegantly placed charge had almost quietly blown the tree clean out of its root system with just enough force to bring it sliding down topmost first upon this point on the trail. It would require a sizeable work force to push the fallen tree downhill, over the ledge of the trail. Haskell watched as the entire enemy company marched single file in and out of several switchbacks that delineated their kill zone. As leading elements of the enemy file finally approached the fallen arboreal blockade, Haskell waited, watching as word was passed backward along the stopped, twisted column. Two men started passing up the line to observe and direct an effort to clear the obstacle. Clearly, these were the company leaders, likely the company commander and either his first sergeant or executive officer. A third man, probably a platoon leader, was also moving forward from the front quarter of halted troops. During their long trek around to this observation point, Haskell had rehearsed with his Yards many times the sequence of events to take place at this moment. Fondling a charging handle in his right hand, while clutching the charging box in his left, he gave a sudden clockwise twist to the handle. This set off an explosive sequence, beginning at the apex of each of the gullies, virtually destroying the trail and blowing outward, diagonally to inner sides of "V" switchback gullies. Each charge was carefully shaped, directed to explode outward and downward, thus not disturbing Claymores that had been placed on the upper, outer curves. The effect of this first explosion was near total immolation of the main body of the company that was blown out, away from steep mountainsides toward the ravine, down into a meandering streambed far below. Those located to the outward side of individual gullies, toward the curves were stunned but not quite disabled by the initial explosion. While most were knocked down, they still had a path to stand on and as yet posed a potential fighting force, though stranded between downed sections of trail. As the remaining enemy still holding ground started to recover, each of Haskell's Yards set off a sequence of claymores which detonated downward from upper revetments on outer curves of each of 5 turns covering 4 gullies along the ravine. The result was a cruel peppering of those remaining souls on the syncopated switchbacks. Many were blown off the remaining ledge trail to join fallen comrades below. A few were left squashed against the broken trail, a grim warning for any others who might attempt to restore this mountainous footpath into AO Focus. As Haskell watched from across the ravine, he observed some movement among bloodied bodies left on the moutainside. Six months prior, he might have pitied the poor souls who would finally end their lives abandoned on that distant ridge. However, he had been at *Lo Dao*. He had seen what the communists did to Montagnard children. He had smelt the incineration pits at *Loc Phieu* and was an eye witness to the aftermath of other atrocities committed against the Montagnards. His resentment toward this enemy ran deep now, deeper than the bottomless blue eyes that scanned the present carnage through field binoculars, carefully taking in fine details of the detonation event. Haskell attempted to count bodies, but could only be certain of more than about 100 and would have to trust Bugeyes that there were at least 120. Pieces and parts were distributed all along the steep mountain face, some covered by rocks and debris, which had tumbled down below. This debris would form a sort of dam that was just beginning to back up waters in the stream below. It would take about one and a half hours for the water to build up enough to spill over the dam and replenish its' dried downhill streambed forming in the distant ravine to the east. The shallow streambed below was now reduced from its angry monsoon season torrents to a mere trickle. This made a rather convenient trail for Haskell's patrol to follow as they trekked back down to an open space at the mouth of the ravine wherein they would be picked up by helicopter and ferried back to Swordfish Lair. During the flight back, men on the demolition team quietly savored this thrilling victory over their adversaries. Each man would relate details of the stunning ambush over and over again to friends and relatives, lending more to their collective resolve and assurance that they were indeed capable of defeating their enemies.

November 25th, 1972

With passing thoughts of Thanksgiving turkeys to the west, Sgt. Gabriel McCarthy was doing his best not to grimace at the horrific halitosis of an old Montagnard man presently seated before the American Medic ,mouth wide open, breathing upward into Gabe's blue, ribbed, cup like face mask. The old man's lower set of incisors and cuspids were worn down to little nubbins, evidence of a lifetime of chewing betel leaves and areca nut mixed with lime, a common proclivity among some of the tribes. This old man had worn his teeth down to the point of painful exposure of tooth roots. To many in his tribe, this represented an era in life that occurred most often during the late third or early fourth decades, just before eyesight changed in losing visual accommodation for near-sightedness. The old man (for in his culture, survival of more than four decades of life was considered quite aged) had heard that there was a *Bac Si* among the Americans who could deliver people in his tribe from enduring the suffering of wizened years by painlessly removing the lower teeth. This seemed a remarkable thing. If true, it would deliver the old man from many months of suffering until the teeth finally wore away. Because the old man was a tribal elder, as were most who survived to an age worthy of this oral tribulation, his influence was important to Operation Fisherman. Accordingly, Sgt. Gabriel McCarthy was preparing to accommodate the old man by pulling out four of his lower front teeth.

Bac Si McCarthy probed with the index finger of his left hand, into posterior recesses of the old man's mouth. Gabe felt for a "V" shaped area at the back of the jaw, just behind the lower rearmost molar. After locating the area by touch, using tactile coordination between his left index finger and right hand, Gabe advanced a metallic, sleeve shaped, thumb ringlet syringe containing a pre-filled, disposable ampule of local anesthetic mixed with epinephrine to control bleeding. Ca Rangh handed it off from just outside the limits of this old man's peripheral vision. She spoke softly to the old man in a Bru dialect as Gabriel plunged the tiny gauge needle into the apex of his "V" shaped lower jaw recess. Although that particular dialect was foreign to the young American, Gabe had heard Ca utter in similar tones many times to other patients and knew exactly what she was expressing at this moment:

"Old father, please do not be tense. You will feel a stinging in the back of your honorable jaw and if you are very fortunate, you will experience the touch of Buddah which *Bac Si* is inviting to bring peace into your speaking mouth."

She referred here to what might happen if the mandibular blockade, which Gabriel was attempting at this moment, caused the tip of his needle to come in contact with the mandibular nerve.

This did not occur on the right side blockade. However, while advancing into the left mandibular notch, Gabriel did manage to hit the big nerve, causing a sudden shock to rush down the old man's jaw. The sensation was followed almost instantly by numbness as local anesthetic flowing from the needle tip worked directly on the nerve bundle without having to absorb from neighboring tissues. The old man gave a slight start, which was carefully controlled by negative counter-pressure from the outstretched fourth and fifth fingers of Gabriel's right hand as it injected.

"Ahhh, there, you see soon-to-be-prodigious grandfather? Buddah smiles on you and takes the pain away from your jaw for this time while you give your lower teeth to his gracious condolence," Ca reassured him.

As Gabriel worked plier-like dental extractors to remove each of the worn down lower incisors, he reflected at how, in his own American culture, this would seem so strange. And yet, all these instruments, designed by western technology, accomplished the same purpose. In the west, teeth were sacrificed to caries and peri-dontal disease whereas these people, who maintained diets high in fiber and virtually without refined sugars, sacrificed their teeth to Buddah and a lifetime of chewing their foul smelling mixture of Betel juice. Having looked into the mouths of many Montagnard and Hmong tribespeople by this time, Gabe was convinced that the betel leaf/araca nut mixtures worked about as well as toothpaste in preventing tooth decay. It was rare for Gabe to have to fill cavities, something he could only do here in the field with a temporary IRM (Intermediate Restorative Material) mix of zinc oxide and euginol. However, even without tooth decay, these people still had their fair share of dental problems. The brittle araca nuts were very hard on human tooth enamel. Many Montagnard tribes made the peppery mix a condiment at weddings due to the heart shaped appearance of the nuts. However, this particular tribe used the mild herbal stimulants on a regular basis, considering them a daily confirmation of virtue and fidelity to tribal marriage vows.

After taking out the lower teeth, Gabe squirted the area again with a local anesthetic mix of lidocaine and 1:100,000 epinephrine. This helped control bleeding in the area. Ca also provided the old man with a few rolled dental sponges that he could bite down on gently, providing compression. As usual, her charm and grace in dealing with patients enamored the old man to her. This reassured Gabriel that instructions on post-operative care would likely be understood and followed.

Subsequent to the demise of Michael Glickman, there had been a regional lamentation among Montagnard communities in the area. During the short season he had served these people, many had grown to love and respect *Bac Si* Glickman. News of his death was the final straw that brought the Northwesternmost village of *Loc Phieu* into the protectorate of Swordfish lair. By Fall of 1971, virtually every target village within AO focus had turned to the combined American/Montagnard leadership evolving out of Operation Fisherman. They were now attracting people from outside the geographic Area of Operations. Already, Swordfish Lair had become densely populated with trainees and liaisons from outlying villages. That broad expanse of open plain to the west, southwest was now dotted with several longhouses in construction as nomadic tribes settled closer to the security of the mountaintop L-site. So-called "pacification" of this area had proceeded remarkably well, despite the crucial losses of Glickman and Brooksly. At this point in late November, Gabriel was alternating a week in camp and a week on patrol. At first, *Bac Si* McCarthy doubted his own ability to continue without the seasoned, ever wise and seemingly all knowing Glickman. But the daily flow of sick and injured people making pilgrimage to Swordfish Lair dispensary had demanded of Gabe a much-needed pre-occupation. During September and October, deep sorrow over losing Glickman could only be swallowed up by work. Gabe would contentedly spend 16 to 18 hours at the dispensary, resisting sleep until the inevitable tide of fatigue drew him into merciful repose without time for laying awake in conscious reminiscence. By late

October, Gabriel began to long once again to go on patrol and mix with the people closer to their roots. He took this up with Captain Fernstead and MSG Briant. They passed his request back up the line. Administrative officers who monitored and supervised Operation Fisherman were keenly aware of the impact Glickman's demise had made on the project. Although they could not replace the Senior Medic, they were able to find a way to succor medical continuance of the mission in the form of a young surgeon by the name of Charles Rivera MD. Dr. Rivera became a part time asset to Operation Fisherman during that Fall of 1971.

Charles G. Rivera MD was the son of an ethnically mixed family. His mother was sixth generation New Englander, his father a native of Spain. His parents married in 1938, giving birth to their only son the following year. Raised in a bicultural, bilingual household, young Charles Rivera graduated from Boston University in 1960. Looking to escape the cold weather he had grown up with, Charles attended the University of Miami School of Medicine in South Florida, graduating in 1964, completing thereafter a first year internship at Jackson Memorial Hospital, also in Miami, Florida. It was clear almost from the start that young Dr. Rivera had gifted hands. He realized very early on in the course of his general medical training that he was destined to become a surgeon. Accordingly, Dr. Rivera applied for a surgical residency with the Federal Government and went on to spend the next four years in residence at Gorgas Hospital in the Panama Canal Zone wherein his ability to speak both Spanish and English became a great asset to the program. It was in Panama in 1968, while serving as Chief Surgical Resident, that Dr. Rivera was told by a colleague about an AMA (American Medical Association) sponsored organization called "Volunteer Physicians for Vietnam." By the late Sixties, virtually every native Vietnamese physician had been drafted and was serving within ARVN. This left nearly the entire civilian population of Vietnam with a dire shortage of trained physicians. In a humanitarian effort to remedy this situation, the US Federal Government forged an alliance with the AMA to recruit US physicians coming out of training for service to non-military citizens of Vietnam. Within the auspices of the program, Dr. Rivera would undergo an additional two years of surgical training and satisfy a draft commitment mandated by the "Berry Plan", a two year physician draft option. And so it was that in 1969, Dr. Charles Rivera arrived in Vietnam as a non-military, Government Service (GS) physician and surgeon. He began working that July at a civilian Vietnamese Hospital located just outside of Nha Trang, ferrying back and forth between civilian hospitals at Nha Trang and Camh Ranh bay. As the only non-military Surgeon in the area, Dr. Rivera distinguished himself in service to the core citizenry of Vietnam; the aged, the women and the children. He received a meager stipend as part of the US Government subsidy program and, for his services, was discharged from any student loan tuition indebtedness left over from his four years in medical school. Educated during the early 60's, that amounted to about $3200.00. As time went on, Dr. Rivera became well known in the area. On occasion, as part of his surgical "training", he was invited to present cases at grand rounds with US military physicians in Camh Ranh bay and China Beach up near Da Nang. He was unmarried and had no close attachments to anyone back in the States.

In early 1970, Dr. Rivera was approached by a "C Team" commander from the old 5th Special Forces Group headquarters, also located in Nha Trang. Because of cultural bias between Ethnic Vietnamese and Tribal Montagnards, 5th Group Medics were finding it very difficult to obtain much needed civilian medical care extending beyond that provided by Special Forces medics. Already, there were rumors that the 5th Group would be leaving Vietnam sometime within the following year. In an effort to acquaint the "Volunteer Physicians for Vietnam" program with untended needs of the aboriginal Montagnards, Dr. Rivera was invited to visit several Montagnard village A-Sites up in the Central Highlands. In February of 1970, he traveled for the first time up to Pleiku via helicopter, visiting several camps at Plei Mrong,

Plei Djereng, Duc Co and Plei Me en route. Along the way, he became educated on a whole new dimension of Vietnam. He became quickly enamored with the Montagnards who, during that first foray, held a feast in his honor, offering up their most prized cuisine of roast dog. Although he would ever after remember with some trepidation the awful yelping which accompanied the preparation of that meal, he would also recall the sweet, child-like nature of these people as they gathered him to the collective bosom of their simple fellowship. It did not take him long to love the Montagnards. Throughout the balance of 1970, Dr. Rivera continued his weekly sorties up into the Central Highlands, dividing his time between assigned duties in Nha Trang on the coast during the week and spending weekends stationing out of Pleiku. Over time, he became well acquainted with Special Forces medics and marveled at the capacity they had to provide intricate health care with a technical background limited to barely a year of training in medicine. Most of what he did was to visit and educate the medics, following through on complicated patients and performing surgery in difficult cases, which 5th Group would arrange to Medevac back to a field hospital at Pleiku. Because Ethnic Vietnamese hospitals were loath to accept Montagnard casualties, Dr. Rivera was called on to render services to CIDG militia members. In the more loosely regulated system established by C Team commanders, casualties were not distinguished as male soldiers verses non-military civilians. Rather, entire Montagnard communities, men, women and children, were considered CIDG militia. Dr. Rivera, therefore, tended to both general surgical pathologies as well as trauma. Aside from gunshot, artillery and land mine wounds, he dealt with cancer, hydatiform cysts, tuberculosis, and the usual genera of surgical problems that exist within any human society, such as appendicitis, cholycystitis, and surgical emergencies for obstetrics or gynecology. In terms of surgical experience, Dr. Rivera obtained from that year more condensed exotic pathology than most US trained surgeons would see in a lifetime. One image he would hold with him throughout the rest of his life was the spectacle of opening a belly following a penetrating abdominal wound, and watching bundles of Ascarid worm parasites wriggling out through perforations in the bowel, almost "like rats abandoning a sinking ship". In 1975, the symbolism would confederate his recollection of Vietnam.

After the 5th Group was recalled back to the States in 1971, Dr. Rivera lost his corridor into the Central Highlands and his beloved Montagnards. While this left him with more time to dedicate to the genuine needs of Ethnic Vietnamese lowlanders in Camh Ranh and Nha Trang, he discovered a great emptiness in the sense of duty he had acquired during that first year. He attempted to make discreet inquiries about how he might get back to the Montagnards, but these fell on deaf ears. It seemed that the mainstream US Military could not be bothered when it came to Montagnards. Finally, over that summer of 1971, Doctor Greg Starr who was also a Special Forces physician and with whom Rivera had worked on occasion in the Central Highlands in 1970 approached Dr. Rivera. Doctor Starr arranged for several confidential meetings in which he outlined to Dr. Rivera the need for a surgeon to support a clandestine mission taking place "in the mountains to the west." Dr. Rivera was assured that he would not be placed in a situation involving greater risk than he was likely to encounter at Nha Trang or Camh Ranh. Should the Special Forces detachment that he would be visiting come under any threat of siege, Dr. Rivera would be promptly removed from the project. Although the offer smacked of intrigue, Rivera did not really care so long as he could get back to the Montagnards. Accordingly, in Fall of 1971, Charles G. Rivera MD boarded a Huey slick in Pleiku and once again ventured back to the mountains, to the enchanting highlanders of Southeast Asia.

Dr. Rivera's role was fundamentally one of camp visitor. He would arrive with the daily shuttle of Huey cargo crews and remain for no more than two days per visit. These visits were alternated every other week, or whenever there was a surgical emergency.

Dr. Rivera was always greeted on the LZ by an extraordinarily competent young American medic whom everyone called *"Bac Si"*. Of course, as a visitor to the camp, Dr. Rivera could not help but surmise the clandestine nature of the location (*probably Laos*) and personnel located on site. None of the Americans wore name-tag or rank designation on their field uniforms. They went by first names, or nicknames such as "Daiwee Gunny", which was what they called the camp commander, or strange transliterations of English epithets such as "Grit" or "Erasor". Dr. Rivera was quite certain that, behind each of these names, there was a great story. He was equally certain that none of these tales could be told for some time hence. Perhaps there would come a day in which he could sit down with these men, collectively or singly, and find out more about what was going on in this remote postern of the Vietnam saga.

For now, the visiting surgeon understood his own part very well. Every visit, the on site medic would present a field hospital brimming with patients suffering from various maladies. Many of these patients were afflicted with tropical diseases endemic to the area, and those seemed to do remarkably well under the sole care of this young American Special Forces medic. Mixed in with these patients were a number of more critical, surgical cases. These fell into the domain of Dr. Rivera. Occasionally, he would encounter something unusual like an adult volvulus or a pediatric intussusception. More often he would deal with mundane surgical maladies such as a parasitic bowel obstruction or ectopic pregnancy. Such cases would be taken in to an amazingly well equipped field operating room made up of sandbagged walls and scrubbed floor surface composed of carefully arranged, flattened streambed rocks grouted with rough cement over a shallow drain field. Anesthesia was limited to Diethyl Ether. It was administered by connecting an intubated patient, via endotracheal tube, to a plastic tubular "T" joint connected on its vertical perpendicular end to the perforated lid of a Mason jar. In this jar, they would place Ether soaked gauze. When the anesthetist, usually a young

Montagnard woman named "Ca," wanted to enhance analgesia, she would place her thumb over one end of the tubular T joint along the same horizontal axis which was attached at its other end to the endotracheal tube. This would cause the patient to breathe from inside the Ether rich mason jar. When Ca wanted to lighten the patient, she would simply remove her thumb from the "T" opposite the endotracheal tube. This caused the patient to breath a richer mix of room air. Occasionally, Ca would supplement the patient with Oxygen doused from a green O_2 tank via plastic hose connected directly into the endotracheal tube. It was a crude, but functional system that seemed to work well in the hands of the attractive young Montagnard woman. Because there was no mechanical respirator, they could not safely drop patients down into deeper levels of anesthesia that would depress respiration to the point of anoxia. This meant that they could not crack a chest. However, many abdominal and cranial procedures as well as any form of extremity surgery were well within reach of the expedient anesthesia system.

During these surgical forays, the American medic, *"Bac Si,"* would scrub in as a surgical assistant. Dr. Rivera was genuinely impressed with young *Bac Si's* steady hands. Some of the other Montagnards were also trained in sterile technique and served as circulators or, on occasion, scrub nurse, limited to holding retractors and cutting sutures. Even had he been inclined to disclose activities here, Dr. Rivera was convinced that few of his medical colleagues would have believed him in describing the facility. It really was quite amazing what this Special Forces medic had accomplished with these people. Within what one might consider at first glance to be a rather primitive physical plant, they had a very well run central sterilizing room (CSR), surgical suite, field laboratory and fourteen bed hospital ward with as caring and competent a nursing staff as any Dr. Rivera had ever encountered. With his first visit to the camp back in early October, helicopters had also brought in a wheeled, columnar portable X-Ray machine and chemical processing tanks. It took decent X-rays limited to

direct image exposures without a buckey grid. Camp engineers
had constructed an additional sandbagged chamber adjoining the
dispensary bunker that now served as a ventilated Dark Room.

It was clear to Dr. Rivera that the Montagnard people in this
camp dearly loved the American medic. It was evident in everything they did, the way they shadowed his every concern, and
attempted to anticipate his intentions. Little gifts of appreciation
were frequently left on *Bac Si's* small field desk, located at the
back of the hospital ward. Staff and patient visitors bowed frequently and almost reverently in his presence. Dr. Rivera felt that
similar courtesies these people demonstrated on his own behalf
were more for the benefit of the American *Bac Si*, to show respect
for one who was respected by their own icon. At one point, Dr.
Rivera found himself thinking whimsically that perhaps this was
what medicine was really supposed to be all about. Every medical
student envisions what it would be like to serve as a small community physician, beloved of the people and prominent in local
cultural circles. Certainly, the mild mannered young American
medic was realizing all the wonder and joy of being well loved as
a healer within this Lilliputian society.

Toward the end of every visit, Dr. Rivera would sit down with
Bac Si and answer a list of questions about medicine or surgery.
These sessions reminded Rivera very much of what it was like to
lecture an eager, third year medical student, hungry for information and knowledge. While some of the topics seemed at times
trivial to Dr. Rivera, he understood that this young medic was
regularly basing life and death decisions on the information shared
between them. For that reason, Dr. Rivera did the best he could
to emphasize and re-emphasize important details, often using
simple pneumonics familiar to every medical student from time
immemorial. Always, they would part after reviewing detailed
post-operative instructions and follow up care on critical patients.
Two weeks or so later, Dr. Rivera would return to discover that all
of his instructions had been attended to with careful deliberation.
Frequently, on first arriving, they would make rounds together on

the inpatients, discussing details of epidemiology, diagnosis and treatment. During one such episode, Dr. Rivera was checking out a teenaged girl who had stepped on a punji stake and incurred a nasty, potentially life-threatening infection. Rivera was quite surprised to find that the girl was being administered high doses of Flagyl, an anti-parasitic. Rivera raised this issue with the Special Forces medic during rounds one day, just prior to leaving the mountain camp.

"So, *Bac Si*, why do you give this girl so much Flagyl? It only requires a couple of days to kill off most protozoans on this medication. I've noticed you dispensing large doses of the drug on several other patients too. You seem to prescribe a lot of Flagyl."

"Well, sir, about four months ago, we ran low on some of our anti-biotics, following a plague epidemic in one of the villages down south."

"A Plague epidemic? As in *Yesernia Pesitis* plague? That's pretty heavy stuff. Did you bring in an epidemiologist to help you out?

"Actually, sir, we had one of the best epidemiologists you could imagine, one of the finest men I have every known in my life, managing the whole quarantine. But he's gone now."

The finality of this last comment prodded Dr. Rivera to detour on that issue and move back to the original.

"So, why do you dispense so much Flagyl? Flagyl is used as an anti-parasitic, not an anti-biotic."

"Yes, sir, I realize that it is listed as an anti-parasitc in the 1969 edition of the PDR (Physician's Desk Reference). However, we've found that it seems to have anti-biotic properties as well, particularly among gram-negatives like we frequently encounter in these punji stake infections. Back when we were running low on antibiotics, I started noticing that patients whom I had dosed on Flagyl for amoebic dysentery also seemed to be getting better with wound infections caused by gram-negative bacteria. So, I started using titrated Flagyl tablets on our Kirby-Bauer diffusion discs in checking cultures and sensitivities. It seems like very often, Flagyl has greater sensitivities than any of the other anti-biotics we use here. Come, I'll show you. You can check for yourself, sir."

Dr. Rivera followed *Bac Si* to the small field laboratory wherein a cabinet was opened revealing several petrie dishes. One side of the cabinet had an air-tight canister for testing anaerobes and from this, Gabe extracted two petrie dishes with a black grease pencil identifier containing the same number as that used to label the punji stake infected teenage inpatient. Looking through the clear, circular glass cover, one could see a medium which appeared sort of reddish-brown in color, filling the lower cup-side half of the petrie dish. Covering this medium was a sort of opaque, brownish green film emanating out from swirls that had obviously been contact streaks for bacteria growing thickly over the surface. Deposited in four sections of this medium were four tablets with drug company ID imprints facing upwards, identifying the medication. These were Penicillin, Tetracycline, Streptomycin and Metronidazole (Flagyl) tablets. The penicillin tablet sat smack dab in the middle of an opaque growth of surface scum. Clearly, it had no effect on the bacteria. Surrounding the Streptomycin and Tetracycline tablets were small zones of clearing within bacterial colonies on the media, indicating that bacteria were not growing or thriving in the vicinity of these discs. Surrounding the Flagyl tablet was a circle of clearing much larger than either of the other tablets on the media. Dr. Rivera observed this with great interest.

"*Bac Si*, do you realize that you may just have discovered a whole new genera of anti-biotic activity against gram negative infections? Aside from Chloramphenicol and Amino-glycosides, both of which have awful side effects, we've been pretty helpless against gram negatives. You may have really come up with something here."

"Sir, all I've done is use a field expedient to resolve an ongoing battle with infection out here in the bush. It's what we do."

"You may consider it a field expedient, but you seem to be using sound, scientific methods for checking your data. Have you had many like this?"

"Well, I've had a few patients like this sir," *Bac Si* replied, reaching into the cabinet and extracting a marble-back log. He opened it, revealing to Doctor Rivera the contents consisting of careful notations on 32 patients who had received the medication, Metronidazole (brand name Flagyl), while treating for gram-negative infections during the previous three months. Alongside each name was a classification of the micro-organism. This had been determined by different types of growth media and Grams Stain results used to confirm bacterial genus and species. Detailed figures were included about how much Flagyl had been given and what the patient's responses were. Doctor Rivera looked on the young American enlisted man with renewed respect.

"*Bac Si*, did you do this on your own initiative?"

"Yes sir, it seemed like the best way to be sure that what I was doing was the best thing."

"*Bac Si*, may I ask of you a favor?"

"Certainly, sir, anything that's within my power."

"Let me borrow this record you've been keeping? I would like to show this to some pharmaceutical people I know in Camh Ranh."

A cloud passed over *Bac Si's* expression as he wrestled with mixed emotions. Clearly, he wanted to please Dr. Rivera, but at the same time, he felt a conflict that Rivera could easily read.

"I'm sorry, sir, I really would like to oblige you on this, but you know the rules here. We're a deep covert operation. You can't communicate this with anyone."

"But, *Bac Si*, you don't understand. A discovery like this could save hundreds, maybe thousands of lives."

"Sir, if it's that good, I'm certain someone a lot smarter than I am will figure it out soon enough. In the meantime, if you reveal anything about your sources on this back in Camh Ranh, we could be compromised here, and that might also mean the loss of hundreds of lives. Please, sir, don't discuss these things with anyone outside of this compound." The young American medic seemed to be particularly imploring on this last comment, and for a moment, Dr. Rivera found himself feeling toward this young man as though he were something of a colleague instead of a very young enlisted American soldier.

"All right, *Bac Si*. This will be just our secret. But, it's a shame. You could get the jump on a very good thing here."

"Sir," he replied, pausing and looking around the little, fourteen bed, sandbagged hospital ward, "I've *got* a very good thing here".

Dr. Rivera smiled, looking around as well at the clientele of shy, hardy, doting little people who filled the tiny field hospital. He nodded sincerely, "Yes you do, *Bac Si*... you do indeed."

December 11th, 1971

Finally, Field Commander Muc Bo Thau had some reliable information on his own devil's triangle. Only a week ago, Commander Thau had started to believe in the devil when an entire company of seasoned troops simply vanished into the mountains. Prior to the ill fated company's departure, Commander Thau had ensured that the departing company took along good field radios and competent leadership. He ordered them to keep up radio contacts at least twice daily. They had maintained radio sitreps (situation reports) regularly up until entering that diabolic pass into the highland territory. Following a day without news, Commander Thau considered it possible that the mountains were simply obscuring transmission. However, by the time a week had passed without contact, he feared that yet another patrol was lost, this a sizeable troop of experienced soldiers. His fears mounted that perhaps the Americans were indeed marshalling a large force in the area. Now, a Judas agent named Huong Vang had managed to make it out of a small village called *Bai Lo Dui* along the westernmost limits of the mountainous territory. The agent, Huong Vang, traveled only during daylight hours and by so doing managed to find one of many North Vietnamese way stations along the Ho Chi Minh trail within

Commander Thau's area of responsibility. Huong Vang had been hustled up here to Regimental Field command headquarters, in which place he was presently undergoing a thorough interrogation.

Muc Bo Thau sat back in a shadow of the interrogation chamber as three of his political cadre grilled the agent, Huong Vang. Up to now, the interrogators had learned that there was a movement to turn a Hmong Village to a small American Special Forces advisory force. There was also some pretense about a fledgling Montagnard/Meo Civil leadership structure. In addition, this Judas agent revealed the proximate vicinity of Swordfish Lair as well as a general area within which the Americans operated. Could it be true? Could it be that only a single American Special Forces team had so impeded his occupation of this area? What was this nonsense about Montagnards and Meo tribesmen forming an independent state of their own? A transcriptionist was taking careful notes of everything being said. Later, the conversation would be reviewed over and over again, but for now, Muc Bo Thau began connecting events in his mind. *"First, the Cambodian invasion in April of 1970, then that Cooper-Church Amendment passed in the American Congress, which supposedly forbade U.S. troops from entering Cambodia or Laos... No, that was not right. It forbade U.S. troops from accompanying <u>Vietnamese troops</u> into Cambodia or Laos. Hmmm, there must have been a reason for that distinction. Let's see, Operation Lam Son 719 in January of 1971. If the puppet army of the South had continued toward their more apparent objectives, they certainly would have taken Tchepone and cut the Ho Chi Minh trail. Why did they not do that? They could have secured an enfilade which, with the assistance of American air power, would have been very difficult for the people's army to break. Why, why, why? And what was the portent of this notion of a Montagnard/Meo state? What ramifications would that have on the ultimate goals of Communism and domination of the Hanoi Politburo over Southeast Asia?"* These were troubling questions, to Commander Muc Bo Thau's analytical mind. As he reviewed events that had followed over the last half year, he could begin to make out strings of a logical fabric, which wove something ominous over his area command. This much was certain. The Americans must be stopped, along with any pretend Meo/Montagnard leadership to which they may be aligned.

One of the most important bits of information received by Commander Thau as a result of Huong Vang's disclosures was information on a Polygamous New Zealander "Kiwi" Agent. Commander Thau had of course read the file on this vile New Zealander before, a man called McClary. McClary's practice of marrying principal operatives was certainly a novel approach. Undeniably, McClary was having enormous impact in recruiting people for the American led venture of promoting a Montagnard/Meo independency. One of the principle reasons Huong Vang had left his assigned village was because one of McClary's wives came perilously close to sniffing him out as a communist implant within their Meo/Hmong community. There was a price on McClary's head, but due to his polygamist family associations, he had a ready clan of extended, trustworthy kinsmen who always seemed to keep him one step ahead of communist retribution ... Regimental Field Commander Muc Bo Thau's retribution. McClary was a very clever intelligence agent. Like all such agents, McClary had established cells of reliable people from whom he could gather information and pander influence. The best thing of all would have been for Muc Bo Thau to place a reliable female communist agent within McClary's harem as a wife. But the wiry Kiwi New Zealander had been far too cagey to let his glands trick him into marrying an unsubstantiated woman. All of McClary's wives came with a rock solid pedigree of local ties and family history, most women related to Montagnard or Meo village leadership. Clearly, McClary had no interest in women without a well-established, verifiable pedigree, stemming from childhood in their own communities; something communist agent operatives could not furnish.

So, how does one conquer such an adversary as McClary? Muc Bo Thau's reputation had risen in large measure due to his own work as an intelligence officer during the early sixties. He was well acquainted with counter intelligence tradecraft. Commander Thau looked over several requisitions set out on his desk, noting orders from Hanoi to increase the volume of traffic in human labor on those portions of the Ho Chi Minh trail under his command. Perhaps there was a way in which to solve both problems, find cheap "coolie" labor and deal with McClary. *"If there is no way to infiltrate McClary's network, than the other alternative was to simply eliminate McClary."*

Chapter 7 – Bridal Shower

December, 1971

Monday, December 13th – Wednesday, December 15th, 1971

In a small Hmong/Meo village, located just beyond the western periphery of AO Focus, Gerald Dowd McClary was tying the matrimonial knot for only the seventh time in his life. The present object of his affections was a charming young Hmong/Meo woman named Ha Vo D'uong, niece to the village chieftain of *Bai Lo Dui*. Because the village was located well into Laotian Hill tribes country, there was no confusion over old territorial disputes between Montagnards and Hmong in this area. The Mountains were Montagnard land. The Hills belonged to the Hmong.

McClary had been properly introduced to Ha Vo D'uong back in mid November by the uncle of his fourth wife, a Bru Montagnard woman named Sh'ra. In fact, McClary had originally ventured into the vicinity of *Bai Lo Dui* nearly two months prior, in early October. Upon locating a decent water source deep in the jungles east of *Bai Lo Dui*, McClary constructed a simple, expedient shelter out of hardwood, bamboo and palm-like thatch. It much more resembled a sort of mahogany chickee hut than a genuine Montagnard longhouse, but for its location mid jungle, far removed from any trails or settlements, it served quite well. Over the next four weeks or so, the McClary clan lived in that vicinity of jungle, undisturbed by outsiders. Two of the McClary

211

wives were sent on at his behest into *Bai Lo Dui* village proper, located about four kilometers west-southwest from their jungle abode. While McClary hunted and foraged for the rest of his family, the two agent wives entered into Bai Lo Dui, seeking out distant relatives, accepting the proffered, customary hospitality of these simple Laotian hill people. The senior wife, Sh'ra, had relatives in the village. Sh'ra, had introduced her younger companion, Justine, as a sister by marriage. Justine was a Katu Montagnard whose family had come under colonial French Jesuit influence during the mid 1950's, shortly before she was born. She was McClary's sixth wife, and all of eighteen years old. Together, these two plain looking women functioned as an exceptionally competent intelligence team. They were as clever a duo as had ever taken the field in any game of espionage. Sh'ra was older, a more mature woman in her early 30's. She had four children, three by her first husband, now dead, and one by McClary. In her assignment to this village of *Bai Lo Dui*, she left her children in the care and keeping of her husband and his remaining harem of four wives. Sh'ra had absolutely no reason to be concerned about the care and sustenance of her children while attending to the task of infiltrating *Bai Lo Dui*. She had been married to Gerald McClary for just over four years now and in all that time, he had never failed to be an excellent provider. Her children were never left untended and always had shelter as well as regular meals and constant nurturing, courtesy of clan McClary et.al. . One of the great prerogatives of polygyny in a society without birth control is the liberation of gravid women to pursue contributory occupations outside of the family. The formula seemed to offer great balance in fostering time and opportunity for such missions as this one in *Bai Lo Dui*.

Both Sh'ra and Justine had outgoing, interactive personalities. They were gifted with an awareness of their femininity and how to use charm as well as matriarchal prowess in winning over friends. McClary had also carefully indoctrinated them in the arts of confidence and subterfuge. Although Sh'ra was clearly the senior agent, Justine was a quick study. Both women regaled in this intricate game of spy crafting or "scouring" of a village. Their first tasks were making contact, and then integrating with the people. Thereafter, they could sniff out any communist agents planted within the village and deal with them accordingly. This was really not so difficult once accepted into village gatherings, which took about two weeks. Both women were well aware of the power of a familiar name. Following introductions from Sh'ra's Uncle , a half caste Hmong/Montagnard, Sh'ra and Justine worked together memorizing names and profiles of all the villagers, especially women and children. Both of the McClary wives had been taught by their husband that the women and children of a village pose the clearest image of community heart and soul. Sure enough, it was less than two weeks before Sh'ra and Justine became privy to all the richest gossip in town. They learned how most of the women had been courted by their husbands, which children were most spoiled, and a whole host of other seemingly trivial bits of information. With this information, came discovery. Among the Hmong/Meo hill-tribes, communism was very unpopular. Perhaps this was due to communistic disdain for religion, or perhaps simply the heavy handed tactics of Pathet Lao and/or NVA who treated the Hmong people with much the same bias as all Ethnic Vietnamese treated Montagnards. For this reason, communism could only be advanced by intimidation. Intimidation necessitates information on what, where, when and how. The intimidators needed this information. So it was that Sh'ra and Justine became suspicious of a man named Huong Vang. Huong Vang had moved into the village about 18 months prior to that October of 1971, claiming to be the nephew of a lately deceased village widower. Huong Vang took over the widower's farm. He commenced to plant and harvest a meager rice crop. Sometime last year, Huong Vang had taken a wife, one of the ugliest girls in the village and without dowry. In the discourse of small talk, sultry gossip-mongers mentioned how Huong Vang had been increasingly contrary to counsel from the village leadership.

Justine and Sh'ra devised a stratagem wherein Justine, on the premise of being a young, impressionable woman, would draw out Huong Vang in public discussion about the village chief. As Huong Vang expressed his disdain over the non-communist chieftain in front of this increasingly attractive young woman, Sh'ra arranged a ruse to have the chief and several of his village elders passing by within earshot of the discussion while en route to offer counsel on a property negotiation. Huong Vang's invective opinion was unknowingly revealed to the village hierarchy as the two parties passed on opposite sides of a reed partition. With similar artifice, McClary's women managed to progressively reveal the true nature of Huong Vang. Finally, Huong Vang was confronted by the village chief on a question of ownership. In essence, Huong Vang had claimed the property he now lived on by verbal affirmation alone that he was related to its former owner. When pressed to prove the relationship by other means, Huong Vang was unable to answer specific questions about either family lineage or his own origins. Accordingly, he was told to leave the village. However, he would be permitted to leave his wife behind until he should be able to send for her.

During this time, in the normal discourse between communities of common language, other visitors to the village had brought news of an American led movement in the east. There was talk of an independent State for the Hmong/Meo/Montagnard peoples. Typical of any community without television or radio, such word of mouth information was passed through a timeless chain of cross fence conversations and neighborly gossip. In a manner that would amaze Westerners unaccustomed to communication methods among "uncivilized" people, rumors flew, carrying the seeds of independence and self-governance. It fired the Hmong people with a sense of possibility that, perhaps they really could liberate themselves from their communist oppressors to the north. Huong Vang had done everything within the power of casual conversation to discourage these notions. He was himself a dedicated Pathet Lao, trained in Hanoi for just this assignment. It would be a terrible loss of face for him to return to his superiors, having been rejected from the very village he was supposed to groom and ripen for communist transition. Huong Vang was informed by dead letter drop in early November that the village was scheduled for a political indoctrination session sometime within the next few weeks. And so, rather than return to his superiors right away, Huong Vang remained outside the village, living in the scrub and fringes of jungle to the west. He depended on his wife to bring him food and supplies, which she did because he was the only man in her life who had ever shown her any real attention as a woman.

It was just a few days after Huong Vang left the village that Gerald McClary and the rest of his family made their grand entrance. His two agent wives, Sh'ra and Justine, had preceded this with encouraging rumors about the independence movement, reaffirming that they had themselves been aware of it and that their husband, who would shortly rejoin them in this village, was playing an important part in the process. In most isolated civilizations, visitors are received with some mix of hospitality fired by curiosity. However, curiosity is perhaps too mild a word to explain the absolute amazement of the people of *Bai Lo Dui* when this tall, darkly tanned Caucasian in a loincloth arrived one day, carrying a crossbow and speaking in their own language. McClary represented a confirmation of the rumors of independence. He counseled with the village chief and elders, surprisingly well informed on names and local issues. With a rich, endearing charm of his own, McClary filled these people with a vision of what Operation Fisherman was intended to accomplish. After only a few days in the village, McClary managed to win most of the people over to his vision. Yes, they would like to visit with the Americans and yes, they would be very much committed to an independent state of their own in tandem with their Montagnard cousins to the east. A delegation of villagers from *Bai Lo Dui* was sent to Swordfish Lair with specific instructions on location of the L-Site. They took with them formal requests for resources that the Americans could offer their village. Among other things, *Bai Lo Dui* was promised a visit from the growing legend of *Txiv Neeb* (pronounced 'Tsev Nang'), the American *Bac Si* so highly revered among Laotian Montagnards to the east. This information was shared and circulated among the villagers of *Bai Lo Dui* and served as introductory incentive for the delegation.

During those first few days in *Bai Lo Dui* by the entire McClary clan, Gerald McClary and his family had been received in the home of Sh'ra's Uncle, a village Elder. While abiding in the Uncle's household, the McClary clan had set about helping with community chores and shoring up the labor force of Sh'ra's Uncle during harvest season. Also living in the same household was a young woman in her late 20's, a daughter named Ha Vo. Ha Vo was a widow of three years, having lost her husband during the battle of *Dai Do* in 1968. Ha Vo's first husband and nine-year old son were conscripted as coolie labor to re-supply the 48th regiment of the 320th NVA Division. She was advised of their disappearance following an American Marine counterattack on NVA supply lines near the DMZ during what some had called Tet II, or the mini Tet offensive. Like so many widows left alone in the simple villages of the Hmong, she had hoped against hope that her husband and son would someday return. They never did. During the bitter years of uncertainty, Ha Vo registered blame with many compurgators, the North Vietnamese and Pathet Lao who had conscripted her husband and son into their slave labor force; the Americans, for launching airplanes and bombs which had vanquished her family; to her own people for idly permitting the communists to dictate policies over them. Now, after three years, the bitterness had acquiesced to a household filled with children and hope. Gerald McClary and his family drew Ha Vo out of the introspective, self-effacing life she had been living. They reminded her that she was yet a young woman, filled with the potential for new life, able to love and be cared for. It was easy to fall in love with Gerald McClary, particularly while viewing him surrounded by others who loved and revered him. With the tacit approval of

Sh'ra and most of the other wives, McClary and Ha Vo began a sort of courting ritual. This started formally during a *pom-poj*, or sort of flirting social dance circle in which McClary responded to Ha Vo beckoning him into the dance. From there, the romance blossomed without intimacy, both parties constantly chaperoned by the other wives. Eventually, Gerald McClary requested from both Uncle and wives the honor of taking Ha Vo into his family. The majority agreed, and a date was set for what western calendars would call December 13th, 1971.

Following Gerald McClary's arrival in the village of *Bai Lo Dui*, the wife of communist exile Huong Vang was able to provide not only food and sustenance, but information, something potentially much more valuable to Huong Vang. Just after the first week of December, 1971, Huong Vang took leave of his faithful, ugly wife and traveled west. He would make contact with distant communist comrades on the premise that this information was too important to let pass without personally informing superiors about the American presence and plans for the area. With growing confidence that the import of this information would justify abandonment of his assigned village, Huong Vang tied up the only loose end remaining to his restoration of face. After laying with his ugly wife one last time as a reward for her fealty, Huong Vang strangled the only person in *Bai Lo Dui* whose disclosures to either villagers or communists could compromise his opportunity for gaining great prestige among his true comrades.

Upon disposing of his wife's body, Huong Vang headed west and north. He traveled only during the mid-day, because McClary had explained that the Americans and Montagnards were laying ambushes for anyone returning to the west at night. Huong Vang did not know that the perimeter of AO Focus ended just east of *Bai Lo Dui* and so he was not really in jeopardy of tripping an ambuscade at any time. En route during his long walk, Huong Vang had ample opportunity to rehearse his story. He would explain to communist superiors that his mission in the village had been a successful one. *"Your humble servant Huong Vang has been so successful, in fact, that the village leadership has confided in him regarding their intentions to betray themselves to the Americans."* Huong Vang would assert that, despite everything he had argued to dissuade the villagers of *Bai Lo Dui*, they had given into promises of fortune and decadence from the Americans. The most important information that he would bring to his superiors could be corroborated and that would be enough. Should he be called upon to return to the village, any aspersions the people of *Bai Lo Dui* might cast on Huong Vang from this point forward could be easily explained away. Within four days, Huong Vang was apprehended by Communist patrols near a primary artery of the Ho Chi Minh trail. He wound up at the headquarters of Commander Muc Bo Thau. It was there that Huong Vang divulged some of the best intelligence information Muc Bo Thau had received in many, many weeks.

Gerald Dowd McClary looked positively resplendent. Dressed in traditional Hmong wedding attire, he sported a black satin cap with a broad sash and vest hung with silver coins. The bride to be had been carefully prepared and pampered by other McClary wives in a sisterly ritual few Westerners could ever begin to understand. The wedding was set for late morning. Many people, family and friends of the McClary clan, had arrived during the preceding days from other villages he had similarly visited over the previous several months. Everyone shared a sense of great optimism. There is, of course, nothing like a wedding for bringing a mood of joy and rebirth into any society. In addition, these people were filled with hope over the new paradigm of an independent state and nation. The marriage of this tall westerner, McClary, with the noble, lovely young widow, Ha Vo, seemed to symbolize a reassurance among the people that if such a union could happen in their midst, anything was possible. At about 1030 hours local time, McClary stood at his place in front of the old village shaman. Ha Vo made her entrance on the arm of her Uncle and in the company of her soon to be "sister wives" who represented a symbology of what Westerners might call the "wedding party". All the wives were present except Justine, the youngest. For

Justine, who had up until today been the newest wife, it was still difficult to deal with the idea of yet another woman with whom to share her grand husband. Justine realized that, perhaps after she had borne children and lived as long as the other wives, she would appreciate more fully what benefits lay in the expansion of their burgeoning nuclear family. However, she simply could not bring herself to participate in the wedding and chose instead to secrete herself off in the jungle, back at the chickee-like hut, which had been the family's last abode prior to the *Bai Lo Dui* occupation. It had also been the last place in which Justine made love to her husband as the favored youngest wife.

They were in the process of listening to the old Shaman utter his traditional community proclamation of good cheer to the gathered host. It was McClary who first sensed the danger. He may have delayed acting on his feelings sooner because of a faltering uncertainty over whether these were instinctive feelings, or seventh time wedding day jitters. He knew that, although all the wives had consented to his marriage, Justine was hurt by it and her absence was quite conspicuous to him. Gerald McClary's last recollection would be a sense of solace from his fears, attained by looking over at each of his wives, finally settling upon the adoring gaze of his most recently betrothed Ha Vo as their world dissolved around them.

Swordfish Lair, 13 December, 1971

Staff Sergeant Thomas Gowen violated both protocol and etiquette by breaking in on negotiations in progress between Fernstead, Briant and Johnston with the delegation from *Bai Lo Dui*, now in attendance at Swordfish Lair. Normally, Lieutenant Erickson would have been in on the parlance, but he was presently on patrol. The Americans were once again impressed with McClary's remarkable success in recruiting yet another strategic village hamlet to the mission objectives of Operation Fisherman. Fernstead had quickly confirmed McClary's promises regarding material and medical aid to the village of *Bai Lo Dui*. They were presently discussing various aspects of the affiliation when Gowen whispered something into the ear of Captain Fernstead who was in a translation pause while Briant forwarded exchanges in Hmong using a broken Montagnard dialect.

"Sir, we just received a flash message from Bugeyes. Didn't you say these people are from that little village way out on the western fringes of our AO? The one called *Bai Lo Dui?*"

Fernstead did not break eye contact with his guests, instead, he replied with a somewhat distant, but polite, demeanor over the intrusion.

"Yes, they are. So, what of it?"

Gowen was aware of the tempered nature of his commanding officer as he replied.

"Well, sir, Bugeyes says they are getting a lot of hot spots at this little village way out on the western periphery. It looks like the communists are pulling off a raid on *Bai Lo Dui.*"

This last comment succeeded in breaking Fernstead's reverie of diplomacy, something members of the delegation from *Bai Lo Dui* had been quite impressed with. Fernstead turned to Gowen, seeking confirmation of the information just passed to him.

"Are you certain about this? Did you ask Bugeyes to confirm the flyover?"

"Yes sir, they confirmed both the village and heat signatures with an angels twenty flyover, looking straight down at max resolution from a secure altitude. There is definitely some heavy ordinance coming down on that village right now, as we speak."

Fernstead looked over at Briant who had himself paused in the translation, aware that something substantial was occurring.

"Ask the delegates if McClary is still in their village, today... as we speak."

Briant forwarded this translation and received back an answer.

"They say that he most certainly is, sir. In fact, he's scheduled to be married, again, today to a widowed daughter of one of the village elders."

With this news, Fernstead rolled his head back looking up for a moment at the ceiling in some apparent distress. Briant broke in:

"Sir, they want to know if anything is wrong. What's going on?"

Fernstead looked back down at the delegates, fixing his eyes on them as they sat with confused, uncertain expressions. "Something very bad, Top and the timing couldn't be worse."

Fernstead proceeded to convey, between agonizing pauses for translation, that word had just arrived about *Bai Lo Dui* being under attack from a large communist force. Gowen conveyed the Bugeyes estimation of a batallion sized or better enemy force. At first, the delegates could hardly believe that the communists would spend so much manpower on their little village when, really, it would take no more than a platoon of well armed communists to overwhelm the unarmed villagers at this point. As an intelligence matter, SFC Johnston probed the delegates about possible leaks of information. It did not take long to understand the communist reaction.

At first, all the delegates insisted that none of the villagers in *Bai Lo Dui* had any love for the communists and certainly would not willingly offer information in any way to compromise plans for this new Montagnard-American-Hmong affiliation. However, on pointed questioning, they mentioned that one of their group, a certain Huong Vang, had recently been exiled from the community after McClary's wives exposed him as a critic of village leadership. Although Huong Vang had been expelled from the village prior to the arrival of McClary, Huong Vang's wife had remained behind and could possibly have informed her husband about McClary's arrival. In the end, Johnston pieced together a pretty accurate picture of events up to this point. Clearly, the communists were unaware whether or not a link up had already taken place. They attacked the village allowing for possible American/Montagnard occupation based on limited intelligence provided by this Huong Vang. If they had taken the time to surround the village and cut off escape lanes, then McClary was almost certainly captured or dead by now. Knowing McClary, none of the Americans could imagine him surrendering.

Sgt. Gabriel McCarthy was making rounds on his hospital patients when the camp alarm sounded. He hastily checked the charts on two people suffering from malaria, observing that their fevers were down and the repetitive spiking cycle so typical of *Falciprium* was resolving since both patients had started on Chloraquine-Primaquine two days ago. Gabe made a quick note and dashed on over to the gathering assembly near the landing strip. Fernstead stood aloft on a sandbagged berm, explaining the situation to everyone present. They only had available one on site Huey C slick that could not ferry more than six people with gear in one load. The helicopter would start shuttling groups of six people to a marshaling area off to the west within the next 20 minutes. In addition, one flight wing of six additional Huey C slicks assigned to Operation Fisherman was inbound from a primary support depot in Pleiku. McCarthy was told to hustle out on the first lift and hastened to get his medical go bag, already stowed and prepared for just such an occasion. In addition, Winkle was advised to go along with his sniper rifle and a Yard spotter. Briant would round out the first lift along with one of the senior yard trackers and a member of the *Bai Lo Dui* delegation group, a slightly built, middle-aged man named Hol Mei.

The Huey deposited its small advanced party about two and a half kilometers east of *Bai Lo Dui*. Briant and McCarthy had all they could do to restrain Hol Mei from rushing to his village in search of wife and family. They explained that if he failed in maintaining absolute sound discipline, they would have to leave him behind, bound and gagged. This sobered the older man, who reverted into a quiet cadence, moving within the well-spaced squad of men who seemed to trek soundlessly along rising and falling hammocks of jungle. Gabriel had a bad feeling about this situation from almost the moment they all caught scent of pungent odors of smoke, drifting back at them on a moderate breeze from the west. It was tainted with an unmistakable smell of burning flesh, yet another poignant reminder to Gabe of the epidemic at *Loc Phieu* and the demise of Glickman. Briant advised that they find some high ground to take advantage of Ron Winkle's sniper scope, survey the village and send communications back to Fernstead, en route with the balance of a sizeable strike force, numbering about 90 men.

Bai Lo Dui, like many Meo hill country villages at dusk, was situated within eastern shadows of low rising hills to the west. It was constructed on contoured, sloping ground, segueing ever so gradually to a broad, shallow river located west, southwest. Briant made communications with an F-4E Bugeyes overhead, which identified the heat signatures of his reconnaissance team and started feeding information about direction and distance to other warm bodies in the area of the village. As they approached the upper elevation of one particularly prominent hill overlooking the village from the east, Bugeyes warned them of another two supine bodies in the area. McCarthy and Winkle moved perpendicular to the reported signatures as Briant formed a skirmish line that he advanced slowly toward the occupied summit. Both lines of advance were rearward of the enemy observation post, facing down, looking toward the village. From a viewing screen aboard Bugeyes, the E/O watched fascinated as two friendly formations advanced, like a pincer, on the dual, prone shaped observers. There was a pause as one member of the friendly line stood up, apparently catching site of an enemy observer. Following this, the enemy heat signatures swiveled and one emitted a bright white light in the direction of the advancing pincer. Both phalanxes of the friendly skirmish line returned this display with bright, white heat signatures from their own weapons. Within a few seconds, the two enemy observers were prostrate, within growing pools of warm fluid.

"Bugeyes, this is minnow advance. We have two bad guys down. Do you scan any others in the area, over?"

"This is Bugeyes. Negative, not on that particular summit, however, there are, isolated thermals on other elevations in and around the village. If you like, I can direct fire into them, over."

"This is minnow advance. Negative on that, Bugeyes, we have no way of knowing who are good guys and who are bad. We'll have to smoke them out individually. Perhaps you can help spot for our sniper..."

Gabriel McCarthy made silent hand signals, asking Briant to query for wounded down in the village.

"Bugeyes, can you give us an idea on possible wounded down in the village, over?"

"Hard to tell, minnow. We've got several signatures cooling down to ambient temperature as well as some distorted by blood pools, but that's about as specific as we can offer, over."

Gabe felt strongly that he belonged down in that village right now. Briant could sense his impatience.

"*Bac Si.* I know where you want to be right now, but we've got to secure the village before sending you down there. We can't let you get hurt, you understand that."

"Top, I understand what you're saying, but I also know that I don't need to be here right now, I need to be there. Do you suppose we could get Bugeyes to find a corridor down, at least get me closer to the fringes of the village?"

Briant turned this over in his mind. It would be at least another hour before they could muster a company-sized element to secure the area. An hour could make quite a difference in the final tally of survivors. Pensively, he keyed Bugeyes once again.

"Bugeyes, can you find a corridor down to the village from our position? Is there any way we could get someone into the village while avoiding contacts, over?"

"Sure, minnow. Send your man out from your location on an azimuth of about 310 degrees for about 200 meters, then turn back to about 140 degrees and that should take you right in. I can't offer you much on terrain, though, over."

"OK Bugeyes. We'll send our team in with the second radio. Let us both know if you see any movement toward our people, over."

"Roger that"

Briant dispatched Gabe with the Montagnard tracker and the *Bai Lo Dui* delegate, Hol Mei. Instructions were given for Sergeant Ron Winkle, along with his own Montagnard spotter, to keep a sharp lookout and over-watch the medical team down into the village. Gabe set out with his two compatriots. He emphasized once more to old Hol Mei, that sound and movement discipline must be maintained on this approach into the village. He reaffirmed this with eye contact to the Montagnard tracker who nodded, taking a position in the lead with Hol Mei in the middle. They put the radio on Hol Mei's back while Gabe carried the headset at the end of a curly chord, next to his ear.

As they navigated irregular terrain leading down into the village, Bugeyes kept them informed of any thermal movements toward them. It was necessary for the three-man group to top one particular crest which offered no good concealment or cover. They passed over it quickly, professionally, with the tracker darting across first, setting up a covering position on the other side. The delegate, Hol Mei, then rushed across the open space while Gabe set up a cross-fire position from the near side. Finally, Gabriel himself dashed across, but in so doing drew a sudden "ping" into the earth off to his left rear, followed about a second later by a loud report from the northeast. Being separated from the radio during the crossing, he only heard the last part of an exchange between Briant and Bugeyes, locating the enemy position as Winkle zeroed and fixed the communist sniper.

The standard sniper weapon for the U.S. Army in 1971 was a 7.62 mm rifle designated "M-21". This was essentially a modified semi-automatic M-14 with a high power, Redfield 3-9 variable power sniper scope over iron sights. Sgt. Ron Winkle had attended sniper school in Great Britain wherein he was trained to use an L42A1 7.62 bolt-action single shot rifle in preference to semi-automatic. After settling into Swordfish Lair, Winkle had requested the closest thing to an L42 in Southeast Asia, a Winchester Model 70. However, due to administrative logistical constraints on Operation Fisherman, they had been unable to obtain the preferred Winchester bolt-action sniper rifle, which was primarily a U.S. Marine inventory item. In the end, he resorted to the M-21.

Laying in a prone position, with perhaps the best field of view overlooking the valley, Winkle was thinking right now that if only he had a bolt action rifle, all would be well with the world. He had located an enemy sniper pod on a distant, lower elevation hilltop to the north and slightly west. He had a side view sight picture on the reclining enemy sniper that exposed both upper torso and head. Winkle also caught a glimpse of at least one other body close by the communist sniper and Bugeyes had confirmed that only two human thermal signatures were located on that particular hill top. Ron Winkle planned his shots carefully. The first he would place directly into the enemy sniper from about 400 yards (In 1971 American snipers continued to think in yards instead of meters). Following the first shot, he would violate normal rules of engagement for snipers and place a series of shots into the vicinity of the enemy spotter. Winkle decided to do so because he could not get a clear sight picture on the spotter, and even if he could, he was certain the spotter would move quickly once his sniper partner was hit. Unlike a typical sniper observation post, Winkle had the enormous advantage of Bugeyes looking down from above. This gave the Americans an opportunity for sniping in conjunction with overhead spotting intelligence, which Winkle had the privilege of exercising for the first time ever. Sgt. Ron Winkle had not realized this when he took his first shot. It appeared to strike clean, into center of mass on the upper torso of the enemy sniper. Winkle did not have time to ascertain the lethality of his first shot before swinging his sight reticle just a couple millimeters into the adjacent bush wherein he placed three quick rounds. The total of four shots were issued in a sequence of "bang.... bang, bang, bang!", in about three seconds. After finishing his volley, Winkle very carefully changed his own position along with Briant, lest any other enemy snipers be drawn to their location by the loud, multiple reports. Bugeyes confirmed that both targets had scored blood pools and there was no movement on the thermals, a strong indication that both were solidly down.

Having now grasped the nature and disposition of enemy sniper deployment around the village, Winkle and Briant commenced using Bugeyes for spotting any similarly dual signatures located at various vantage points around the village. The system worked well. Winkle grimaced over one first shot miss, which he attributed to the looseness of his rifle's semi-auto receiver group. However, the advantage of a quickfire series following the "loose" first shot quite compensated for any subtle deficiency in trajectory. Over the next 20 minutes, as Sgt. Gabriel McCarthy's trio made their way down into the village, Winkle and Briant zeroed in on and eliminated four other enemy sniper positions with the help of Bugeyes.

As Gabriel made his way into the village, Hol Mei, led their group toward the town center. En route, it was apparent that Hol Mei was very anxious, constraining himself from breaking away and plunging off to his own household. Despite this worthy display in self-restraint, Hol Mei could not prevent himself from letting out a tragic, sustained, low pitched moan as they ventured toward the town center. From a secluded vantage point, they could see bodies scattered all about, some obviously dead. Men, women and children in bright colored, bloody clothing lay in a cortège before scattered clusters of grieving women and young children.

For a moment, Gabriel stood transfixed, poised over the gruesome spectacle from a secluded distance. He was unable to grasp the meaning or consequence of such random brutality. They found concealment next to a habitation occupying a corner that opened up onto the town square. It seemed that closer to the epicenter of the town, the density of carnage increased, culminating at a pile of riddled bodies among which, Gabriel McCarthy recognized with great anguish, was the body of Gerald Dowd McClary. It appeared as though Gerald had attempted to use his own body as a fragile shield for his bride along with her attendants, who were also his other wives. McClary lay, sprawled over toward the six women, hands clutching at arms and shoulders.

3 hours earlier

Justine McClary had been far out in the jungle when the shots first started. Breaking her reverie of self-pity over acquiescing to another honeymoon bride, and refusal to attend the wedding, Justine rushed back through the two kilometers of jungle toward her family, eventually joining a throng of other women being re-strained by Pathet Lao and NVA soldiers. The communists had formed a picket around the town center. The square itself was surrounded by soldiers and in the middle of the square, an officer stood with a bullhorn. He was announcing that in consequence of betrayal against the people's cause of liberation, all men and boys of this village were being sentenced to hard labor from which, if they served out their terms faithfully, they would someday be permitted to return home.

One of the things Muc Bo Thau understood very well about forced coolie labor was that slaves must have some hope or purpose for survival. If they were told the truth, that very likely all the men and boys from this village would die of malnutrition while laboring as beasts of burden, then many or all of them might at-tempt some form of mass suicidal charge on their captors. Aside from that, laborers will always work harder if they have some-thing of consequence to believe in. Commander Thau was giving them something to believe in, namely, that some day they would be permitted to return to this village. To such end, Commander Muc Bo Thau would also leave behind the women, mostly alive and relatively unmolested except for a few scapegoat examples that the rest would remember. Leaving behind the women also gave the men something to come back for. Additionally, it would serve in leaving behind testators to the retribution of communist indignation over disloyal peasants.

Justine clawed and wriggled her way to a vantage-point among the village women until she could see the village center and the communist political officer proclaiming his judgements over the loudspeaker. There, at the feet of this officer, lay the bullet riddled body of the old village Shaman and immediately beyond, virtually every member of the wedding party, dead. All of the bodies had been pepperd with small arms fire and lay where they had fallen. The communists trod among, on and over corpses of dead villagers littering the town-square. Bloody boot and shoe prints were everywhere. There, on the raised dais of the village center, alongside Commander Muc Bo Thau, stood a triumphant Huong Vang, former villager and Judas Agent. After Muc Bo Thau finished his pronouncements, he turned the microphone over to Huong Vang. Huong Vang explained in conciliatory, placating tones how he had tried to warn the people of this inevitability. How foolish the people of *Bai Lo Dui* were to place their trust in the illusionary Americans and their ridiculous notion of a separate state or nation. Some of the women thronging the village square periphery shouted back at him with cursings and accusations. The most vocal women were apprehended by soldiers and led off. These were raped or humiliated with calculated deliberation.

Communist forces had stormed into the village like a tempest. In like manner, NVA drovers herded the hapless males of *Bai Lo Dui* off to the west less than an hour and a half after assaulting the wedding service. Most of the officers and troops departed with them, including Commander Muc Bo Thau. He left behind Huong Vang with a squad of communist soldiers dressed in peasant homespun clothing. In addition, communist sniper teams were placed into hills round about the city, anticipating a visit from American/Laotian patrols sometime in the next few days or weeks. From the village square, Huong Vang continued vocalizing his long winded revisionist policies to the remaining population, made up largely of women, children and very old men. He advised the people not to be distressed by the sounds of gunfire from various hills surrounding the village. It was simply the brave communist snipers ranging their weapons, a necessary process in protecting this village from the Americans. However, no villager should attempt to leave the village as it might be necessary to use them as target practice in preventing any betrayers who might want to alert the Americans. Although Huong Vang noticed absently that most of the fire seemed to be coming from the highest hilltop due east, he attributed this to the fact that he knew the sniper teams commander was at that particular location. Understandably, in deploying his teams, the sniper leader would want to situate his own position highest up among sentinel like hills surrounding the village. This would provide him an accurate roost from which to direct fire down on the Americans should they arrive sometime during the next few days or weeks.

As Huong Vang concluded his diatribe, village women gathered mutely about the square. None dared speak out against him, subsequent to the return of several women who rejoined the gathered throng weeping and obviously violated. This was a powerful inducement to submission for the remaining women. Justine stood to the rear of the female villagers, furthest away from Huong Vang and his gathered henchmen, who had changed out of their NVA uniforms into village homespun clothing, taken from ample wardrobes of conscripted men, presently being force marched away from the village. Justine had not yet approached the body of her husband for fear that Huong Vang would recognize her as the only member of the family still alive. She believed that her sole chance for survival, and hence revenge, would be to melt back away from the town center and thence into the jungle, hoping that she could find her way to one of the patrols from Swordfish Lair. She was in the act of shrinking back onto a side street and had just turned her head away from the perturbing voice of Huong Vang when she literally stumbled across Hol Mei and two other armed men. To her utter astonishment, she saw crouching alongside Hol Mei an American in Tiger Striped fatigues. She further recognized him as the young medic who had been so embarrassed during that commencement feast they had all participated in last Spring. How could the Americans be here this quickly? And where were the rest? She only saw Hol Mei with two men, one obviously a Montagnard and the other this American. She was careful in pausing for too long, quickly dropping down beside them and looking deeply into the eyes of the American. Gabriel looked back at her, reading in her countenance her anguish and seeming to hear her thoughts. *"Where have you come from? Have you been here all this time?"* Of course, Gabriel could not read the more subliminal sobriquet of her deepest recrimination... *"Were you witness to my dishonor in not being slain along with my family?"*

In the few seconds passing between them, Justine and Gabriel reached a quick, silent consensus about the situation. Without words, it was clear what needed to be done. Justine realized that the American and his companion could not distinguish who was who in this scenario. Although Hol Mei knew most of the villagers, from their present vantage point the rescuers had no way of singling out communists from villagers. Justine was aware that presently, only communists occupied the center of the square. Once those men mixed with the villagers, it might be very difficult to assault them as a liberating *force du jour*. Also, village survivors might be fearful of crossing Huong Vang again. With all the instinct she had so confidently acquired as a competent intelligence agent, Justine sensed that if the people of this town had any chance at regaining their independence and their men, she must act now, quickly. Somehow, she knew the snipers would not be a problem. Justine reached out and took hold of the M-2 Carbine Hol Mei had been entrusted with. Somewhat to McCarthy's surprise, after exchanging a few whispered urgencies, he let her take it. She was familiar with the weapon. She had fired it with McClary during their stay at Swordfish Lair. Justine understood where the selector switch was and how it operated. Setting it to full automatic, she wrapped the small rifle up among stalks of long stemmed flowers that had been dropped on the street from the wedding celebration. Further concealing the small rifle within a paper wrap, she turned and strode toward the town center again, gathering flowers into a larger bundle as she went. As Justine approached the village nucleus, Huong Vang stopped mid sentence during one of his pompous diatribes. He recognized her right off as one of the two women who had been identified as Mc-Clary's wives and one who had probably played a role in driving him out of the village. She was the young, attractive one and he hesitated another moment to take her in while his comrades in peasant clothing took her to be a receptionist presenting them with flowers in acquiescence to their occupation. Although still armed, the civilian clad soldiers had shouldered their weapons in a gesture of conciliation toward their new occupation. Justine approached to within three meters of the group, consisting of Huong Vang plus eight enforcers. She reached into her floral bouquet, grasping the stock handle of the carbine and swinging it up toward the communists, squeezing the trigger as flowers dropped away from around the barrel. The little weapon spit retribution back at the *Bai Lo Dui* occupation committee. At that same moment, Gabriel McCarthy and his Montagnard tracker rushed forward from their concealed positions to reinforce Justine's ambush. She had just finished the magazine as they raced into the square. Four communists were down and of the four remaining, two were fumbling to get rifles off their shoulders. Gabe and his tracker took out two each of those remaining with bursts of semi-automatic fire. This left only Huong Vang standing, unarmed on the dais.

Justine had hardly broken stride as she unleashed the carbine's entire magazine of 30 rounds on her enemy. Through some fluke, Huong Vang had not been shot. After emptying her weapon, she continued her relentless trek right up to Huong Vang who was looking incredulously down around him at his fallen comrades. As he gazed back at Justine, she swung the butt of her rifle full force into his left cheek. He went down with a thud and as he did so, other women in the area advanced on him kicking and beating him to a violent demise with all the savagery of a pryde of lionesses.

Hol Mei was making inquiries among less frenzied villagers about what had happened. They told him that the communists had placed sniper teams into surrounding hills to harass any possible reaction force. These communist sniper teams anticipated several hours or even days in which to set out their positions and await the arrival of any Americans. Not expecting such a rapid response, enemy positions were still somewhat disoriented when Winkle and Briant started picking them off one by one at the behest of Bugeyes. As it turned out, the highest hillock, which they first assaulted, also contained a dead NVA lieutenant with radio, apparently the leader of these five sniper teams surrounding *Bai Lo Dui*.

Gabe enlisted his Montagnard tracker to go around the village, locating any wounded among the villagers. The women quickly caught on to what he was doing and started forming groups to bear the wounded back to a triage station in the town square. Gabriel knelt over several older men and checked for vital signs. It became quickly apparent that the communists had made double sure all male village leadership were killed with a bullet to the head. There were virtually no living young or middle-aged men left in the village. There remained, however, a number of women who had been collaterally wounded by random munitions as well as a few others badly mauled during gang rapes. Gabriel tended to one middle-aged woman whose rectum had been mutilated by a rifle barrel inserted to hold her still as she resisted being ravished. She was hemorrhaging profusely from a traumatic fistula, torn between rectum and vagina. Cognizant that his patient was in great pain, Gabriel administered 10 mg. of morphine before gently irrigating and packing her lower quarters with compression dressings. He also started an IV with plasma expander. Finally, he started her on high doses of Crystalline Penicillin and Streptomycin. This was necessary because, after wounding her so, she was no longer fit to rape, and therefore, her tormentors threw her, bare-bottomed, into a muddy pigsty.

By the time Fernstead arrived with his reaction force, a triage had been established with 15 wounded patients, four of them critical. Using his radio, Gabe requested that Ca Rangh be transported in along with two other reliable, medically trained Montagnards. Ca arrived on scene with the next airmobile rotation, bringing several parcels of additional medical supplies. Gabe found that, without even being told, she had brought along most of the materials he needed. With Ca at his side, it seemed a certain order and confidence settled over things. Aside from the rectal mutilation, they worked to save a penetrated abdomen, a head wound and a chest injury. Working in concert, Gabe and Ca stabilized the first critical patient, a woman struck in the abdomen by a ricochet. She also required pain management with morphine while replacing lost blood volume with intravenous fluid expanders and arranging for her to be transported back to Swordfish Lair wherein Doctor Rivero had been summoned. There was another woman with a head wound. She had been struck with a rifle butt as the advancing enemy force was breaking through to the village square. The woman showed signs of a skull fracture with increased intracranial pressure. Gabe treated her with mannitol as well as intravenous steroids. She was also transported back to Doctor Rivero, but without benefit of any pain relief, due to the head wound. The fourth critically injured patient was a child, a little boy about eight years old. He had also been knocked over during the initial assault. In the process, some communist foot soldier had stepped on his thorax, creating a flail chest wound. When they brought him to Gabe, the boy was gasping for air. His lips were blue and he was dying of asphyxiation. With every breath, as the cavity of the little boy's chest attempted to inflate his lungs with expansion of the diaphragm, a circular area of several broken ribs in the right chest wall would convolute, recessing deep into the chest wall contrary to the expanding rib cage. The same thing happened in reverse as the child attempted to exhale. Gabe rolled a field bandage into a tight pack and settled it over the flail segment, wrapping it tightly into place with adhesive and a four-inch ACE wrap. The effect was a mechanical stabilization of the supple chest wall. This prevented contra coup movement of the flail segment. Although the boy could still not take a deep breath, at least he could take in enough air for respiratory exchange. Ca started the child on 100% oxygen from a small green canister, administered through a clear green plastic mask with bag reservoir. Gabe listened to his chest and found that there were no breath exchange sounds on the side of the flail chest. Worried about some sharp rib fragment puncturing the right lung, he put in a chest tube using a, foley catheter. The procedure was painful, being limited to field site intercostal blockade with local anesthetic. This only provided local anesthesia for the stab incision into the lung. Snaking in the small, French guage catheter was always very painful, however, once in place, it would assure that air could not build up between lung and chest cavity. With no reverse vacuum apparatus available in the field, Gabe constructed a makeshift Heimlich valve with the latex finger of a surgical glove. After snipping off a long middle finger glove segment he snipped off the tip and adhesive taped in place the tip of the latex finger piece around an expansion sleeve end of the Foley catheter. Then, on the more supple, wider, palmar end of the cut latex glove finger, he wet half the finger sleeve, causing the wider end, away from the Foley catheter, to slurp together and effectively create a field expedient, one way valve. The tip of this he put into a canteen cup of sterile saline. Each time the boy coughed or made an effort at a deep breath, small bubbles would issue out of the end of the Heimlich valve. In this way, the damaged right chest wall would decompress the Pneumothorax while en route to Dr. Rivero.

After evacuating the four criticals, Gabe returned to assist with various extremity wounds and fractures that remained on site in *Bai Lo Dui*. He was forming a plaster arm cast with 90 degree bend at the elbow for a shattered Humerus when SFC

Johnston approached, addressing Gabe in the now familiar appellative:

"*Bac Si*, we're going after the men taken from this village. From what the women tell us, the communists have about a two and a half-hour head start. Captain wants to know if you feel up to going with us? He thinks we're gonna need all the Americans along in order to pull this off."

Gabe did not hesitate to assent, confident that Ca could manage most of what was left. He gathered his weapons and quickly restocked his medical go bag before joining Fernstead who was briefing officers and NCO's.

"… Bugeyes reported a batallion sized enemy force. That means somewhere in the neighborhood of eight hundred field troops. We only have about 90 men. That means they probably outnumber us by eight or nine to one. However, they certainly won't be expecting us to come after them so soon. It has never happened to them before here in Laos. We'll have the element of surprise on our side, which is a big advantage. The people of this village, *Bai Lo Dui*, came to us. They expected us to help protect them. We cannot permit the enemy to snatch this village away from us. It would be a major blow to all of our efforts here. The up side is that with the advantages of surprise and good intelligence from Bugeyes, we have a decent chance of intercepting the enemy column driving those villagers. If we can separate villagers from enemy, we can call in air support and pour some real hurt down on the troops who did this. The bad news is that the closer we get to *Ho Chi Minh Trail* complexes further west, the more anti-aircraft they will have up. Bugeyes will not be able to get in real close.

Our order of march is bounding overwatch until we reach their trailheads. Half our element will be forward, spread out into a "V" formation, the other half behind in a reverse "T". We don't have any really good maps on the area we'll be going in to and so we'll hold our limited air wing in reserve. With only the three birds we have left, it doesn't make much sense to ferry the whole group in consecution, so we need to move out ASAP." With that, Captain Fernstead started to organize his columns. Just prior to heading out, he called a conference with his own American NCO's:

"We need a way to separate those villager coolies from the enemy herders. Do any of you have an idea on how we can do that without shooting up our villagers in the mix?"

Gabe had been thinking about this and spoke up.

"Yes sir, I think I have a way of separating them, but it will require the delivery of some supplies from Swordfish Lair."

"You know we have a time constraint here, *Bac Si*. It will take at least 45 minutes to cover a round trip to and from Swordfish, but go ahead, let's hear your idea."

With that, Gabriel outlined his plan. Fernstead was impressed and after considering it for a few seconds concluded that there was no other practical way of separating the two groups. A Huey was dispatched to retrieve the items needed with all haste. It made the round trip in just under 40 mintues, also making a quick refuel from the large rubber fuel bladder cached near the LZ at Swordfish Lair.

As soon as Gabe had his supplies, SFC Estrada started out with point elements at the spearhead. Volkert and Haskell, who organized either wing of the V component, joined Estrada. SFC Johnston took command of the reverse T, which followed in reserve along with McCarthy and Winkle. Sgt. Winkle was positioned forward in the throat of the V where he could quickly communicate with Fernstead who stayed right behind the point element. They moved quickly over ground that thickened considerably in dense, bush like vegetation as compared with the mountainous climes of AO Focus further east. As they progressed westward, they encountered jungle that was honeycombed with high-speed trails and intricately camouflaged waypoints. Fernstead's group set out at dusk and moved at a brisk pace with Bugeyes directing their movement from skyward. As the shaped column moved deeper into progressively more dense jungle, the order of march necessarily thinned down to a column, which followed a high speed trail route, clearly laid out by communist engineers. The trail was invisible to aerial observation, but incredibly well maintained for rapid movement in thick foliage. This eliminated any hesitation over azimuth taking or concerns about flank security. The trails in that part of Laos at night were generally quite deserted. Moving in this manner, the distance between Fernstead's relatively fast moving ground column and Muc Bo Thau's encumbered, human cattle drive, closed over about four hours. The communists never suspected that they were being pursued and took necessary rest breaks in their march west about every hour, again confident that their victim snatch would not be realized for several days yet.

About 0200 hours in the morning, Fernstead's column closed to within 1500 meters of the bivouacked communist battalion and conscripts. Fernstead moved slowly on the trail from that point on, until about 0245, when he had to reposition his people using Bugeyes for orientation. The enemy had driven conscripts from *Bai Lo Dui* without benefit of food or water for over six hours. Orders were finally issued to provide water to the weary villagers. Muc Bo Thau did so only because he understood that he must either water his human cattle now or face the prospect of killing off a portion before returning from this mission. After receiving a detailed description of their deployment from Bugeyes, Fernstead instructed Briant to envelop a right flank north of the west bound enemy column. They then sent the intrepid Hol Mei forward into the camp. He had accompanied them from *Bai Lo Dui* and, en route, Gabe had explained the plan in detail to the hardy little *Bai Lo Dui* village elder. Within his tunic, Hol Mei carried several dozen packets of pills and two dozen small vials of liquid. Among other things, their plan depended heavily on the coolies having already been searched so that, when Hol Mei stumbled across a communist perimeter guard, he could claim that he had dropped out of the column to relieve himself. He would probably then be returned to the conscripts without being searched again. The ruse worked. The perimeter guard had been facing inward, toward the bivouac to prevent any conscripts from fleeing outward into the hills around their rest stop. The guard was momentarily startled to encounter Hol Mei coming back into camp from outside the main group. He treated Hol Mei roughly, pushing him back among the other coolies without thinking to re-search him.

The other male villagers immediately recognized Hol Mei. They were uniformly surprised at his rejoinder with them. He quickly quelled any stirring within their ranks and carefully disseminated the plan among huddled, seemingly inattentive, gatherings. Every man in the conscription group was provided a measure of pills and in addition, many received a small brown, glass vial. These were distributed along with the water the communists had made available. With the water ration, each man from *Bai Lo Dui* took a packet of 8-10 pills. These were mega dose B vitamin and Niacin tablets, each tablet contained a particularly high dose of Vitamin B_{12} –Niacin and Folic Acid. Effects of this massive ingestion of Niacin became apparent about 25 minutes later as the communists were taking an hourly head count. Several of the Bai Lo Dui conscripts began coughing and moaning. They were punished for this with kicks and cursings from the drovers, but as time went on, it became apparent that many of these villagers were genuinely sick. Communist medics looked in on the conscripts and found them to be bright red in complexion with apparent swelling in the face and hands. While Hol Mei was examined by one of the communist medics, he confided, "Perhaps it has something to do with when the Americans visited our village a few days ago".

"Americans? In *Bai Lo Dui* a few days ago?" Commander Muc Bo Thau had just been informed by one of the communist medics of this disclosure. *"It was possible, after all, Huong Vang had only provided intelligence on the village up to about two weeks prior. Certainly, it would make sense that the Americans would attempt contact with the village, especially after the village had been so foolish as* to send a delegation. *Could it be that the Americans had already vis-ited the village? There certainly were no Americans present when they had stormed the village that day before, during the wedding. But, why, why would the Americans come and leave that fellow McClary behind alone?"*

From his field tent, Commander Thau instructed the medic to bring forward this villager who had mentioned the American presence. Hol Mei was presented before Muc Bo Thau a few min-utes later, bowing and submissive.

"Tell me about these Americans who visited your village re-cently!"

"Well, most honorable sir, they visited our village and spoke with the chief. They left us gifts and a most strange offering, hon-orable sir, they left us with gifts for our children. The Americans have very strange customs for children's gifts, sir."

"What do you mean, what strange customs? Speak up man." Commander Thau's suspicions were beginning to rise.

"Well, they left our children with pets, honorable sir."

"Pets! What sort of pets!"

"Mice, honorable sir, little white mice."

Muc Bo Thau looked at the man in horror. "Mice! Did you say mice?"

"Yes, sir. Our children of course thought the little animals were interesting, but most of the mice were lost almost as soon as their cages were opened."

Commander Thau backed away from the placating Hol Mei, instructing communist medics to return him immediately to the rest of the conscripts. Upon his arrival back among the other men of *Bai Lo Dui*, Hol Mei issued a signal for those who had them to drink the small brownish vials containing Syrup of Ipecac.

At the same time, Commander Thau was summoning his field officers around him.

"It is possible that the Americans have intentionally infected these people anticipating that we would be conscripting them! Several months ago, we attempted a similar ruse on them at that small village down south, *Loc Phieu*. It is possible that we have played right into the hands of the Americans by taking these coolies and mixing them with our own men!"

This caused some considerable stir among the officers. Many rumors had circulated about the Russian Bacteriologist and his mission in this area last summer. There had even been discussions about the use of Plague-black-death, being deployed. Every officer present had a genuine superstition about Plague and wanted nothing to do with bacteriological warfare. In the midst of this reverie, one of the NCO's supervising the conscripts, brought grim tidings:

"Commander Thau, many of the conscripts are vomiting."

"Vomiting? How many?"

"Very many of them are vomiting. They are throwing up all of the water which we gave them along with a yellow bile that is most disagreeable."

"Captains! Separate our men at once! Instruct them not to have any contact with the coolies! Any of our own men that have touched or had close contact with the coolies must themselves be quarantined from the main body of our battalion. Make it so immediately!"

The NVA officers did not need any additional encouragement. They hustled off to their respective troop commands issuing hasty orders to subordinates. Those officers responsible for drovers called back the perimeter guards separating drovers and guards into groups well removed from the main body of the NVA Batallion. To Bugeyes, looking down from 25,000 feet above, it was an interesting sight. The A-6 E/O turned to his pilot and remarked.

"I don't know what our boys could have done to get the enemy to cooperate so much with us, but you wouldn't believe this. If I'm right about which group are the coolies, those commies are compartmentalizing their column almost as though they wanted us to know who are the good guys and who are the bad. It couldn't be better for an air strike!" Almost on cue, a radio communiqué from the ground requested that Bugeyes summon a Spectre gunship.

During the next ten minutes or so, it appeared as though their communist taskmasters consecutively abandoned the men of *Bai Lo Dui*. Hol Mei had begun moving his fellow villagers in slow; halting movements back toward the east as NVA perimeter guards from that side were recalled. Many of the villagers who had taken syrup of ipecac were genuinely distressed but none hesitated to follow the lead of Hol Mei, as he directed his people eastward. They were amazed to find Americans and Montagnards waiting for them only a couple hundred meters distant.

Fernstead gathered the sick looking villagers into a column and while marching them eastward toward home. He addressed them through Hol Mei.

"Men of *Bai Lo Dui*.... You have shown great courage in following our instructions... I know that many of you feel ill right now... Our *Bac Si* assures you that this will shortly pass... None of the medicines you have taken contain any poison.... The prickly feeling and sensation of heat will pass away within half an hour or so... Those of you who were called on to take the liquid should know that once you have thrown that liquid back up, you will no longer vomit... In a few minutes, we will give you more water and you will be able to hold it down... For now, we must quickly move away from the communists who may shortly discover that you have gone." The men of *Bai Lo Dui* seemed very much inclined to cooperate and began moving expeditiously back down the overcast, beaten, high speed trail in the direction of their village.

Back in the communist camp, Commander Thau was receiving reports from his staff on quarantine efforts. In the midst of this, he asked if anyone knew whether or not the coolies were attempting to mix in with his men. One of the NVA NCOs replied.

"No sir, I went down to check that all our men were separated from the villagers. I found the villagers going back toward their village, good riddance. But, sir, I found several bottles of medicine lying about from where they had been. I do not believe that we have given them medicine for their sickness."

"Of course we have not! I gave no order for any medicine to be distributed among the Hmong people! Where could the medicine have come from? They were all searched before we began herding them back here. Arrange for some of our intelligence officers to examine this medicine at once!"

About 25 minutes later, one of the English speaking intelligence officers assigned to the battalion brought back news that the vials contained labels in English. The name on these vials was pronounced EEPIKAK. Communist medics had been summoned. They informed the intelligence officers that ipecac was a medicine given to cause vomiting after taking a poison. The logic of this finally broke through to Commander Muc Bo Thau. While as yet not quite certain that his troops were safe from contagion, he nonetheless decided to contain the villagers of *Bai Lo Dui*, if for no other reason than to observe them in quarantine. Commander Thau issued orders to overtake the fleeing villagers and bring them back, but to be careful not to touch or make direct contact. If they needed any encouragement; "shoot a few so as to set an example for the rest to follow."

In the meantime, Captain Fernstead was closing up a rear guard on his recovered villagers. He directed Hol Mei to take his people home and sent a radio along with two squads to accompany the villagers as well as inform Erickson and Gowen back at Swordfish Lair. They were to keep in touch should there be any trouble on the way back. Bugeyes remained overhead observing the delaying elements of Fernstead's company who were now being deployed along higher ground paralleling the return route of march. An advance patrol of about 30 NVA regulars had been sent back to intercept and turn the withdrawing villagers. The enemy formation was described by Bugeyes to Fernstead as he led the communist patrol file on into a long ambush corridor occupying about 50 meters in length. SFC Arnold Estrada initiated the ambush just as the last part of the enemy patrol came inside the long killing zone. Most of the strike force was positioned within 5 meters of the path, looking down on to the enemy. At each end of the ambush corridor, they had emptied into the earth plastic jugs of a highly explosive substrate called Astrolite, mixed together in two long parallel lines on opposite sides of the trail.. The mix formed a very unstable compound, capable of detonating virtually any material soaked up by it. That night was cloudless with one of those clear, mid season quarter moons. The ambush triggered with Astrolite detonations at both ends of the killing zone. Collectively, the strike force emptied two complete magazines per man of small arms fire down on to the hapless communist patrol. Each man tossed two grenades into the melee between magazine changes. The result was a near total disintegration of the advance NVA patrol occurring in the space of less than one minute of massed small arms fire. Commander Muc Bo Thau heard the eruption of gunfire back down the trail. The quick cessation of it signaled a very poor outcome for those being ambushed as typically; broken ambushes result in a much longer exchange.

Captain Fernstead moved the majority of his force out quickly, but not before sending down several men to leave grenades with pins pulled and set at spoon tension under what was left of several NVA bodies. In addition, Fernstead laid out several "Toe Popper" mines in ground around the trail so that when other enemy NVA followed, while stepping around the dead, they would encounter the nasty little anti-tracker devices. Three klicks downtrail, Captain Fernstead received word that an AC-130A Spectre gunship had arrived on station. Two HARM bearing F-4E Wild Weasels had also swept the area for SAM signatures, but most of the SAM ordinance was in short supply due to stepped up bombing farther north since President Nixon had commenced Operation Linebacker. Aside from gun mounted anti-aircraft, useless against high fliers, there were no real SAM sites in this area of LAOS except right along the Ho Chi Minh trail itself. That was yet about 45 kilometers off. While the hill country was laced with foot trails, this had been a light infantry foot patrol operation. Most of the communist armor and troop trucks were still deployed far to the west and south, anticipating another incursion from Cambodia. So, when Spectre arrived on scene, they had no tangible air threats and a screen full of enemy thermal signatures under their guns. Captain Fernstead remained with the rear most guard having taken up position atop a prominent mound, providing him clear line of sight to the west. Commander Muc Bo Thau heard the big Hercules aircraft overhead, but did not consider it much of a threat at night with his troops invisible to American spotter aircraft. The communist commander was again confounded that fateful evening when torrents of 7.62 caliber rounds came raining down through the overhead jungle canopy on his deployed battalion with withering accuracy. It was as though the communist column was right out in the open, in broad daylight. Despite efforts of the officers to disburse, the dreadful gunship rained its merciless deluge directly in to the massed main body of troops. Muc Bo Thau remained nearby his own command tent, established back where the column had been bivouacked. What saved him was the fact that he had already ordered most his troops to follow up on the ambush. Commander Thau had remained behind with a relatively small command structure. Although the NVA commander could not fully appreciate it at the time, his disposition of the main body of troops was what preserved him from coming under the guns of that dread American sky dragon. In the end, his 838-man contingent was nearly obliterated. Two days later, 121 mostly wounded survivors returned with Commander Thau to regional HQ back along Ho Chi Minh trail. They left behind the bodies of several hundred dead veteran NVA and Pathet Lao communists in a debacle which Commander Thau's staff and field officers would carefully analyze for many weeks to come.

Chapter 8 – Conspiracies

December, January-February, 1972

Washington DC, Wednesday, December 23rd, 1971

Those who truly know Christmas week in Washington, DC, might contrast the season with images of an heir apparent poised under some proverbial mistletoe, awaiting kisses from deep pocket benefactors for services rendered. It is a city that bristles with quintessential power, oozing from every nook, cranny and office party, which there are more of this Yuletide season than any other. To those who feast on the rush, Christmas season is a sumptuous repast in which Potomac party favors come in all sizes, shapes and forms. Congressman Riley Hathoway was giving and receiving his fair share. Accompanying this particular reception were two old Congressional colleagues, both party members, one of whom served on the powerful Congressional Defense committee. Riley Hathoway stood with them in a conversational circle of four, all toting champagne in plastic cups designed to look like stemmed glassware. Seasonal libations had loosened everyone's inhibitions within the group to a point that all felt this warm, cozy sense of being among friends. In addition to Riley Hathoway and the two other Congressmen, former Ambassador Sylvester Williams, recently discharged from his post as U.S. Ambassador to Laos, filled out the quartet. Hathoway was leading the conversation.

"You know, Ambassador Williams, I just returned back last month from a fact finding tour of South Vietnam. I had the opportunity to visit personally with President Thieu and General Minh. I was rather pleasantly surprised. They struck me as exceptional statesmen, far more considerate of the U.S. legislative branch than Creighton Abrams, I should say."

Sylvester "Sully" Williams was a tall, thin man with receding hairline. He returned Hathoway's comments with a glassy eyed look that signaled loose lips to an inside straight. "Please, Riley, call me Sully. General Abrams is all right. At least he isn't fixated on chasing snakes like his predecessor, Westmoreland was."

"Chasing snakes?"

"Yes, a favorite metaphor of the former Commanding General William C. Westmoreland. According to Westmoreland, when one is committed to a fight, the enemy must be treated like a snake in the grass. One must chase it down no matter where it goes in order to cut off its head. Obviously, he's more of a soldier than a statesman. In this case, chasing the snake into the grass means crossing over into someone else's back yard, and that could cause some major problems."

"What kinds of problems?"

"Well, problems like getting China into another shooting war with the U.S., violating Geneva Conference mandates about the sovereignty of Laos and Cambodia, that sort of thing." Williams paused to sip his champagne. Congressman Hathoway carried on the conversation.

"Well, we are all agreed that U.S. troops have no business in Cambodia or Laos." (To which Ambassador Williams replied with a short slurp as he hastened in reply.) "Not all of us, my friend, not all of us."

"Like who? You mean Nixon?"

"Nixon, along with all those military geniuses he's been listening to. For five years I managed to keep Westmoreland mostly out of Laos."

At that, one of the other Congressmen quickly interjected. "Is that like being *mostly* not pregnant, Ambassador?" This roused chuckles all around the group. The other Congressman, the one on the Defense Committee segued into the next comment. "From what I understand, Studies and Observations Group has been in Laos almost from the beginning, not to mention CIA operatives up in the Plain of Jars."

"Well, I couldn't do much about the CIA or Air America, plausible deniability and all that. But SOG was for the most part directly under military command and, at least up until Nixon, I had some influence there," Williams replied.

"What kind of influence?" Hathoway followed up.

"Back in 65' I started right off letting the military know who was boss by insisting that U.S. led reconnaissance teams confine themselves to non-heliborne insertions within two small boxes of geography along the South Vietnamese border with Laos. I also demanded that supporting air strikes could only launch from Thailand."

"And the military bought it?"

"The military squawked like plucked ducks. But President Johnson understood that it was much better to let diplomats handle diplomacy."

"Then, why did you let the military cross over at all?" Hathoway inquired.

"Well, any diplomat needs terms for negotiation. Westmoreland convinced me that we needed to know if in fact the North Vietnamese were in Laos, despite their absolute assurance that they would respect the Geneva conference resolutions not to invade Laos."

"But, the North Vietnamese *are* in Laos aren't they?"

"Well, of course they are. They had to use Laos as a corridor in which to construct the Ho Chi Minh Trail. But, we knew that. I didn't need Westmoreland sending in bird dogs to tell me about the Ho Chi Minh Trail."

"So, why did Westmoreland want reconnaissance on Laos?"

"Because he believed the Ho Chi Minh Trail was essentially a supply line intended to support an eventual invasion of the South and he wanted to know how close to that eventuality Hanoi was getting. If Westmoreland had his way, he would have invaded Southern Laos and dismantled the Ho Chi Minh Trail."

"And how would that have affected the conflict."

"Well, if he had succeeded, he probably would have extended the McNamera line all the way to Thailand. In order for the North Vietnamese to get around it, they would have to go through Thailand. "

"But, Sully, I thought Westmoreland didn't care for the idea of a McNamera line."

"You're quite right. Westmoreland doesn't believe in static defense lines. He was always fixated on the failed French Maginot line during World War II, which the Germans walked right around and through. Westmoreland would have probably built more of a dynamic wall made up of high speed access roads and dispersed armor units that could quickly coalesce in response to massed assaults. But, once the line was approved through all the red tape, he agreed to get behind it. Personally, I think he expected to make it simply an early warning system with high speed resources to mobilize massed troops anywhere he wanted them along the DMZ."

"Now, Sully, I heard you were the one who decided how far U.S. troops could go into Laos," one of the third person Congressmen chimed in at this point. Williams responded by equalizing eye contact among the other three in the circle as he replied.

"During the Johnson administration, they had the good sense to realize that as Ambassador to Laos, *I* was the best person to set policy for U.S. military intelligence gathering within Laos. I placed limits on men in the field. Sometimes it was necessary to re-evaluate these limits over time as we found out that the North Vietnamese do indeed have a substantial presence in Laos."

"And the military followed your directives?"

"Yes they did. I'll give this to Westmoreland. He and I may not see eye to eye on many things regarding the Vietnam War, but he knew how to follow orders."

Congressman Hathoway fueled the conversation at this point; "What do you think about having U.S. troops in Laos?" Williams replied: "Well, frankly, every military force in history has had to provide pawns from time to time, to use as cannon fodder for some higher cause."

"Cannon fodder?"

"Yes, you know, military fanatics who volunteer for suicide missions because they want to go out in a blaze of glory. The British call them "forlorn hopes". Believe me, gentlemen, better to let them have their wish than come back home and become card carrying voters eh?" To this, everyone in the circle chuckled, accepting the comment as satire without any real animosity. Hathoway recovered from the political witticism by following up with a serious question.

"Tell me Ambassador Williams, what are your genuine thoughts on U.S. troops in Laos?"

Posed in the proper mantle of title, the Ambassador sobered and directed his gaze in soliloquy with Hathoway.

"The fact is that I do genuinely regard those missions into Laos as suicide missions. I insisted that the only U.S. troops to be involved would be volunteers, no draftees."

The Congressman who served on the Defense Committee piped in here, "Do you mean to say that because these men volunteered, you considered them like expendable kamikazes? You actually intended for them to die in Laos?"

Sully Williams replied rather curtly, "not necessarily, but I was willing to accept that there would be a very high casualty rate. That about sums it up." He then ended the discussion, "gentlemen, if you'll excuse me, I am expected home soon."

To this terminus in the conversation, Riley Hathoway could only respond by nodding in acquiescence. After Former Ambassador Williams departed, Congressman Hathoway drew aside one of his remaining congressional colleagues, the one on the Defense Committee.

"You know, Jim, I turned up something during this recent trip to South Vietnam about some American Special Forces team or teams working with Montagnards in Laos. Have you heard anything about this?"

"Well, Riley, that is all classified stuff you know. But, just among friends, there is a hush-hush initiative going on about what to do with the Montagnards. We have set aside some special project funds to support a military think tank panel based at Fort Bragg. They've inserted a single Special Forces A Team to work with the Montagnards in Laos, sort of a Beta project. As you probably know, the Vietnamese don't really much give a damn about the Montagnards."

Hathoway put on his most aghast expression: "But, but Jim! You know as well as I do that the Cooper-Church Amendment specifically forbids American Advisors from entering Laos with Vietnamese military personnel!"

"Believe me, Riley, we took all that into consideration before allocating a dime to this project, *Fisherman* I think they call it. The Green Beret advisors are only permitted to work with Laotian Montagnards, you see."

"But, I got the impression that President Thieu considers all Montagnards to be Vietnamese citizens!"

"Oh, he may say that, but it's just not so. We completed several cultural assessment studies before dedicating funds to this project. You see, most Ethnic Vietnamese could care less about the Montagnard people, except that the South Vietnamese all seem quite willing to spill Montagnard blood instead of their own in fighting Communism. Montagnards do not consider themselves Vietnamese. They do not recognize the same geographical boundaries for their traditional homeland that North and South Vietnam have established. The fact is that many so-called Montagnards are born and raised in the highlands of Laos and are technically citizens of Laos. That means that our U.S. military advisors are only working with Laotian citizens and therefore abide by terms of the Cooper-Church amendment."

"That seems to tread a pretty thin line, Jim."

"Well, Riley, it's only one team of about twelve men. They only have approval for one single deployment with no replacements. If they lose over 50% of their U.S. ground force contingent while in Laos, they have to shut down the mission. They do have a considerable air support and unit resource account. They're using some slick new look down technology with electronic flyovers that lets them see human and animal heat signatures on the ground under canopied jungle. I think they call it *Bugeyes*. Amazing technology! They can actually see enemy troop movements from nearly invisible altitudes. Evidently the L-Site is in such a remote area of Laos that there are no roads for enemy vehicles to get at them. From what I hear, they're using up the project budget funds pretty fast. However, the project is only slated to last a year after which, it's due to be re-evaluated. Everything depends on how well the American Advisors fare during this first evaluation period. It all may be a moot issue, after all. You know those Green Beret types. They're all suicidal. As the ambassador said, they'll probably all get killed or captured."

"You may be right. It's unfortunate, but every conflict requires pawns, what did he call them? Forlorn hopes? It sounds as though they are fanatics in a position to be sacrificed for the greater good of the game, so to speak. Look, do me a favor Jim. I promised President Thieu that I would get back with him on this. Please keep me informed so that I can let him know we're not tampering with South Vietnamese citizens."

At this, the other Congressman abruptly changed his good old boy demeanor, shifting gears into a state of more alert concern, finally penetrating through his fifth glass of champagne. "Now listen, Riley, this is very hush-hush stuff. I probably shouldn't have told you any of this. You mustn't discuss it with Thieu or anyone else outside of myself. It's a matter of National Security."

"Pawns, Jim, military pawns whom we allowed to be put where they are precisely so that policy makers like ourselves can use them to bring about the greater good. I have a chance to help get us out of Vietnam thanks to this relationship with Thieu. He confided to me that he really wants to be independent from the U.S. It's our own military that is perpetuating the U.S. presence over there, too many U.S. Generals putting stars on their shoulders. In order to stop our involvement in Southeast Asia, including Laos and all the other places that we *don't* belong in, it may be necessary to sacrifice a few pawns. This trip to Vietnam has really opened my eyes. Most of us don't understand the oriental mind. Everything with them is face. They don't care about human or political life the way we do here. All they care about is saving face. At this point in history, if we embarrass any of the Southeast Asian powerbrokers, Allied or Communist, it will not be good for either them or us. It may be necessary to bargain off a few expendables in the process, but in the long run what we can do here will certainly be for the good of our own great nation."

The other Congressman was not ignorant of political rhetoric when he heard it. Clearly, Riley had preached this issue in the soapbox of his mind many times to a mental body politic. Although Congressman Jim was a bit impressed with Riley Hathoway's passion on the topic, he was not impressed enough to forget his own oath of confidentiality, a pre-requisite to any member of the Congressional Defense Committee.

"Now look, Riley, I can see you feel strongly about this. But, I'm still going to have to insist that this matter remain strictly confidential between us."

"Well, if you say so, Jim. Of course, I'd never do anything that you would feel uncomfortable about."

Looking at the two men in quiet discourse from a distance, no one would have suspected that the seemingly casual, Washington Christmas feté had just lain a foundation for the loss of so many distant lives in the now formative future.

South Vietnam, Saturday, December 26*th*, 1971

President Nguyen Van Thieu hung up the telephone with an air of triumph. Since conversing face to face with Congressman

Hathoway last November, there had been at least half a dozen exchanges by phone between Hathoway's office in Washington, DC, and the Presidential Palace in Saigon. None of these had come through on secure lines and it was simply another testament of the arrogant American Congressman's naiveté that he would share such sensitive information over a simple long distance phone connection. Presient Theiu was well aware that most of his phone lines were tapped. He had a special, secure line he had purposely not disclosed to Hathoway, hoping for the tet a té that had just transpired. Thieu reached for his secure line now, picking it up and dialing code numbers that would connect him directly to General Minh's headquarters. The tinny, artificial sounding voice which answered on the other end identified itself as General Minh's office. President Thieu identified himself, knowing that his own voice would be similarly unrecognizable on the other end and so he included a number and codeword resulting in his being patched directly through to General Duong An Minh. When Minh came on the line, he exchanged a similar number and codeword. Thieu responded without prelude.

"It seems, General, that our Montagnard issue has a name, *Operation Fisherman*. As we suspected, the operation is being run directly from Fort Bragg and supported by adjacent airfields here, most likely both Da Nang and Pleiku. The Americans have a new toy. It is most impressive and I think we should take them to task for not sharing it with us."

The tinny secure voice mask reply could not conceal an edge of irritation in General Minh's voice: "Just what is the nature of this *new toy* as you put it?"

South Vietnam, Friday, January 1st , 1972

New Years Day, January 1st, 1972 was celebrated, as were most western holidays in South Vietnam, with a hot meal for troops in the field, and time off for non-essential military personnel. To the eastern mind, it was a day of vulnerability for the Americans, a day in which Americans simply seemed to take time off from the war. It was on this day that General Duong An Minh chose to launch his first offensive against *Operation Fisherman*. The initial salvo landed with a phone call to the office of Brigadier General Dwight Elkins, commander of Special Air Operations over I Corps, headquartered at Da Nang air base.

"This is General Duong An Minh, I must speak with General Elkins immediately." The enlisted CQ on duty conveyed this telephone call directly to General Elkins' private quarters. In less than two minutes, General Elkins was on the line.

"General Minh, good morning to you sir. May I take this occasion to wish you a happy Western New Year!"

"Thank you General Elkins and the same to you. I am calling to advise you that several of my attachés will be arriving this morning to be briefed on your new Bugeyes system. I am sorry I cannot be there myself to receive the briefing. I hear it is most impressive." The pause which followed from General Elkins had been summarily anticipated by Big Minh and served to assure the Vietnamese military commander that his mini-coup was on track. Even following a full 6-second pause, General Elkins seemed quite the bantam diplomat as he replied:

"Why, I'm sorry General Minh, but I am not aware of any briefing scheduled for this morning."

General Minh decided it best to deliver another knock down punch while Elkins was still reeling from the first pronouncement. "Oh, yes, the new look down imaging technology that you are field testing with that Special Forces A-Team in Laos at this time. I hear you can see right through the jungle with it."

General Elkins was completely caught off guard. How in the world had such a major breach of security developed after all the extraordinary precautions taken to service the Bugeyes system in far off Okinawa? Da Nang had only been used as a refueling station for reconnaissance aircraft tasked to support Operation Fisherman. How, HOW could Big Minh know about this project? General Elkins himself was the only person at Da Nang to understand the entire concept of *Operation Fisherman* and had indeed even been on the consortium panel that evaluated and selected Team A-321. In nearly 8 months since the insertion, nothing about the routine of the base had been exculpatory in revealing Operation Fisherman except for an incident in which that Medic had absconded with a wounded Montagnard from some Vietnamese field hospital. General Elkins had half-expected a breach in security to follow the occurrence last summer, but the incident was neatly subterfuged into non-existence. Now, nearly six months later, Big Minh apparently had some major parts of the big picture, and was pressing for disclosure under a façade of diplomacy.

"I'll have to get back with you on this, General Minh."

"Oh, no need to get back with me. I will get a full report from my Air Liaison Officers when they return. Good Day, General Elkins.... *Click*", a declivitous disrupt cut short the American Brigadier's reply.

Within twenty minutes, a delegation of four ARVN officers presented themselves to General Elkins' office, demanding an audience with General Elkins. They had with them a letter from General Duong Anh Minh as well as a letter of introduction from a U.S. Congressman. General Elkins had only just arrived at his office and was beginning an attempt at coordinating some strategy with the rest of the general staff for Operation Fisherman, most of whom were on New Year's furlough. He was again interrupted by his secretary to be informed that he had a telephone call from Washington DC.

"General Elkins! This is Congressman Riley Hathoway, good day to you, sir, and Happy New Year. I am conducting an investigation into alleged violations of the Cooper-Church Amendment and am directing you to offer your full cooperation to members of a delegation from the Army of the Republic of South Vietnam. The information they are seeking will certainly help allay any allegations about your involvement with *Operation Fisherman*. This ARVN committee is acting in response to both my own inquiries as well as orders from our ally, General Duong Anh Minh who is collaborating with me to obtain full disclosure in this investigation."

"Sir, I have no information to substantiate either your identity over this *non-secure* telephone line, nor any congressional investigation which would normally be coordinated through the Congressional Armed Forces Sub-committee. If you are who you say, you must understand that I cannot proceed to discuss any matters which may involve classified information without appropriate preparations."

"General Elkins, that is ridiculous! I am a well-known elected federal legislator of the United States government and your cooperation is mandated by that fact. Now, you are to disclose all pertinent information that you have on both Operation Fisherman and the new electronic lookdown technology code-named *Bugeyes*. Do I make myself clear?"

General Elkins was for the third time that morning, momentarily stunned. Could this Congressman be so stupid as to openly discuss highly classified information over an unsecured line like this? Was this really a Congressman or simply somebody posing as a Congressman, taking a shot in the dark? If so, where did the Viets come up with an intro letter on Congressional letterhead and how had this supposed Congressman timed his phone call with the arrival of the Vietnamese delegation? How could they possibly have procured the terms *Fisherman* and *Bugeyes*? There was nothing to do but break the conversation and launch a security inquiry.

"Congressman, sir, whoever you are, I am terminating this conversation at this time and declaring your call as a potential security violation in accordance with Department of Defense Directives section 5200. I am reporting this call as a violation of National Security to the National Security Agency. Sir, before you make a call such as this again, you should seek legal counsel and understand your liability for breach of National Security. This conversation is ended."

With that, General Elkins hung up the telephone. He then confiscated the document on Congressional letterhead presented by the Viets and dismissed them, explaining that they had been misinformed. The ARVN officers were skilled at tactful resistance toward being dismissed, but in the end, General Elkins was quite insistent and the Viets left with thinly veiled threats concerning the dissatisfaction of General Minh.

In Washington DC, Congressman Hathoway hung up his own telephone in a livid rage. How *dare* this upstart Brigadier deny a *Congressional* inquiry! How *dare* he accuse a United States Congressman of breach of National Security! Hathoway spent the rest of that evening and most of the next morning making telephone calls, exercising all of his considerable political influence in sabotaging the character of General Dwight Elkins. Among other things, Hathoway laid the blame on General Elkins for revealing details about Operation Fisherman and Bugeyes technology thus reversing the curse of security violation back onto the General. An investigation would ensue during which General Dwight Elkins would be relieved of his command and spend many months in a legal quagmire. In the end he would be exonerated, verifying that it was in fact Congressman Hathoway who had violated security. By the time this was all proven and dredged through the obtuse quasi-legal Judge Advocates Group (JAG), a process which took the better part of nearly two years, General Dwight Elkins' career was pretty much ended. Concurrently, Congressman Riley Hathoway would retain his constituency, who would be favorably influenced by their candidate's increasingly skeptical attitude about military policies in Southeast Asia. This played a considerable role in his successful bids for re-election.

General Creighton Abrams relieved General Dwight Elkins of his command in Special Air Ops about ten days later. By that time, Congressman Riley Hathoway had stirred up enough vindictive political muck that General Abrams had no choice. Abrams had been strongly advised to replace General Elkins with another military commander who better understood the political climate between Washington and Vietnam. One of the great advantages of having a Brigadier over Special Ops section was the ability to intimidate subordinate commanders into getting things done. By 1972, there was a growing apathy among many U.S. military personnel about exposing themselves to unnecessary political or corporal peril. As always, there remained a stalwart core of gallant men and officers quite willing to go and do what they were told. Cross border flights into Laos were considered quite dangerous at any time, but by 1972, so much of the border was dotted by anti-aircraft emplacements, the daily sorties to Swordfish lair were becoming more and more difficult to coordinate, even with Bugeyes. General Dwight Elkins had done a splendid job of assuring that A-321 was well coordinated with both air-ground support as well as the ever-essential Bugeyes flyovers. General Creighton Abrams had, of course, been briefed on operation Fisherman. But, he could not dedicate a great deal of his attention toward what seemed a small, clandestine mission within the grand theater of operations over which he had command. General Abrams considered Brigadier General Elkins to be a competent, effective military leader who was doing a remarkable job of managing several very difficult operational objectives, and so it was with some trepidation that General Elkins was relieved.

Over the ten days preceding relief of command, Congressman Riley Hathoway had taken ample time to build some bird dog relationships with a cadre of politically expedient military officers. Most of these officers were West Point graduates. Most of them were also stars in a rising generation of what eventually became referred to as West Point Protective Association (WPPA) general officers. WPPA officers would be characterized as skilled tacticians who masterfully practiced the fine arts of shifting blame for error to others while stepping forward to take sole credit for worthy accomplishments of subordinates. Many of these officers had spent little time in forward line commands, although most had completed the process of making a career essential presence in Vietnam. A common theme among this unusual fraternity was looking after fellow West Point graduates no matter what the issue. One such WPPA officer materialized to take over the Special Air Operations position. Colonel Julius Ignatius Schultz was a New Englander from Hathoway's own home district. Colonel Schultz had risen within the military largely as an entity of the Quartermaster Corps. Schultz had managed to complete three tours in Vietnam, the first two of which were absolutely noncombatant. Feeling it would be a good career move, he wisely volunteered along the way for Airborne school and Special Forces Officers Basic Course. On his most recent Vietnam tour, more than four years prior, Schultz had managed to obtain command of a SOG Hatchet force company. Following his most noteworthy mission, Captain Schultz recommended himself for a DSC while commanding a mission in which he lost nearly a third of his command and abandoned his own men on the premise of being wounded himself. His WPPA colleagues assured that his requisition for the citation was properly forwarded. Since that time, Schultz had managed to rise in rank to Major, Lieutenant Colonel and finally, Full Colonel while occupying a cushy job in the Pentagon. He had risen as high as he could within military plutocracies passing in review before the Washington political parade circuit. Congressman Hathoway managed to get Schultz endorsed by two Federal Congressional Representatives and one Senator, all from the same party politic.

Prior to surrendering his command, General Elkins had briefed General Abrams on the nature and progress of Operation Fisherman. When General Abrams realized the urgency of keeping the project clandestine, he stood firm against continuing pressure to reveal the nature of the project beyond members of a Military Congressional Defense subommittee, who were already apprised and who sustained Abrams in his quest for confidentiality.

While Congressman Hathoway could not penetrate the veil of Operation Fisherman from without, it became clear to him that he stood a very good chance of doing so from within if he could influence the commissioning of Colonel Schultz. So it was, that under extreme pressure from several powerful political advocates within Hathoway's sphere of influence, Colonel Julius Schultz was recommended for command of I Corps Special Air Operations effective January 17, 1972. Prior to departing for Vietnam on January 15th, Schultz had a farewell luncheon at the Marriott Hotel in Pentagon City. Among guests and well-wishers in attendance was one Congressman Riley Hathoway, who took the occasion to speak privately with Colonel Schultz for about 25 minutes.

Swordfish Lair, January 15th, 1972

A large council fire had been constructed mid plain in the valley below Swordfish lair. By this time, much of the western plain was dotted with Longhouses and primitive agricultural efforts toward beginning a crop-line. Presiding over this council was Philip Suvete, the Bru Montagnard chieftain who had so capably kept up with growing populations in and around Swordfish lair. Seated about Chief Suvete were Captain Fernstead and MSG Briant as well as a number of village elders from various communities within AO Focus, including Hol mei, representing *Bai Lo Dui*. Gabe had been summoned to offer testimony before the group. At this present moment he sat back amid shadows in the fringe, alongside ever-cognizant Ca Rangh as she translated for him during the field congress. She was as always, leaning slightly toward his ear, whisper-speaking the words of various Montagnard dialects spoken before the grand council. The consortia represented an aria of fellowship between various villages within AO Focus, united together for the first time, here in this place, to discuss liberty, fired with the temperance of justice. Guided by American leadership, the notion of accountability for injustice fostered from an idyllic concept and grew into a mounting tempo of intention. As an awakening ethos within the people rose up against the heels of their political intimidators, they met in order to form agreements over accountability for transgressions of the powerful over the powerless.

The present subject of this grand council was NVA Regimental Field Commander Muc Bo Thau. Laid before the council were testimonials of various atrocities committed against people in the region. Throughout his tenure as regimental overlord, Commander Muc Bo Thau had made it clear that he was designated regent. Any act of brutality or authority performed by Communist soldiers within the limits of AO Focus had been willingly, publicly affirmed by Commander Thau. Through the vehicle of Propaganda and Harassment Patrols, Muc Bo Thau had terrorized these people in the name of Communism, forcing both Montagnards and Meo tribesmen into subservience. The Americans had come to this province and demonstrated that the communist provocaturs of Muc Bo Thau could be beaten. In the process, the Americans had also shown this people how to live with greater dignity. The Montagnards had more rice to silo, more food to distribute than at any time within the life-spans of most present. They were physically living better, organizing schools, primitive legislatures and a basic form of common judiciary with mutual codicils. Now, they were meeting collectively, united for the first time in congress over this area, to issue an indictment against the guardian of their adversity under communism, Regimental Field Commander Muc Bo Thau.

With bold determination, delegate village elders spoke out, decrying the horrors directed by Commander Thau. Throughout that late afternoon, and now well into the evening, survivors' testimonials were collected and transcribed. After all, Muc Bo Thau believed strongly in leaving behind survivors to tell the tales, so that fear might circulate as the true taskmaster over his serfdom. Survivors from the three largest villages; *Bai Lo Dui, Lo Dao*, and *Loc Phieu*, sequentially filled the docket on a sort of primitive, elevated dais, located in the center of the horseshoe shaped amphitheater constructed of rough timber and hewn earthworks. There were a great many indigenous citizenries present. Fernstead attempted to count, but lost track around a thousand and had to estimate in masses or blocks of humanity occupying square sections of the open-air forum. He was not a man given to exaggeration and so he estimated conservatively about 6,750 people present. In fact, there were closer to 7,500 men, women and children filling the broad plain west of Swordfish Lair.

Everyone present knew that by now, Muc Bo Thau would have infiltrators among the milieu of villages in attendance. One of the reasons why such gatherings had not taken place in the past was precisely because communist agents would infiltrate and subsequently report on potential ringleaders. In the past, whenever village councils had criticized, communist overlords were swift to punish democratic initiative. However, this congress had convened for the express purpose of revealing outrage, broiling in the hearts of these people. The principles of this grand encounter not only expected, indeed, they intended for news of their public denouncement to travel back to Commander Thau. It was a powerful statement of resentment, from a supposedly meek and perpetually impuissant people, now rising up against their masters. In this part of the world, it carried a poignant message that elevated a sense of being among the Montagnards and Hmong/Meo people, something referred to in the west as "Face". In so doing, their council cast a gauntlet down before Muc Bo Thau. It could not be ignored, particularly in the wake of events at *Bai Lo Dui* and *Loc Phieu*. Fernstead, Briant and Chief Suvete knew of a certainty that handing down this indictment would wave an anti-red flag right in the face of the communist bull from which only one of two consequences could result. Either the communist leader would back down and stop interfering with the people of this region, rather unlikely, or Commander Thau would come down on them full force in a resounding, high profile action that would certainly expose the violation of North Vietnamese invasion forces in Laos. The mission profilers for Operation Fisherman had projected this eventuality, anticipating an inevitable confrontation from the beginning. Vast air assets had been marshaled for on call mission support. Carefully planned firezone grids, long since laid out, were by this time clearly designated to various strategic forecast scenarios. If the communists came into these mountains, they would have to do so on foot. The rough mountainous terrain would not support track vehicles and it would take months, possibly years to cut roads into all of AO Focus. History had proven that enemy artillery could be brought in piecemeal on foot but, unlike Dien Bien Phu, artillery emplacements against Swordfish lair would be confined to ground strategically lower than the L-Site base camp. This geography left ballistic advantages of distance and accuracy to the defenders of Swordfish Lair. A natural cistern cut deep within the mountain would assure a continuous water supply. Food and ammunition stores stockpiled during the previous six months could sustain a very long siege. However, Operation Fisherman tacticians did not anticipate a sustained confrontation. With massive air assaults, the enemy could not hold unimproved fixed positions around Swordfish lair for long. Without their own air support, communist re-supply routes would be land bound and vulnerable to air raids along inbound arteries. With the incipient advantage of Bugeyes, enemy fusiliers could not conceal movement into or out of AO Focus.

Concurrent with Operation Fisherman, similar Lima sites had been established further north in Laos, scattered about the Plain of Jars. One such Lima site was already engaged in a life or death struggle at Long Thien. These camps were supplied out of Thailand via CIA funded, Thai based facilities such as Air America. They had also been engaged for many years in a back and forth struggle with the Pathet Lao, which, at this point, was inciting similar distractions for NVA units to the north. The overall scheme was to draw North Vietnamese enemy units illegally occupying Laos into several large, offensive maneuvers spread over diverse fronts. The resultant chaos of large troop engagements would certify North Vietnam as a Laotian invader. Then, with the deployment of U.S. air power, massed enemy units could be depleted. This engagement would eventually force Southern Laotian based NVA into withdrawal. As the communists regrouped, linkups between Montagnard and Meo elements would establish a defilade, eventually drawing a line between Thailand and Vietnam that would become the northern border of an independent Montagnard/Meo nation. As a fringe benefit, it would also eliminate the Ho Chi Minh Trail and thus leave the South Vietnamese with a secure western flank.

January 25th, 1972

Regimental Field Commander Muc Bo Thau held before him a document from his own military superiors up north. Nearly two weeks had passed since the request for reinforcements was passed up the line. Muc Bo Thau catalogued actions at *Bai Lo Dui* as well as *Loc Phieu* and the patrol lost at Buzzard's Gultch. His conclusions were that the Americans had established a large base camp in the mountains west of Aterat and that they would be shortly launching offensive operations to cut the Ho Chi Minh trail. The specter of such an action could not help but evoke a response from Hanoi. Although a bit exaggerated in content, the report he had forwarded provided Commander Thau with several essential bits of administrative leverage. First of all, it protected his own "Face" in the audience of his superiors who were well aware that he had taken a great many casualties over the previous few months. Secondly, it provided an impetus to reinforce his command for an all out assault on the American Base camp, now clearly located by agents who had attended the indictment council. *"Imagine those impudent Montagnards issuing an indictment against a high ranking Communist officer!"* Making such things public ran contrary to every doctrine of proper protocol in communist propaganda policies. Via forbidden public forums, it made the communists appear evil and oppressive. Commander Thau could not permit such notions to be circulating among his peasantry, at least, not out loud. The Communist propaganda machines tread a strange party line from western perspectives. This dichotomy was one of the problems that the American press had in narrowly focused interpretations of events during the war. While Communism did indeed employee brutality and cruelty as a matter of policy, it expressly forbid any open discussion about this, as such brutality and cruelty were forbidden by Mao Tse Tung's little red book of doctrine. What that book said was what the peasants were supposed to believe, taking in the centuries old form of a state-mandated philosophy, which had always existed, albeit previously in some sort of religion. This uprising among the border Montagnards would have to be crushed in a decisive manner that would send a clear and resounding message to all the other peasants who might be in doubt as to their proper loyalties.

Among other topics discussed within the document which Muc Bo Thau now read again, were details of the engagement at Long Thien in which Pathet Lao forces, heavily reinforced by NVA, had finally overrun the base and scored a decisive victory up north on the Laotian Plain of Jars. General Giap now intended to redeploy his troops for an all out offensive against South Vietnam come Spring. The action was described as something that would even surpass the Tet offensive in sheer manpower and overwhelming force of arms. The Politburo was virtually guaranteed that by the end of April, 1972, North and South Vietnam would become a single nation, united under Communist rule. With this mandate, Muc Bo Thau was assured of a troop presence within his area command. He would have to maneuver carefully to assure his retention of control over various command elements, distributed under his influence.

January 27th, 1972

The first salvo to launch the demise of Swordfish Lair came not from the West, but from the East. This arrived in the form of one Colonel Julius Ignatius Schultz who was holding his first meeting with a panel of officers from First Special Air Operations. Schultz had arrived in South Vietnam on January 17th per schedule. Three days later, on January 20th, a Change of Command ceremony took place, which formally passed command of I Corps Special Air operations from General Elkins to Colonel Schultz. Over the three days preceding this change of command ritual,

Elkins' staff had accounted for all assets within the outgoing command as well as past, present and ongoing mission designations. General Creighton Abrams had arrived for the command transition to review signatories, which relieved General Elkins and assigned Colonel Schultz to each aspect of his new command. It became clear right off that Schultz would be obtuse on every detail of assets and accountabilities.

While it was customary for some courtesy to be extended toward the outgoing CO, Schultz made it clear that because General Elkins was under congressional review, every item of inventory, every account budget line item, every personnel file, every bit of minutiae conceivable for scrutiny be revealed. Like an obnoxious IRS auditor, Schultz ungraciously pried into every possible administrative nook and cranny, searching for some evidence of disclosure prior to signing over on Special Air Operations. What he found was a meticulous command structure, well administered and entirely accounted for without fault. Although this should have warranted some degree of respect toward the outgoing General Elkins, Schultz's disingenuous manner left a bad pallor hanging over the entire change of command ceremony. General Abrams was quite certain he would have problems with Schultz, but he could not submit a request for another change of command without at least giving Schultz a chance. Now, one week after assumption of his new command, Schultz was finally getting around to covert operations, a responsibility currently under his authority. The present briefing was all about Operation Fisherman. Schultz necessarily had to be briefed now that he had near total control over air assets for the mission. After the briefing, as was customary, the briefing panel offered to answer questions about the nature and concept of the mission. Schultz had listened to the entire presentation with an air of mounting tension. He now burst open like a spurned bride: "Do you mean to tell me that this operation has been going on since last May in direct contravention to the Cooper-Church amendment? And, how in the world did General Elkins justify all of these expensive air assets to just this one mission in support of one illegal Special Forces A team operating up in those mountains? And, why the hell isn't this new system, what do you call it, Bugeyes? Why isn't it being made available to support regular ground troops where it could be of much greater use as an asset to South Vietnamese forces?"

The panel of briefing officers for Operation Fisherman collectively paused to regain a moment of lost composure. Each man in the panel wondered if this new Commander of Special Air Operations had even listened to their brief. The spokesman for this group, a Lieutenant Colonel Carlock, looked back at Colonel Schultz with a deep, somber gaze that Schultz found himself having trouble trying to stare down. The Lieutenant Colonel responded: "Sir, I thought we made this clear from the beginning. The personnel with whom this Special Forces team are working have all professed themselves to be Laotian citizens. Most of them were born in Laos. Therefore, there is no contravention of the Cooper-Church Amendment. That fact has been thoroughly reviewed and certified by the U.S. Congressional Defense Committee. The purpose of this mission is to give the Montagnards an even chance of surviving as a race after the United States becomes divested of Southeast Asia. There is a very real chance they will be subjected to systematic genocide once Ethnic Vietnamese resolve their own conflicts."

"Look Lieutenant Colonel Carlock, or whatever your name is…. I understand you are a CIA liaison assigned to this project because someone supposedly important thought you had some expertise in these matters. Let's get this straight. First of all, I don't like anyone impersonating an officer under my command. I'm not even certain your rank is official and if it's not, I want those Silver Leaves off today. If you are a legitimate officer under my command, you will be identified with a proper name tag. Secondly, as far as I'm concerned, Montagnards are Vietnamese. That means they are a Vietnamese problem. I think it should be up to the Vietnamese how they expend their military assets with respect to the Montagnards. Finally, and let me make this clear from the start, this is *my* command. I and I alone will make the final decision on all ops that deploy out of I Corps Special Air. *Are we clear on this?*"

The nametagless Lieutenant Colonel Carlock was silent for a moment, obviously exercising some inner Chi to reign in his rising rage. In the silent few seconds that ensued, he did not wither at all before Schultz's attempt at intimidating glower. Carlock weighed options on a number of responses. Unlike others on the committee who were fuming at this point, LTC Carlock had a gift for keeping himself detached in such situations. Although only words, his response must be measured, and most important, it must be for the good of the mission, not a vent for his own personal feelings toward this obsequious new Commanding Officer. Actually, this was not the first time they had confronted one another, though Colonel Schultz did not realize it at the time. In the end, the Lieutenant Colonel determined that his best tack was simply to walk away quietly and muster whatever external influences would be necessary to remove Colonel Schultz as a roadblock to Operation Fisherman.

"We are clear sir."

Something in the unexpected timidity of the response tweaked Schultz. Perhaps it was the rock hard, cold blue eyes that even now refused to back off. Schultz decided to push the envelope a bit. "As of now, fixed wing air support for Operation Fisherman is suspended. I am limiting rotary wing air assets to Pleiku, meaning there will be no, I repeat, no fixed or rotary wing air support for this project deploying out of Da Nang. I am also shutting down any ARSP's (Ammunition and Refueling Supply Points), which may be illegally stationed along the border. You contact the Americans on that L-Site and get them out. That is the only air support I will authorize. I am shutting down Operation Fisherman!"

Several members of the committee for Operation Fisherman started to respond at once, the no name Lieutenant Colonel silenced them all by raising his hand. "With all due respect, sir.

You do not have the authority to shut this mission down. Project oversight comes directly from a Congressional Defense subcommittee. Administrative supervision comes directly through the JFK Center at Fort Bragg. Your role in this is one of support. If you feel that you are unable to do your duty in this, we will be happy to convey your position back through our own administrative chain of command."

Colonel Schultz rose from his desk, red faced with livid rage. "Listen *Lieutenant* Colonel! As of now, in this little piece of the pie *I* call the shots. In case you haven't noticed, *I* am the ranking officer in this room! You are not the only ones who have a legislative ace in the hole on this matter. I am acting on direct orders from Congressman Riley Hathoway of New England who's trying to get us out of this abortion you all have cooked up across the border! Now, you do as I say or I'll see to it that all of your tickets are punched on your way out of here!"

Lieutenant Colonel Carlock remained calm in the face of Schultz's tirade, quietly digesting this latest bit of information on the new player, a New England Congressman? All the while, the Lieutenant Colonel maintained an unblinking continence in response to Colonel Schultz, which of course only further aggravated Schultz. One last attempt was made at reasoning with Schultz. "Look sir, I understand better now what sort of pressure you are under if there is an unauthorized Congressional delegate attempting to interfere in this operation. This Congressman Hathoway, Riley Hathoway you said? He most certainly does not sit on the Congressional Defense committee, which is the only Federal authority with whom we are authorized to communicate on matters concerning Operation Fisherman. Please sir, understand that this mission has been very carefully planned and coordinated. It satisfies every legal tenant of the Cooper Church amendment as certified by both Congressional and legal scholars. Sir, with all due respect, you do hold the influence at this time to cause considerable damage to the mission. But, why would you want to do so? Fisherman is the single most credible mission within your theatre of command at this time. If you review your budget, you'll find that more resource funding has been allocated in support of Operation Fisherman than any other single mission designation. Why would you want to lessen your resources by closing down this project?"

Colonel Schultz sat back down in his seat, no longer even attempting to meet the penetrating eyes of his subordinate. "Well it's like this. You see, Lieutenant Colonel, I've been playing this game long enough to know that figures lie and liars figure. By the time we finish reviewing the funding allocations for this command, I am quite certain we will find there has been a misallocation of funds in support of this illegal and unauthorized operation, no doubt encouraged by my immediate predecessor. I have it on good authority that's why he *is* now my predecessor and I am in command here. Once these facts are proven, the previous Commander of this base will have to face the music. If you are not all careful, you could go down with him."

Clearly, it was pointless to discuss anything further with Schultz. Someone, probably this Congressman Hathoway, had influenced the new commander to believe it was in his own best interest to play the zealot. Of course, Schultz would have to be replaced. That was obvious to everyone except Schultz. However, all the committee members of Operation Fisherman knew that, *"whilest the wheels of the gods turn with great resolve, they turn ever so slowly."* It would take some time to cycle out Colonel Schultz. The rising imperative at this juncture was to secure his removal before he did irreparable harm to Operation Fisherman.

January 28*th*, 1972

SSG Thomas Gowen entered the CP with a distinct wrinkle of concern on his suntanned brow. Captain Fernstead sensed the welcome intrusion of another body in what he considered his own administrative dungeon and looked up from a partially typed report to greet the communications NCO with a smile.

"Sir, something I thought you should know about. For the first time since we been here, Bugeyes is off the net. I got a transmission from the last flyover this morning at about 0540, telling me that they was at Bingo fuel and no relief had arrived on station to replace their watch. Bugeyes had to head back to Da Nang to refuel and we got no eyes in the skies."

Although this news raised an alarm in Fernstead's mind, he replied calmly as always, which put Gowen transiently at ease. "Well, it's been almost nine months now and they've never missed a guard post once. It was probably inevitable that they would make a little screw up sooner or later. Let's give them a shift change, six hours, and if no replacement has arrived on station, send an AM burst back to Bragg alerting them of the discrepancy. In the meantime, as soon as the next bird takes station, let me know."

"Yes sir." Gowen went back to the commo bunker, a domain of electronics and radios. He felt secure within his own den of transmission and reception technology. He was confident that the most powerful weapon known to man was still communication. Over the next four hours, SSG Gowen maintained a vigilant scrutiny over the Bugeyes net, awaiting a call-sign alert that they were again watched over, but it never came. Being fastidious in his duty, Gowen had the AM transmission burst ready to go five and a half hours later. He confirmed the message with Fernstead before sending it and in the process, could not help but noticing just a shadow of concern in the staid L-site camp commander.

It was nearly 20 hours later, the following morning, in which a reply came back from Fort Bragg, half a world away. Gowen prepared the report after deciphering it through the NEBO code system, using a key phrase from page 122, line 14 of Louis L'Amour's Western Novel, "Galloway (The Sacketts, No.13)". He took it in to Fernstead as soon as the entire message was broken out. Captain Fernstead read concern in the eyes of his senior communications NCO as he accepted and signed for the logged in message.

Classified – Top Secret Document, COVER-SHEET REQUIRED

Dispatch # <u>1072</u>

From: USAIMA, Special Operations Command

L Site-321 HQ Area Focus

Code Name: Fisherman

Saturday, 29 January 1972.

SUBJECT: Bugeyes surveillance over AO Focus

TO: Fernstead, Ronald, Captain, Commanding

II. GENERAL:

BE ADVISED THAT EFFECTIVE 0530 HRS. 28 JANUARY, 1972, BUGEYES SURVEILLANCE AVAILABILITY HAS BEEN INTEREFERED WITH IN PROSECUTION OF MISSION OBJECTIVES FOR FISHERMAN. EFFORTS ARE UNDERWAY TO CORRECT THIS DEFICIENCY. SUGGEST IMPLIMENTATION OF CONVENTIONAL GROUND RESOURCES INTELLIGENCE GATHERING METHODS DURING FORSEEABLE FUTURE, IE LRP, LP AND LOCAL ASSET INQUIRIES.

    A. IN ADDITION IT MAY BE DIFFICULT TO OBTAIN DEDICATED AIR SUPPORT AT ALL HOURS AS HAS BEEN AVAILABLE UP TO THIS TIME. RECOMMEND YOU DELAY TIMELINE TOWARD CONFRONTATION WITH ULTIMATE ENEMY RESOURCES.

    B. MAINTAIN CONTACT WITH THIS UNIT COMMAND POST THREE TIMES DAILY ON EIGHT HOUR SEQUENTS USING BRAVO DELTA CODE TIME SEQUENCE FOUR LIMA CHARLIE

    C. RECOMMEND YOU BRING IN AS MANY INDIGENOUS NON COMBATANTS AS CAN BE ACCOMMODATED WITHIN THE PERIMETER OF SWORDFISH LAIR.

Chapter 9 – Siege

February, 1972

Tuesday, February 8th, 1972

The explosion happened suddenly, unexpectedly, knocking down sterile packs and liter bottles of saline from shelves in the hospital bunker. Gabriel had been making rounds, checking on a patient recovering from Schistosomiasis, when he was rocked along with everyone else in the bunker by the concussion. Prior to the loud intrusion, he had been distantly aware of the daily chorus of helicopter rotors as mission designated Huey Slicks changed station every other morning. Typically, one of the Americans would assume the role of LZ landing guide in clearing the departing Huey as a replacement hung in the sky just northwest of Swordfish Lair. Fortunately, the enemy mortar round missed both helicopters, erupting on a sandbagged southern wall of the hospital bunker, situated south of the landing pad. Although the hardy structure effectively shielded any impact on the helo LZ, the effect on helicopter crews was obvious. Both crews on the lightly armed slicks knew that an enemy mortar crew zeroing in on a fixed LZ was a very bad thing. Both pilots immediately waved off the LZ and proceeded to fly off, outside any perceived trajectories into the Lima Site.

Over the previous week and a half, since losing Bugeyes, the Americans had taken all possible local precautions toward gathering intelligence on a growing enemy presence that seemed to be

rising like a menacing, insidious flood tide from the west. Without the extraordinary reconnaissance advantage of their high-fly-
ing observer in the sky, camp defenders of Swordfish Lair were
limited to reconnaissance in force using radio linked listening and
observation posts. Patrols which had previously roamed with remarkable cunning given all the advantage of foreknowledge, now
had to be more cautious, with greater dilution of friendly probing
forces than had been previously necessary. The loss of Bugeyes
reconnaissance could not have come at a worse time. Because
the enemy had previously been distracted by events in Cambodia, there was little focus on this desolate, mountainous terrain
in Southern Laos. Now, communist units were returning to Laos
for R&R as well as reinforcements for the Ho Chi Minh trail. It
appeared from what intelligence Fernstead had available, that the
Communists were positioning for an all out siege. The Americans
received information about enemy construction going on around
the far fringes of AO Focus from the area of *Bai Lo Dui*. Track
vehicles had been able to move at least that close. However, it
would take many months to construct adequate roads in these
mountains and many more before they could get heavy vehicles
any closer than *Bai Lo Dui*. What concerned everyone most were
reports of massing ground troops and the more numerous enemy
reconnaissance patrols that had by now most certainly located and
targeted this, the heart of AO Focus. Today marked the first time
since its installation that Swordfish Lair had come within range
of a Chicom 82 mm mortar. When the first round exploded,
SSG. Philip Volkert had been near by the chopper-landing pad,
occupying the role of LZ guide-on, assisting in the exchange of
outgoing and incoming helicopters. The 1st enemy mortar round
hit about 50 meters away from Volkert's location at the landing
panels, striking on the other side of the hospital bunker. SSG.
Volkert knew at once what was happening. He correctly anticipated that a second round would follow, about 45 seconds later.
When it hit, that second round landed southeast of the landing
pad. It exploded on open ground. Fortunately, it did not injure

anyone because the entire camp had responded to shouts of "Incoming!" Almost everyone had scurried off into well-rehearsed trenches and/or foxholes dug around the perimeter of the camp. During the three-quarter minute bracketing round lag, Volkert dashed over to one of the western mortar pits. Although a designated Combat Engineer, Volkert was very good with mortars. He had this intuitive sense for perceiving a conus arc in space. Some tube gunners in Vietnam just seemed to have such a gift. It took him less than 30 seconds to drag out a box of six High Explosive 81 mm projectiles in a sequence well rehearsed during numerous incoming reaction drills over the previous months. As he pulled out the first round, his eyes began surveying the western landscape down below. Without distracting his gaze, Volkert's right hand fingered a lightly crimped cotter pin fuse. He pulled it out, dropping it unseeingly to the ground. This activated a point-of-contact detonation fuse on the projectile warhead. Volkert had already hung the rocket shaped charge with both hands, fins down, just caressing the upper, innermost lip of the tube. There! He caught it as a subtle, telltale puff of dust arising from a slight clump of jungle on fringes of the western plain. In the few milliseconds passing between eyes, brain and hands, Volkert recognized the location of the enemy mortar site and mentally bracketed the position. He could almost recognize it just for sheer strategic logic. Nudging the ribbed cylinder of his 81mm aiming tube momentarily with his left hand, Volkert let the explosive round drop down the tube. The primer behind the fins struck a pin at the base of the tube. This resulted in a loud "WHUMP!" along with a violent repercussion against the baseplate. The tube belched a blurry, dark wad of energy skyward and before it even hit, Volkert had another round hanging precipitously over the tube orifice as his keen eyes sought the impact point of his first round. Just about that time the enemy's third round hit within 20 meters of the landing pad, but by this time, both helicopters had risen up in a wide, high racetrack course around the perimeter of Swordfish Lair, pilots maneuvering desperately to avoid flying a perpendicular track under dueling parabolic mortar trajectories.

Scanning for the mortar-site, which he had already pinpointed, Volkert watched as his 1st round struck; "There!" Just to the left of where he perceived the enemy gunners to be. He instinctively calculated the slight movement necessary to adjust his tube. He realized at the same moment that his own position was now evident to them as well. This was confirmed as an answering round from the brier patch below caused another puff of dust to rise up within the lush jungle. During 5 seconds or so that it took before the enemy 82 struck, Volkert had dropped two rounds and was in the process of dropping his third when he felt the enemy round's impact behind and to his right. They were attempting to walk their tube from the known last impact point to his position here in the mortar pit. But they were doing it methodically, adjusting with small turns of cranks on the mount of their tubular gun. Volkert was answering instinctively, not waiting for one round to strike as he adjusted the tube with nudges and tugs. WHUMP!... WHUMP!... WHUMP! By now, the recoil baseplate of the tube was settling into a deepening recess within the pit. The tube itself had become scalding hot and was burning his hands, but Volkert was oblivious as he watched for the strike of his barrage. The first round of the volley hit. It was just off right of where he believed to be the exact location. The second round hit just a bit behind. The third round landed dead on, lighting the very patch of jungle from which telltale dust clouds had heralded the enemy's position. That third round produced an extraordinary fireworks display as secondary explosions cooked off, creating a sudden umbrella of smoke and blast, cratering the jungle floor.

Lieutenant Erickson had climbed up to the observation platform atop Swordfish Lair's central crag. He was in communication with the two Huey pilots on a common frequency net dialed in at number 72 on his PRC-77. One of the birds was circling over the blast site, headed northwest, passing over just as the secondaries burnt off. Turbulence caused the pilot's cyclic to bounce in his right hand and the entire helicopter shuddered from the intensified atmosphere over the obliterated enemy position below. Both pilots reported at once, jamming the net.

Estrada was first to run across and jump into Volkert's mortar pit, embracing his smaller comrade in a big bear hug.

"HEY! AMIGO! Dat was some shooting eh?"

Volkert was occupied at that moment with trying to secure two remaining 81 mm rounds he had lying at his feet back into their wooden rack, when he found himself plucked up into the bigger man's arms. Estrada's embrace took away his breath for a moment, and when Grit Volkert finally shrugged himself loose he grumped back,

"Yo Compadre! Let's not get all warm and friendly while I'm juggling live rounds here, huh?"

Estrada had incidentally noted that the safety pins were in place and considered that secure enough to unleash his unbridled *machisimo* for the smaller framed Volkert.

"You got some eye with that tube, *hermano*. Good thing you was closest to it. I think we need you in the pits when all hell begins to break loose around here eh?"

By this time, others had gathered around to congratulate Volkert on his exceptional duel. Fernstead resolved to put in yet another recommendation for commendation, which due to the clandestine nature of operation Fisherman would probably never get reviewed. Gabriel came out with Ca to survey damage on the hospital bunker. Once again, the legacy of Glickman was felt in the nature of this structure that the senior *Bac si* had been so much a part of designing. Gabe recalled having thought back at the beginning when they were sandbagging everything in that Glickman was overdoing it by building out the lowermost, first layer of sandbags 12 wide and sloping up from there to a hipped roof, cross gabled into the central crag. Nowhere in its construction was the field hospital bunker less than 6 sandbags deep. The ceiling weight had been enormous, necessitating extra reinforcement with steel load bearing I-beams, and two large upright column supports. However, the wisdom of this foresight could be surveyed now as everything held together under the concussion of the 82 mm warhead. None of the patients within had been worsened by the event. It appeared that the only thing to repair would be about four sandbags, blown open by the initial impacting round.

As it turned out, repairing the hospital bunker was perhaps the least of contingencies enacted as a result of the incident. It somehow came to the attention of Colonel Schultz that air-crews under his command were being placed in what he considered to be unnecessary jeopardy by leaving a "cold" helicopter daily on the ground deep in enemy territory. He thereafter issued orders that from that time on, any designated helicopter support teams would have to station out of DaNang or Pleiku without ever turning off their engines at Swordfish Lair. These meant that Huey C Slicks tasked to Operation Fisherman could in essence only fly into Swordfish Lair and either pick up or drop off after which, due to fuel constraints, they would have to return immediately to their ground station at one of the two secure airbases within South Vietnam. It meant the loss of immediate aerial support for rapid response teams and squad sized deployments. It extended the time necessary for a ground unit to walk from the top of Swordfish Lair to the valley below from just a few Heliborne minutes to over half a day. It was another considerable setback for the mission.

Over the next couple of weeks, Fernstead had to withdraw his reconnaissance elements back in closer and closer to Swordfish Lair as evidence of advancing enemy probes reached deeper and deeper into the mountains. The enemy was detailing with increasing clarity the exact location and nature of the L-Site stronghold. One of the greatest disadvantages of static, fixed defensive positions is the capacity for a dynamic offensive force to have complete superiority of intelligence over defenses, which do not move with time. While Spectre gunships were still available, smaller echelons of helicopter attack units could not remain on station for long. Without the advantages of Bugeyes to track and coordinate delivery of air support, by the time air assets arrived on scene, situations on the ground could change considerably. Radio links with field reconnaissance units on the ground could not consistently direct accurate fire without disclosing their own presence. In any given area, handheld Radio Direction Finding (RDF) equipment used by the communists could quickly pinpoint transmitting positions. In well-rehearsed communist field enclavement maneuvers, the Montagnards and their American Advisors would be quickly cut off. Being savvy to this, the Americans and their Montagnard/Hmong allies took every precaution to assure contingencies but despite it all, several reconnaissance units had some very narrow escapes. It is quite difficult to see without being seen in mountainous jungles. The jungle was neutral. It favors neither side. It created hardships for both Communists and Allies. But the communists were so much more numerous, theirs became the advantage of attrition. It is very difficult to direct fire with any considerable accuracy while running for your life. Although upbeat and exercising every available field asset with amazing expediency, it was quite clear to the entire camp administration that a noose was closing around Swordfish Lair.

Thursday, February 10th, 1972, Da Nang, South Vietnam

"That is absolutely correct. No aircraft deploying out of Taiwan will be refueled at Da Nang without my express consent. Specifically, no aircraft dedicated to any clandestine missions involving this new look down technology will be serviced under my command until such time as I and my South Vietnamese counterparts have been further briefed on the nature of this air asset." Colonel Schultz clamped down the phone with a derisive bang, which he imagined would make the "click" heard on the other end sound all that more ominous. *"This will send them a clear message about who's in charge here,"* It had taken just a week and a half to ferret out and shut down all the cleverly disbursed resources for Operation Fisherman. Someone, probably that no-name CIA spook posing as a Lieutenant Colonel, was clearly at work distributing physical assets in such a way as to make them less visible to Schultz's withering scrutiny. Just yesterday, Colonel Schultz had discovered a bevy of four old Huey C model helicopters with an elaborate maintenance pod located in one of his own hangers here at Da Nang. On paper, they were simply four old helicopters listed under secondary maintenance and support roles. Had he not been keenly aware of other veiled assets supporting Operation Fisherman, he might also have overlooked this one for all its meek appearance on administrative paperwork. These helicopters were evidently being used to rotate in and out of an on site heli-pad located at the clandestine L-Site. Upon discovering the presence of the covert flight bay, Colonel Schultz had gone directly over to the old hanger, located diagonally opposite his command post at the other end of the air base compound. On arrival, Schultz encountered an impressively efficient maintenance crew, surprisingly well supplied. Posing as an interested commander, he queried the flight and maintenance crews in a cordial manner, extracting from them considerably greater detail about their role in Operation Fisherman than he had previously been aware of. Schultz even discovered that just a couple days prior, an enemy mortar barrage had fired on two of these helicopters, involved in their remote site station rotation. When asked why he had not read a report on this action, Colonel Schultz was informed that the flight logs and reports were always forwarded directly to a courier from Fort Bragg who transmitted them back to the States during bi-weekly shuttle flights. Again, the enormity of this project resource allocation astonished Schultz who directed the flight crew to forward him a carbon copy of all paperwork concerning Operation Fisherman as well as all flight logs and after action reports filed with the courier. Colonel Schultz then returned back to his headquarters wherein he proceeded to disband the C-Slick maintenance hanger on paper and reallocate its inventory among other air assets within his command. In addition, he went back over flight tower logs of all incoming and outgoing aircraft using the airstrips at Da Nang. It did not take him long to find the courier aircraft, a civilian Lear jet on consignment to the U.S. Army of all things! One of these aircraft arrived twice a week and had to be refueled there at Da Nang before returning back on a three-leg flight path with refueling stops in Hawaii and Travis AFB in California. It seemed truly amazing that they would dedicate such expense in just fuel alone to this one mission! He could not fathom the concept of compartmentalization on this issue and simply figured they were taking assets away from his own command. To his way of thinking, these were budget line items that he should have been able to use at his own discretion. He had already stopped the Bugeyes overflights by simply refusing to refuel blackbird surveillance aircraft. During an earlier era, these aircraft might have been able to use Thailand as an alternative fueling station, but with the decline of Air America and pressures from Washington to eliminate CIA presence in Thailand, that corridor was shut off as well. It was virtually impossible to cross any aircraft over I Corps without coming under Colonel Schultz's scrutiny. And Colonel Schultz also made it clear that in an effort to improve US-South Vietnamese military advisorship, he would entertain a liaison from the office of President Thieu who would be informed of any activity involving over-flights of Vietnam. By the end of the first two weeks of February, 1972, Colonel Schultz was able to report back to his good friend, Congressman Riley Hathoway, that he had fulfilled his directive to eliminate essential air assets for this illegal clandestine operation code named Fisherman. Over the phone, Hathoway praised Colonel Schultz for his leadership and dedication to the laws of the United States. With all the eloquent diction of a professional politician, Hathoway assured Colonel Schultz that he was demonstrating a special kind of courage in standing up to misguided and renegade influences within the U.S. military. Hathoway assured Colonel Schultz that work was already in progress to issue the Brigadier's star that he so justly deserved. Colonel Julius I. Schultz just ate it up.

Monday, February 14, 1972, Swordfish Lair

Captain Ron Fernstead made a simple command decision. He set aside everything else on his encumbered field desk and imposed an essential task into his very busy schedule. He feared that, if over looked now, it might never be properly attended to. He sat poised over a yellow legal notepad, using the same lined yellow pages, which had occupied so many rough drafts of ideas, directives, orders and communications over the previous 10 months. Again he thought how un-elegant it must seem to his wife when she should read his letters on such complacent stationary. There was simply no chance to obtain any decent formal stationary here in the field. And so, he was left with writing, oftentimes-intimate thoughts, on a very plain medium. All private correspondence out of Swordfish Lair was sent in plain, white, unsealed envelopes. This was because every personal letter had to pass through a mail censor back at Fort Bragg. The censor consisted of an intelligence officer, Major Julien Scadlock, who would decide what could and what could not be sent on through. Often, letters were delayed while segments of the letter were read and occasionally blacked out or retyped, eliminating what might be considered compromising information. Knowing this, it made any expression of deeply personal sentiments rather difficult. However, on this occasion, Valentine's Day, Ron Fernstead felt it absolutely necessary to compose a very personal letter to his wife.

14 February, 1972

My Darling Diane

This evening I am in a place far away from you, but know that I am very close to you in my heart. Again, I am so thankful for the fine details of your face and body that are inscribed upon my heart and mind.. You have given that to me during the precious little time it has been my greatest privilege to spend with you. In my minds eye, I feel you here with me now, the twinkle in your eyes, the posture of your walk, the sweet smelling fall of your hair, which summons me away from all other concerns. From the moment I laid eyes upon you, I have loved you and been all amazed that you could love me back. That you have accepted this old soldier into your life, knowing me for who I am and what I am made of is certainly the greatest joy I have ever known..

You once said that you loved me for the sum total of all that I am and that you had decided even before I asked you to be my wife that it would make you very happy to "take on the whole package of everything that is Ron Fernstead". I can only hope that over these last few years, you still feel the same. You must know by now that a great deal of what I am has to do with command and the responsibilities that come with command. I have been called away from you to serve this command. It is to a noble cause. One that I believe you would approve of if you could know all the details of our mission. While you must know I cannot tell you a great deal about why, where or what I am doing here, suffice to say that a great many very good people are relying upon me to bring them through a terrible crisis that may demand considerable sacrifice. I want you to clearly understand that the most important thing in my life is our family, you and the kids. However, a vital part of what has made us a family, the things that have caused us to love each other, involve duty, honor and country. I have been called to this duty. You have similarly been called to serve our country, to honor all of my burdens in absentia, which I clearly understand must be more difficult for you than anything I have been called upon, or will be called upon, to do here.

As a soldier's wife, you must know that we may both be summoned to share a soldier's fate. Whatever happens here over the next few weeks, please know that I will do my best and that I shall measure every decision by the gauge of what would make you proud to say that you are my wife. Please know that I am so proud to be your husband, and shall always be.

I do not wish to bother you with these concerns, but it is most important to me that you convey to our children some few things I want them to always know. First and above all, that their Father loves their Mother. Secondly, that they are very, very much loved by both their Mother and their Father. Third, I want them to know that they are fortunate to have been born in our country, the United States of America. It is a nation that will offer them all the opportunity they might be willing to strive for, which will empower them to be all they can be in this life. But they must understand that such privilege does not come without sacrifice.

A great many good men and women, some of them our own ancestors, have been willing to give all, up to the last full measure, in order to assure that their children, and our children, will have the privilege of being born into a nation that is truly a free land. Our children must never take this for granted. They must never be lulled into complacency over privileges which they will grow up with through no effort of their own. They must know their legacy, a legacy that is handed down to them through a veil of blood, sweat and tears from many others who have gone before. Our children must know that all the sacrifices which will have gone before shall be justified, shall be honored, if they succeed in attaining something of value with their lives, something that can only be defined by the substance of their individual talents and efforts.

Beyond these things, what it all comes down to is this. I love you Diane. I will always love you with every fiber of who I am and what I may become. Please forgive me for those times in which I have not been there to shoulder the burden of our family. Fortunately, you have been blessed with a strength, which I know can carry us all through no matter what happens.

And now, this one last thing; if something should happen to me, I want you to go on. I want you to live and love, to care for and to be cared for by whatsoever, or _whomsoever_ your best judgement and a benevolent providence might provide. Know that I will always be with you, through our children, through our memories, through whatever fate lies beyond the limits of this mortal sojourn, you shall always be:

My most beloved wife

All my love

Ron

Wednesday, February 16th, 1972; NVA 639th Regimental Field Headquarters

Commander Muc Bo Thau was present throughout the siege of LS-85 at *Phou Pha Thi* in 1968. He had served as intelligence officer, feeding information to siege commanders who ultimately tore down the "unassailable sky fortress". Muc Bo Thau was a field Major at the time. He had argued against the use of Soviet

Biplanes which, above his objections, the North Vietnamese engaged anyway in a most remarkable attempt to emulate World War I tactics on the mountaintop fortification. The North Vietnamese Air Force was eager for a victory and wanted to demonstrate their own capacity to use air power against their enemies. Soviet surplus Anotov AN-2 Colts, single engine bi-planes were used against LS-85. They circled overhead firing machine guns down on the camp and dropping mortar shells as bombs. It took only a single Air America helicopter door gunner to take out both planes, thus humiliating the anachronistic North Vietnamese air force in yet another example of American dominance over the skies. Almost exactly two months after the biplane debacle, three battalions of 766th NVA overwhelmed the site by launching a diversionary ground assault against the sloped compound entrance while several hundred NVA commandos scaled the 5600 foot cliff side. In so doing, they overran the compound, capturing and/or killing several of the American Air Force advisors as well as their indigenous support troops. Muc Bo Thau had planned the details of the cliff-side assault. He spent most of February, 1968 training NVA commandos and working out climbing logistics. It was in large measure his success at that venture that propelled him upward and onward to his current command within the North Vietnamese Army.

At the present moment, Commander Thau was experiencing a bit of Deja Vu as he studied rough sketches of the mountain atop which, Swordfish Lair was situated. Unlike LS-85, which had at least some scanty aerial intelligence from the Anatov's, as yet, Muc Bo Thau knew little about the upper surface geography of Swordfish Lair. *"This will surely prove to be an even more challenging fortress than the one they called Lima Site-85,"* he thought. Like LS-85, it posed sheer cliff walls on the western side, but unlike LS-85, other sides of the mountain fortress were sharply contoured with one, relatively small land bridge leading into the compound from graduating jungle elevation on the east. "What was it they called this place? 'Swordfish Lair?' What was that...the den of a swordfish?" Muc Bo Thau wondered absently if there really was such a thing as a "swordfish". In any event, he had learned a great deal about this bristling mountain retreat during the last few weeks. Interestingly, some of his most useful intelligence had come from Saigon instead of Hanoi. The South Vietnamese military regime was like a great leaky sieve of information. It was one of the benefits of a corrupt society that secrets could be purchased by the highest bidder. Interestingly, in the matter of this "Swordfish Lair", it was almost as if the South Vietnamese *wanted* him to know about what they considered to be yet another Montagnard insurrection. This time, it seemed as though ARVN was leaving it up to the North to extinguish the scoriae of Montagnard independence once and for all. In the process of gathering data on the bold American venture to support development of a separate Montagnard state, many questions had also been answered about a new spy weapon the Americans were using for monitoring body heat. They called it "bugeyes", a most appropriate aphorism. Clearly, it altered the scales in their favor far too drastically to leave the Americans with such an advantage. Already, steps had been taken at the behest of Hanoi to shut the system down through covert means, including the recruitment of unwitting allies in the United States itself. "That is the greatest weakness which the Americans have. Their systems are so impressively complex that it only takes one small part to make the whole machine malfunction," Commander Thau mused, not for the first time.

With the same cunning, calculating talent for tactics that propelled him up through the ranks of his countrymen, Commander Thau set about assembling elements to absolutely assure the destruction of this base camp, Swordfish Lair. His first step was to secure approval for added manpower and supplies from Hanoi. In order to do so, he'd had to exaggerate by a rather wide margin, the size and force of the enemy. However no matter what the size of the enemy, Hanoi understood the strategic importance of displacing this American grown hornet's nest right in the middle of their own Laotian fairway to the south. In the present circumstance, it seemed to Commander Muc Bo Thau that squashing a bug with a boulder was in order. Accordingly, he requested to lay siege with the entire resources of his own regiment as well as a reserve regiment to run operational re-supply routes and take the place of his own support structures along the Ho Chi Minh trail. Between the vast resources of two entire regiments, he could construct a most impressive assault force. It so happened that in addition to his own 639th regiment, he was provided the 766th for support. This same 766th had successfully assaulted Lima Site-85 four years earlier. Stories of the historic siege had grown to legendary stature among the men of the NVA 766th over time. Of course, veteran NVA NCO's who sustained the core leadership structure within the 766th knew better. Some of them had participated in the 5600 foot ascent up the exposed western rock face of that complex. They were keenly aware of how vulnerable they had been, naked to gravity and whatever horrors could have been rained down upon them from the Americans and Laotians up above. However, thanks to Buddha or whatever, LS-85 defenders had remained preoccupied, fighting off a feint attack from the east. It was certainly one of the most impressive vertical assaults in military history, although in the end, they had to win; simply out of sheer numbers. Commander Muc Bo Thau intended to use these veteran mountain climbers to train a whole new generation of intrepid mountain troops, even larger than the assault force used against LS-85. As a mark of distinction, soldiers of the 766th were permitted to wear the so-called "black pajama" commando uniforms instead of characteristic chartreuse field uniforms of NVA regulars. The simple, black homespun tunic and trousers made famous by the Viet Cong, provided better freedom of movement and would blend in with contour shadows for the night climb. They had begun training in mid January and were by this time a formidable force of stout, muscular, spider like soldiers eager to test their mettle against the arrogant American squatters.

That first mortar barrage on February 8th was the beginning of a series of ploys to harass and bracket the base camp. The Americans and their allies, however, had been very clever about clearing out ranges from western and southern elevations, particularly following that first barrage. Because of the remote location of Swordfish Lair, without roads, larger communist artillery such as wheeled 130 mm guns could not be transported into the mountains. The only really practical artillery the Communists could bring by mountain trail back into so primitive an area were Chicom 82 mm mortars, which were pretty evenly matched with the US 81 mm, given a level playing field. The problem for Commander Thau was that this fortress was not level with any decent fusillade corridors below. Following that initial mortar duel, the Allies had expanded their defensive perimeter using detchord and explosive cutting charges to extend western and southern visual fields down below Swordfish Lair. There were jungles to the east, but they were quite dense and the trek around to them initially required a four-day hike over elevations south and east without any hope of vehicular re-supply. There were lesser mountains to the north and northwest, but they were hardly more than impassable rocky crags above the vegetation line. Within that line, there were few decent ledges and these had quite clearly been bore sighted by the Americans. The surrounding elevations offered little in terms of any reliable mortar platforms. Limiting himself to mortar artillery as a matter of face, Commander Thau had ordered a half-dozen breech loaded 160mm mortars, the ones Americans designated "Type 43". The big guns were presently en route to specific deployment sites under commander Thau's orders. While such weapons would certainly offer an added dimension in terms of extended range, they were huge, cumbersome artillery pieces, very difficult to haul into this part of Laos. Once deployed, it was virtually impossible to hide their large tube signatures and so they would be well within reach of any large 4.2 inch mortars that the Americans might have available to them, not to mention the possibility of 105 howitzers and/or air support. Muc Bo

Thau doubted (correctly) that the Americans would spend precious space on wheeled artillery pieces when they were limited to such a small piece of high ground real estate. As for air support, he would have to test the limits of the American support network to determine how much of a threat the intimidating US warbirds would be during his assault.

Mortar engagements resumed sparring again in earnest on February 12th, four days after those first probing rounds had been fired from the mortar crew immolated by Grit Volkert. Multiple cannonade exchanges started midmorning Saturday, continuing steadily for nearly 36 hours. Elevated American 81's answered back at Chicom 82's disadvantaged by lower elevation and a lack of concealment. With withering accuracy, the defenders of Swordfish Lair bracketed and destroyed communist 82 mortar crews methodically, relentlessly. In all this, Commander Muc Bo Thau found the means to study his counterpart (almost certainly an American officer) defending the high base camp. First of all, Commander Thau was impressed by the cunning of his opponent. The American 81's were extremely well coordinated, and invisible up over the precipice to any line of sight from below. During an entire day and a half of almost continuous barrage, never once did a 4.2 mortar sound off from the summit of Swordfish Lair. If the defenders had any large mortars in their arsenal, the American commander would not reveal it until he absolutely needed them. Commander Thau would, of course, assume they were available, but there remained that grain of uncertainty which is so much a part of the vital battle of wits between commanders in all ages of war.

Commander Thau also learned that the defenders were very, very good mortar marksmen, usually bracketing and blanketing within four rounds. From the sound of the tube pops on the mountaintop, it seemed as though the US 81's were pretty much evenly disbursed around the perimeter, and Muc Bo Thau placed the number of 81 mm Mortar pits on that summit at about 12. This information had cost him 19 medium size mortar tubes along with most of the crews servicing them. Predictably, it cast a pall over his own artillery units whom he had to constantly reassure were playing an essential role in probing the Americans, a necessary sacrifice to the people's cause. There was one other discovery during this period. Commander Thau was rather amazed when he realized on the second day of the campaign that not once in 36 hours of on and off cannonading, did any air support come to assist the Americans. That was a drastic change of tactic.

On Sunday evening, the 13th of February, Commander Thau called a temporary halt to his bombardment, spending three full, quiet days thereafter re-supplying troops and assembling his larger artillery pieces. It was on the fourth day, Wednesday, February 16th, that he had finally staked out his 160 mm mortar tubes in an irregular series of four pits concealed well back within the western jungle. In addition, two of the big tubes had been hauled, at considerable sacrifice, around the southern mountains over partially or uncut trails to a position due east of Swordfish Lair. It had taken nearly two weeks to engineer paths which would place the two mortar crews and their big 160mm tubes within striking distance of Swordfish Lair from both east and west.

Wednesday, February 16th, Swordfish Lair

Gabriel McCarthy and Ca Rangh had kept busy throughout that week, dealing with shrapnel wounds and all the trappings of a siege environment. Although they'd encountered several nasty shrapnel casualties during the initial volleys fortunately, no one had yet been killed by the mortar barrages. Gabe was especially thankful for the means to generously distribute flak jackets in diverse sizes. It had been necessary to make daily surveys of the fresh water supply and assure that it was well separated from waste sites disbursed around the camp. In total, Swordfish Lair now domiciled a population of over 3500 men, women and children. During the 18-hour bombardment episode, most women and all the children had remained huddled within covered trenches and sandbagged structures about the compound. Throughout intermittent bomb-storms, the inevitable process of normal human physiology proceeded. Although attempts were made to provide buckets and cans, after the first day, smells and consequences of concentrated human waste began to permeate the camp. Gabe intercepted two cases of Cholera on Sunday evening, which he quickly quarantined into the field hospital, necessarily driving out some uninjured Montagnard families who had been sheltering there. Remarkably, there was no hesitance or discontent from the Yards in this directive. They trusted their *Bac Si* implicitly and realized that he would not move them into the stinking holes unless for a very good reason. After the sporadic bombardments ceased, around mid-afternoon Sunday, it was not until Monday late morning that Fernstead would permit Montagnard dependents to venture out into unsheltered spaces of the camp. Meals were served out and work-groups organized to clean out the bomb shelters and attempt to expand sanitary facilities within. For the first couple of days, everyone remained quite alert, hovering close by shelters and maintaining careful surveillance over children who would inevitably seek out playful intrigues if left to their own devices.

By the third day, Wednesday, despite mandates from camp leadership, everyone generally began to relax their precautions. Some Montagnard families went back to live in damaged longhouses while carrying out structural repairs. The camp seemed to come back on line as the sound of children playing mixed with crackles of open-air hearths in native meal preparation. By the third day despite every contrary logic, there was a growing sense of hope that led to complacency among the normally stoic inhabitants of Swordfish Lair. Many within camp stopped wearing their Flak Jackets as they engaged in the heated manual labors of reconstruction.

The aura of complacency was broken abruptly on Wednesday mid-afternoon when the first 160 mm shells began raining terror and destruction down on to the camp. Fernstead , Briant and Estrada had all been urging the Montagnard leadership to sponsor reaction drills, which had been carried out on a daily basis, but with less fervor as complacency grew. With the first desperate shouts of "Incoming!" punctuated by a repetition of loud bangs from east and west, a tragic pause settled on non-combatants throughout the camp. The more professional instincts of healthy youth resulted in a quick migration of all assigned warriors to their respective battle stations in mortar pits or bunkers. From thunder to impact, this barrage was different. The big shells hung in the air longer, creating alternative time continuums between dependants and soldiers. From their quickly attained battle stations, both American and Montagnard combatants viewed with horror the delayed reaction of matrons separated from children and elderly struggling to understand what was happening. Sgt. Ron Winkle had taken his own station at a communications post within the perimeter bunker line, while SSG Tom Gowen remained in the main communications annex bunker. Together, they would ensure a steady flow of commo throughout the camp should any particular communications node be disrupted. As Ron donned his landline headset to listen in on ready reports from stations throughout the camp, he observed a five year-old Montagnard boy chasing after his oblivious three year-old little brother. Evidently, the five year old had a sense for what was happening and, absent his mother, was attempting to secure the three year old who was running for their father, stationed in a perimeter bunker, unaware of the unfolding drama now staged before Sgt. Winkle.

The first 160 mm shell hit from the west, neatly bracketed just north of the helipad. The big shell pounded into the mesa alongside a trenched walkway, causing earth and debris to collapse in on the ditched pathway. The enormity of the explosion was immediately clear to everyone in camp who had become accustomed to lighter impact signatures from 82 mm rounds. Within a 25 meter radius of impact, everyone standing, even within a trench, was knocked down. The children presently visible to Ron Winkle were about 35 meters from the first impact. They were both knocked down from a diminishing concussion wave surrounding that initial explosion. Ron Winkle tore off his headset and made a sudden, mad dash across 25 or so open meters separating him from the two children. As he reached, them, he huddled the two of them together behind him as he scanned the immediate area to find the nearest dependent shelter. As he did so, a second 160 shell impacted to his front, about 20 meters away, hurling earth and metal fragments in his direction. The impact tossed Ron backwards, along with the children who were mercifully shielded by the American's body. Off in the distance, the mother had been frantically searching for her two missing progeny. She correctly anticipated that they might run for their father and she was in the process of chasing after them when the second shell detonated. She became the first siege fatality of Swordfish Lair as the same shell which toppled Ron Winkle and the two children, disintegrated their mother.

Even though Captain Ronald Fernstead had anticipated 160mm Mortars he was still jolted, along with everyone else, over explosive forces from the big warheads. He had heard the distinctive, heavier, more hollow sounding bang down below. From his post atop the dunce's cap promontory, he observed a muzzle flash far out, into the western jungle, well beyond the enemy perimeter of 82 mm tubes. Fernstead had already grabbed the land-line field phone and was dialing up his Fire Direction Control crews when the first detonation event took place. He had purposely held in reserve his 4.2 mortars for this eventuality. The big pits were separately dug into a cornice on each of four compass quadrants surrounding the central camp promontory. By the time four impacts had registered within the camp, Allied crews from the northwest and southwest pits had repeated tube adjustments from Briant and Estrada manning Fire Direction plot boards along east and west summits. The loud retort of American 4.2 inch tubes thumped loudly back at the enemy with the first two rounds igniting almost simultaneously. Just as these first two ranging shots were impacting down below, two more ominous thuds echoed from the east, again startling the camp into momentary distraction. Lieutenant Erickson was situated on the eastern perimeters of the camp, along with Volkert and Johnston, who also used plot boards to run mortar crews on northeast and southeast cornices of the central camp promontory. One of the big 160 rounds landed squarely on a trenched shelter, collapsing it down on huddled dependents within. Erickson called for Haskell, stationed in a perimeter bunker, to do what he could but cautioned him to keep his head down until the barrage let up. It was an unnecessary admonition. Haskell was well aware of the devastation that the big warheads were causing. It was foolhardy for anyone to venture across camp during the barrage.

Over the next 20 minutes or so, several more salvos pomped in from enemy gunsites, located both east and west. In response, Swordfish Lair methodically walked their tubes in to the muzzle blasts below. As the 4.2 tube crews worked in harmony, west and east respectively, Fernstead watched as each of his FDC teams directed fire onto the enemy crews below. Again, the communists were disadvantaged by not being able to see up and over the summit of the American/Montagnard stronghold. They were simply lopping shells onto the top of the plateau, hoping they would strike vulnerable targets, whereas the Allied Defenders maintained an immense advantage by spotting their own impact signatures. It took approximately 25 minutes to obliterate communist mortar crews to the east and west of Swordfish Lair. During that time, random munitions dropping indiscriminately within camp wreaked considerable havoc. When it was over, four Montagnards were dead and one American, Sgt. Ron Winkle, seriously wounded.

Sgt. Gabriel McCarthy initially received notification by radio report from Fernstead, within seconds after Ron Winkle went down. Braving the turbulent impact zone, Gabe grabbed a quick pack M-3 aid bag and ran across the compound, doing his best to stay within ditchlike trenching networks interconnecting the compound. Somehow, Gabe made it to his fallen comrade within a minute of Ron Winkle being hit. Upon arrival, Gabe found that Ron had been pulled, along with the two children, into a bunker, manned by the children's father. The tearful Montagnard striker had done what he could to assist the fallen American while coping with his own children and the incipient loss of his wife, not to mention an ongoing bombardment.

Gabe found Ron on his back, clutching his face, peppered with shrapnel all up and down his front. Upon forcibly prying away Ron's hands, Gabe looked down in horror at what had once been a familiar countenance. Part of Ron's lower jaw was blown away, along with a stellate gash involving most of his nose. With tissue debris occluding both nasal and pharyngeal airways, Ron produced a gurgling type sound with each attempted breath. He was suffocating to death. Gabe recognized immediately what was happening and instantly reached into his shirt pocket, taking out a Bic fountain pen. While thumb flicking off the plastic cap using his right hand, Gabriel palpated with his left middle finger for a small "V" shaped structure just below Ron's Adam's apple, the Crico-Thyroid membrane. On finding it, Gabriel stabbed the inktip of his Bic pen through, momentarily distracting Ron's facial grip. Upon puncturing the membrane, in one quick motion, Gabe withdrew the pen, biting down on the pen nib, pulling out both nib and ink reservoir tube. He then bit off the plastic cap on the opposite end. With the clear plastic housing that remained, he quickly slid it back into the puncture wound in Ron's throat. Although relatively small in diameter, the ½ centimeter circular, clear plastic tube provided Ron Winkle with the means to draw a full breath of air without aspirating bits of tissue from his mutilated face. He stopped gripping his lower face and reached down with both hands, holding the Bic pen shaft erect as he drew breath. During the reprieve, Gabriel rummaged through his M-3 Aid Bag, locating a crico-thyroidotomy set. Contained within the sterile plastic bag was a curved, stainless steel tracheostomy tube filled with a curving, trocar-tipped cannula and obturator. The instrument was designed to perform exactly the same maneuver Gabriel had just done on Ron Winkle. Gently separating

Ron's hands while offering reassurances, Gabriel deftly replaced the Bic Pen shaft with the metallic tube, using the obturator tip to seat the curved tube down into tracheal portions of Ron's windpipe. After removing the obturator, Gabe then used a string like umbilical tape to tie the apparatus around Ron's neck, securing both ends on cleated flanges located either side of the seated Tracheostomy tube. Although the deeper penetration of the curved stainless steel tube caused a momentary gag, once seated, Ron Winkle was able to breath comfortably, without straining. This accomplished, Gabriel proceeded to pump 10 mg. of morphine sulfate in to a thigh muscle. He then tied a large, sterile battlefield dressing in four corners around Ron's disfigured face.

Using gentle compression along with hemostats and tie lengths of chromic gut suture, Gabriel was able to stem profuse facial bleeding within a few minutes. He thereafter set about cutting off loose portions of Ron Winkle's shirtsleeves and shredded portions of his jungle fatigue trousers. As he did so, Gabe located multiple shrapnel wounds, some with metallic fragments visible right at the surface. These, were removed with a forceps taken from the canvas instrument kit contained in his M-3 aidbag. Deeper fragments of shrapnel would have to wait. In the meantime each wound, ranging from the size of a bee bee all the way up to the size of a lemon, was cleansed and irrigated with fluid from a half-liter bag of sterile saline, used sparingly on each site. All the while, Gabe attempted to verbally comfort the now trembling Ron Winkle. Gabriel counted about 32 wounds spread over upper legs, arms, face, neck and throat. Fortunately, Ron had been wearing a flak jacket that protected his chest and abdomen. The flack jacket was itself peppered across its front side with what could have been potentially fatal, low velocity projectiles of shrapnel. After checking to make certain there where no wounds underneath, Gabriel decided it best to leave Ron's flak jacket on while they remained under the 160 mm mortar barrage. About half an hour later, the shelling finally stopped as camp Fire Direction Controllers silenced the last of the big enemy tubes. Upon receiving an "all clear" from Fernstead, Gabriel secured a litter and transported Ron across the pockmarked compound, back to the intact field hospital. Miraculously, none of the 160 rounds had been able to significantly damage any of the primary bunkers, including the hospital, now fast filling with siege casualties.

Sunday, February 20, 1972 Da Nang

Colonel Julius I. Schultz hung up the telephone beaming with a sense of insider hegemony. *"How many U.S. Commanders in Vietnam have the straight track to a US Congressman?"* He thought, not for the first time. Since assuming his new command, Colonel Schultz had been on the phone almost weekly, offering "on the scene" perspectives to Congressman Riley Hathoway. The fact that this interchange took place directly with the Congressman, and not with a Congressional aid or advisor, simply lent credence to Schultz's sense of achievement. Always, their brief conversations would end with some bit of praise or acclamation from Congressman Hathoway… "I cannot begin to tell you, Colonel, what a great reassurance it is for me as representative of the people of this nation to know that we have a link with some form of responsible military leadership in Vietnam! Please, continue to keep me informed, and rest assured that I am working tirelessly to use whatever influence I can offer toward your receiving a well deserved promotion."

"Well deserved promotion…" the words echoed repeatedly in Schultz's thoughts as he went about routine tasks of supervising Special Air Operations at Da Nang airbase. His primary task, as he saw it, was to assure that everything under his command was scrutinized and accounted for. This was a busy time for Vietnam airbases. In other base commands at Da Nang, sorties were being dispatched around the clock in support of B-52 raids, launched primarily from Guam. President Nixon had stepped up aerial bombing of the Ho Chi Minh trail in an attempt to halt the torrent of supplies rushing south from Hanoi and specifically, from Haiphong Harbor on the northern coast. Each wing of three

B-52's assigned to carpet bomb the trail, required air support from a host of smaller aircraft deployed out of Da Nang, including F-4 and F-105 fighters, as well as "Wild Weasel" classified electronic surveillance aircraft. For Special Air Operations, it was an era of relative inactivity, although Colonel Schultz had no perspective of this from his short tenure. There were occasional support missions to extract a downed pilot or limited in country reconnaissance, but by Spring of 1972, Command and Control North, now referred to as Task Force 1, was well on its way to standing down in South Vietnam. There had been incidents. One wing of helicopters all but refused to support a SOG extraction when a sensitive listening post had been overrun. Schultz had distracted the implications of this by constructing a careful paper trail of excuses, maintenance problems, battle damage etc.... He had even gone so far as to interfere with Thailand based rescue aircraft, threatening the Thai based crews with courts martial if they interdicted personnel which his own support wings were supposed to recoup. By mid February of 1972, Colonel Julius Schultz had quite effectively shut down the US air umbrella over Operation Fisherman. He took great satisfaction in a sincere conviction that he was making a "contribution" toward dealing with this "unconventional war" in his own unconventional way.

Colonel Schultz was basking in his own medium of self-contentment on Sunday morning, going over reports from the previous week. He was at first only mildly irritated when interrupted by an announcement from his CQ that General Abrams had just arrived for an unscheduled appointment. Schultz reassured himself that, since assuming Special Air Ops, he had maintained all of his records in order while managing to lower maintenance expenses without the loss of one single aircraft under his command. Confident in his own administrative house of cards, he went out into the foyer to greet General Abrams. As Colonel Schultz ventured into the adjoining foyer, he was momentarily surprised to see the Four Star Abrams in company with the no-name Lieutenant Colonel spook who had been pestering Schultz about that ostensibly illegal Special Ops mission going on in Laos. *"Perhaps General Abrams has finally gotten wind of this thing and is stepping in to formally shut it down..."* thought Schultz as he greeted Abrams.

"Ah, General. What a great honor it is to have you visit us here at Special Ops Air. I wish you had let me know about your arrival so that I could have prepared something for you."

General Abrams shifted stance from his right leg to his left, as though transferring from static to dynamic burdens.

"Yes, well, Colonel Schultz, the nature of this visit is not particularly prone to predisposition. Are we able to have a private discussion in your conference room?"

"Of course sir, let me lead the way." With that, Schultz led the pair into an adjacent conference room containing a long, gray table, surrounded by 20 chairs. There were two doors, both along the same wall within the room. One of these doors opened into Schultz's own office to the rear of the room, closest the head of the table. The other door opened from the foyer toward the front of the room, closest the foot of the table. They entered the conference room closest to the foot of the table. As the room was empty, Colonel Schultz switched on lights and a wall mounted air conditioning unit located also on the foot end of the room. The air conditioner announced its meal of electricity with a rhythmic humming sound as it started filling the room with a cool, advancing thermocline. Schultz headed the trio up to the head of the table, still almost stiflingly warm and humid, farthest removed from the noise of the air conditioner. There were no windows in the room. All walls were covered with retractable map curls or blackboards with cork pin strips lining their upper margin. Nothing was displayed at the moment, and the oblong room seemed sterile, almost desolate. Colonel Schultz paused at the head of the table, as this was his customary place in the room. However, he quickly acquiesced to a distinct body language signal from General Abrams who clearly intended for Schultz to be seated directly across from the Spook Lieutenant Colonel while Abrams positioned himself between them at the head of the table.

The three of them stood just behind chairs with backrests flush against the table's edge, anticipating General Abram's invitation to take seats. Schultz decided to make a conversational initiative:

"General, why don't we excuse the Lieutenant Colonel here so that you and I can discuss the nature of your visit in private for a few minutes."

Abrams responded to Colonel Scultz with a cold, directed stare that bored in right to the bone. "No, Colonel, actually this man IS the nature of my visit here. He is about to make specific charges against you for negligence and dereliction of duty. I thought it best to verbalize these accusations in your presence so that you can respond to them in an informal setting."

Colonel Schultz was visibly dazed. He caught himself in a perplexity of expression ranging between shock and outrage. "Negligence! Dereliction of... General, surely you... Why, this is.... I can't believe that you would take this man's assertion seriously! Surely you are aware that he is most likely CIA. He's probably not even a legitimate US Officer. I'm afraid I'll have to insist that he leave this room so that you and I can discuss this matter directly!"

General Abrams blinked once on an otherwise steel continence as he replied: "Colonel Schultz, this man will *not* be dismissed until after he has stated his allegations. You will, for the time being, be silent and listen to what he says. You may speak when I tell you to speak and not until I tell you to speak."

"But sir! He is at best a junior officer and he has no right to...."

"*Colonel*! Do I have to give you a direct order? Not another word, or so help me, you will be held on charges of insubordination!"

This last retort stunned as well as silenced Colonel Schultz. While the others remained standing at sort of a relaxed parade rest, Schultz leaned forward on the backrest of the chair in front of him, letting his gaze pass back and forth between the two other men in his conference room. General Abrams turned his head to the Lieutenant Colonel. Without addressing him by name or rank, Abrams simply nodded. This gesture turned the conversation over to the tall-statured Lieutenant Colonel who spoke evenly and clearly as though reading from an invisibly prepared text.

"Sir, I do hereby charge Colonel Julius I. Schwartz with negligence and dereliction of duty respecting aspects of his command having to do with *Operation Fisherman*. As you and he are both aware, this mission has direct oversight from the Congressional Defense committee. As such, it has been independently budgeted and tasked by a chain of command which rises to the authority of the United States Congress. Colonel Schultz has been negligent by refusing to confront or even consider attempts on the part of myself and other commanders designated to coordinate mission objectives with respect to *Operation Fisherman*. He has either ignored or denied acknowledgement of ongoing reports respecting the mission, apparently using this subterfuge as a basis for neglecting allocation of essential air assets. In assuming command as Special Air Operations chief over I Corps, Colonel Schultz became a responsible member of this chain of command and was specifically tasked with supporting *Operation Fisherman* to the limits of his resources and ability. Colonel Schultz has failed in this duty. He has not only withheld resources vital to prosecution of the mission, but he has actually sabotaged existing assets essential to protecting United States advisors and their allies who are, as we speak, in imminent peril of being overwhelmed by the enemy. Colonel Schultz has compromised security by repeatedly carrying out briefings and regular disclosures with a member of the U.S. House of Representatives who is not on the Congressional Defense Committee and therefore has not been designated the appropriate security clearances for such disclosures. In addition, since assuming command, vital intelligence that had evidently not been available to the enemy prior to Colonel Schultz's designation within this mission has since been leaked by either direct or indirect duplicity from Colonel Schultz's administration.

At this moment, enemy elements of the 639th and 766th NVA regiments are converging on a US supported Lima Site well within the air umbrella of both DaNang and Pleiku. US advisors and their allies have withstood enemy artillery barrages for the last 11 days. There have been casualties among both allies and US personnel. These casualties have been denied medical evacuation as a result of Colonel Schultz's specifically refusing our repeated entreaties to deploy mission designated Medevacs and Gunship support elements from this command. Should the Lima Site in question be overrun, Colonel Schultz will be directly culpable for the deaths of over 3000 people presently under siege. These include Laotian citizens who are US allies as well as US advisors under orders to support this mission."

During the last part of the oratory, Colonel Schultz had risen up to stand as if at attention before the Lieutenant Colonel. He scowled with indignation and outrage at the accusatory lessor colonel. General Abrams kept his own gaze fixed on the no name Lieutenant Colonel like a supportive audience waiting for the finale. When the oratory was finished, a short silence followed, broken by General Abrams:

"Thank you Lieutenant Colonel, you may be dismissed now. Please wait for me in the foyer."

"Yes sir," and with that, the no-name officer made a smart right face, exiting the same door from which they had all entered at the foot of the table. By this time, the room had cooled down considerably as the wall mounted air conditioner extended its curtain of influence to this far corner of the conference room. With the heat, went the humidity and somehow, the valedictory dankness gave way to a sense of cool resolve within the room. After the door had shut in the two remaining officers, Abrams turned to Schultz:

"Are these accusations true Colonel Schultz?"

Schultz found it difficult to meet Abram's directed gaze. "Sir, I can only say that from my inception as commander on this base, I have not been properly informed with respect to the total concept of this mission, which I considered to be speculative and possibly illegal."

Abrams replied, "Look, Colonel, if you want to assume a defensive posture right now, I will turn this matter over to a board of inquiry tomorrow morning. But, let me remind you Colonel, this operation is designated Top Secret. Because of that, you will be immediately relieved of your command and the entire matter turned over to a group of General Officers with appropriate security clearances to consider whatever evidence surrounds the issue. During the board of inquiry, you will not be provided access to regular legal counsel nor will you be placed before the JAG until such time as the board has made its conclusion as to whether or not these allegations are true. Upon recommendation of the board, because much of the evidence deals with sensitive issues that can not be presently entered into public record, JAG will serve only to pass sentence on you should the determination of the board fall against you. If you appeal, you will have to wait seven years before the evidence is declassified at which time, you may appeal at your present rank, but until such time, you will be relieved of all active duty within any branch of the United States military. Now, do you want to discuss this matter with me candidly or shall I convene the board?"

Schultz withered before his Commanding General, once again leaning on the chair back before him. "Look, General Abrams, you and I are both West Point graduates. That man is not one of our breed. I suspect that he is not even a legitimate officer... He doesn't even wear a name tag..."

"As it so happens, Colonel Schultz, that man *is* a legitimate officer and is duly commissioned a Lieutenant Colonel in the United States Army. His real name is Carlock and because of the sensitive nature of this mission, he has been advised to maintain anonymity while carrying out his mission directives. Those directives come all the way from the US Congressional Defense committee, something that has been confirmed to you in writing and which should have been held within your classified files. I assume you have by this time reviewed all the mission files within your command?"

"Well, of course sir."

"Is it true that you have been communicating with a US Congressional Representative who is not a designated member of the Congressional Defense Committee?"

"General Abrams, you have to stop this now. Again, let me remind you sir, we are both graduates of West Point. We have a unique responsibility to one another as a result of our common fraternity. I will speak with you candidly, sir, but I must be assured that you will keep this matter within our mutual confidence despite any potentially controversial disclosures on my part."

General Abrams looked down on his now whimpering subordinate with mounting disdain. "Colonel Schultz, at this moment, I am frankly ashamed to consider that you are indeed an alumnus of West Point. Your entreaty is offensive to me personally and demeaning to your commission as an officer and a gentleman. Now, Colonel, without further obfuscation, is it true that there are US and allied personnel under imminent danger of enemy conquest, who have been denied the resources of your command?

This last interrogatory struck Colonel Schultz like a howitzer. In seconds, Schultz realized that he had indeed been duped, played like a willing marionette from the very beginning by a campaign motivated US politician not at all dedicated to the US military. His own duplicity with the process had indeed compromised his command and would most certainly ruin his own career. He broke out into a cold sweat, chilled further by the cooling room. "General, if you will excuse me for a moment, I will gather from my personal notes any pertinent information I may have on this matter." Without waiting to be dismissed, Schultz staggered around behind General Abrams, clutching at the doorknob opening into his own office adjacent the head of the table. General Abrams looked on as Colonel Schultz staggered through the door, taking care to close it quietly behind him.

Alone in his office, Colonel Schultz sat at his desk and unlocked the secured right lower drawer for his personal note files. Located also within the drawer was a loaded .45 automatic intended to act as a final measure of security for protection within his own office. Schultz looked down at the pistol, knowing it to be locked and loaded for quick action if needed once the drawer was opened. He thought momentarily about the symbolism of that weapon, intended to protect his command as a last ditch measure in the event of attack or attempted compromise of sensitive documents.

General Abrams had finally taken a seat within the adjoining conference room. He was mentally reviewing the allegations that had been presented and castigating himself for his own preoccupations, which had delayed intervention on this matter. He had known from the start that Schultz was at best a marginal officer. Abrams was also well aware of a debacle that had been covered up during Schultz's role as a Hatchet force commander with SOG back in 1968. General Abrams had hoped that perhaps Colonel Schultz learned something from that former travesty and would take the opportunity of this new command to make amends in a professional way. It was clear now that Schultz was innately lacking in competence as a leader of special operatives. Abrams was just shaking his head to this realization as a shot reverberated loudly from the adjacent office, informal notice that Colonel Julius I. Schultz had just voluntarily relinquished his failed command.

Chapter 10 – Circumvention

February–March 1972

0430 hrs. Monday February 21ˢᵗ, 1972

Sgt. Gabriel McCarthy leaned back from a gangly, cross-legged sitting position against sandbagged walls, spent beyond all limits of exhaustion. Curled up next to him on the tamped floor of the ward area, head cradled on his left thigh, Ca Rangh dozed. Gabe calculated that it must be the first sleep for her in about 72 hours. As always, she remained near him throughout the chaos of the previous week. Together, they'd tended shrapnel wounds, performed debridements with delayed primary closures, monitored food and water distribution, and made rounds in the stinking bunkers all about camp. Within the dark bomb shelters, Gabe and Ca did their best to reassure and encourage huddled dependents. By this time, the bunker people had assumed a sort of stoic, eerie calmness as they looked to their *Bac Si* with sunken, hopeless eyes. Even the children had stopped crying and many were starting now to show signs of malnutrition. This was not for lack of food, which remained quite plentiful within the camp, but rather for lack of appetite. Parents had attempted to feed the little ones, but except for infants who could still find solace from breast-feeding, most children between 2 and 12 could not hold down solids. Gabriel had concocted a sort of broth and powdered milk formula, sweetened with sugar, which seemed to hold within some of the little stomachs. Most children, however, could do little more than huddle in their parent's arms, increasingly dazed for lack of sunlight, activity and absent a desire to eat.

It had been thirteen days since those first enemy mortar rounds intruded upon the inner perimeter of Swordfish Lair. Open areas of the mountaintop plateau were now pockmarked with craters bearing the signatures of 82mm or 160mm parabolic artillery. Although the big 160's had been silenced, it seemed as though the communists had an endless supply of scattered 82mm tubes from which they randomly lobbed harassment munitions onto the mountaintop, firing sporadic, single round, probing shots to discourage return bracketing fire from topside defenders. There was constant tension, heightened by a grim, lightless nighttime silence broken occasionally by these sudden, violent, shuddering explosions. This non-circadian rhythm made effective sleep all but impossible. Gabriel looked down at Ca as she slumbered fitfully, her body tensed to the next explosion, which her lightly dozing mind anticipated. Repeated code bursts informing mission administration back at Fort Bragg had been unsuccessful in raising any additional air support and without air support, clearly, Swordfish Lair could not hold out. The relentless mortar pillory of the last few days had been clearly intended to deny the defenders any significant REM sleep so that, when a final attack came, defensive efforts would be hampered by fatigue. Gabe reviewed the physiology of this in his mind. Sleep is really a biphasic activity that involves a light trance-like state at both the beginning and end of a sleep cycle. This light trance is an entrée into a deeper state of sedation called REM sleep, named after characteristic "Rapid Eye Movement" that occurs while dreaming. Dreaming is an essential part of sleep. Without dreams, the human mind cannot really rest. While dreaming, neuro-transmitters are released which deeply sedate the body, almost to a point of paralysis. This protects the body from physically reacting to perceived events while dreaming. These neuro-transmitters also neutralize the body's chemicals of mental fatigue and restore the conscious human mind to a state of heightened capacity. When under constant threat, the brain withholds these neuro-transmitters and thus preserves the ability to awaken quickly in response to a need for fright, fight or flight. While not privy to the exact physiology of this process, the communists were well aware that sporadic harassment fire for extended periods prior to an all out attack would weaken any quarry.

Gabriel observed the consequences of extended fatigue all about camp, little fumblings that made fine motor movements difficult. It was more challenging, for example, to dial the correct frequency on a radio, or to do a venipuncture for starting an IV. More often as not, proud, otherwise competent, Montagnard medics would defer back to him after several unsuccessful sticks on patients needing IV access. It seemed, inevitably, to come down to the *Bac Si*. No matter how carefully he trained nursing and technical staff, whenever confidence lagged, they always preferred to rely on him. At times, the burden was enormous. Just the process of mentally prioritizing what needed to be done first could be agonizing. In all of this chaos, Ca was there. She had in essence become the junior *Bac Si*. She made prudent decisions, buffering him against distractions, allowing him to focus on more pressing, critical tasks. Both patients and support staff respected her nearly as highly as they regarded him. All of this ran through his mind, during those few quiet minutes that early morning.

As he detailed tiny features of her face resting in profile on his lap, Gabe realized, almost with some amazement, that in fact he deeply loved this amazing young woman of such courage and stamina. He considered for perhaps the first time, that he loved her not only as a close friend and confidant, but as a sensual, attractive female and a companion. Gabriel McCarthy felt his body stirring with a sense of her close femininity and was thankful for her repose, trusting in its discretion to deliver her from any physical notice of his musings. In considering this, he realized also that these feelings, which he had developed for her, were essentially virtuous. Gabe and Ca had never crossed that delicate threshold between familiarity and passion. Not that she had ever been cold toward him, or done anything to be defensive toward his masculinity. It seemed, rather, that during the 10 months of their relationship, they had both been so consumed with a common purpose; there simply had never been time to explore one another's feelings beyond the immeasurable tasks at hand. If there should be such a thing as the future, he would want to spend it with her among these, her people; his people, the people that united them both in a sense of commission and belonging. It seemed fitting he should remain with her here through to the end, as the camp collectively settled into an unspoken resolve that it was only a matter of time now. Gabriel watched with some satisfaction as Ca's delicate eyelids began a stuttering movement on her slumbering features. He wondered what she was dreaming about, while at the same time, wishing he could be sharing in her dreams.

Ca Rangh was not destined to enjoin her sound sleep for long. At precisely 0425 hours, Regimental Field Commander Muc Bo Thau issued a key word by radio to subordinate commanders located at deployment points all around Swordfish Lair. For over a week, NVA troops had been marching southward and east, around the southern mountains of Swordfish Lair so as to station themselves in foothill jungles east of the camp. At the same time, special NVA troops from the 766th had been training in the north, practicing on sheer rock face mountainsides. They had worked at scaling rock as fast as humanly possible, laden with weapons, ammunition and climbing gear, nothing more, not even water. Theirs was the honor of leading the true assault on Swordfish Lair from the west, though it was Muc Bo Thau's intention to give the impression that the primary assault would come from the east. Of the topographic intelligence the NVA had about their objective, they knew that it was shaped like a triangle, with the apex pointing east and its base facing west. That apex ended at a narrowly filled land bridge, which most certainly had been set for demolition by the Americans. Although it was possible to assault up sloped sides of the northeast, that approach avenue had been heavily wired and clearly prepared as a deadly killing field by the defenders. On the southeast side of the triangle, there were rough, irregular ravines with dense, nearly impenetrable vegetation, which made it impossible to estimate elevations from any approach within 1500 meters. While it would be a steep climb for an attacking force from the west and his troops could take high casualties, it was the boldest and most unlikely lane of approach. His plan was, therefore, to launch an attack from the north and south eastern perimeters, with an artillery barrage from the west. This should draw the defenders to the eastern sides of the compound and hopefully leave the western side, set atop a sheer drop of over twenty five hundred feet, less tended. Commander Thau planned several feints to draw attention away from that western elevation which he intended to scale with his 766th mountain troops.

In constructing Swordfish Lair, careful consideration had been given to its strategic location. Similar, supposedly impenetrable, mountaintop fortresses established in other parts of Laos and on the Vietnam-Cambodian border had all been ultimately overwhelmed by massive NVA communist assaults. During the briefing phase of the mission in Tan Son Nhut, both officers as well as senior, Operations/Intelligence NCO's, had studied these other locations in detail. Over the 10 months they had been able to fortify their position, Captain Fernstead, Lieutenant Erickson, Sergeants Briant and Johnson had carefully evaluated their defensive options. The overall plan had always been to draw the enemy into this place and then use massive, repeated air strikes to pound the enemy into submission as had been done in Khe Sanh. Evidence of Communist invasion and occupation of Laos in an operation conducted specifically against Laotian citizens encamped at Swordfish Lair would have been an undeniable confirmation that North Vietnam was violating terms of the Geneva Conference. Hanoi had always contended that, aside from engineering assistance to the people of Laos, an NVA invasion force had never occupied Laos. They even denied that the Ho Chi Minh Trail was in Laos, insisting that it was constructed entirely in South

Vietnam. This of course was absolute nonsense. SOG long-range reconnaissance had confirmed repeatedly that NVA troops occupied Laos and that they actively trained and cooperated with pro communist Pathet Lao, one of three ethnic segments within the complex Laotian culture. Technically, this gave the US and South Vietnam absolute justification in doing the same. However, by 1972, the war was so unpopular that without some sort of dramatic evidence running contrary to North Vietnam assertions, such as a great defensive victory by US led Laotian resistance forces, any prospect of US support for expansion into Laos was virtually impossible. It had been the intent of Operation Fisherman planners from the beginning to prepare for this confrontation. Had all the elements of Operation Fisherman remained in place, particularly General Elkin's command over special air ops, air support sorties would have begun just a few days after the siege began. Instead, the entire, massive instrument of combined ground and air campaign forces had been systematically disassembled by Colonel Schultz and, by extension, Congressman Riley Hathoway.

While frantic administrative efforts were being entreated in Da Nang to restore the original operations plan following the demise of Colonel Schwartz, Swordfish Lair received the first assault waves on its eastern positions. Predictably, the first wave attacked the land-bridge entrance into the compound. Crisscrossing M-60 and 50 caliber machine gun fields of fire supporting the entrance to Swordfish Lair began engaging at 0447 hours. Mortar tubes thunked out parachute flares revealing many small groups, doggedly throwing bamboo ladders over wire embrasures for comrades to dash over, disappear into the earth and give fire cover as more, small groups rushed forward. They moved skillfully, hugging the terrain, and many survived to press ever-deeper aggregate formations assaulting the main gate. Coordinated machine gun fire raked advancing troops who had trenched their way up to the base of the mountain. Angled bunker positions along northeast and southeast perimeters offered excellent firing positions for assigned marksmen to engage the charging NVA.

Fernstead directed return fire from his own command position on Dunce's cap rock while Briant and Estrada directed killing fields from perimeter bunker lines. Communist 82 mm mortars began shelling in earnest from the west, seemingly short in their range, falling on the western side perimeter. This was intended to make the defenders think that they could not be reached by the limits of the 82's, thus emboldening the eastern defense lines. Also, it was figured that the Americans would not imagine the enemy could dare to bombard from that western side if communist ground troops were being deployed from the west, up the mountainside, into the barrage.

However, the ruse did not deceive. Commanding the western wall Lieutenant Erickson with SFC Daniel Johnston monitored visual and seismic sensing devices placed along the cliff faces many months prior. As the 766th NVA troops began their frantic scramble up multifaceted rock faces of that western elevation, Johnson tracked their progress on both a map-board and horizontal sand table, representing the vertical surface of the western wall. By 0510, over 350 NVA troops were distributed along various vertical climbing lanes. Unbeknownst to these troops, concrete down facing bunkers had been poured into the upper perimeter of Swordfish Lair. Settled within these bunkers were diagonal slots, lipped on the downhill side to contain large canisters of incendiary, military Foo Gas. So-called Foo Gas is not really a gas at all. It is an incendiary explosive which, when vapor disbursed over a given area, can be detonated, literally causing the "air to explode". At 0512 hours, SFC Daniel Johnston cranked a detonator handle, which sent the first wave of Foo gas down the western side of the mountain. Once emptied, the large drums were quickly replaced with others lined up in columns along the inner bunker walls.

The effect of the Foo gas torrent was devastating. Erickson had to remind himself that these pitiful creatures below him had just been doing their level best to scale this mountain for the express purpose of killing everyone in Swordfish Lair. Now, the enemy beneath him seemed like so many fiery insects dropping off the mountainside, human beings who were dying in an abrupt, terrifying manner. Some managed to hug themselves into nooks and crannies within the rock wall and actually survived that first dreadful torrent of fire and explosion as it swept down the mountain face. Montagnard marksmen manning horizontally facing bunkers took up down facing firing positions that enabled them to fire at oblique angles along the western face using night vision riflescopes. For the climbers below, if they fired upward, their rounds would strike solid concrete. The only possibility the communists had of returning fire would have been to shoot in angles up the sheer rock walls. However, in the pre-dawn dark it was impossible to realize this and so most of the first wave of NVA 766th mountain assault troops were swept off the mountain face as Commander Muc Bo Thau observed in trepidation. Clearly, these Americans and their willing Montagnard/Hmong lackeys had prepared themselves very well. Commander Thau had taken to thinking of them only as Americans. He could not accept that Laotian born primitives could raise such a formidable resistance independently. As far as he was concerned, they were all Americans, using their clever weapons of war to both kill and harden his own communist troops. This was further confirmed as radio reports from the eastern front assaults announced that the first waves had failed in taking the land bridge before the Americans blew it up. In imagining the scenario, Commander Thau gazed down at his own carefully constructed miniature sand table of the visible compound. He visualized in his mind that the allied defenders had waited until the last possible moment, when the bridge was packed with assault troops, before the Americans detonated their front door into the compound. He was correct in this perception. Now, it would be necessary for the majority of his troops deployed on that eastern approach, to charge up steep slopes of the northeast and to a lesser degree, the southeastern sides of the triangular compound. This meant a more costly engagement and eliminated any possibility of reducing the butcher's bill. By that time, however, Muc Bo Thau was quite willing to pay whatever it cost in human lives under his command to extinguish these arrogant, pugnacious Americans.

In deliberating over these things, Commander Thau considered counsel from the brilliant Chinese strategist Tzu Sun in "The Arts of War". A common premise to Tzu Sun's philosophy concerning war was that knowledge and information are power. Always keep an unknown thing in reserve from your enemy, while at the same time, probing your enemy to discover his position and weaknesses. These were the keys to successful campaigns. Clearly, Commander Thau had been unsuccessful in surprising the Americans with his dual-fronted attack, but he had learned a great deal about his adversaries over the previous two weeks. He knew the number and proximate location of their mortar pits as well as the orientation of their defensive perimeters. As time went on, more and more intelligence became available and Muc Bo Thau had processed every bit of it. He thought of all this as he looked down at the sand table erected for analysis of his deployment. *"So, American Commander, who is so clever and fights so bravely, I am finding out all your secrets. Do you think you know all mine? Why haven't you called in your fearsome air power over all of these last 10 days? Can it be that you are constrained from doing so? Is your country forbidden to fly over this part of Laos? Perhaps you are keeping it in reserve, a surprise, like one I am keeping from you. Well, that is all right. Because each day my men dig their holes deeper, and your vicious warplanes cannot go into the earth after them; you cannot burrow so deep down into the earth as my men can to transform your terrible weapons into loud noises and nothing more. So, what are you thinking right now American Commander? Are you so confident of yourself up on top of that mountain, surrounded by a necklace of death, all safe with your famous Bac Si to mend your wounds and strengthen your resolve?"*

The assault continued throughout that next day, Monday. Although it was clear that there was little benefit in attempting to scale the western wall en masse, Commander Thau continued to send up small climbing groups of men hoping to sneak sappers in under nooks and crannies within the vertical mountainside.

The majority of remaining troops from the 766th were sent around to join their compatriots along the eastern approaches. While it had taken nearly two weeks to place those first communist encampments on the east, Muc Bo Thau had also set engineers to work, forging high-speed avenues through jungle and across mountains. Thus, the trek around Swordfish Lair had been shortened to about 18 hour's force march along improved trails with up and down steps cut into mountain passes further south. As the 766th marched, NVA troops already positioned on the eastern side divided their efforts between trenching and probing. Under radio command with their commander to the west, eastern side troop commanders instructed their men to make feints into the perimeter all that day long, attempting to expose strengths and weaknesses. What they encountered was a 300-meter open kill zone sloping steeply downhill from the upper northeastern battlements. The last 100 meters of that zone, all uphill, closest the actual perimeter was laced with successions of concertina and barbed wire set on metal posts. Beyond the three lanes of wire, a picketed, zig zag wall of sandbag and concrete reinforced bunkers had been set up running from both ends of the base side, toward an apex at the entrance. That entrance was now a gaping hollow, cratered by the immense explosion, which sealed off the land bridge entrée. The no-mans land between strata of concertina had of course been mined and so it became an impact zone for 82mm mortars attempting to detonate pressure activated land mines. This was relatively successful. The communists were less successful, however, in taking out Claymores, which had been carefully sighted within sandbagged mounds with clear, 120 ° exposures to the outward perimeter. The only practical, passable approach to the southeastern perimeter was through a lane transit from the northeast. And so, it all came down to that northeastern corridor, three hundred meters of graded, open, sloping ground, devoid of cover or concealment. It was a brutal killing field.

It was customary for the Americans to leave lanes within their defensive approaches, invisible areas devoid of mines, with inconspicuous spaces in the wire that a man could pass through during a nighttime escape attempt. By mid-day, Muc Bo Thau was quite convinced that the Americans had not constructed any such options into their fortress. By late afternoon, Commander Thau had as clear a picture of the defensive network around Swordfish Lair as if he had constructed it himself. The price for this understanding was high. It cost another 171 brave NVA soldiers, now corpses left hanging in the wire. NVA officers directed their mortar barrages into those outermost layers of concertina, using the corpses as sighting posts to zero in on the wire while at the same time blowing the bodies to bits so that they would not serve as morale flags to dispirit living communists. Something about seeing a comrade blown to bits, even by one's own artillery, seems to deepen rage and served as seasoning for the assault troops.

Rows of concertina stretched out on either side of northeast and southeastern berm-lines. As barbed wire curtains approached the northernmost corner of the compound, slopping terrain became steeper, wrapping around a northern crag onto the more vertical western face. The southeastern perimeter sloped as well, but with much more dramatic changes in elevation, dropping off about half way down the berm-line into a series of draws which emptied toward a deepening jungle gully several hundred feet below. The southeast was navigable up a draw, about halfway down that side, but posed impossible terrain to the extreme southern end. The final attack would have to be concentrated along that northeastern perimeter. In the meantime, Commander Thau continued all day and early evening with feints and probes on all sides, attempting to find weaknesses and, if possible, deplete strong points. He went back to dueling with the 82 mm mortars, drawing return fire from mortar pits within Swordfish Lair. Even from the eastern approaches, it was difficult for the Communists to bracket anything inside Swordfish Lair as the camp was uphill and actual mortar pits were still invisible to observation from below. Communist spotters were sent to adjacent peaks with the most powerful telescopes or binoculars they could muster, hoping to spot muzzle flashes or locate hits for their crews. But Swordfish Lair was the highest elevation in the area and remained largely shielded from line of sight observation anywhere down below. Over the balance of the day, that Monday the 21st of February, NVA mortar crews simply peppered the plateau above them hoping to hit something on top. They were in fact successful over several hours' worth of shelling. All told, they hit four of the US 81mm pits, as well as taking out one of the invaluable 4.2 mortar tubes. From their higher elevation, the defenders continued to effectively spot and bracket enemy mortar crews down below as the frequency of fire out in the jungles relentlessly exposed communist gun crews to Forward Observers along the perimeters.

2315 hrs. Monday February 21st, 1972

Sgt. Gabriel McCarthy had been awake continuously for over 96 hours. The last time he had done anything like sleep, it consisted of a stop and go series of naps over about a four hour period, during which time Ca had managed to rearrange patients to make more space in the hospital bunker. Gabe stood by now, bleary eyed and bedraggled, at the operating room table in the forward part of the hospital bunker. They had been taking casualties in spurts throughout the day. About mid-afternoon, several criticals came in from mortar pit crews hit by enemy artillery. Three had lost all or part of an extremity. There were four with serious leg injuries and eight who had taken shrapnel in arms and legs. Another two died of head wounds before he could do anything for them. Had he time or energy to despair, Gabriel would have deeply lamented these latter casualties. However, the all consuming process of preserving life left him absent any time to mourn. For those patients with visceral wounds, there was little he could do for them beyond chest tubes and colostomies. Gabe had learned enough from Dr. Rivero to open a belly and run a bowel segment. However, he was unable to differentiate Mesenteric and Aortic arterial circuits. He could not effectively track circulation servicing kidneys, liver, pancreas, or spleen. If any of these organs was damaged, about all he could really do was ligate and remove a spleen. He had no means to provide mechanically assisted respiration in serious chest wounds. He had neither whole blood reservoirs nor the means of efficiently typing and cross matching, which demanded careful supervision. While he could depend on medically trained Montagnards using Ambu bags to temporarily respirate some of the more serious chest wounds, any patient taken deep enough with Ether to crack a chest never came back up again. Repeatedly, Gabriel chastised himself for all that he could not do, for that he did not know.

Several times during the day, Gabe contaminated futile sterile fields with petulant tears as he wept over the mortally wounded, dying under his hands. Ca continued on beside him, seemingly stoic to the blood and horror all about. She realized that this pose was necessary to keep *Bac Si* going, for she knew that if she hesitated or shrank from her theater of tragedy, he would have nothing left to sustain him. In reality, she was quite concerned about him, standing tall in an arena of agony, ministering with a degree of empathy she believed to be more than any single person could endure. She worried about *Bac Si*, not because he was indeed a fallible surgeon, but rather over the iconoclastic image he struggled so hard to sustain in reassuring the people. Somehow, there was a perception among the wounded and their loved ones in this camp, a perception that, if they could bring their sorrows to *Bac Si*, everything would be all right. Live or die, it did not matter so long as they did one or the other within sight of him. And the indigenous mountain people accepted death quietly, unceremoniously, as they had always considered it, just a part of life. Whether the dying, or loved ones who could not be denied a presence with parting loved ones in the crowded bunker hospital, *Bac Si* embraced them all, living or dead, with a calm, caring deliberation of labor and circumspection. Somehow, that was enough. This tall, fair skinned man from another place, with all his learning, his medicines, his undeniable, genuine love and concern for their people; that he would make such an effort, that he would shed tears for them… it was enough. Ca knew this. She also knew that her *Bac Si* was quite unaware of the heights to which adulation towards him could soar and so, guilelessly, he suffered with them.

As the ordeal wore on, Ca Rangh longed to take him in her arms and comfort him, to offer him some respite from the stream of broken, mutilated bodies brought before him for solace. By around 2250, the communist shelling stopped and over the next hour or so, the flow of wounded slowed to a trickle. At about 2345 hours, Gabriel finished pushing a chest tube into the last critically injured patient of the day. Instead of a Foley catheter, he used the more rigid urethane chest tubes designed for the task, most of which were gone now. During the last couple of hours, he had been shaking his head and force blinking his eyelids, struggling against irresistible fatigue. Finally, with the tube in place, he handed the needle holder with threaded silk suture back over to Ca, trusting her implicitly to seal the edges of the puncture wound with airtight ligatures around the tube. With unspoken acknowledgement, Ca took the suture and started to throw stitches as Sgt. Gabriel McCarthy stepped back from the OR table. He trundled back against the sandbagged wall, crumpling slowly down to the wet, flat rock floor falling asleep in his surgical gown, assuming a sort of cross legged, sitting position with his head tilted forward, over his knees, hands in bloody gloves crossed over the front of his chest.

Ca finished sealing the chest tube, connecting it to a Heimlich valve and summoning help from other members of the hospital detail to assist with the patient. She turned to find her *Bac Si* asleep on the floor in the awkward sitting position that she knew would leave him with a terrible kink in his neck. Tenderly, also as yet in gown, gloves, mask and cap, she bent over him, tilting his body to the left, lowering his head down onto her own lap as she seated herself next to him on the bloody floor. As Ca loosened the surgical mask from around his head, she could feel a dampness from the bloody floor seeping into her trousers and knew it was also soaking his left side. She was, however, insensible to anything save the vital purpose of protecting *Bac Si*'s slumbering head on her lap. Satisfied that she had accomplished this, Ca leaned her own head forward and down, coming to rest on her own right arm, which rested on his upturned right shoulder. As the two of them slept, several Montagnard attendants came in and cleaned the Operating room, washing away most of the blood into a shallow drain field beneath the floor. They took care not to awaken their sleeping *Bac Si* and his valiant woman.

Commander Muc Bo Thau called off the harassment artillery at 2250 hours. Over the course of the siege, he had hardly allowed his own troops time to rest. He wanted them all to get a good night's sleep, for he knew that come morning, he would launch the final assault. In order to do so, Commander Thau wanted his troops awake and alert. In the morning, he would distribute amphetamines, French made Benzadrine tablets, which would fill his men with vigor and bravado, following their sound sleep. Many of them would have nightmares about the events of the last day or so. Troops from the 766th wearing black pajamas, had by this time force marched to join the main force on the eastern side. They would stir all night with visions of their comrades being swept off the western mountainside by the terrible explosive gas used on their elite sappers. The rest of the communist troops, mostly members of Commander Thau's own 639th Regiment, would sleep with contorted dream-vistas of their comrades being blown to pieces in the eastern concertina wire entanglements. Commander Thau knew that among the majority of his siege troops, there was a sense that dawn would bring some sort of closure to this ordeal. The communist foot soldiers would be ready, he thought. They had been subjected to weeks of marching and digging and apprehension. His troops were ready, and they could well afford to give the American defenders a few hour's undisturbed sleep also. Muc Bo Thau hoped the defenders would sleep deeply, right through the first assault waves he would launch in the early morning hours when a man's senses are most dulled.

The Americans were indeed all very tired, along with the rest of the camp. Within 15 minutes of the cessation of shelling, nearly everyone in the bunkers was asleep. Fernstead recognized the insidious lull for what it was and made rounds on the perimeter, letting the men sleep in their bunkers for at least a few hours. He found Erickson, Johnson and Briant. Together, they set a graveyard watch, assuring that at least two of them, an officer and a Senior NCO, would be awake to rouse the troops at 0230 hours. From 0230 on, they would maintain a 50% alert along the perimeter, anticipating a full force frontal assault sometime before dawn. Just after midnight, Fernstead went to the communications bunker, wherein he found a dozing SSG. Gowen. Captain Fernstead instructed the senior communications NCO to send out a single code word, repeated three times: *Diadem, Diadem, Diadem.*

Da Nang, Tuesday, February 22, 0038 hours

The call came from Fort Bragg via secure comlink. Operation Fisherman had reached its climax. The team commander was informing higher mission command that they anticipated a final assault as imminent within the next six hours. When the operation had originally been conceived, Operation Fisherman planners imagined that it would take up to six hours to marshal all of their air assets. They had planned on using air power to break the final confrontation between NVA invasion troops on Laotian soil, and Laotian citizen defenders with US advisors, also on Laotian soil. Although the distinction seemed a bit querulous at first review, all the congressional legal advisors were quite certain that when examined in light of the July 62 Geneva Conference, North Vietnam would certainly be exposed as invaders on the soil of Southern Laos. Such would legitimize advancement from a successful phase two outcome for Operation Fisherman. Administratively, all the briefs had been prepared to argue the issue before US and International forums. With the utterance of *"Diadem"*, a mammoth switch was supposed to actuate that would set in motion the fulfillment of Phase II for Operation Fisherman.

The problem was that the essential foundation upon which Fisherman was constructed was, after all, a paper algorithm. All of the assets needed to put that algorithm into play depended on human leadership set in a reliable, consistent poise. Had Brigadier General Elkins been in command when the clarion sounded, he would have activated elements of machines, fuel, munitions, communications, flesh and blood necessary to launch the maelstrom. Without implicitly saying he intended to do so, Colonel Schultz had meticulously set about re-allocating those air assets geared up to support the *diadem* summons, that he never even knew about, when it broadcast. The death of Colonel Schultz left a vacuum in command that could not be hastily filled. There was an Executive Officer, a Lieutenant Colonel by the name of Amos Jenkins. Lt. Colonel Jenkins had been brought in by Schultz and knew nothing about any deep covert support missions under the aegis of Special Operations command. Jenkins was awakened very early on the morning of February 22nd, 1972 by an orderly bearing written instructions from General Creighton Abrams.

Lt. Colonel Jenkins had been thoroughly consumed supervising an investigation into Colonel Schultz's suicide. Jenkins had himself only just retired after midnight and so was somewhat disoriented and not a little ill tempered when awakened at 0303 hours with instructions to receive a classified briefing committee as soon as possible. He rose, showered, shaved and dressed in what he considered a relatively impressive set of dress greens, stopping to have coffee before joining the briefing committee in the conference room alongside what had been Colonel Schultz's office. It was by that time nearly 0400. It would take just over half an hour to explain the precepts of Operation Fisherman sufficiently to impress upon Lieutenant Colonel Jenkins the significance of the mission and what his default role would be in activating a response.

To his credit, Jenkins clearly grasped the urgency of the situation and started issuing directives about 0500. Had these mandates come from a known authority, such as General Elkins, or even Colonel Schultz, the spin up would have gone a lot more smoothly. As it was, Lt. Colonel Jenkins was issuing orders to aircraft and crews, most of whom he had never before interacted with. Some of these human elements were equal or superior in rank to himself. Human communication depends on a great many things beyond simple spoken words. Urgency and enthusiastic trust are a combination of attitude that cannot be so easily deployed without some introduction. While support assets had been in place for these many months, they existed as sets of unknowing, unrehearsed players in a grand scheme, which very few were even aware of. Mobilization of these naïve assets would take some finesse and would have relied heavily upon an experienced command personality. Accumulating aircraft involved contacting airfields all over South Vietnam as well as Thailand and far away Okinawa. It necessitated cross-compartment diplomacy between Army and Air Force, something Lt. Colonel Jenkins was totally unprepared for. Off site commanders wanted explanations as to why their aircraft were being prioritized away from scheduled mission designations. The simple exhortation "To support a classified, combined-Corps mission per orders directly from General Creighton Abrams…" was not nearly enough to uniformly inspire prompt attention. General Abrams could not himself offer more than tacit support for the operation without drawing down premature scrutiny on the highly classified mission. And so, the process of mobilization of air assets continued on into forenoon watches of the morning and even later, into the afternoon. Most of these latter sorties would be recalled before even arriving on target.

At 0410 hours, A wing of B-52's lifted off from Okinawa as the first phalanx of airborne response to *diadem*. They were hastened in part by other staff members of the original Operation Fisherman think tank, which remained with the 1st Special Forces Group in Okinawa. Lt. Colonel Jenkins was able to locate a group of Air Force support helicopters, new Echo models, which he was assured would be made available. The Air Force air wing commander only released his group of neophyte pilots on condition that an experienced US Army Heliborne Commander be on scene to direct the mission. They understood that mission might possibly involve the extraction of US personnel and Laotian allies as well as wounded casualties from some skirmish just over the border in that mountain country referred to by aviators as "the Parrot's Beak". From the air base at Plieku, a group of six DivArty (Division Artillery) Cobras armed with rocket pods and two gun Cobras armed with 7.62 mini guns lifted off at 0550 hours. They were accompanied by one single Loach. For this mission, they were advised there would be no need to track or snoop close to the ground. Therefore the Airborne mission commander opted to only take one of the smaller Light Observation Helicopters (LOH, pronounced "Loach"). Evidently, a Special Forces Lima Site was under siege and the environment was already "target rich" without the need to send in scout pilots. What was needed was heavy ordinance favored by the Cobra gunships and so, scramble crews were dispatched with all the ready munitions they could muster on very short notice. In addition, a heliborne on site air wing officer lifted off in one of the new Bell Rangers, an aircraft most scout pilots considered nearly worthless. His job would be to circle high overhead and direct fire for the Cobras. That left the one single Loach scout ship as a lightly armed backup for any "what if" contingencies. The wing commander was a Major Stanley Plinder. Major Plinder had completed one previous tour in Vietnam and was something of a short timer toward this, the end of his second tour. Major Plinder wisely opted to bring along his Senior Chief Warrant Officer scout pilot, Mr. Roger Cox. CW2 Cox was approaching the end of his third tour in Vietnam.

Swordfish Lair, Tuesday February 22, 1972 at 0445 hours

Commander Muc Bo Thau ordered the main assault to begin at precisely 0348 hours. He selected that time, knowing that it is the most difficult time of a 24 hour human sleep cycle in which to arouse suddenly from deep sleep and respond to quick thinking situations. Commander Thau had held something in careful reserve from the defenders of Swordfish Lair. Far removed, up in these mountains, the largest artillery that could be hauled in were Chicom 160 mm breech loading Mortars. To test the American's response to this artillery, he had used up his first six of the big tubes in a mortar duel just six days prior between his own 160's and the American's 4.2 inch mortars. This had cost the Communists all six of the precious 160's they had deployed at the time. However, it revealed the final measure of heavy weapons armaments mounted atop the summit fortress. Evidently, the Americans had no more than four of the big tube guns. Commander Thau expended the best efforts of his combat engineers to bring in a dozen more of the big 160 mm tubes along with ammunition and gun crews. Over the last couple of days, they had been laying out the mortar pits, distributed on either side of Swordfish Lair, east and west. Like all mortar crews, communist gun crews consisted of essentially three components. Fire Direction Control (FDC), which calculates tube angle and charge loads, a Forward Observer (FO) who observes the fall of the shots and recommends adjustment back to FDC, and finally, an actual Gunnery Crew (GC). A big gun tube, such as the 160, normally occupies a total crew of between four and six men incorporating all three components of gunnery, FDC and FO. Each communist FDC crew gets together with other FDC crewmembers when a barrage is planned and together, they proof tube calculations to assure a better fall of shot. For much of the preceding three days, FDC crewmen had been working on crude plotboards. While primitive by western standards, they were nonetheless potentially accurate. On these boards, using abacus calculations, NVA FDC teams had been plotting the difference between their 82 mm tubes and the 160 mm tubes in terms of trajectory and charge. All of the twelve big tubes had been laid a fixed distance to the rear of 82 mm tube pits. The 82's had thus served as spotter rounds in setting the angle and charge on larger mortars. In this way, Commander Muc Bo Thau depended on all twelve large mortars being able to strike nearly dead center of the mountaintop wherein he estimated both the American Command Post and the majority of the American 4.2 mortar pits were dug in.

At 0348, the 160's went off almost simultaneously in a single huge, stereoscopic "Boooo..oooo..ooommmm!" This awakened those people in Swordfish Lair not already on alert. The explosions that followed did indeed strike nearly dead center of the mountaintop plateau, knocking the tip off of the dunce's cap prominence, occupied at that moment by First Lieutenant Ron Erickson on watch as spotter. His last conscious action prior to painless disintegration was to call in the coordinates of flashes on the eastern side to the 4.2 crews below, none of whom were injured in the initial salvo. Surprisingly, there was an enemy pause following that first catastrophic cacophony. This occurred while the communist gun crews adjusted their tubes to the northeast and southeastern perimeter bunkers. In the interim, the American 4.2 crews started answering and two of Muc Bo Thau's precious 160's were lost in the return salvo. This left ten intact large guns firing when they opened up about three minutes later on the outer perimeter, laying hits on the zig-zag bunker system. So well had these bunkers been constructed, no one was injured for over 20 minutes, until the upper caps of some of the bunkers started to collapse under the repetitive pounding. All the while the American 4.2's were answering back and taking out bright flash points revealing 160 pits off in the black jungle void. After 20 minutes, another four 160mm tubes had been taken out. By that time, communist 82's had joined in the fray and were being engaged by the American 81mm mortar tubes. Two of the US 4.2's had been hit, one totally demolished, the other repairable but out of action. The first human assault wave trumpeted at about 0505 hours. Parachute flares, fired by US 81mm tubes revealed a massed wave of men in mixed black pajamas and regular NVA uniforms advancing toward the northeastern perimeter. They passed through the first layer of wire that had been all but removed by shaped, pipelike charges and artillery fire in advance. When the enemy approached the second layer of concertina, M-60's began crisscrossing fields of fire that was absolutely devastating. Men caught in the wire could not effectively go forward or backward and many in the front line became human ramps as their bodies were used for bridge-like treads into the wire. However, the Concertina had been carefully laid for this very scenario. While it was possible to create small alleys through the second layer, these alleys became murder holes wherein massed automatic fire from the bunkers mowed down files of assault troops coming through. Only because of relentless sacrifices on the part of the communist assault troops, the corridors grew, and as they did, the second layer of wire had just started to give out when enemy trumpeters sounded the first withdrawal. The communist first assault wave was broken. Their troops withdrew, dragging wounded and dead with them. As they melted back into the invisible jungle 250 meters back, enemy mortars again began shooting in on the center of the camp, licking out for US mortar pits and their soft target crews. Massed artillery fire continued over the next hour or so, in a relentless bombardment. By 0510 hours, there was only one 4.2 remaining, that was the one which had been repaired and was only just able to begin returning fire into the fray. Of the 81mm tubes, there were four left. They could not reach out to the big 160's but they continued to drop ordinance into the far jungle as well as engage visible 82mm tube flashes. Captain Fernstead did not have even a few moments to mourn the loss of Lieutenant Ron Erickson. Fernstead had been totally occupied directing the defense from his command bunker, venturing out to check the perimeter and keep tabs on his assets. Big Daniel Johnston was killed along with all the indigenous crew of one of the 4.2 mortar pits. Sgt. Kip Haskell took station on the southeast perimeter bunker line while Volkert directed the 81 mm pits from an FDC post out on the northernmost corner of the northeast bunker line where he had a clear field of view over the primary enemy approach.

Estrada was also out around the middle northeastern perimeter while Briant took up station on an M-60 at a bunker near the "spearhead," closest the demolished entrance to Swordfish Lair. Gowen remained in the all important communications bunker coordinating communications between Fernstead and various commo links around the camp, directing the distribution of munitions and collection of casualties. McCarthy remained in the hospital, again swamped with dead and wounded. The next direct assault began at 0628, just as the sun began peeking around the upper right corner of Mount Aterat to the east. Muc Bo Thau hoped to blind his quarry with the sunrise in their faces. He deployed his troops simultaneously against the northeast while directing a side bar to the southeast sides in a pincer movement intended to occupy both fronts thus extending defenders' resources as much as possible. On the southeast, Haskell directed his defensive line with exceptional cunning, directing fire into massed charges, driving the assault front toward an impassable southernmost gully, wherein communists instinctively ran for cover from shepherding machine gun fire. At one point, three or four platoons of NVA troops were crouching within the main gully. Their officers went in after them, screaming at them not to falter in their orders to assault. At a crucial moment, with the gully full of cowering NVA troops, Kip Haskell detonated a series of charges connected by detcord buried into the sides of the gully. The effect was sheer havoc. The detcord blew outward in a cleaving blast, which cut many of the troops in half. The result was almost a lesson in following orders for the communists as those who survived joined with others to charge once again into the wire, firing their assault rifles impotently toward the crisscrossed bunker slits on the southeastern line.

Meanwhile, the northeastern perimeter was engaging at the innermost strand of concertina. Several bunkers along that line had been breached by this time as numerous combined hits from 160 and 82 mm mortar fire gouged holes into their covers. This disrupted the meticulous crisscross killing fields. Sensing in the heat of battle weak points within the defensive wall, communist officers directed their troops in lateral movements toward less concentrated killing zones. NVA bodies littered the field, but Muc Bo Thau had troops to spare as he called in his reserves to reinforce the assault. From his distant command post to the West, He could feel the fabric of the defense beginning to break as radio reports came in. He was just starting to feel some confidence, a smell of blood, when the air filled with that dread sound. He realized that the American commander had held back one last trump card as the first American airplanes came in from the southeast.

The air assault was ushered in by a wing of Phantoms, F-4's deployed out of Da Nang. The flight leader, a Major Jim Casey, had been scrambled at 0525 hours that morning. His flight wing of four fast movers was provided almost no briefing on this mission whatsoever. It was the sort of mission that caused him to grow a few more "distinguished" gray hairs on the rims of his 36-year old crew cut temples. They were flying from south to north up a valley with a mountain range off to their eastern right, centering on a large, flat-topped mountain atop which *another* Special Forces A-camp, supposedly not here in Laos, was clearly in a non-entity crisis. What Major Casey needed most right now was a spotter, an observer who could give him the low down on this situation and call in ordinance. Just as he was thinking this, his radio squawked to life.

"US Flight wing commander on my frequency, this is Minnow One do you read, over?"

"Minnow 1, this is Gunslinger 1, we read you five by five minnow. How can we help this morning?"

"If you are able to take out the big guns on the east and west sides, that would be most obliging Gunslinger."

From his birds eye position, Major Casey had seen the big Communist M-43 (160 mm mortars) muzzle flashes farthest out in a rough circle with its epicenter a series of bright flashes atop the mountain plateau to his right front.

"Gunslinger Wing, line up on the big tubes. You probably won't see much more than flashes. Just line up on the guns furthest from that L-Site. Two and Four, you take this western side. Three, you follow me around to the east. We'll take out the M-43's on that side."

Two of the stubby jets drifted away from their compatriots as they lined up on the big mortar emplacements, visible by their flash characteristics in this pre-dawn light. The other two planes flew a wide racetrack around, turning back east and then north to south, paralleling the eastern side of Swordfish Lair. There were only five 160 mortars left of the original ballistic dozen. All five were immersed in a transient firestorm of napalm dropped along the rumbline of their ranged pits. Both planes expended all of their hardpoint ordinance in accomplishing this. They came around a second time, however, braving gun runs with their big 20 mm "Gatling gun" M61A1 cannons, chopping up the invisible jungle just outside eastern perimeters of the Lima Site where the few remaining 81 mm mortars were entrenched.

Having spent their munitions, the Phantoms disengaged and flew back to Da Nang to rearm, refuel and, if summoned, to return for another sortie. Just as the Phantoms departed station, a flight of six-fixed wing, Douglas A-1 "Spad" Skyraiders, also out of Da Nang, made their approach, along the same south to north corridor the Phantoms had just flown in from. Fernstead once again exchanged short directives by radio with the flight leader of the Skyraiders, asking to prioritize any remaining Mortar tube targets as well as to soften the assault wave on the eastern front. The Spads offered a tremendous tactical advantage over the fast flyer Phantoms. In contrast to jets, the fixed wing, big propeller driven Skyraiders could fly relatively low and slow. Not as low or slow as helicopters of course, but they were capable of delivering much greater payloads. By this time, enemy 12 mm machine guns set atop lower elevations on mountains north and south of Swordfish Lair came into action. They had been momentarily stunned by the appearance of the Phantoms, but now began fulfilling their intended role as anti-aircraft weaponry. While the Skyraiders circled around to the north, several machine gun crews on that side got a piece of one of the big, prop driven attack aircraft. Billowing out streamers of grey-black smoke, the airplane wheeled over as it flew in low, cresting the northern mountain and crashing horrendously into an upward extended crag. The other Skyraiders found their targets, as enemy 82mm mortars continued to pepper Swordfish Lair from various pits on eastern and western peripheries. One Skyraider wheeled in over the eastern perimeter, dropping a Cluster Bomb in the midst of enemy assault units along the southeastern perimeter, reeking havoc on that front. The smattering of explosions and secondary explosions sent formed assault troops into chaos, scattering troops once again toward southeastern gullies wherein Haskell ignited successive tiers of detcord cleaving charges. It only took a few minutes for the Skyraiders to spend their ordinance. As they reformed for their return leg to Da Nang, they were minus one with two others shot up enough to be out of action for at least a few days.

As the Spad Skyraiders withdrew, helicopters came in from the sun around the northern side of Mount Aterat, following a northeast to southwest approach.

Captain Fernstead had moved to what high ground remained in the camp epicenter, sequestering himself among disordered sandbags atop the crumpled dunces cap promontory. From there, he communicated a relay through Gowen as best he could while firing a .50 caliber machine gun over the heads of his own troops into communist waves below. At this point, communist anti aircraft gun crews who had scaled adjacent peaks to the north and south were attracted to his firing position, just visible to their declinated line of site. First from the south, then from the north, gun crews reached out with their 12 mm heavy machine guns. They could place rounds just within range, over 1500 meters away, into the besieged campsite. Throughout his maneuvering about camp during the siege, Captain Fernstead had the constant, welcome company of Montagnard chieftain, Philipe Suvete. Chief Suvete helped relay messages in native dialects, which eliminated the expediency of tortuous translations during critical moments. He had been wounded himself by shrapnel, which peppered his left side. Fortunately, nothing had penetrated deep enough to injure any vital structures, however, he was obviously in pain. Fernstead was aware of this and insisted that Chief Suvete visit the *Bac Si*. The hospital was by that time overwhelmed. Casualties lay everywhere on beds, on the floor, littering the archway entrance into the medical bunker. Bac Si seemed to be with everyone all at once. He also was everywhere, ranging from patient to patient, trailed by his assistant, Ca Rangh, toting packs full of battle dressings and supplies. As Chief Suvete waited his turn for medical triage, he evaluated the man and woman who labored together with one heart and soul. There is a capacity in every culture to admire something noble. To the old chief these two young people, man and woman, epitomized the virtues of all he had wished for in this venture; the tall, caring, odd colored foreigner alongside this selfless, faithful young woman from his own race. All around them, the couple were surrounded by pain and suffering, which they worked determinedly to alleviate. *"What greater cause than this?"* he thought.

"Ah, Chief Suvete, I see you have been indulging in shrapnel this morning! You must be more careful. Your people need you," said *Bac Si* when he finally got around to Chief Suvete.

"Well, *Bac Si*, I am like my people this morning you see, wounded but not down. I can see them here, so many coming to you for your blessing, then returning to the perimeter. What is it you do, *Bac Si*, to make my hurt people go back for more?"

At this, Gabriel McCarthy paused, looking deeply into the now sunken, dark rimmed eyes of the old chieftain. "I tell them, Chief Suvete, that they are still members of this living world, that while they yet live, they are among others who have left us to go on to a world beyond. I offer them the opportunity to remain here among their wounded kindred or to return and fight the good fight; for it must be a good fight given the price it has cost among those we love. I tell them, Chief Suvete, that we will care for them as long as they need us to do so, but beyond that, they must care for themselves and I leave it with them." Chief Suvete looked over *Bac Si*'s shoulder at the reclined Sgt. Ronald Winkle, face covered in bandages, metal tube protruding from his throat. As he felt the sting of his own wounds being cleaned with disinfectant, Chief Suvete reflected mentally, *"Who are these men, these American, who are so willing to come here for my people and sacrifice so much?"*

The old Chief met the gaze of the revered young American medic before him, and then looked away without grimace as *Bac Si* bent to tend his wounds. There were several pieces of shrapnel visible sub-cutaneously. These, Bac Si removed with forceps and hemostats, dressing each wound as he moved expeditiously from one to the next. There was no time to administer local anesthetic and so prior to starting, he gave Chief Suvete an 8 mg. injection of morphine, resisting a full dose of 10-20 milligrams, knowing that the old Chieftain must not be rendered senseless during this critical time. The morphine loosened somewhat the feelings of old Chief Suvete, at the same time making him feel warm. When *Bac Si* finished, the old Montagnard chieftain attempted to thank him, but already *Bac Si* was off tending another casualty.

When Chief Suvete limped out of the hospital bunker, he went into the adjacent communications bunker. Inside, Staff Sergeant Thomas Gowen was transmitting sitreps back and forth between various defensive sites around the compound relaying command information between Captain Fernstead and Master Sergeant Briant. Chief Suvete looked around the bunker, lit by three bright Coleman lanterns. Gowen explained that Capt. Fernstead had stopped transmitting and suspected his radio might be out. Chief Suvete settled on a row of unused radios, mounting one of the PRC 77's onto his own back via harness and rucksack frame. Evidently, Captain Fernstead up above needed another radio. Thereafter, with bullets whizzing around him, the old Chief climbed up atop the communications bunker, stepping sideways onto a climbing platform and clambering over the lip of a low-lying wall of sandbags. On the other side, he found that it was not a radio failure that had broken communications with the American Commander.

Captain Ronald Fernstead, was lying on his back against a ledge rock surface of the promontory top. He had a hole through his chest about the size of an apple. Through a sentient haze of emotion, still affected by morphine, Chief Suvete knelt over the dead American Commander, shedding tears over the lapels of Fernstead's camouflage fatigue blouse. Evidently, one of the communist .51 rounds fired uphill from NVA crews on adjacent peaks had haphazardly found the valiant American officer. Old Chief Suvete realized with a flood of emotion that the big bullet had struck squarely in the heart of the American; *'how symbolic'*, he thought while nodding a silent farewell to his friend.

Chief Suvete reached for the handset on his radio in response to repeated calls from Major Plinder.

"Minnow One, Minnow One, I say again, can you read me? This is Saber Leader, over."

Chief Suvete put the handset to his ear, pressing down on the transmit button as he did so.

"You come for your people! You come! We have them ready!"

It was all he could say. He knew nothing about directing close fire from attack aircraft or how to coordinate an airmobile withdrawal. About all he could do was attempt to get the Americans to the landing pad and get them out. With Fernstead gone, Chief Suvete had not the slightest doubt that this place was lost. His people would hold out to the last man, woman and child. He knew the communists would exact a terrible price for Montagnard resistance. Leaving the radio strapped to his back, Chief Suvete climbed down from the blunted dunces cap promontory. His first stop was almost directly below. He went straight to Ca Rangh, pulling her aside from tending to a Montagnard warrior wounded in the proximal thigh. He explained to her the situation. He advised her to get *Bac Si* and the wounded Sgt.

Winkle to the landing pad. He explained that by whatever wit or stratagem she could devise, she must get *Bac Si* on a helicopter or he would surely die. Old Chief Suvete then went directly south, into the weapons bunker. He collected as many rifles as he could and went from there into the bunkers wherein the women and children huddled.

"Come children, it is time to meet the enemy." With that, he handed out what rifles he was carrying, directing the women to collect more from the weapons bunker and pass them around. Without any formality, certain women were handed grenades and silently designated as caretakers for the very little children. All the rest of the women, along with all the children over the age of about seven years, trundled off to the weapons bunker to secure more rifles and ammunition.

Chief Suvete left that bunker and went to the landing pad, wherein a single, small helicopter, shaped like a large egg with a tail was just landing. Evidently by some stratagem, Ca had managed to get *Bac Si* to leave his precious patients long enough to carry Sgt. Winkle over here to the landing pad. The Montagnard chieftain approached Ca Rangh with an extra rifle, setting both weapons down in a conspicuous place that she could clearly see, understanding what he meant by the act. They were both positioned behind *Bac Si*, who was huddling in front of them with Sergeant Winkle draped over his shoulders. As the little helicopter touched down, Chief Suvete and Ca pressed forward, urging *Bac Si* toward the helicopter which, having approached from the east was now landed with its single left sided crewman's door facing them. As he ran, *Bac Si* lifted his friend over his shoulder from a fireman's carry position, while preparing to fit Winkle into the small Loach compartment. As they ran toward the aircraft, Chief Suvete and Ca Rangh followed close behind. It was quite clear that this little helicopter would not hold more than two additional people and so it would be quite senseless to attempt to bring the other Americans in at this point. As *Bac Si* unloaded his friend into the Loach bay, Ca and Chief Suvete pushed him in from behind, causing him to fall headfirst within a far recess of the helicopter bay, at the same moment, Chief Suvete stepped around to the cockpit; "*Di Di!* Go Go!" he shouted, observing the pilot acknowledge with a nod of his helmeted head. Ca leaned in and whispered something into *Bac Si's* ear, then hopped back, off the skids. The other American crewman had grasped *Bac Si* by the back of his web belt and was holding him in the helicopter bay as the tiny warbird lifted off. Ca Rangh could see Gabriel kicking and struggling to twist around from his awkward, headfirst position. For a moment, she feared that he might actually get loose and jump back down to them. Just as he was turning to his side, she gasped as she saw a red splash erupt from under his left side, knocking him back face downward. In the only display of emotion Chief Suvete had ever heard from her, she groaned out loud as she realized that *Bac Si* had just been wounded. Evidently, he had taken a hit near the groin. She had a momentary flash of thought, a review of intimate fantasies she had considered briefly in times past. She hoped for those few moments that he would live, that he would come to know a woman someday. She was quite certain he had never known a woman intimately in that way before. She believed that if he ever did in some future, more gentle age, she would somehow know from wherever she was bound beyond this life, and somehow she would share also in that part of discovery with him.

For now, Ca Rangh turned and hurried back, accompanying Chief Suvete to where he had cached the two rifles. They involuntarily dropped down as a loud explosion came from the communications bunker. Together, Ca and Chief Suvete rushed the communications bunker, killing a team of four sappers rampaging through the camp with satchel charges. They changed magazines in their weapons and headed over to the northeastern perimeter, now starting to fenestrate with breaks in the defensive line. What few 82 mm mortar tubes the communists still had were pounding relentlessly into the sawtoothed bunker line. Communist mortar crews were actually hitting their own men, now just beginning to overrun the bunkers. All the defenders became vaguely aware of a loud rending crash as one of the larger helicopters, a big Huey, swung around and plunged downhill, crashing loudly into the inner strand of concertina. The explosion produced a transient gap in that part of the NVA assault wave. Chief Suvete, with Ca close behind, went directly to MSG Carmen Briant at the tip of the perimeter apex. They found Briant firing an M-60 with a bright red barrel that sizzled as it scorched fibers of the sandbags around his portal. When he finished the belt, Briant had to pause a moment to switch barrels. He was alone in the bunker, and Chief Suvete stepped forward to help mount the second barrel which, while not red hot, was still warm enough to burn his hands. Briant had an asbestos glove on his own left hand and used it to pop out the superheated barrel, turning to see Chief Suvete.

"Sergeant Briant! Captain Fernstead is dead. *Bac Si* and Winkle have been medevaced out by one of your little helicopters. You, Estrada, Haskell and Volkert are all that remain. You must try and leave now!"

Briant turned to him, speaking in Rhade dialect as he loaded the next belt into the feeder slot without looking.

"*Chief! Go tell Volkert to call in an Arc Light. Tell Estrada and Haskelll what you have just told me. I leave it to them to make their own decision but for me, my place is here!*" With that, Briant turned back to the firing port and commenced directing fire into the numberless enemy, now breaching the innermost wire only 25 meters or so from his position. Chief Suvete turned to Ca Rangh.

"Go, find Estrada, and tell him. I will tell Volkert and Haskell."

Ca left to find Estrada, who was closest down the northeastern bunker line. Chief Suvete had to detour back into the trench system to get to Volkert who was on station in the only remaining, active mortar pit nearest the camp epicenter. He was firing from his tube within direct line of sight of the advancing enemy. Philipe Suvete explained the situation to Volkert who nodded, then reached back into his LBE buttpack for the beacon device. He activated a power switch, dialed in the correct coding sequence then, checking to assure that the device was functional, he turned on the beacon, setting it for point of contact, indicating that the bombing strike should hit at the very spot the beacon was broadcasting from. He set the beacon at his feet, and then resumed efforts with the 81mm mortar tube, hanging and dropping repeatedly with the aid of a Montagnard loader.

Ca Rangh found SFC Estrada at the middle bunker on that northeastern perimeter. He had expended all of the M-60 ammunition within the bunker. The roof of the bunker had been nearly opened up by repeated impacts from both 160 and 82 mm enemy mortars. Directly to Estrada's front, the enemy had successfully opened a body-strewn corridor through the innermost wire. He could not see them, however, because his firing port faced off at an angle to the left toward a sector wherein the enemy was rushing around the flaming helicopter to assault the bunker line farther north. SFC Estrada only had time to empty a single magazine of M-16 rounds, firing on semi auto at point blank range, maintaining sufficient control to resist the temptation to flip on full automatic. As he fired off the last round, the first pajama clad hoard overran the bunker. They swarmed up and over, into Ca Rangh's field of fire. She was not quite so well controlled in her management of the M-16 she had in her hands. She flipped the selector switch to full automatic and shot point blank into the wave of NVA communists, emptying the 20 round magazine in just under two seconds. As the weapon emptied, she conjured up a recollection of *Bac Si*, gazing at the rising sun, which she could now see full orb over the heads and shoulders of enemy assault troops. It left her with something good, something she could fill her mind with during these last few moments. Enemy soldiers continued to flow over and on top of her, shooting down at both Ca as well as their own fallen comrades in their haste to kill up close. She went down under the stampede.

All the bunkers were placed at angles to the line of attack and so none of the enemy had yet been able to shoot straight back at

Estrada. As he heard shots to his left rear, he whirled to see Ca Rangh firing from the explosion gouged bunker entrance, upward toward the top of the bunker. Estrada could see waves of black pajamas and chartreuse uniforms dropping onto her as she fell beneath gunshots and bodies. Issuing a roar like the toro he was so often compared to, Estrada seized his ever present machete in the right hand, while grabbing an M-16 bayonet up in his left. Head down, he plunged into the host of enemy surging over the bunker with their backs to him. He struck, slashing with the large blade and stabbing with the shorter bayonet. He had a vague, slow motion, strobe like sense of stabbing and gashing. Pieces of clothing containing body parts fell at his feet. He pushed his way into the hoard slashing and thrusting. NVA soldiers who had overrun the bunker and were now inside the camp whirled to see the big American actually rise up under a pile of kicking, struggling communists dropping over the bunker tops, driven forward by the rush of others to their rear. Communist soldiers inside the camp turned and fired their own AK-47's at full automatic, back into their own soldiers, crossing over the bunker line, now inseparable from the raging Mexican-American. Nearly a dozen NVA "insiders" formed a reverse skirmish line, firing back toward their own line of advance. They expended a full load, changed magazines and fired again, all the while shooting at the terrible American samurai as he cut his way through their own comrades. He finally went down, taking no less than four dozen rounds, collapsing under a weight of enemy dead who continued to pile on top of him as the terrified skirmish line kept shooting into this seemingly invincible warrior.

Enraged NVA assault troops swarmed through camp from the northeastern perimeter breach. Instead of charging into adjacent bunkers, they rushed toward the center of Swordfish Lair, shooting and bayoneting their way into the hospital and command bunkers, which had already been demolished by some of the first sappers to break through the perimeter. Women and children fired random patterns of M-16 rounds at full automatic, before being mercilessly cut down by assaulting troops. SSG. Volkert remained with his mortar crew to the end. His last conscious thoughts were of the arc light strike, now finally responding to the beacon. He stood within the mortar pit, 81 mm shell in hand, looking up into the morning sky, he could just see the a pattern of blurry projectiles dropping through a light shroud of cumulous clouds above, raining down toward the beacon at his feet.

20 minutes earlier

Ron Winkle was only vaguely aware of the world around him. For the last twenty-four hours, he had been kept deeply sedated by Morphine administered liberally from *Bac Si*. Even Winkle had come to know his friend by the appellation *"Bac Si"*. During those last few weeks in Laos, it would have seemed almost strange to call his former best man "Gabe" or "McCarthy" any more. He was *Bac Si*, and the voice of *Bac Si* was what kept Sergeant Ronald Winkle connected with a world seemingly far removed from his other senses. Ron could neither see nor smell nor talk. He could hear and he could certainly feel. Even through the morphine, he could feel. Pain. Shooting pain, alternating between burning, electricity and, whenever the morphine started to wear off, sheer screaming misery. Two of the big three sensory-motor branches of his facial trigeminal nerve had been damaged when the lower half of his face was blown away. He drifted in and out of consciousness heralded by that pain. At one point, he heard something, or someone that brought him back. It was the sound of a name, his wife's name, spoken by the voice of *Bac Si*.

"Ron, this is Gabe. I have to carry you now over to the Med-Evac. There's no one else to help, so we're gonna have to do this the hard way, on my back. It's gonna be uncomfortable, but you've go to bear with me buddy, I have to get you home, back to the world, back to Kath."

Ron Winkle nodded at this, vaguely understanding that it meant he would be moved. Moving was painful and he tensed with the realization of it. Had he a voice, he would have groaned as he was hoisted up onto his friend's shoulders and bounced relentlessly for several minutes. Ron could express nothing more than wheezes through his cricoid tube, agonizing, exhalatory wheezing from the up and down motion of riding on his friend's shoulders. He felt himself drop at last, falling backward into something mechanical and loud, a helicopter. It must be a helicopter. They had come for them at last. They were leaving, but under what circumstances? Sounds of battle permeated all around. He could feel *Bac Si* squirming and struggling over him as a sensation of lifting began. There was an increase in weight and a tilting. At the same moment, a blast of wind struck him from below and also from his right side, from the front of the helicopter. He wondered if they were being shot down and analyzed this for a moment. If they were, he would certainly die. Perhaps that would not be so bad. At least he would be finally delivered from this pain. However, he might not see Kath again either ... his Kath. Although he had known her throughout most of the last decade representing half of his entire lifespan, it seemed as though he had only just really begun to discover her. If there was any reason for living, that was enough. To return to Kath and to discover all about her that time and circumstance might offer. But, would she want him like this ... with only half a face?

Ron Winkle was aware of a finger probing at his throat, seeking out his carotid artery. He knew it was *Bac Si*, recognizing the closeness of his friend who was now packed in against the tiny confines of the helicopter, probably a LOACH. There, he could still reason and think after all. Yes, it must be a LOACH. Winkle felt wet warmth soaking his right thigh and realized it was blood. He could not feel any new wounds on his own body and wondered if it was perhaps *Bac Si*. Was *Bac Si* wounded? Could that happen? *Bac Si* who cared for all the other wounded. Somehow no one considered the possibility of *Bac Si* being wounded. But, it must be, after all, *Bac Si* would never have left Swordfish Lair otherwise. How badly was *Bac Si* wounded? Winkle wondered about this, reaching out with his arms, embracing his friend, holding *Bac Si* as the shattered little war bird rushed eastward. There was someone else in the compartment, probably a crewman. He was trying to help them stay in the aircraft, but there was so much wind! Everywhere there was wind. It was as if they were flying in a very fast convertible with the top down. The noise was too great to hear anything but the sound of the engine and the wind rushing by. And so, Ron Winkle held on to his friend, because it was all that he could do. The morphine was wearing off and the pain was coming back and his friend was limp in his arms. Then, it occurred to Ron Winkle that there was one other thing he could do, and so he prayed.

When the LOACH finally landed, Sgt. Winkle was aware of attendant hands prying free the tight grip he maintained on his friend, *Bac Si*. Winkle felt *Bac Si* being lifted off of him and could sense also that the pilot and crewman were exiting the aircraft. Thereafter, Winkle was lifted onto a stretcher and placed in a Crackerbox ambulance. He was transported from one place to the next throughout that day. At one point, he was aware of someone, probably a doctor, removing the bandages from his eyes and for the first time in several days, he could see. The realization came upon him with a flood of tears. He had not been certain if he would be able to see again. His eyes had been swollen shut and bandaged since the explosion. He had not been able to actually focus on anything. His eyes felt puffy still, but they could definitely see. He heard a voice.

"Listen Soldier. We don't know who you are. You came in here sterile, but you must be an American. We realize you cannot talk, but I believe you can hear and probably see. If this is so, I need you to blink twice for me."

Ron blinked twice to the blurry form of his inquisitor.

"Good. Now, whoever put this tube in your throat did a good job but clearly, it was done in a hurry. In order to give you any chance of talking again, we need to move your breathing tube down to a regular tracheostomy site. The wound has destroyed part of your jaw and your nose, but you still have a tongue and most of a hard palate. That means we can maybe rebuild your jaw and perhaps you will be able to articulate again in the future. But, in order to do that, we must minimize the damage to your larynx, your voice box. So, we are going to put you out now, and when you wake up, this thing in your throat will have moved down a bit. You may be able to swallow again, although that will still be difficult until we can work on that jaw. You'll be going to sleep now, son.

"*Son*", an appellation of affection, coming from a paternal voice; that was the last word he could remember. Now, it was... later. How much later, he didn't know. He was in another vehicle, a large plane this time. There was a feminine presence next to him, strange how he could sense that it was a woman without even opening his eyes. When he did, he saw that he was in the bay of a large aircraft, suspended on litter hooks beneath another litter similarly suspended above him. There was an Army nurse tending to him, taking his blood pressure and pulse by palpation.

From the Evac Hospital at Pleiku, Sgt. Ron Winkle had been transported to Cam Ranh Bay where a first tier surgical team went to work. There was really very little for them to do aside from transitioning the Cricothyroidotomy to a regular tracheostomy. Surgeons were impressed that somewhere, this unnamed soldier had received excellent care. Evidently, he had been given massive doses of antibiotics as well as a cut down IV access portal placed into the greater saphenous vein of his left ankle. He had clearly undergone careful primary debridements of numerous shrapnel wounds along the front of his body. The face would require extensive plastic surgery and for this, Ron Winkle was being transported back to the United States, where he ultimately wound up at Brooke Army Medical Center in San Antonio, Texas. Brooke Hospital had acquired a reputation for plastic surgical reconstruction based largely on the burn center located there. In the case of Sgt. Ron Winkle, he was quickly certified for the plastics team due to the nature of his injuries. Over the next few months, his jaw would be reconstructed using segments of rib and iliac crest. In addition, numerous shrapnel wounds on his body would undergo delayed primary closures with some necessitating skin grafts harvested from his back.

February 25th, 1972

Kathleen Marie Winkle was in her sophomore year at Florida State University. After Ron had disappeared into isolation back at Fort Bragg, she remained in Fayettville for about a month, sharing time with the other wives. They encouraged her to go back to school while Ron was "down range". So she departed for Tallahassee in Ron's green VW beetle that Spring of 1971. She arrived in time to commence the summer term at FSU. She had since corresponded with the wives regularly. It almost seemed as if she needed their reassurance, their approval, for this move as she felt very much the need for contact with their particular sorority. Accepting financial help from her parents, Kath attended school at FSU over that summer in order to make up for the semester she lost out on following the impromptu nuptials with Ron. It was late in the summer of 1971 when she read a letter from Diane Fernstead, informing Kath that Gena Glickman had been notified of the death of her husband, SFC Michael Glickman. Kathleen Winkle took the news very badly. Prior to this, she had considered the Green Beret A-team to be invincible. They were all young, strong, intelligent men, and she nurtured a subconscious conviction they could survive anything. Although she knew, of course, that they were soldiers, she simply had not equated it with the possibility of one of them really dying. For several days after hearing the news, she was unable to focus on her studies. She had been writing back and forth to Ron during that time through censors via an APO at Fort Bragg. When she next received a letter from him alluding that all was well, it somehow comforted her. Later the following fall, she discovered in a letter from Roxanne Briant that Kirk Brooksly had been wounded, how badly no one knew. Hungry for information on her husband, Kath used some of the money she was now receiving as a military service dependent to secure plane tickets for herself and Roxanne. The two women met in Atlanta and flew out together to San Francisco over the 1971 Thanksgiving break. They visited with Kirk in Letterman Army hospital at the Presidio. Again, Kath was devastated to discover the handsome, athletic Brooksly just having undergone an amputation above his right knee. During the two-day visit, Roxie and Kath stayed in a cheap motel on Pacific Avenue just off post from the Presidio. Brooksly remained an inpatient, as yet he was unable to check out from the hospital, still receiving a powerful anti-fungal medication, Amphotericin B. She had heard one of the medical interns attending Brooksly refer to the medicine contained in an aluminum foil wrapped IV bottle as "Ampho-terrible B." It caused awful side effects, but at the time was the only thing effective against San Joaquin Valley Fever, the disease that had somehow infected his leg. Although he obviously suffered from constant nausea and generalized aching, Kath found Brooksly to be polite and respectful with her and Roxanne, eager for their company, answering those questions which he felt did not compromise any part of the security of his comrades. He spoke positively of Ron Winkle, about how much he had grown and accomplished during their mission. But below the guarded demeanor, Kirk Brooksly had changed somehow. Both Kath and Roxanne sensed this and discussed it in their motel room after visiting hours. It was more than just the terrible amputation, more than the ravaging drugs scourging his system. Sgt. Kirk Brooksly was quiet, despondent, somehow more primitive in character. Kath had known him previously as a shy, charming young man who frequently grinned and seemed totally confident in himself as well as the US Military. He still expressed absolute fealty for the Army. However, he seemed less devoted to the concept of civil patriotism. He seemed to place the Army and the US mainstream in separate camps, almost like enemies. It seemed as though he had lost faith in the citizenship of his country. As military dependents, Kath and Roxanne shared a Thanksgiving dinner at the Presidio Hospital mess hall with Kirk. He was still connected to an IV pole on wheels. He was only able to pick at the food and clearly, attended the mess hall banquet more for their benefit than his own. Kirk Brooksly bordered on bitter whenever Kath mentioned anything about her college life and the attitudes that seemed to prevail on campus about the Vietnam war.

Returning back from San Francisco, the two women took separate fights to their respective destinations in Fayetteville, North Carolina and Tallahassee, Florida. Kath had more time to herself than she really wanted. She wondered what would become of her husband. Would he come back similarly maimed physically, emotionally? Would he return to her the same man she remained so deeply in love with? Contrary to some of the other servicemen's wives she had met on campus at FSU, Kath found herself not at all attracted toward other college age men. Over the months preceding the visit to Kirk Brooksly, the only contact Kath had with Ron was via a weekly letter, which she looked forward to with rapt anticipation. In almost every one of his letters, Ron opened up in some new way that endeared her to him more and more. Except for his letters, which she read and reread over and over, she would immerse herself in studies, shunning the considerable social life available at Florida State University except perhaps to go out to a movie or concert from time to time with other female acquaintances in her dormitory, DeGraf Hall. Shortly after arriving back from Letterman hospital, Kath was invited by another coed to attend a concert during the first week of December, 1971. She thought it might be a good way to get her mind off mounting concerns about the well-being of her husband. The concert headliners were a popular contemporary band, *Country Joe and the Fish*. As she sat in the packed campus football stadium among masses of academic peers, she began picking out isolated lyrics with a sense of growing incredulity:

> *Yeah, come on all of you, big strong men,*
> *Uncle Sam needs your help again.*
> *He's got himself in a terrible jam*
> *Way down yonder in Vietnam*
> *So put down your books and pick up a gun,*
> *We're gonna have a whole lotta fun.*

And it's one, two, three,
What are we fighting for ?
Don't ask me, I don't give a damn,
Next stop is Vietnam;
And it's five, six, seven,
Open up the pearly gates,
Well, there ain't no time to wonder why,
Whoopee! we're all gonna die.

Well, come on mothers throughout the land,
Pack your boys off to Vietnam.
Come on fathers, don't hesitate,
Send 'em off before it's too late.
Be the first one on your block
To have your boy come home in a box.

And it's one, two, three
What are we fighting for ?
Don't ask me, I don't give a damn,
Next stop is Vietnam.
And it's five, six, seven,
Open up the pearly gates,
Well there ain't no time to wonder why,
Whoopee! we're all gonna die.

She would recall listening to the other students gleefully singing along with the melody during the open-air event held on the football field at Doak-Campbell Stadium. As Kath looked around at long-haired youth all about her, she saw them in a new light. They were all children, really, just spoiled, naive children, conceited offspring of a baby boomer generation who had reaped terrific good fortune as progeny of self-sacrificing, World War II generation parents. Here they were, a generation of youth her own age, satiated with drugs and sex and music, gleefully shouting satirical lyrics in defiance of the incredible sacrifices of other young men and women from their same generation. It seemed to her that they were defiling American military men and women in service to a country that measured its greatness in large measure by such liberty as would tolerate the blasphemy of this chorus. American servicemen, sacrificing for these ingrates, were suffering and dying halfway around the world from where they all gathered on that beautiful late autumn night in 1971. It was so ludicrous, so narcissistic, so... so... *profane.* What was even more poignant was the fact that she recalled herself with the same callow attitude just a few months prior. She had not understood before and thus had been caught up in the contagious fervor of an eclectic generation of pampered youth, the largest single generation ever known, with a powerful market force able to enrich and reward contemporary skeptics of an inconvenient war.

Over Christmas break, 1971, Kath drove up to North Carolina, spending the holidays with other wives and family members of Team –A-321. Notably absent was the family of Michael Glickman, who had by this time left Fayettville and Fort Bragg for good. After Christmas, Kathleen Marie Winkle drove from Fayettville, back down to Miami and spent New Years with her own parents, as well as Ron Winkle's family. She shared with his parents some of the things he had disclosed to her about how his feelings for them had matured and grown over the previous year.

Following Christmas break, Kath returned to FSU and launched into the new Semester, which began January of 1972. She was attending a lecture in Child Behavior on Friday, February 25th, 1972 when a secretary from the office of the Academic Dean interrupted her class. She was singled out among her classmates and asked to accompany the secretary back to the Dean's office. From the moment she was summoned, a sick feeling began to grow in the pit of her stomach. She silently stood up, departing the stone quiet classroom, leaving behind books and lecture notes. In the hall, she grasped the secretary's arm, while trying to control a rising panic.

"Is it my husband? Tell me, is it my husband?" Hysterical tears started to fill her eyes.

"Well, I, I really can't ... you should really speak with the Dean." The secretary turned and started walking away. Kath noticed a wedding band on the secretary's left ring finger and with this, halted her again, spinning her around, meeting her face to face.

"Listen, you're married. If you love your husband, you must know why I have to know here and now. Surely, you understand this. I have to know right now and I don't want to hear it from some Chaplain. Is my husband alive or dead?"

Again the woman faltered before meeting her gaze, then looked her back straight in the eyes.

"He's alive Mrs. Winkle, but he's wounded. That is really all I can say now, more than the Dean would have wanted me to say. You know how sensitive an issue the Vietnam war is here on campus right now. If word got out that one of our full time student's husband was wounded in Vietnam, there might be another demonstration. Please, just come with me now."

Kath did accompany the woman across campus to red brick administrative offices off College Avenue. They were greeted in the Dean's office by the Academic Dean as well as a military attaché from Fort Bragg. Upon entering the room, Kath did not even acknowledge the presence of the Dean, meeting at once the stony countenance of an officer with a scar running the length of his left eyelid and cheek. He bore gold oak leaves and a nametag, which read "Scadlock".

"Where is he, Major? Where is my husband?"

Major Scadlock met her inquiry without hesitation, almost as if he expected her to be this forthright with him.

"He's at Brooke Army Hospital in San Antonio, Texas ma'am, and he's going to be there for a while. Now, you and I need to talk about what must be done in order to finally bring him back home."

Chapter 11 – Recovery

Late March and Early April 1972

March 23rd, 1972; US Army Hospital Psychiatric Ward, Da Nang, South Vietnam

Major Sydney Shia Schwartz settled in to his usual roost at the bedside of a young man dressed in faded blue pajama bottoms and a dull-patterned hospital gown, tied in the back. It was Major Schwartz's 12th session with this particular patient and the Army Psychiatrist was beginning to fade in his initial resolve that this soldier could be returned to the fighting force. The patient had arrived four weeks prior with a bloody wound in soft tissues of his flank between pelvis and left hip. It had bled profusely en route to a MASH unit in Pleiku. For several hours, survival had been touch and go. Evidently, some ricocheting enemy bullet disrupted the series of vessels running between a cruciate shaped anastomosis encircling the femoral neck and several branches of the Superficial Iliac artery. Although fuzzy in his recollection of much of the anatomy he had learned in Medical School many years ago, Major Schwartz recalled a mnemonic about that particular artery. One of his old med. school dissection partners had nicknamed it "The Great Anastomoser" because the Superficial Iliac interconnected so many vessels in the Iliac Plexus. Fortunately for this young man, the wound had clotted down before he bled out, due in large measure to someone applying direct pressure over the area. The wounded soldier had arrived with an H&H

(Hemoglobin/Hematocrit) of about 7 and 22 respectively, both confirming the more apparent physiologic signs of shock from loss of blood. A team of surgeons clamped and ligated several severed pelvic arterial branches, essentially stopping the most serious hemorrhaging. Because of an extensive interchange of collateral circulation within the pelvis, there would be no need for a complex vascular reconstruction. Undoubtedly, the lateral hip would be painful as a scarifying wound had been created very close to the large obturator nerve that serves both Hip and Knee. However, careful muscle testing had confirmed that there was no motor deficit. Several pieces of ricochet bullet fragments still remained strewn throughout the area. Being inert metal, the damage it would cause to remove them all did not justify the inconvenience of leaving them in situ. Once the surgical team in Pleiku managed to rebound the patient's H&H, as well as bring his electrolytes back on line, they collectively determined that this young man should recover sufficiently to return to his own local unit, whatever that was. He was subsequently transferred here to Da Nang US Army Hospital, ultimately winding up in the psychiatric wing.

Uncharacteristically, the patient had arrived at Pleiku in sterile camouflage field uniform without dogtags. Shortly after his admission in Da Nang, a very abbreviated 201 file with basic medical records jacket arrived from MACV SOG. The young man's name was McCarthy, first name Gabriel, though he'd not responded to either name at any time throughout these several sessions with Major Schwartz. During the first couple of encounters, Schwartz suspected that the young man was catatonic. The patient, McCarthy, would not take food or drink, of his own volition. The patient did, however, attend to his own bodily waste functions, after the Foley catheter had been removed about a week following his admission. Aside from trips to and from the latrine, which practically nobody had been witness to, McCarthy did little else but lay in bed. During conscious times, McCarthy would recline in one single, supine position, looking straight up at the ceiling.

When he slept, he would twist and turn violently, screaming things in mixed english and foreign dialects. Doctor Schwartz enlisted the aid of a Vietnamese linguist who worked part time in the hospital. The Viet had informed Major Schwartz that the words being shouted by the young American casualty during his tortured nightmares were not Vietnamese. They sounded more "*Moi,*" meaning savage, or Montagnard-like in nature. With very little background, Major Schwartz pieced together that this young man must have been on some sort of clandestine mission, in which he had worked or lived with Montagnards. More than that, the aging psychiatrist had not the slightest idea. McCarthy would not respond to Dr. Schwartz's questions, even under sedation. Doctor Schwartz had attempted various hypnotics, anti-psychotics, tranquilizers and sedatives, always injectables, as the patient would not co-operate with any medication offered by mouth. Among other things, an attempt had been made to induce some response with Thorazine, but all that had accomplished was to produce a characteristic "Thorazine Shuffle," which Schwartz actually observed on one rare occasion when the patient went to and from the latrine. Presently, Dr. Schwartz was considering whether or not to attempt Electro Convulsive Therapy (ECT), shock therapy, in an attempt to break through the young man's neurotic introspection.

During the first session with patient McCarthy, Dr. Schwartz had conducted the usual cognitive testing, which included a specific test to determine the patient's level of psyche by response to pain. The Army psychiatrist had knuckled his patient over the sternum, a certain and precise way to elicit pain response among patients capable of feeling pain. There had been a slight grimace in the eyes, but no attempt to physically resist, to turn his body or prevent the noxious stimulus. It was almost as if this patient was tacitly accepting the painful stimulus like an obedient but emotionless child would accept a spanking. Somehow, the response had softened the Doctor to this young man and over these ensuing weeks, on each occasion in which they had visited together, the psychiatrist found himself becoming somewhat inured to the case.

"Gabriel, this is Dr. Schwartz again. How are you today?"

No response.

"Gabriel, we have been visiting together for quite some time now, surely, I have earned the right to speak with you?"

No response.

"Gabriel, I am not the enemy. I am here to help you. We have to communicate in order for me to help you. I know you can hear me, and I have heard you speak out loud while sleeping. I have the power to help you. Do you want to return to your unit? Do you want to go home? Do you want to live? Do you want to die? Tell me, what is it you want?"

No response.

"Gabriel, does the feeder tube bother you? If you would like, I can remove it right now, if you will just tell me that you'll eat voluntarily."

No response.

It had been like this every other visit. Doctor Schwartz attempted all sorts of verbal ploys to get a reaction. On one occasion, he even discussed a concern about cowardice with the young man, but all that had done was elicit one of those painful, subtle grimaces about the eyes, which was even more pathetic than the response to physical pain stimulus. As with the sternal pain response test, Dr. Schwartz never repeated any reference to cowardice again.

To compound matters, there was so little information in the 201 and medical records file that Doctor Schwartz had none of the usual characterizations with which to establish some rapport. Where was this kid from? What unit had he been assigned to? Did he have family back home? Where were all of his buddies? Normally, a wounded soldier had at least a few unit comrades come to visit in the hospital. But, with this young man, no one had been by to see him. Doctor Schwartz requested more information through the local Provost but had been politely informed that what he had was all he would be provided in order to treat this patient. When the Doctor protested, he was advised that if he wished to be released from the case, someone else could be assigned in his stead. Somehow, the thought of being removed from McCarthy's treatment caused the seasoned, middle aged military psychiatrist to feel a pang of regret on his own and simply renewed his desire to unlock the puzzle of this unusual young mind.

"Gabriel, if you continue to be unresponsive, I shall have to consider electro convulsive therapy in your behalf. Do you understand what shock therapy is?

No response.

Well, he had attempted everything else. Perhaps it would be the best thing for the patient in order to bring him out of this stupor. Balanced on Major Schwartz's left knee since the beginning of this session, was a medical record chart on the patient, McCarthy. Dr. Schwartz had opened the chart to a Physician Orders sheet and was struggling with a decision whether or not to sign the "zap" order. Finally, however, Dr. Schwartz's mind was made up. A session or two of ECT would certainly bring the patient around, perhaps at the expense of a few thousand-brain cells, but so be it. That was surely preferable to this semi-lucid neurotic state McCarthy now seemed remanded to. The order needed only be signed and Sergeant McCarthy would be taken straight away to a place in this hospital where such treatment could be administered in relative safety. With a grimace of his own, the military psychiatrist signed the order, following which; he stood up and exited the room to initiate the process.

Out in the hallway stood several officers, all dressed in starched OD jungle fatigues with folded green berets tucked under shoulder epaulets. One of them stepped forward to enter the room as the psychiatrist started to walk down the hall. Major Schwartz turned and addressed the officer, a Lieutenant Colonel with no name on his uniform.

"Excuse me... sir, but unless you can tell me something about your relationship with that patient, in order for you to visit with him, it will have to be in the presence of either myself or one of the psychiatric nurses. His condition is too fragile to risk any emotional strain."

The Lieutenant Colonel turned, leveling a deep, penetrating gaze in Schwartz's direction, not unlike some of the psychotic looks Major Schwartz had encountered among his inpatients. Another officer stepped forward. This one was a full bird Colonel and wore Medical Corps insignia on his lapel. Schwartz read the name "Starr" over his right shirt pocket.

"Actually, Dr. Schwartz, we will need to let the colonel spend some time with that patient alone. I have read over his chart and your progress management notes on him. We appreciate your efforts thus far in his behalf. He is a very important asset to us."

Dr. Schwartz was a bit perturbed by this unexpected intrusion on his patient, particularly after just having arrived at his own rather difficult treatment decision.

"Those notes are confidential and who are you people anyway? If you have something to do with his former unit assignment than I need to speak with you about what preceded his admission here. This is a very sick young man. I am about to order ECT on him in an attempt to bring him around. If you have anything to offer that would help me avoid shock therapy, please let me know. Otherwise, I shall have to insist that you leave, ... now."

The medical officer, a Colonel Starr, exchanged glances with the no name Lieutenant Colonel. He then looked back at the Army psychiatrist. "Doctor Schwartz, we will permit the colonel here to speak with that patient, alone. If after they have finished, the patient still has not responded, than I will cooperate with you in any way possible and fully endorse your decision to use electrocortical therapy. However, until such time as we have had an opportunity to speak with him in isolation, I must ask that you forestall your order. I have here a signed affidavit from your Commanding Officer as well as the Commandant of this hospital facility. These documents give us full authority to assume care for this patient. We do not want to usurp your role here Dr. Schwartz, but it is vitally important that we arrange an interview in private between this officer and that young man in there."

Major Sydney Schwartz looked disbelievingly at the documents before him. In 18 years as a Military physician and psychiatrist rendering service that stretched all the way back to Korea, never had he been shanghai'd on a patient order such as this.

"At least let me be present when your man speaks with him."

"I'm sorry, Doctor, but we cannot permit that."

"Than you will have to sign off that this is being done against my professional advice."

"I am prepared to do so, Doctor," with that, Colonel Starr wrote a statement on the order sheet, indicating acknowledgement of Dr. Schwartz's reprimand, and signed it, handing it back to the military psychiatrist. After doing so, Colonel Starr again glanced over at the no-name officer and nodded his head. Without further word, the Lieutenant Colonel entered the room, closing the door behind. Major Schwartz looked on in frustration for several moments, and then stomped off to his own commanding officer, who was prepared and waiting to receive him.

Inside the hospital room, the Lieutenant Colonel looked around. He noted four stark walls painted a sort of light green color with single, grated window looking down from the second story building level on to a grassy court below. There was a second door in the room that opened into an adjoining latrine. The latrine opened into two additional doors, one into the hallway as well as another leading into an adjacent cubicle, which was a mirror image of this one. The latrine contained facilities for restraining and washing a patient if necessary. The colonel could not know for sure whether or not restraint had been necessary with McCarthy, but he strongly suspected it had not. After closing the latrine door, he pulled up the same chair Major Schwartz had just been using. Reversing it, the light colonel sat with the back of the chair facing forward, straddling the seat as he leaned forward on the backrest.

"Sergeant McCarthy, do you recognize me?"

Although McCarthy did not acknowledge in any obvious manner, the voice pattern triggered a movement on the patient's brow and semi-closed eyelids opened perceptibly.

"We were introduced once before during a committee interview at Fort Bragg just over a year ago. Perhaps you recall?"

There was no response to this, and after several seconds, the officer continued.

"I have news for you, news about Operation Fisherman, and what has become of Swordfish Lair. Do you want to hear this news?"

There was a slight, ever so slight, response to this, an inclination of the head just a few degrees in the direction of the Lieutenant Colonel who accepted the movement as an affirmative response. For a few seconds, he weighed his next words. *"Was this kid capable of hearing the truth right now?"* he thought. If McCarthy could be of any further value to the mission at hand, it was now or never. With measured words, in as gentle a voice as he could muster, the lieutenant colonel went on.

"Swordfish Lair is gone. The camp was overrun just as we dropped massive arc light ordinance in response to a beacon activation signal from within the L-site. Subsequent aerial reconnaissance has confirmed that most people around"... he paused before going on... "and within.... the site... are dead."

With that, for the first time in weeks, emotion broke through the cold, pathologic reticence of Gabriel McCarthy. His eyes filled with moisture that cascaded down the sides of his face, mixing with a shallow growth of sideburn on either side as he directed his gaze straight upward toward the ceiling. The colonel continued.

"Your patient and friend, Sergeant Ronald Winkle made it back to the States OK. He was sent from Travis directly to Brook Army Hospital at Fort Sam Houston because of extensive facial damage. They have some of the best Plastic Surgeons in the world working there in the Brooke Burn Center and at last report; they expressed confidence in being able to adequately restore most of his facial features, eyes, nose, and jaw. His wife Kathleen, the one you all snatched from that church down in Florida, she's there in San Antonio with him right now. I have to admit," he mused, "we had our doubts about her given the sudden change of heart at that wedding and all. But it seems she has turned out to be an extraordinary young woman. She'll ride this out with him … all the way."

Gabriel responded with a very slow, diminutive nodding of the head, which signaled also a stemming of the cascade of tears flowing down the sides of his temples. Seeing the impact of familiar names scoring some cognition with his one sided interview, the lieutenant colonel continued.

"You did a good job with him. You saved his life. You need to hang on to that."

To this, Gabriel's head stopped nodding and transitioned into a similarly diminutive wagging, back and forth in the negative. For the first time since leaving Laos, he spoke. His voice was hoarse and strained at first.

"They're all dead… and I should be… back there… dead with them. They were my patients … my people. I didn't… didn't want to leave them. The Yards … they pushed me into a Loach while I was loading Ron. The door gunner … he held me in. I tried to jump out, but took a hit that knocked me back into the crewspace. He wouldn't let go. … I have no right … no right to be living, with them dead…, all dead" He closed his eyes as again, a flood of tears began to cascade up from under the eyelids.

The lieutenant colonel watched as emotion and personality slowly coursed back into the young man lying before him. Again, the Lieutenant Colonel paused a few moments before measuring his next reply.

"We think maybe they're not… *all*… dead."

This opened the eyes of Sergeant Gabriel McCarthy and motivated a directed gaze toward the colonel. "What do you mean, sir? Some are still alive? Who? Where? Did you bring them here, to Vietnam?"

"We think there is at least one person still alive, Master Sergeant Carmen Briant. We've received a beacon device frequency signature from deep within Laos, near the trail. It is set to repeat with a sixty second flash cycle once every 24 hours on unique, amplitude modulated frequencies that could only be from Operation Fisherman."

"But,... how do you know it's Briant? How... how do you know he's still alive? It might be an enemy soldier experimenting with one of the devices."

"Only the officers and senior American NCO's knew how to use those devices. They are very, very sensitive items. The frequency pattern had to be set by an American. No one else would know how to key in the correct number sequence to activate the device. Son, once, I was very close to Carmen Briant. Close enough to read his mind. If he were dead, I'd know; body or no body, I would know. He's not dead. I know that. I'm here to find out if you're willing to go back with me to get him out."

Slowly at first, but with more energy as he completed the movement, Gabriel McCarthy sat up and swung his legs over the edge of the bed, facing the officer. There was a Naso-Gastric (NG) tube running from his nose, clipped to his hospital gown by pinching between a safety pin. It imparted to his voice a nasal resonance as Gabe posed his next question:

"Sir, who are you anyway?"

The colonel looked away for a few moments, letting his eyes take a far away look before they came back and met squarely with the querying eyes of young Sergeant Gabriel McCarthy.

"In another lifetime, I was like you. I was an NCO who got involved with something that I believed in, something that was very important to me. When an opportunity came to score what seemed to be some real influence for this cause, I took it."

"Sir, with all due respect, that doesn't answer my question."

"No, it doesn't. Well, I suppose it's about time to show the whole deck. You've earned that much. Once upon a time, the name was Shriver, Michael Dalton Shriver."

"As in Sergeant Shriver? Mad Do....", Gabriel broke off the refrain, fearing it disrespectful to the officer seated before him.

"Yes, son, the one they used to call Mad Dog Shriver. Of course, the name grew with the legend and as with most legends, tended to outlive and outgrow reality. Actually, that's the fundamental reason Mad Dog Shriver had to die, you see, so that his legend could grow and serve a much more significant purpose."

"But ... you're alive, sir. You're not an enlisted man, and it doesn't look like you're a field operative."

"No, but that's another story. Perhaps someday, I will have an opportunity to tell you. For now, I need to know this. Can we get you out of this bed and back into the field? You're the only asset I have in Southeast Asia right now who's been on that access trail out of *Bai Lo Dui*, to the west."

Gabriel followed events backward in his mind to the place and time referred by the surprise visitor. That trail they had taken following the death of McClary and the pillaging of *Bai Lo Dui*. The last major action they had engaged in prior to the siege on Swordfish Lair. He had a clear recollection of the episode, indeed it was one of the myriad memories he had relived over and over in his mind during the last few weeks.

"Yes sir, I recall it well. Is that were we're going?"

Major Sydney Schwartz sat apprehensively in a lumpy gray cushioned metallic chair under a squeaky ceiling fan in the office of his Commanding Officer. Major Schwartz situated himself across from a name block centered on one edge of a similarly gray colored desk. It read *Colonel James H. Reid MD*. Colonel Reid was an Internist with over 22 years time in service to the U.S. Army Medical Corps. The two military physicians had exchanged a lively conversation regarding this patient named McCarthy in psychiatric isolation. Colonel Reid had received written instructions regarding disposition of the patient and was nearly as puzzled as Doctor Schwartz over this gross breach in protocol regarding psychiatric patient care.

"I'm sorry, Syd, but my hands are tied by these damned spooks. I have a directive here all the way from I Corps HQ to defer to the SOG people on care and treatment of this patient. We're instructed only to provide support staff and facilities."

"But Jim, look, this kid is as close to la la land as any patient I've ever worked with over here. Have you seen his hair? He's only 20 years old and already, his hair is turning white. I'll bet he came over here without a single gray hair. Do you realize what it takes to cause that kind of physiological change in a person? I believe that inside his head, there's still a workable human being, but unless I take drastic measures, and soon, he may become so reclusive that we never get him back. None of these sneaky petes identified themselves as a psychiatrist. The one that went into that room for a solo interview didn't even wear Medical Corps branch insignia. The whole thing reeks of intrigue that has no business in a hospital."

Colonel Reid was about to reply when interrupted by a soft knocking sound at the door. The Colonel's secretary, a freckle faced enlisted kid, stuck his head around the partially opened, creaky, hinged door.

"I asked not to be disturbed, Parker."

"Yes sir, but one of those SF officers is here and asks to speak with you. His name is Colonel Starr."

Colonel Reid exchanged glances with Major Schwartz before directing his attention back to the timid Spec Four Parker, still peeking diminutively around the door. "Very well, show him in."

Colonel Starr strode into the room as both Reid and Schwartz rose to meet him. In starched jungle fatigues with spit shined jungle boots, Starr had the advantage of "presence" in the confined office space. Both Reid and Schwartz were dressed in plain, poplin, short-sleeved khakis with white lab coats. Not wishing to diminish his own authority figure, Colonel Reid spoke up first.

"What can we do for you Colonel Starr? I trust you understand that we are somewhat disturbed by your intrusion within our facility here."

Colonel Starr was a thin, blonde haired man with heart shaped face set atop squared shoulders. He responded with a disarming smile that expressed sincerity without condescension. "Sir, I have come at the request of your patient, Sergeant McCarthy, who would like to speak with Doctor Schwartz here."

"What? What do you mean speak to me? That patient hasn't uttered a word in the four weeks he's been here. Has your man somehow gotten him to respond?"

"Apparently so, perhaps you, yourself, could come and conduct an interview with him now?"

Doctor Schwartz erupted from his seat, brushing past the starched Colonel, swinging around the creaking door with one pendulous motion and quickstepping back to the psychiatric isolation wing. Both Colonels Reid and Starr followed him in close tow.

Doctor Sydney Schwartz was not at all prepared for the vignette that greeted his return to McCarthy's room. The patient was sitting up on the side of the bed, slowly stretching his arms and legs. As the psychiatrist entered the room, McCarthy looked up.

"Oh, hello, sir. Thank you for coming so soon. I was wondering if your offer to take out this feeding tube still holds? I'm ready to eat now."

Major Schwartz kept the patient another two days. His decision to do so was not in any way contested or interfered with by the SOG group. During those two days, McCarthy quite satisfied all objectivity testing as to mental competence. Schwartz was amazed. On the second day, just prior to signing the discharge order, Schwartz had one last interview with the young man McCarthy, now a much more imposing figure in starched camouflage jungle fatigues with green beret in hand.

"Sergeant McCarthy, I can find no reason to keep you here any longer. You've satisfied every cognitive examination criterion I can offer. Although I understand why you can't discuss with me what it was that brought you to us in the state you were at only two days ago, I must confess, I remain concerned. You understand, in your mind, the trend has been set. Whatever happened to you before has demonstrated the capacity to render you a psychiatric cripple. Should those events or similar events recur, you could be thrown back to the near catatonic state in which you presented here. You realize this?"

McCarthy stifled a bit of wry grin, which transitioned into more of an expression of gratitude for the earnest Major. "Sir, believe me, those circumstances are not likely to recur ever again. I only wish I could explain to you why that, in itself, is such a tragedy."

Schwartz searched the sincere, yet grim, expression of the young man before him and replied, "Well, tragedy, or mystery as it must remain to me, I wish you the best. Good luck Gabriel." With that, the military psychiatrist exchanged a firm handshake and immediately thereafter, signed Gabe's discharge order.

They were again waiting for him in the hall, five officers patiently standing in a quiet, non-conversational group. As McCarthy emerged from the room, they all turned, almost as if on cue and proceeded without a word down the long corridor, out of the hospital. While climbing into the waiting jeep outside, Gabriel felt a weakness that had pervaded body and soul during the previous four weeks of incapacitation. He would spend the next few days working aggressively at restoring muscle strength, coordination and fine motor skill, particularly in his left leg, which constantly ached in the knee and hip, although he would admit it to no one.

Four days later, Sergeant Gabriel McCarthy sat, transfixed by red glowing gauges, set to protect night vision for pilots and crew. These were the only lights visible within the wind-shrouded bay of a Huey D model slick rushing them headlong westward, into the night, back into Laos. Gabriel carried the now familiar feeling Car-15 along with a .45 ACP Colt service automatic shoulder holstered under his left armpit. In addition, he carried an M-79, hung from a sling which draped it muzzle down, just behind his right arm, suspended in such a way that he could easily swing it forward by reaching down and back. This was the way Estrada had taught him to carry the weapon back at Fort Bragg when they went through their first weapons familiarization together as a team. Was it only a year ago? So much had happened, a lifetime of events. And now, Estrada was gone, along with most of the rest of A-321.

Reconnaissance flyovers had confirmed that Swordfish Lair remained in an area so remote, the communists, lacking heliborne support, could not stay for long without running out of supplies and logistics. They did not even bother to haul out their own dead, but left the entire area a stinking, scorched necropolis. Evidently quite certain that the Americans would characteristically make an effort to catalogue their own dead, and not inclined to pack out carcasses, the enemy had left bodies of dead Americans lined up outside the hospital bunker. It would take an Army pathologist some time later to decipher that the enemy had switched parts among the bodies in one last, spiteful quest to antagonize the Americans; "*Estrada, Glickman, Gowen, Haskell, Johnston, Erickson, Fernstead, Volkert ...all gone. Still alive, back in the states, were Winkle and Brooksly, both maimed for life,*" he thought. To Gabe's count, aside from himself, that left Briant. Was Carmen Briant still alive? Shriver was quite certain that he was. According to a bugeyes flyover, no one living was left at Swordfish Lair. So, then, where was Carmen Briant? Shriver had a theory about where Briant was at this time and why. It went back to their days operating together as a Special Ops team. Together, Shriver and Gabe exchanged conversation on a closed circuit "David Clark" headphone system, especially wired within this Huey to permit conversation between passengers without members of the crew listening in. Shriver was speaking into a boom mouthpiece attached to the headset:

"*Operation Fisherman has been effectively shut down. With more than half the team dead, a circuit breaker clause went into effect that prohibits further activity except for SAR resources necessary to get survivors out of the AO. That is how we've been able to justify tasking this helicopter to take us in and later, hopefully, to get us out. It will probably be one of the last times US aircraft cross into Laotian airspace for a long time. This is a mission to recover Master Sergeant Carmen Briant, based on the assumption that he is still alive.*

"You see, son, Briant and I were more than teammates. It got to a point where we could read one another's thoughts. Probably came from spending so much time in the field communicating with nothing more than hand signals. There were eight of us, two Americans and six Montagnards. Our team became like a single entity and we could sense one another in the field. Pitch black night, jungle so thick you couldn't see your own hand in front of your face, it didn't matter. It was like we each had this radar inside our minds and we could sense the rest of the team like dots on a screen. We were united in our purpose, destroying angels sent to dish out retribution on the ungodly. We knew our targets were bad people, and sensed a feeling something akin to what it would have been like to take out Adolph Hitler the day after he started killing Jews. Just before Briant left on R&R in 66, I was given a mission to go after a series of targets that were described to me as American traitors, U.S. servicemen who had gone over to the gooks and were conducting raids on SOG teams in Cambodia and Laos. Although we were advised that there might be several Americans in collaboration with the enemy, we only knew about one for certain. He was a Marine with blonde hair, named Welker, Stuart Welker. We had a dossier on him that catalogued several incidents in which he had been observed dressed in black pajamas and a gyrene cap, leading enemy patrols. They found the remains of three ambushes resulting in dead Montagnard strikers and U.S. advisors, attributed to this Welker.

I was ordered by a Lieutenant Colonel, name of Carlock, to take out Welker along with any other Americans working together in collusion with the enemy. We'd had other run-ins with this light bird Colonel Carlock. He was assigned as S-1, intelligence officer for C&C North. A couple of times, he had left us dangling after a contact. He would take his own sweet time to get us out. When word came down on this mission, he got the bright idea that he would help earn himself a full bird by going out in the field with us. I didn't like the idea and said so, right up front. I also was not convinced about the mission. You see, son, I had always trusted Briant. He was the conscience of our team. He would research the dossiers more carefully than you could believe. Oftentimes, he would find additional information on a mission that not even our own S-1 intel people preparing the report, had turned up. That always irritated this colonel Carlock. It was OK with me, because it just made the colonel work his people harder and that improved our field security. Of course, it drove Carlock nuts that we had the option of turning down a termination if we were not convinced the mark had committed actions worthy of 'extreme prejudice'. But that was the standing order. Any special ops team not convinced of the severity of their target were not required to carry out the mission. We were all strictly volunteers.

"Anyway, Briant was gone on a well deserved R&R. I could never return to the United States as Michael D. Shriver because of some trouble down in New Mexico back in 62. In another life, I came home once on leave to find my ex-wife badly beaten by a live in boyfriend. He was a psychopath who liked to beat women and play with civilian firearms. To make a long, sad story short, I wound up in a New Mexico state penitentiary. There were some people in the government, who felt that I was more valuable as an asset in Southeast Asia. They managed to get me out. That was on condition that I would not return to U.S. soil as Michael D. Shriver. It meant ending all former associations. No more childhood acquaintances, no more contacts with anyone back home, including family. I suppose one of the things that drew me to Briant was the strength of his family. I always wanted to meet his wife and kids. Have you ever met Roxie?"

"Yes, sir, Top Briant pretty much made us a part of his family and his wife always made us feel at home. She's quite a woman. The whole team loves her.... loved her. It sure would be great to salvage something out of this mission by returning Briant to his family."

"I agree with you, son. Your understanding that is another reason why I consider you essential to this E&E recovery."

"E&E? So you're convinced Briant is presently Escaping and Evading?"

"Well, let's just say E&E fits as a bucket into which we could file this mission. No, I do not believe Carmen is E&Eing. I believe Carmen Briant is stalking a mark. He is hunting the enemy."

"Field Commander Muc Bo Thau?"

"That's right. I think Briant is convinced that he has one last score to settle before he can go home to Roxie."

Gabe responded; "That sort of makes sense, except that I can't understand how he would put it ahead of returning home to his family. If ever there was a man that needed killing, it's Muc Bo Thau. We had a file on some of the atrocities that he's been responsible for among the Hmong and Montagnards. I think he must be the worst human scum of the earth. What you said about Hitler rings true. If this guy were to rise in power, he would be every bit as bad, maybe even worse, than Hitler. The problem is, given the fog that settles over everything communist, the rest of the world might not know about him until it's way too late. But, sir, you were telling me about how you and Sergeant Briant got separated."

"Yes I was. Well, son, some things are not easily explained without a foundation. My foundation was Carmen Briant. He was always rock steady in the field. I could always count on his good, common sense while at the same time, never doubt that he would be there, where I needed him to be. The Yards loved him even more than I did, which is saying a lot about the man. So it was December of 1966, and Carmen was in Hawaii with Roxie. I was left with this garret trooper light colonel Carlock who ordered me to take him out into the field on an operation about which I did not believe we had nearly adequate intelligence.

"We inserted deep into Cambodia, West of Ple Djereng. No sooner were we in the bush than this jackass Carlock starts screwing things up, insisting on radio checks every couple of hours, sloshing around with half a canteen and less of a brain. After I took the radio away from him, we managed to make our way along this river towards Helo Charlie Michael Tango. On the third day, we found their camp, late in the afternoon. As usual, Colonel Carlock wanted to sitrep HQ until I finally put the barrel of my .45 against his temple and told him the next time he used that radio without express permission, he would become KIA. After that, I never caught him at it, although we think they were listening in on a transmis-

sion he made during our RON that night. It's possible that Welker even helped the gooks translate some of what Carlock said, although I doubt they knew exactly what our mission was. We reconned their base camp all that next day. Sure enough, in addition to the blonde haired Marine, Welker, there were three other Anglos and a Negro in the camp. The blonde kid and the Negro wore black pajamas. The other three Anglos wore blue jeans and khaki safari type clothes. They were taking a lot of pictures. It turns out they were a trio of photojournalists trying to do a documentary on American deserters in the field. Charlie was cooperating by showing them a case of white and black soldiers working together with the communists against the U.S. . I had no idea what the two journalists had been promised at the time, but found out later that some U.S. magazine had offered a quarter of a million dollars for an article showing proof of U.S. deserters working in the field. Maybe Welker and the Negro soldier had struck some kind of deal with the press, I never found out for sure. During the fourth day of our mission, the Black soldier took off on patrol with a platoon-sized group of NVA regulars. We waited two more days for him to return, finally, on the sixth day after insertion, we agreed to make the hit that following morning, which would be the seventh day of the mission. We only had rations for seven days and the longer we stayed, the more at risk we were of being discovered, especially with Carlock so useless in fieldcraft. He and I had an argument about how to make the hit. He wanted to initiate the shot, something I always did as designated One Zero with the Yards. Finally, the Colonel seemed to see reason and agreed to wait until I took the first shot. We got up early that morning, way before sunrise. We made our way into the camp until we could make out the canvas hooch in which we had seen the blonde headed American Marine sacked out the day before. I crawled up close enough to toss a pebble into the hootch, which woke up Welker. He took a step out of his hootch and I drilled him dead center with the .45. What happened next was chaos. We had come to anticipate these situations, when a superior enemy force, during the sleepiest hours of darkness, receive reveille by gunfire from within their own camp. Carlock went for the other Americans, the Journalists. That was something I didn't expect. I had figured that since they might be civilians, they were excluded as targets.

Evidently, the journalists had been rehearsed about what to do in the event of a bombing or air raid. They ran into a shallow bunker nearby the field tents they were sleeping in. Carlock runs over and tosses a Wille Pete into the bunker. That pretty much turned those three journalists into hot plasma. I couldn't believe it! We never discussed anything about killing non-military. In fact, I had mentioned that we'd have to be certain they were clear of the deserters when we took the shots, for fear of getting them into a cross fire. Evidently Carlock made the decision on his own before we even snuck into camp.

We knew how to get out. We'd done it before under worse circumstances. The Yards started several fire fights among the gooks while I searched Welker's body and found that he still wore his dogtags. We evaded northeast about a klick, calling for exfiltration from an LZ we had pegged out the day before. For someone who'd left our rear ends high and dry on more than one occasion when he was directing missions from a far away safe house, Carlock was in an all fire hurry to get to that LZ. The straightest path was back along the way we had come. I advised him not to take that route. He was feeling his oats as the mission was winding down. Maybe he felt his rank coming back on line. We had no choice but to either abandon him, or follow him back to the LZ. I had our Yards spread out as it was getting light and I didn't want us bunched up. That's what saved the rest of us. Carlock walked right into a counter ambush set up by the Negro soldier, whom I later found out was a kid from Pittsburgh named Dudley. When Carlock tripped the ambush, we were back about 25 meters. I brought the yards onto a skirmish line perpendicular to the way their ambush was laid out. Fortunately, the bush was just light enough to let us stay more or less linear. With our combined firepower hitting their right flank, they broke ranks. We got about six of them, one of which was the American deserter. I got his dogtags, along with Carlock's. By that time, the enemy had regrouped and were starting to counter-attack. I lost four Yards during those last 20 meters to the choppers. I took a little nick on the left shoulder, but through luck and pluck, the rest of us managed to get out."

At this, Shriver paused and gazed off into the somber night, rushing by outside. *"I don't have to tell you, McCarthy. When you lose people, especially when you're real close to them, you'd pretty much rather die than go on wondering why you didn't go down with them. Later, a hatchet force went back in after the bodies. They found the Yards along with what was probably Carlock. One body had been skinned, decapitated and both of its hands cut off. With no finger prints or dental impressions there was no way we could get an absolute identification on him..*

After the debriefing, our staff people were most concerned about the journalists. They figured it was necessary to do something to draw attention away from the mission yet acknowledge that there had been a mission. Something that would so distract people about the mission itself, nobody would be likely to look closely at the purpose of the mission. They contrived the death of Mad Dog Shriver. Carlock was about my size and height. He had no real family back in the states. His mother died when he was a kid and his old man had been killed during WW 2. He had no living grandparents, aunts or uncles, and wasn't married. It presented a somewhat enigmatic solution. I would become Carlock. Carlock's corpse would become me. The communists unwittingly cooperated by mutilating the body, particularly after word went out that my patrol was lost in the area. Lieutenant Colonel Carlock was transferred on paper back to the JFK center at Bragg, which was were I eventually wound up. Carlock's actual remains are catalogued at Central Identification Laboratory in Hawaii (CILHI), near Tripler, on Honolulu. As I understand, he is listed as BTB (Believed To Be) Shriver, Michael D. But without confirmation, Michael D. Shriver remains officially missing in action. Carlock may actually someday be buried at Arlington, under the headstone of an unknown soldier from the Vietnam war.

After that, I spent another year in and out of Vietnam, mostly down in Saigon. I made visits as a spook advisor to South Africa, Panama and even made a little snorkeling trip into Cuba. Because of my experience with the Yards, my handlers let me head up a task force to try and think tank some sort of solution to the Montagnard problem. I continued to use Carmen Briant from a distance, though he couldn't know that I was pulling the strings. As always, he came through on whatever task we gave him. In a way it was as if we were still working together. It was painful, almost as painful as losing the rest of the team, to let him go on thinking I was dead. But the people who put me in a position to head this task force made it an absolute precondition that I never again have direct contact with him or anyone else who knew me. They even did plastic surgery to change my facial appearance, although I don't think it would have fooled Briant.

We planned to launch Operation Fisherman back in 68, but were sidetracked by Tet. Then the South Viets became suspicious and started trying to infiltrate our think tank. It became more and more clear over time that we would have to conduct the operation from Bragg, only using Southeast Asia for essential staging and distribution of supplies. It might even have worked if Big Minh hadn't gotten wind of it. As things turned out, it was just plain arrogance for us to believe we could keep the thing confidential until the U.S. State department would announce that Montagnards were forming their own Independent State. We did all we could, given available resources. You were doing it too, son. If we could have kept you and the rest of the team up in those mountains another six months, fixing them up, improving their quality of life, building their confidence toward self governance. The Meo and Montagnard people always had a fierce sense of independence, a cultural identity. FULRO demonstrated that the Yards could form their own separate political system. All we needed was something to build a thread of continuity among their various tribes. Something that had been proven during the Buon Enao experiment was medical civic action. One of our biggest mistakes during the Special Forces era in Vietnam was rotating A-Team medics every six months. The Yards could readily adjust to new military and civic leadership. What they needed was a sense of continuity in health care. They needed Bac Si's who were part of the community, who didn't have to start all over again every 6 months getting to know the sniffles and sneezes of the people, so to speak.

The Montagnards trusted us as healers and organizers. What they needed to unite them was a sense of promise in deliverance from the more brutal enemies of illness and disease. Those adversaries have plagued them for as long as they've been a people. We grew to believe that overcoming disease and malnutrition would also unite them. You and Glickman were intended to be the harbingers of all that. When we lost Glickman, we all wondered if you could follow through. We considered breaking protocol and trying to smuggle in another medic. We even considered sending in a permanent officer, but increasing pressures from the Cooper - Church amendment scuttled us. Then that MD sawbones, Dr. Rivera came along. For a while, we thought things would work out. Until this US Congressman, Riley Hathoway, back home, started interfering and managed to shut down Bugeyes. We had to pull Dr. Rivera out of the project. If he were to become KIA, there was no way we could have covered up a dead MD. While he was there, he helped ..." to this, Gabe nodded listlessly "*...but right up until the end, you were what they really needed, son. With Glickman as martyr, and by your teaching the Yards to care for themselves, it hardened their sense of identity. Most societies develop a sense of cultural identity as a result of meeting some essential organizational pre-requisites. Those pre-requisites include civic and religious or moral leadership, both of which can be composed in relatively short order. The other component of even primitive societies is some form of community healer. That particular designee requires greater endorsement than any other essential cultural job description. If we had sent in a trained physician, it would have taken us at least 10 years to fully train the first Montagnard replacement for that physician. While we all hoped it would happen someday, we relied on you and Glickman to lay a foundation on the magic of western medicine among the Montagnards. You have to understand this, son, that in accomplishing that particular objective, you were absolutely successful.*"

With this last comment, Gabriel found himself again fighting back a wellspring of tears. After being discharged from the hospital, he had begun to think himself immune to any further emotion. Shriver had not presented his dialogue as so much patronage, rather, a simple statement of fact. At that moment, a tap on Shrivers's shoulder from the crew chief broke in to their conversation. The crew chief held up ten fingers, indicating that they were about ten minutes to the infiltration point. Shriver reached over to a communications panel into which all the headphones were connected and switched to a common onboard net.

Conversation was exchanged between the pilots and Shriver as they approached their first objective and infiltration point, an open area just west of the village of *Bai Lo Dui*.

The Huey came sweeping in from the southeast, having taken a long, circuitous route over the mountains to avoid both observation stations and anti-aircraft fire. Pilots on board the chopper flared to a brief hover about twelve feet off the ground, descending to three feet over the same ground from which the Mike force had deployed just three months ago. As they hopped off the skids, Gabe felt the ground rise up to meet him and found the old instinctive movements within his body coming back, absorbing the weight of rucksack and gear. In addition to weapons, Gabe brought along a single M-3 "small" aidbag. Although limited in volume, it carried a decent assortment of essential medical supplies, battle dressings, morphine, 250 liter canister of serum albumin and two 500 milliliter bags of Lactated Ringers along with two cutter sets and 18 gauge butterfly needles. In addition, he had a field surgical set with instruments rolled in an OD canvass casing, suture materials with disinfectant, local anesthetic and a common pillbox dispensary of oral, suppository and injectable medications. Although he carried a fair diversity of medical items, he carried none of them in any particular quantity. In this way, he felt prepared to deal with a greater variety of single casualty injuries, but realized he was not at all prepared for multiple casualties. This was not a support mission. They were on their way in to discover if Briant was still alive and if so, to get him out. MSG Carmen Briant, if alive, might possibly be wounded. He might be sick from having to survive in the jungle. This was the only potential casualty Gabriel had constructed his medical contingency plan for. Both Gabe and Shriver had attired themselves with explosive mechanisms to booby-trap their own bodies in the event they should be captured. Neither would permit themselves to be taken alive in Laos. For Gabriel, if there was no living Carmen Briant at the crux of their mission, he had no particular motivation to come back. His world had changed so much over the last year. The elations, hopes and ambitions he had constructed during Operation Fisherman were so all emotionally and personally consuming. Gabriel McCarthy could no longer conceive of any life worth returning, to what seemed the imaginary world of, "back home." The reality, what he believed in most, was here in this landscape. He felt it in the bite of shoulder straps, in the familiar hand-holds of weapons, in the confidence of his medicaments. As he shadowed Shriver toward thicker forest back in from the LZ, Gabriel once again sensed his body chinking and swaying under nylon and canvas burdens, moving to the rhythm of the bush. Shriver felt it also. The rush of effort and sound and vision and smell, all came together in a primitive terrain communicating with primeval genes. They moved noiselessly along trails now grown over, but surprisingly fresh in the mind of Sgt. Gabriel McCarthy. He recalled the same trek, back around the end of rainy season, following Fernstead and the courageous little old Hol Mei back to the Hmong Village that had been savaged by NVA scalpers. The team was strong then, fearless, confident of their technology and their supporters, unafraid of the enemy, eager avengers ready to mete out retribution for the cruelty the Montagnard people had suffered. How much had changed since then.

April 2nd, 1972

MSG. Carmen Porter Briant attempted to open his eyes, but was only successful in bringing vision to his left side. The right eye and lid were caked shut with a mix of dried blood and vitreous humor. As his port sided view struggled reluctantly with the input of a new day, Briant started momentarily from a faraway dream of Roxie and the children, wishing to hold them in his thoughts as sleep faded to restless consciousness. Time no longer had any significance as a continuum in this present world. There were no reviles, no alarm clocks, no kisses good morning. He awoke because something within prompted him to arise from the dark, dank jungle floor that had been his resting-place during part of the night. For the sum total of days numbered without count, Carmen Briant had awakened to pain in his right eye as well as a need to complete the mission. *"The mission, what was the mission now?"* Over the course of his life, he had served so many missions; they all seemed somehow jumbled up in his mind. Carmen rubbed a filthy hand over his head, transiting down to his face as he idly scratched six week's worth of unchecked beard. He struggled mentally to clarify this present mission, what was it? He had a mission, clearly, there was a mission it was... what? To preach the gospel? To carry out orders from his military superiors? Perhaps the question was so puzzling because there was more than one mission. Yes, that's it, there are many missions, so many missions. How does one know what to do? Prioritize, of course. One must prioritize the mission by reviewing the objectives. What are the mission objectives? To defend Swordfish Lair ... No, that mission is over with. He had defended Swordfish Lair to the limits of his resources and ability. So, what now? There was something.... Oh, yes, to take care of his troops while completing the mission. What troops? Let's see, *"Officers are all dead,* so the chain of command is down to me."* He whispered out loud. With the officers dead, his next, most immediate responsibilities were those troops under his command. *"Dead, dead, dead, dead, dead, dead...,"* he mentally ticked off the names of each man on team A-321.... *"...dead, Medevaced out during monsoon season, Medevaced out two during the final engagement at Swordfish Lair, dea.... No, not dead. There was one more alive. There is one more I have a responsibility for before I can go home to Roxie... Who?"* As he pondered this, light began filtering down onto the little space in which he had been sleeping and with the light, came recollection. *"Yes, young Haskell, he's still alive and not far away. I must find him and take him home with me, back to Roxie. So, the primary mission is to get Haskell so I can go home to Roxie. What is the second mission? Yes, but what? The second mission is the mark and who is the mark? Oh, yes, The second mission is justice, or is it ... retribution?. It's all as simple as that... Haskell is the road back to Roxie and in the process, if the opportunity* *presents itself… there is, a man from whom to exact retribution by blood atonement, the termination of life. "That man's name is Regimental Field Commander Muc Bo Thau. He is an evil man who has been responsible for great suffering and injustice among the Montagnards, so many of whom are now also dead, by his hand."*

Having recited the logic of this daily litany, MSG Carmen Briant roused himself for the day's task at hand. He had been living like this since the final assault on Swordfish Lair. After the firestorm from that last beacon guided, Arc Light bombardment, Briant awakened within a false tomb of sandbags and bodies. He had been in an apex bunker on the outermost northeastern perimeter, firing from a sawtoothed portal at the advancing tide of NVA, pouring over the wire and into the camp. Briant had known that Volkert would call in the arc-light at the end, when all was hopeless. There was absolutely no option for surrender. The communists would kill everything living within the camp, especially after their protracted defense infuriated the enemy beyond any possible quarter. Briant knew that when the moment came, he would feel the earth quiver and rage with the ultimate decimation of Swordfish Lair. He thought that he would take some last satisfaction in knowing that they had done their best to fight their enemies and… to defend their indigenous charges? But, as the huge bombs began to disintegrate the mountaintop, Carmen Briant's last conscious thought was one of failure, failure to keep his promise to Roxie, a promise that he would return to her and the children. On that thought, Carmen Briant dropped into a state of catalepsy, knocked unconscious by a levee of sandbags, hurled in upon him with great force. He was thrown under the lintel of the firing portal, the one through which he had been discharging the red-hot barrel of his ardent M-60 machine gun. When the bomb blast from behind threw Briant against the opposite partition, his face was pressed into the proximity of the framed portal, which, somehow, preserved a breathing space within the sepulcher of collapsing sandbags around him. The arc light had been called in sometime around mid morning. Briant lay in state under the collapsed bunker, unconscious for about twelve hours, his tired body making up not only for injury, but massive fatigue as well. When he awakened, he was brought to bear consciousness again by a searing pain in his right eye. Evidently, as he had been bodily tossed about within the collapsing bunker, his face came into contact with the heated barrel of the M-60 and specifically, with the forward aiming post of the barrel. The elevated metal post had driven hard into his right eye, penetrating and cauterizing the orb as cascading sandbags blanketed the rest of the barrel and gun. As the gun buckled, it remained enough of a strut that it preserved a space around Carmen, sufficient for him to expand his lungs. The framework of the firing portal left an irregular duct through which fresh air continued to circulate around him.

It had taken Carmen Briant more than 30 minutes of persistent struggling after regaining consciousness, to crawl out of the would be tomb. Initially, he was able to free up his right hand, first tending to the aching eye. There was little time for mending as a simple palpation of the area revealed enough about the injury to give up on the eye itself. For the next half-hour, Briant painfully worked his way out of the bunker space, straining against burlap and poly-fiber layers of cloth stratified within a dirt mound, all that remained of the bunker. When finally he emerged, like a cyclops mole, he took careful, monochromatic stock of the carnage left around him. There were bodies and parts of bodies everywhere. Off in the distance, there were living people, milling about what had once been the center of camp. The dented dunce's hat peak still stood, but had been altered by heavy bomb ordinance. NVA soldiers were sifting through the rubble, looking for battle trophies or anything that might render salvageable intelligence information. In the immediate vicinity wherein Briant had broken surface, there were no enemy soldiers, perhaps because it was so close to a perimeter completely enshrouded by fragmented bodies. Somehow, Carmen Briant snaked his way down into the gully below. The ground was strewn now with remnants of the former land bridge entrance into Swordfish Lair, as well as a carpet of dead bodies to bolster his descent. Once down below, he made his way around the summit, moving warily under a dull, misty, reddish half moon. By dawn, MSG Carmen Briant went to ground, crawling into a hole, which offered decent concealment while still providing him a mono-vision vista of the western plain below. That geography had also been subject to the arc light bombardment and now appeared as an eerie, lunar like surface with huge craters surrounded by areas of stripped vegetation. Briant estimated that there must be many thousands of dead communists. There were so many dead that the living who remained were not even making an effort to organize or bury corpses, something the NVA would normally tend to so as not to give the Americans any satisfaction in body counts.

Carmen Briant had on his person a .45 caliber colt automatic pistol sidearm. This was holstered to his personal load bearing equipment (LBE), along with a Naval Survival Knife in a whetstone-containing sheath, and several other web gear items. Contained within a small butt pack, he carried a single beacon bombing emitter device and four cans of assorted C-Rations. He also carried on his web belt a canteen full of water, and four extra magazines for the .45. He consumed small amounts of the food and most of the water during the next 36 hours, finally working his way down to a meandering stream on the northern side of the western plain. From a small, brown, wax capped jar, taped on to the looped plastic cap retainer of his canteen, he dropped two water purification tablets into the refilled canteen, giving them time to dissolve before satiating his thirst with water smacking of a strong iodine aftertaste. While pausing nearby the stream just before dusk on the second day after the battle for Swordfish Lair, Briant noticed a delegation of NVA soldiers passing off in the distance. Having stalked general officers many times over the previous decade, Briant recognized the minion-supported ranks of a field officer and staff. What particularly drew his remaining eye into focus on this hoard was a single, tall figure dressed in tiger stripes, bound with arms behind his back, being prodded along by the group. Obviously, it was an American.

With the advance of night, Briant crept stealthily after the assembly. Clearly, the NVA troops remained stunned over their losses. There was very little in the way of perimeter security around the command post and Briant was able to get close enough to hear conversation as well as recognize the prisoner. It was Haskell. Throughout the night, Briant pieced together bits of information as he listened in on the NVA speaking in their own tongue. Vietnamese was a language Briant picked up over the years along with his Montagnard dialects. Evidently, the communists had accounted for six dead Americans, all in sterile uniforms and therefore without any insignia of rank or identification. One of the dead Americans was a negro, something that always seemed to fascinate the North Vietnamese. Six dead. That meant both officers, Fernstead and Erickson, as well as Estrada, Volkert, Gowen and Johnston. Briant was aware that Winkle and McCarthy had been med-evaced out. For a time, Carmen Briant was blinded by a welling of moisture in his remaining eye, along with a stinging lacrimal duct within the right eye socket. He lay most of that night just outside of visibility from a bonfire glare near the command post. Finally, as dawn was creeping over Swordfish Lair Mountain to the east, he came to rest within a hide made up of broken vegetation and clumps of displaced earth. Briant slept fitfully throughout the next day, awakened once by a small group of NVA soldiers passing within 15 feet of his hide. They were transiting to and from the stream carrying and filling a couple dozen canteens.

For the next few weeks, Briant trailed the field command post as they made their way west, back toward Ho Chi Minh Trail. The circuitous four-week march had finally ended at a compound located about a kilometer east of the main trail thoroughfare. It was one of many such way stations situated along the trail. NVA soldiers in chartreuse uniforms mixed with coolie laborers wearing plain, pajama like tunics and trousers. There was a cleverly camouflaged pipeline pumping station set up within a cluster of structures surrounding some kind of central above ground command bunker. Because of occasional bombing in the area, there were also numerous below ground bomb shelters dug within the compound. Although there was no real security perimeter around the place, Briant had to be more and more careful as enemy elements became more soldierly in the vicinity of the trail. By that time, he had consumed all of the C-Rations in his kit. He had been able to refill his canteen several times en route but finally ran out of the water purification tablets, resigning himself to hoping that he would not develop the runs. En route to the trail, the communists had bivouacked for three days at a huge, concealed rice cache from which they replenished their own field rations. After they left, Briant took the occasion to do the same, using all his pockets as well as what space remained in his butt pack for rice. He had returned to the cache on two occasions since to replenish his food stocks. Dried rice, along with a few dead snakes and small animals had made for meager fare throughout most of that month of March 1972.

Carmen Briant started with diarrhea sometime around the fifth week after the fall of Swordfish Lair. That was almost a week ago. It was clear that his body was waging a losing battle with dehydration as it mounted a mind-altering electrolyte imbalance. Briant spent his days accumulating intelligence on the holding station in which they retained Kip Haskell. He hoped to be able to somehow break out Haskell, but as time went on, the likelihood became more and more absurd. With little more than a .45 caliber pistol, there was no practical way to assault the camp directly. The best plan Briant could come up with was to activate the beacon, which, he hoped, would bring in an air strike. Perhaps in the ensuing confusion, Briant could make his way into the enemy headquarters and retrieve Haskell. With the advent of incipient diarrhea, Carmen Briant realized that his strength would be progressively sapped as time went on. The snatch would also have to take place before Haskell was moved, something that would surely occur after the communists had extracted all information they might consider him to be good for. The NVA were patient interrogators. They would let mounting sleeplessness and a state of continuing misery work as co-conspirators to break their prisoner.

Everyone, including the Americans, knew that breaking any man was essentially a matter of time over resolve. Haskell had himself been through SERE (Survival Evasion Resistance and Escape) school and and understood communist interrogation tactics very well. During the forced march back toward Ho Chi Minh Trail, Haskell had time to mentally repair himself from the loss of his teammates. He found some solace in occupying his mind with the process of mentally constructing an elaborate "cover within a cover within a cover" story for his captors. One of the painful lessons learned from Korea by US military POW's was the futility of rock hard, stubborn resistance to advanced methods of communist interrogation. The notion of "Name, Rank and Serial Number", became arcane conventions for US servicemen faced with ruthless communist interrogation techniques that had no respect for either the Geneva Convention nor those who would bind themselves to any precept precluding use of torture. Haskell understood this. His SERE training had prepared him as much as possible for what was to come. He would not give things up to his captors all at once. Instead, it is better to build a show of graduated resistance in the face of such an enemy, giving up bits of construed information in protracted segments, forming a relationship with the interrogators, who would be trying to do the same thing in reverse. Haskell had been well rehearsed to accomplish this through his SERE school experience. They permitted him no more than four hours of sleep for every 24-hour period. Kip was provided the barest diet of rice and water. As a POW, Haskell was subjected to constant noise and sight stimulus as well as a full time attendant to slap him in the face during most of those times in which he was inclined to doze off. Every few days, several soldiers would come in and shave Haskell after tying his arms and legs.

To oriental people, the sight of a furry Western face is considered foul and objectionable. It gave the appearance of a filthy face, one not fit to bring before officers. They had taken his tiger stripped camouflage fatigues on the second day of his captivity, replacing them with a light gray, rough textured homespun tunic and trousers. He had been left with his boots because they were frankly too large for any of the captors, there were no shoes big enough to fit Haskell and they needed him to march all the way back from Swordfish Lair. It took nearly four weeks, entirely on foot. After arriving at what appeared to be a way station or marshalling area with above and below ground bunkers (bomb shelters), Haskell began attending sessions at random hours during which he was bound with arms behind his back and suspended off the ground from his wrists. This was inflicted at regular intervals of what the interrogators referred to in their own language as "directed punishment".

The story that Kip Haskell ultimately intended to give up in small segments, usually toward the end of these sessions, left the communists believing that he was the son of a poor, West Virginia farmer, a proletariat. Pursuing an understandable desire to better himself, the imaginary Kitson Haskum (it was better to use subtle derivations of actual names which could be easily pronounced by the North Vietnamese) had applied to become a student of engineering in the United States. In order to pay tuition, he was required to join an ROTC organization on campus. By attending a series of seminars, he was trained as an officer while also studying to be an engineer. After completing his schooling, he was required by rich American politicians, bourgeois, to pay for his education by serving as an officer. He was assigned to this mission within the Laotian camp, not even being advised of his exact whereabouts. His purpose on the mountaintop was to build and maintain a portable, fresh water resource in the mountains. All of this was extracted little by little under a relentless campaign of misery and controlled consequences. By giving out the information only after a commendable degree of inflicted misery, his cover story was all the more believable. This satisfied the communists, while at the same time, endearing them to the benefit of Kip Haskell, who represented himself as an officer, a Major in the US Army Corps of Engineers. During one of the sessions, a particularly cruel interrogator had been clumsy in the way he tied up Kip's wrists. In the process of emphasizing a point of interrogation, the communist grabbed the suspending rope passed over a pulley hung from the ceiling. The sadistic interrogator began jerking it up and down. To resist being dislocated in his shoulders, Kip Haskell twisted himself to one side, absorbing most of the energy of the bouncing in his left arm. Seeing this, the communist redoubled his efforts to break the American and, in fact, succeeded in a physical sense when Kip's left forearm snapped across radius and ulna, leaving both bones protruding like two little sharp, white sticks through the lower, inner side of Kip Haskell's left forearm.

That had been just yesterday. Interrogators treated the injury with a show of minor regard, but afforded Haskell the relative comfort of being returned to his confinement cell, a bamboo cage suspended from a large tree limb within the enemy camp. An NVA medic came to his standing cell and roughly set the arm. The communist medic constructed a splint made of bamboo sawed longitudinally in halves about as long as Haskell's forearm. These were bound tightly together with shoestring from Haskell's own boots. The splint remained in place for the last 24 hours without any dressing to cover the exposed open fracture site. Haskell's arm had started to redden and swell up within the constricting splint. He was unaware of this because the communists permitted him nearly ten hours of sleep for the first time in over five weeks. He was awakened, not by a slap to the face, but by the sudden retort of several loud explosions rocking the entire camp and setting his cage to swinging wildly from the tree branch he was suspended under.

Chapter 12 – Counting Coup

March–April 1972

Beacon bombing was a high tech, highly classified, "concept" weapons system of the early 70's. Research and development of beacon bombing as a unique technology in Single Side Band radio-wave emissions later became the parent subsystem for international EPIRB (Emergency Position-Indicating Radio Beacon) systems developed a decade later. In essence, beacon bombing devices were originally used as sort of "fuse delays" to coordinate a detonation event held in concert with some form of airborne explosive delivery system. The beacon devices used in Operation Fisherman were small enough to fit into a butt pack. They could sight a target as far out as 150 meters. Because of Single Side Band radio energy efficiency, batteries in the system could power a beacon device intermittently over several weeks of short-burst radio transmission sequences.

There were two delivery systems considered "beacon capable". One system was a glide slope construct that essentially added maneuverable fins and a radio guide on to traditional, heavy ordinance iron bombs. These were typically released at high altitudes and essentially glided toward the beacon radio signal. This was the type of beacon signal activated by Grit Volkert during the final siege of Swordfish Lair. The second beacon system had yet to be deployed in an actual combat scenario. It had to do with an Infra-Red (IR) signal, which a self-powered, guided missile could identify and home in on. The concept behind this latter device permitted an explosives team to place the beacon close enough to "paint" the target with a sort of electronic time delayed fuse. That is to say, a supersonic aircraft could fly overhead and launch its payload with pinpoint accuracy long after the human part of the demolition team had been safely exfiltrated. The device itself would emit short burst signal frequencies over preset, irregular time sequences for several weeks if necessary. This signal verified that the device was on station and ready to coordinate a strike. Beacon devices were also limited radio receivers. When the delivery aircraft arrived within a ten to twenty-mile "look down" radius of the device, both aircraft and beacon would exchange "handshake" signals. This activated the beacon to "paint" its target with an IR beam. The beacon could also be set for "point of contact", meaning that the beacon itself became the target for incoming ordinance. Just a few milliseconds prior to a target detonation event, the beacon would receive a terminal "confirm" radio transmission signal. This would then cause the beacon device to detonate itself from a small charge placed within its own casing. The beacon would also detonate itself if tampered with once a non-tamper code had been entered into it via analog keypad.

The concept offered a novel approach to clandestine demolitions. Theoretically, it would no longer be necessary for a covert team to become exposed by placing site charges directly on to an intended target. The demolition team would not have to risk discovery by igniting fused charges in close proximity. By 1972, the concept had just come off the drawing boards and was an experimental reality. Operation Fisherman became one of the first mission designates for beacon bombing devices. SSG Philip Volkert had been the first ground asset to actually deploy a device in live combat during the final throes of Swordfish Lair. There had originally been a half-dozen beacon devices assigned Captain Fernstead to deploy as he saw fit. Fernstead dispensed one each to the senior NCO's, as well as one to Lieutenant Erickson with instructions to set the devices at "point of impact" should situations warrant. MSG Carmen Briant had the only beacon device left.

All the others were destroyed during the bomb firestorm that had engulfed Swordfish Lair.

After trailing Haskell to the regimental commander's field headquarters and temporary interrogation compound, Briant had sighted and activated his own beacon device. He intended to launch a distraction by detonating some vital structure close to Haskell, but far enough away to avoid injuring Haskell himself. Briant hoped that perhaps in the confusion of the explosion, he might have a chance at getting to Kip Haskell. It was a desperate plan with little chance of success. But with no other assets available, Briant had few other choices. He had originally activated the beacon toward the end of that third week in March 1972, four weeks after escaping and evading from Swordfish Lair. Briant set the device for a time window strike to occur between 0200 and 0230 hours at any time following first transmission. Every night, for over two weeks, Briant had waited not far from the beacon transmitter/receiver. When the explosion came, he intended to exploit confusion within the enemy camp as much as possible while locating and snatching Haskell. Beyond that, there was really not much to plan for. He had no radio capable of voice transmission. They would have to move overland eastward through some of the most difficult terrain in the world, surviving off the jungle and avoiding contact with the enemy, until such time as they might come across an American outpost at least 50 linear miles distant.

Southern Laos, Wednesday, April 5th, early morning hours

McCarthy and Shriver had moved quickly. They sacrificed security for speed by risking movement at night along high-speed enemy trails cut within the jungle. They were aided considerably in their trek within the nighttime void by use of a new generation of Starlight scopes, adapted to wearable head visors, mounted over the eyes, dubbed the AN/PVS-3A in military parlance. This revolutionary device permitted them night vision within a narrow field of view directly ahead of wherever they were looking.

The scopes worked by magnifying ambient light, turning the visible world into a luminescent green. Although very little "ambient" lighting penetrated through the canopied jungle in which they traveled, the marginal thinning of overhead cover created by these trails seemed to permit just enough limited reflection from overhead to facilitate their movements. By that spring of 1972, NVA engineers had constructed an impressive latticework of jungle trails such as the ones McCarthy and Shriver were now transiting. The purpose of these cleverly constructed, camouflaged lanes was to enable rapid communist force deployments on foot. Although such high-speed trails were routinely sentried at night, there was mounting apathy among guard posts as NVA soldiers knew, even at the field level, that by now, American SOG teams were no longer running reconnaissance in Laos. Another thing which facilitated their mission was the fact that most NVA troops had been deployed northward, leaving this sector very thinly marshaled. On March 30th, 1972, Hanoi launched the largest offensive against South Vietnam since the Tet offensive. Caught off guard, ARVN troops had initially fallen back, lending impetus to North Vietnam. US air support was hindered by bad weather. On April 2nd, 1972, President Nixon approved *"Operation Freedom Train"*, a massive bombing campaign launched to cut off strategic re-supply both in North Vietnam, and along the Ho Chi Minh Trail. For McCarthy and Shriver, the sound of distant explosions served as subtle advocacy from *Operation Freedom Train*, lending distraction to their rapid night movement. During the pre-dawn hours of that first day following insertion, unable to hide their native Caucasian features in daylight, McCarthy and Shriver reluctantly left the trails and took to hides within dense vegetation just a few meters into the jungle. During that time, in hushed, whispered exchanges, Shriver disclosed more of what had transpired since the fall of Swordfish Lair.

By the time Special Air Ops, under temporary command of Lieutenant Colonel Jenkins, had marshaled sufficient air assets to respond to the *diadem* transmission, Swordfish Lair was already breached. To Jenkins' credit, he had managed to sortie a flight of Skyraiders and Phantoms as well as a pink and white combat helicopter platoon from some DivArty company in the process of standing down out of Pleiku. In addition, Jenkins managed to rouse some Air Force slicks for purposes of evacuating the site. Later in the day, Jenkins counted his losses. One Skyraider, one Air Force E model Huey, as well as the entire contingent of US advisors and indigenous militia on the L-site in Laos. The actual amount of combat air power deployed only represented a small fraction of the original air assets once intended for Operation Fisherman, so effectively had Colonel Schultz dismantled the project. With more than half the American advisory force killed or missing in action, Project Fisherman became technically invalidated as a viable mission. There had been a contingency option submitted during the original brief on the mission objectives which stipulated that in the event the project was compromised, mission commanders were authorized only to use whatever additional assets that might be necessary to extract surviving US advisors on the ground. This did not include allocation of any additional ground forces beyond those already involved. In addition, only limited air assets could be employed and only for extraction purposes. While Lieutenant Colonel "Carlock" (Shriver) had been quite candid in his report to the Congressional Defense Subcommittee regarding the final assault, he'd somewhat exaggerated in one particular. He reported that one member of the American Special Forces A-team had managed to survive and establish radio contact with Project commanders. Shriver was granted permission, with the approval of General Abrams, to conduct an exfiltration mission for the lone survivor. However, that exfiltration was limited to involvement of personnel who had already been briefed on Operation Fisherman. Some members of the congressional subcommittee were quite concerned that news of this mission might leak to the news media, which would most certainly raise a firestorm of controversy over reconciliation with the Cooper-Church bill. Because other personnel involved with Project Fisherman were either too old, injured, or had no training as ground troops, Shriver was left with either recruiting McCarthy, or going back in alone, something he certainly would have done if necessary. This much was clear. Although they still had access to air assets; should they be compromised, there would not be anyone else coming for them. This was to be the last ground operation involving US personnel in Southern Laos.

Both Shriver and McCarthy carried radios. In addition, Shriver had a special radio direction finder set to frequency and time constraints that would read a vector during the few seconds of burst transmission emitted by the beacon at odd hours each night. This would take them in the general direction of the beacon. By combining this with vectors secured from previous transmissions, Shriver was able to confirm that the beacon was still in the same place and that they would likely be close to it within 24 hours. Once they were in the area, Shriver had access to a flyover Bugeyes lookdown that he could call in on request. Of course, the only thing Bugeyes could offer would be to identify heat signatures. It could not tell whether they were emanating from American or Communist bodies. While McCarthy remained concerned about how they could possibly find Briant in this vast landscape, Shriver was quite confident that instinct would prevail.

They slept on and off that day, exchanging four-hour watches. As soon as night settled into the jungle, they set out once again. Upon stepping out at dusk on that second evening in country, Shriver figured they were about 35 klicks removed from the location of the beacon. By using communist high-speed trail systems, they covered that distance in about eight hours. This they did, rarely breaking pace, pausing only to take water en route. About 0330 hours on Thursday, April 6th, Shriver and McCarthy arrived in the vicinity of the beacon. They could determine this to within about ¼ kilometer, thanks to a final radio direction vector taken by Shriver at 0247 hours that morning during a three second burst from the beacon. Upon arriving in the general vicinity, Shriver took them off trail, into dense jungle bush, slowing their progress considerably. They found a small, kettle-like clearing within a depression on the jungle floor, evidently created by a bomb crater. Shriver called in the Bugeyes over-flight. It took about 35 minutes to arrive on station. Most of the communist SAM ordinance in that area was being retained for formations of multiple aircraft. Single aircraft radar blips like this one usually meant Wild Weasels hunting for SAM's with HARM anti radar missiles. Evidently, no one on the ground wanted to take on the highflying Bugeyes. While radio transmissions could be monitored, Shriver communicated with Bugeyes via voice scrambler, making the voice transmissions nonsense to any radio receiving signals without a crystal receiving chip. Shriver limited his own transmissions by pre-arrangement with the Bugeyes aircraft commander. He identified their location to the flyover by igniting a small piece of White Phosphorus, shaped like a matchstick. It burned for about seven seconds at the bottom of the crater. Having identified their location from 23,000 feet overhead, the Bugeyes pilot called down information on location of warm bodies in the vicinity. To their west, about two klicks, there was a large concentration of human signatures, probably a garrison, distributed in various sleeping and deployment patterns. To their east and south, there were occasional heat signatures, a few seemed to be stationed along trails, which gave off a light sentient temperature change from surrounding jungle. Off to their northwest, about 350 meters, there was a single warm body, not moving, apparently mid jungle. By increasing resolution at Shriver's beckoning, they confirmed that it was definitely not an animal, but human. Over the next couple hours, McCarthy and Shriver moved slowly within the jungle, following an azimuth set for them by the Bugeyes over-flight.

Carmen Briant was dreaming. It was the only real comfort he had left. During his conscious hours, he was all too aware that he was dying. Diarreah had sapped his strength and dehydrated him so much that he could not walk for more than a few meters without becoming faint. He had soiled himself beyond the point of caring anymore. He was dreaming of his family. They were all sitting together in Church, singing a hymn. Briant had sung this hymn from early childhood and knew it well, "<u>Lead Kindly Light</u>" by John B. Dykes and John Henry Newman:

Lead kindly Light amid th'encircling gloom;
Lead thou me on!
The night is dark and I am far from home;
Lead thou me on.
Keep thou my feet; I do not ask to see
The distant scene-one step enough, for me.

As the tune played through his mind, he began dreaming of times with Shriver. They were together again, younger men moving soundlessly through the jungle along with their beloved Yards. There had been a certain reckless arrogance in being one with the jungle, part of an elite brotherhood.

I was not ever thus, nor pray'd that thou
Shouldst lead me on.
I loved to choose and see my path; but now
Lead thou me on!
I loved the garish day, and, spite of fears,
Pride ruled my will.
Remember not past years.

If one could ignore the insect bites, the heat and humidity, the constant fear of encountering a ruthless enemy, one could learn to deeply love this land. Few human beings from the West ever paused to take stock of this place, to consider its inherent beauty. As Briant slept on, oblivious to his physical self, he pondered some distant consolation that he would end here in the jungle, one with the earth, finally free from pain and responsibility and worry. Of course, there were regrets about his family, but the only thing he had left to do was consign himself to his Maker. He believed that he and his wife were married for time and all eternity. Therefore, he believed that he would be with Roxie and the children again. That made this whole process tolerable and lent him peace as he surrendered his life force.

> *So long thy pow'r hath blest me, sure it still*
> *Will lead me on*
> *O'er moor and fen, o'er crag and tor-rent, till*
> *The night is gone.*
> *And with the morn those angel faces smile,*
> *Which I have loved long since, and lost awhile!*

Before his single eye, Carmen Briant had a vision. It was Shriver, there in front of him. Briant whispered in a hoarse, cracked voice through vocal chords withered by dehydration:

"Well, old friend, have you come to meet me for this final mission together? Have you met grandpa and grandma? Are they here with you?"

Carmen Briant referred to his maternal Mormon grandparents whom he had known as a child. They had been very old and at one time came across the American Frontier to settle in Utah during the late 1800's. As a child, Carmen had loved them dearly and was consoled by his mother at the time of their deaths, within a month of one another, that both would meet him again someday. Throughout his life, Carmen Briant harbored a personal belief that his Grandparents would be the ones to greet him when it came time to be ushered out of this life and into the next.

He looked up into the face of his old friend, Michael D. Shriver, dead now these five years. Looking over Shriver's shoulder for his grandparents, he was somewhat confused to see the face of *Bac Si*, the medic whom he had also grown to love so much.

"*Bac Si*! Why are you here? I thought you survived. I thought they flew you out. I thought you were still among the living!"

"I am still, very much among the living, Top. So are you. And if I have anything to do with it, you're gonna stay that way."

"But, *Bac Si,* this man here, this man is Michael D. Shriver. He's dead. If he's dead, what are you doing with him?"

Shriver lowered his head as his eyes welled up. He backed away, letting McCarthy take over. They had traveled through the jungle to within about thirty meters of Briant. Even with the night vision visors, they would have searched in vain till morning, had it not been for the hymn. They heard first the melody, then the words. Softly sung in a hoarse voice, somewhat off key, but like a lamp in the dark, the hymn guided them to their quest on that dark night. Their noses led them the final few feet. They discovered Carmen Briant's prostrate form, lying face up on the jungle floor. He had covered himself with foliage. Fearing him dead, Shriver fairly leapt to his old friend's side, feeling for a carotid pulse, finding one thready and weak. *"Thank you God. Thank you for keeping him alive,"* Shriver whispered in an uncharacteristic surrender to spiritual reconciliation. Through his starlight visor scope, Shriver could see the face of his old friend almost indivisible from the surrounding jungle floor. It was hideous. The right eye was a socket of crusted tissue and filth, seared above and below with a linear burn. Briant's face was thick with growth of beard and his remaining left eye was bloodshot and sunken under a half opened eyelid. Gabriel McCarthy moved in, gently tapping Shriver on the shoulder to signal a need for space. When Shriver heard these last words from Briant, it triggered tears all around. Shriver moved aside, holding a small penlight for *Bac Si.* The night vision visors were too limited in their peripheral vision to work up close and so as they had come upon Briant, McCarthy produced the small penlight and they both removed their visors before turning it on.

For the first time, Shriver had occasion to watch McCarthy exercising his medical prowess. The young *Bac Si* was indeed a real professional. He started by examining Briant from head to toe, laying out his own poncho with liner and lifting the emaciated Briant onto it. After ascertaining that there were no wounds other than the eye, *Bac Si* removed blouse and trousers. Shriver had dealt with wounded men in his life. He had seen many spill their bowels in death. Like most human beings, he was a bit repulsed by the smell and presence of human body waste. If it bothered *Bac Si*, there was not the slightest indication. He worked over Carmen Briant with a gentle demeanor. Using a cloth, lightly moistened with Phisohex and a bit of canteen water, *Bac Si* wiped clean, first Briant's face, around the gaping eye socket, carefully examining the area close up under penlight. Eventually, he also washed an area on Briant's right arm. Gabe had trouble finding a peripheral vein because Briant was so dehydrated. In order to start an IV, *Bac S*i had to load a scalpel and cut delicately into the left inner arm, just proximal to the antecubital crease. He located a vein almost immediately as though he knew it would be right there. After securing a flexible Angiocath with ligature, *Bac Si* opened up the IV tubing spin valve all the way, introducing a flow of life giving Lactated Ringers solution into the body of Carmen Briant. McCarthy then went on to examine the rest of Briant, once again assuring that there were no other wounds or injuries. Careful testing revealed that evisceration of the right eye had been complete. What was left of the globe had self-sealed, probably due to the burn. Through some miracle of time and circumstance, the remaining blackened eye socket had not become infected. There was no evidence of sympathetic opthalmia to the remaining intact eye. After finishing the physical examination and giving the IV fluids time to rehydrate, Gabe finally attempted to speak with his pugnacious team sergeant.

"Top, can you hold anything down?"

Briant was reviving almost within minutes of having received the intravenous electrolyte solution.

"Yeah, it's just keeping things from going out the other end that I have a problem with."

"OK, take these." And with that, Gabriel lifted Briant's head slightly assisting him in downing two tablets of Lomotil, and one of Flagyl. The water had a sweet taste to it, unlike jungle puddle water Briant had been drawing from over the last few weeks.

"I guess I must smell pretty bad, huh?" Briant commented lending credence that he was indeed back among the living. "But, *Bac Si*, I could have sworn that you were here with my old One Zero, Michael Shriver, must've been a hallucination. How'd you get here? Where's the rest of your team?"

It was still dark. Briant could only make out small movements with his one good eye. Within the subtle glare of the penlight, his vision was blurred and indistinct. Gabe replied from shadows as he started pumping up a blood pressure cuff to record some vital signs. "There are just two of us who came for you, Top."

"Two of you? But, that's not going to be enough. What about Haskell?"

"Haskell is dead, Top. I didn't come with Haskell."

"No, no, I mean, we have to go get Haskell. He's still alive."

With this disclosure, Gabe paused in his concentration from listening to the blood pressure beat as it opened a systolic/diastolic interval, audible to the stethescope. "What'd you mean, he's still alive?"

"Just that, he's still alive and not far from here. I've been trailing him since they took him **POW** out of Swordfish Lair. We've got to get him out. That's why I activated the beacon. Figured if I could manage a diversion, I might be able to get him out."

"Haskell, alive?" This revelation was almost as stunning to Gabriel as had been the discovery of MSG. Carmen Briant himself.

"*You mean to say, you've been out here all this time trying to get Haskell out?*" The voice came from somewhere off to Briant's blind right side. Again, Briant began doubting his senses as the familiar voice ingram registered with his memories.

"Who is that? *Bac Si*, who is that? Who's here with you?"

Gabe could not answer. He did not have to.

"I'm here, old friend. You should know that you're about the only person on this planet who could bring me back from the dead." Shriver replied in a Bru Montagnard dialect that he and Briant used to communicate with one another in the past. Briant responded in the same tongue.

"But, but you're dead. They told me you're dead. I've visited your tomb at Arlington under the headstone of an unknown soldier."

"You should know that extraordinary necessities warrant extraordinary measures." Shriver replied in English.

They remained there, on the jungle floor, long past daybreak. As the jungle developed a subtle illumination with the new day, Briant kept moving his one eye back and forth between Shriver and McCarthy, still not quite certain of reality. This could be just another dream to dispel with the rising sun. After running in both 500 half liter bags of lactated ringers as well as the 250 cc canister of serum albumin, and draining two full canteens in careful sips over three hours, Briant was definitely back among the living. He took four more tablets of Lomotil the next six hours before trusting his leaky bowels with standing up again. Finally, he was able to consume an LRP ration, the first real food he had taken in many weeks. They waited to see if Briant could hold things in. He was still weak, but able to rise and walk. They moved together slowly through the undergrowth to a place Briant had found wherein there was a meniscus of fresh water on the jungle floor. At that location, they helped Briant remove the rest of his filthy clothing. Shriver had brought along an extra set of black pajamas, anticipating the need to similarly disguise Briant. Carmen Briant spent some time cleaning his undergarments before putting them back on. Under such circumstances, it seemed important to him that he follow a certain ritual in order to feel human again. Shriver provided him with a shaving razor and for the first time in a month and a half, Carmen Briant began to look and feel alive. They huddled there in the jungle for the rest of that day, exchanging quiet conversation. Briant constructed a sand table of the POW interrogation compound and outlined his plan to get Haskell out. They would take another day allowing time for Briant's strength to recover to a point at which he could again move unaided within the jungle. MSG Briant insisted he could carry the extra radio, but neither McCarthy nor Shriver would let him bear more than the radio, which was a lightweight new SINCGARS V (Single Channel Ground and Airborne Radio System) designated AN/URC-78. It was a prototype first developed in 1971 by RCA. They had three of them for Operation Fisherman and Briant was familiar with its use. Shriver had intended to call in an extraction, but they first had to make a decision about Haskell. They reached an easy consensus that if all surviving members of team A-321 could not get out of Laos together, then none of them would leave individually.

Shriver made contact with his flyover Bugeyes liaison that evening, transmitting for less than eight seconds to issue a single code word sequence, *"Fishbill, Gaff, Bait, Arc 023 off flash one K, flash 024"*. From a list of codewords predetermined for this mission, the ALO understood the word *"Fishbill"* to mean that they had located Briant. *"Bait"* meant POW. *"Gaff"* was the code word used for a Prisoner of War snatch. Was Briant a POW? If so, did that mean they had found him? But, if Briant was a POW, perhaps they were going to attempt a snatch? *"Arc 023 off flash one K"* meant to call in an arc light bombing run at 0230 hours, to at least a Kilometer off the beacon. It meant the team on the ground would use the beacon as a safe spot during the arc light. *"flash 024"* meant to also use the beacon device to deliver a point specific payload ten minutes after initiating the arc light. It all seemed rather confusing, but Lieutenant Colonel Jenkins went ahead and approved the bombing run. What he concluded from the transmission was that Briant was a POW and that the two-man team was going to attempt to snatch him around 0245 hours the next morning. It seemed ludicrous. Two men attempting to assault an enemy internment camp nearby the Ho Chi Minh trail. But, live or die, this mission would finally conclude Operation Fisherman and Jenkins was anxious to comply in any way he could.

The beacon-bombing run to follow the arc light would consist of a prototype missile designed by Raytheon Systems Co. It was not due for release into general military arsenals until the following summer when it would be designated the AGM-65 Maverick air to surface missile. As part of their final "beta" testing campaign, Raytheon was anxious to deploy their prototype weapons system in an actual combat situation. They had constructed the first generation "smart bomb" missiles, intended to work hand in hand with beacon bombing devices. The missile had an Infrared seeker located under its nose cap. The seeker would locate and follow an IR homing beacon to pinpoint impact, something never before actually attempted in a live combat situation.

Haskell was located in a bamboo cage visible from outside the camp. Shriver pulled reconnaissance on the site, observing with binoculars from a tree just beyond the perimeter. This particular enemy compound was located about a kilometer from one of the Ho Chi Minh Trail main thoroughfares. It served as a way station and, as such, was not constructed with a ringed defensive perimeter per se. The camp had numerous bomb shelters intended for ready access to troops resting during movement south or north along the trail. For this reason, the "perimeter" was void of any walled obstacles such as one might encounter in a secured base camp. The only real obstacle for the Americans was a wide open, clear field of visibility within the mustering area. This would expose them to enemy observation during their approach. From about noon Friday, April 7th, 1972, Shriver maintained reconnaissance on the camp. He observed Haskell being led to a thatch and earth covered hutment, with concrete walls wherein, Shriver suspected, they were interrogating the prisoner. Shriver was still observing later as they led Haskell out, clutching his left forearm in apparent distress. Four guards shoved him back in to his bamboo cage, hung from a tree near the hutment. Shortly thereafter Haskel seemed to go limp, probably sleeping. Later that afternoon, an NVA soldier approached the cage and manipulated Haskell's arm, pulling it out of the cage and wrapping it in something. From about 1600 hours on, nothing else happened. Haskell again went limp inside his cage. The unusual posture of Kip Haskell within the obelisk shaped cage indicated that he must be either unconscious or catatonically fatigued.

Just after sundown, Shriver rejoined McCarthy and Briant back in the jungle. Prior to doing so, Shriver made one last check of the beacon device. Briant had placed and sited it on a rise overlooking the camp. It was situated high enough so that any personnel walking by between the beacon and the target structure would not likely break the IR directional beam. He assured there was a clear line of sight to the building that Briant had determined to be the command bunker. It was about 50 meters from Haskell's suspenosry cage. The beacon itself was just within range of the optical limits of the beacon's IR pointer, located about 90 meters from the eastern edge of the camp perimeter. Gabe had turned over to Briant the M-79, along with a bandoleer vest containing a dozen 40mm HE projectiles. The three of them were in place at 0215 hours just outside the camp on Saturday morning, April 8. Briant was limited in his vision perspective. He could not judge distance well but with the starlight scope visor, his narrowed field of view offered about as much perception as someone with two eyes using the scope. While wearing the visor, there was no room on Briant's face for bandages to cover his right eye socket and so it was left open, liberally smeared with antibiotic ointment. They only had two night vision visors and McCarthy had surrendered his own to Briant.

By April of 1972, daily bombing runs along the Ho Chi Minh Trail were commonplace thanks to *Operation Freedom Train*. US ground reconnaissance teams were not. NVA troops stationed or moving along the trail were far more concerned over being hit by a bomb disbursement than they were about ferreting out American ground teams. And so, at 0230 hours, when heavy ordinance began falling along the main Trail, just west of the compound, communist troops positioned around the camp scurried, as usual, into various bomb shelters dug throughout the area. Haskell was left swinging in his cage. If he were to be injured or killed by American ordinance, the communists would have considered it just desserts.

Regimental Field Commander Muc Bo Thau was working by candlelight at a desk in his command bunker when the American Arc Light heavy bombs first started falling. Initially, he rose up and walked over to the doorway pausing for a moment, framed against the candlelit opening to his command bunker. Muc Bo Thau was well aware that the chance of his being injured by a bomb this close to the trail was a remote possibility. He was also aware of the impression it left with his troops when he remained at his desk, working during such forays. Troop gossip inevitably followed about their Commander's own seeming disregard for danger. His troops would view him as courageous, undeterred, invulnerable. This impression had immense command value. It made up for harsh discipline and the occasionally cruel orders he would issue them from time to time. He made a grand command presence until most of the troops had already found shelter, disappearing into pitch black holes, below ground bunkers. After assuring himself that many had seen him standing there, observing their quick but orderly movements into the bunkers, Commander Thau turned and went back to his desk. And so it was that he was alone at his desk for the moment, while the rest of his support staff were huddled only a few meters away in adjacent underground bunkers. Commander Thau was confident that the chances of a direct hit on his above ground bunker were slight at best.

On this particular night, Commander Thau had been up late processing information. Along with studying intelligence on the American prisoner, he was reviewing briefs about supply trains supporting actions at Binh Long Province wherein a major offensive was taking place just 75 Kilometers from Saigon. Commander Thau was distracted from his documents by a step fall at the threshold of the entrance to his bunker. Thinking it to be one of his own men wanting to observe their commander's cool demeanor during the bombing, Muc Bo Thau looked up casually.

He was immediately taken aback by a ghastly, one eye'd apparition too terrible to imagine. It was a man, dressed in black pajamas, with a black hole for a right eye socket, holding an American 40mm gun, pointing the huge tube right at the desk in which Muc Bo Thau was sitting. The man walked over to a momentarily stunned Commander Thau. Holding the big gun level at the communist commander, the nightmare said something in Vietnamese.

"*Regimental Field Commander Muc Bo Thau?*"

Commander Thau responded as though in a trance. "*Yes? What is it you want?*"

In a *moi* dialect, the horrible apparition stated something that Commander Thau could only partially understand, something like:

"*For ... crimes... ... condemn ..., Muc Bo Thau.*",

Then, in Vietnamese:

"*HÔM NAY LÀ NGÀY BAN SË PHÁN XÉT - It is the day of your reckoning!*" With that, the ghastly apparition stepped forward and shoved Commander Thau's left shoulder with its right hand. The process of being physically touched seemed to break Commander Thau's reverie. Without taking his eyes off the horror before him, he began shouting;

"*To arms! To arms! I am under attack!*"

6 minutes earlier

Almost as the first loud explosions began sounding west of their position, communist troops had scurried off into holes following well-rehearsed air raid drills. McCarthy and Shriver made straight for the Bamboo cage containing Haskell. It was now swinging in a slow, pendulus manner, swaying to the seismic movements of heavy artillery falling within a kilometer of the site. Shriver shouted to McCarthy as they darted forward into the compound.

"This has got to be another first in military history, *Bac Si*. Close air support from B-52's!"

McCarthy looked over at Mad Dog Shriver as they ran. He actually had a smile on his face, a maniacal, unsettling grin. Shriver seemed to become fluid, moving like a basketball player, darting around obstacles on a crowded court. Of course, the notion of close air support from B-52's was absurd. Even with the primary target area nearly a kilometer away, 500, 750 and 1000 pound bombs were landing close enough to cause immense shock waves that took their breath away and caused McCarthy to topple over at least once. When he stood up again, Shriver was already at the cage, cutting the chords that held it suspended. McCarthy joined him. Together, they lowered the cage down to the ground as another explosive shockwave caused them to sway back on the rope, then fall forward, collectively losing their balance against the charged environment.

The cage fell to the ground. As it did, Haskell fell face downward, away from the hinged door tied shut behind him. Hinged tie downs were located above and below him, but he could not bend or reach within the narrow confines of the cage. Access to opening mechanisms was out of his reach. At first, Haskell believed that for whatever reason, some of the communists had come back for him, to take him into one of the bunkers. He was most keenly aware of his left arm, now throbbing with an agonizing pain. When the cage fell forward, his arm, held outside the cage, became caught under bamboo slats to his front. Kip was pinned by his arm, already injured, at an angle under the bamboo bars before him. He felt the tight bamboo partition behind being loosened, then a hand on his shoulder.

"Kip! Kip! Are you with us buddy?"

It was a voice both familiar and incredible to his ears at the same time, one he could hardly believe. Not trusting his own disclosure, he replied, unable to turn.

"*Bac Si? Bac Si* are you here?"

Gabriel McCarthy realized at once what had happened to pin Haskell within the fallen cage. He motioned for Shriver to go around to the top of the cage and lift, tilting it upward. As he did so, Haskell was able to painfully maneuver his arm back in between bamboo cage slats. With that, he could turn and behold McCarthy. Momentarily oblivious to the searing pain in his left arm, he threw both arms around his American comrade.

"*Bac Si*! You came, you came!" Haskell cried without restraint, like a child. McCarthy embraced him for the moment.

"Come on, Kip. We gotta go!"

Haskell nodded and as he did so, McCarthy broke the embrace, grabbing Kips left shoulder, suddenly aware of the bamboo splints bound about Haskell's left forearm which, clearly, Haskell was favoring. There was no time for it now. They turned and began running back toward the east, as Shriver stayed behind, providing rear security and looking for Briant.

Their plan called for Carmen Briant to hold back somewhat, randomly lobbing 40 mm HE shells onto bunkers in the area. The smaller explosive charge of a 40mm shell could not breach heavily layered bunkers. However, the impact of even the smaller shells falling against the bunkers would render an impression to those within that bombs were falling nearby. This should discourage any peek-a-boo looks from those huddled down in the dark holes. As Briant entered into the compound he viewed the command bunker through the night vision Starlight scope visor. There, illuminated by some backlight coming from within the bunker, was a field command officer who fit the description of Commander Muc Bo Thau.

Without any real thought for his motives, Briant stalked forward as the last few communists between himself and the command bunker scuttled down into their holes. It appeared the command officer did not intend to follow them himself. Carmen Briant observed the Vietnamese Officer take a deep breath, puffing up his chest, then turn and retire back into the above ground command bunker. Briant rushed forward, slipping the night scope visor down around his neck as he entered the bunker threshold, too brightly illuminated by candlelight to use the visor. By the time Briant stepped into the bunker, the Vietnamese officer had already taken a seat at his desk and was in the process of studying some documents. He was alone. Evidently all of his staff officers were in nearby underground bomb shelters. The officer looked up at Briant and was immediately, obviously, startled. Carmen Briant had to be certain that this was Commander Muc Bo Thau. Oblivious of his bizarre, one-eyed appearance, Briant spoke in Vietnamese, using Muc Bo Thau's full title of rank:

"Regimental Field Commander Muc Bo Thau?"

Muc Bo Thau answered in confirmation of his own identity: *"Yes? What is it you want?"*

Within the confined quarters of the bunker, Carmen Briant was too close to use the M-79. He thought for a moment of the .45 pistol, suspended from the LBE web belt at his waist, but hesitated. From memories deep down, going back to his childhood playing with Ute reservation Indians in Utah, MSG Carmen Briant was seized with an instantaneous, insane notion. Briant stated in a low, steady voice, speaking at first in a Montagnard Rhade dialect, the same tongue used to bear testimony against Muc Bo Thau at that last grand council of tribes:

"For your crimes, I stand to condemn you, Muc Bo Thau."

Then, switching to Vietnamese, Briant spoke with a fixed single eye'd fury:

HÔM NAY LÀ NGÀY BAN SË PHÁN XÉT - It is the day of your reckoning!"

With that, Carmen Briant crossed over to the mesmerized Vietnamese officer, palming Muc Bo Thau on the left shoulder, Counting Coup on his enemy. It was the physical touch that sparked a reaction in the Vietnamese officer.

"To Arms, To Arms, TÔI ĐANG BI NGÙÒ I TA ĐÁNH! - I am being attacked!"

The shout was loud enough to be heard in nearby underground bunkers. Already, bomb vibrations from the arc light appeared to be moving off to the south. Carmen Briant darted back, to the bunker entrance, ducking around the edge of the doorway. He stepped off a few meters into the relative darkness of the surrounding night of the blacked out compound. Briant then turned around and stood upright, unhurried, mixing with other confused coolie refugees starting to emerge from the bomb shelters. No one seemed certain of exactly what was happening. North Vietnamese officers and senior enlisted men started coming up out of the adjacent command bunker as Commander Thau shouted hysterically from within his one room office:

"*HÃY ĐẾN VỚI TÔI! - Come in here! Come to me now! The enemy is here!*"

The commander's cadre of officers and NCO's started rushing into the command bunker, weapons raised, while others came behind, crowding into the confined structure from outside, uncertain what to do. Briant started going around in the immediate vicinity from bunker to bunker shouting in Vietnamese:

"*Commander Thau is calling for you! He is under attack! Go to him!, Go to him!*"

Briant checked his watch as he darted back and forth within the compound. He postured his movements in starts and stops, running about in the same confused, disorganized manner as most of the communist soldiers and coolie laborers now emerging from their own bomb shelters. "*0239, only nine minutes since this whole frakas began,*" he thought. Already, ground trembling from the arc light had ceased. People were rushing to Commander Thau's bunker as word spread around camp that someone had been sent to assassinate the Commander. Briant's watch was set from the beacon device, which had a visible time display. He figured he was within 10 seconds of the beacon countdown. He had sauntered back away from the command bunker, toward darker fringes of the eastern jungle, sensing rather than seeing, that Shriver was near by. As yet, there were no lights within the compound. They were still under an air raid blackout. Briant turned his face away from the command bunker, anticipating the final trump card to their raid.

Approaching at supersonic speed from the northwest, a Phantom jet whispered, like its namesake, through the night. Following several miles behind, a loud sonic "boom" pursued the speeding jet with a noisy vengeance, cheated out of its natural noise continuum in time and space. Suspended under the wings from either side of the fuselage, two prototype missiles, streamlined to sustain such speeds, hung from strong points close to the cockpit. The pilot started his run nearly 100 miles distant, turning round to a preset vector and following a time pandect established through numerous short burst transmissions from the ground beacon. Upon receiving thumbs up from the front seat, the back seat Weapons Systems Officer (WSO), nicknamed "Whizzo", opened a special black box casing welded into his already narrow operating space. While the pilot slowed his velocity to accommodate his payload, Whizzo set about activating their as yet experimental weapons system. Within the black box were several switches, not yet normally a part of the F-4 weapons control panel. Whizzo powered up the system by flipping a "power" toggle painted luminous yellow and glowing faintly within the black box. As small lights came on within the box, Whizzo flipped a toggle designated "#1" in front of the power toggle. Outside his cockpit, this caused eyecaps to fall off paired missiles on either side of the fuselage, exposing glass, forward looking "eyes" located on the foremost carriage tips of the missiles. As Whizzo flipped the next toggle, designated "#2", radio frequencies within the missiles came on line, searching for and finding the ground beacon frequency. This sent signals also back into the cockpit, by this time less than 20 miles from the beacon. A small, yellow light came on within the black box casing, illuminating the word "Acquired". Whizzo then raised a small hood at the end of the array. Beneath this, he pressed a button over the letters "FIRE". The system paused, waiting for an exact time synchronization in which to launch. Whizzo felt a moment's panic, thinking perhaps that the system was malfunctioning. This was shortly dispelled as both pilot and WSO suddenly felt vibrations occurring simultaneously beneath them, on either side of the fuselage. Instantly, paired solid fuel missile propellants lit the night sky around, with a bright, whitish orange display, speeding away forward of the aircraft, temporarily taking night vision from both men in the cockpit who jointly forgot to close at least one eye. The paired missiles accelerated to nearly twice the aircraft's own considerable speed. Both pilot and WSO watched fascinated at virtually the only things they could see in the night, twin exhaust signatures from the missiles as they arced forward and downward seemingly in formation. Both pilot and WSO thought simultaneously, *"this has gotta be the easiest bombsight ever pickled."*

When within three miles or so of the target, both missile seeker heads acquired the IR signature painted on the side of a building before them. As the missiles sped onward, communicating in milliseconds with the beacon emitter, both mechanical devices exchanged one last bit of radio dialogue as the beacon detonated itself almost simultaneously with the two missiles striking their target, very nearly dead on. The above ground bunker was at that moment filled with officers and NCO's, coming to the aid of Commander Muc Bo Thau. He had by this time lost all demeanor before his men, shouting insanely about a one eyed assassin.

Briant received short notice of the missiles as a loud "bang" went off from the elevation wherein he had carefully sighted the beacon over two weeks ago. He closed his single, left eye as a loud "B-BOOOOMM-MM!" sounded behind him. Regimental Field Commander Muc Bo Thau had just issued the last order of his mortal command... *"He is out there! He must be an American! After him!!!"*

The blast sent other communists scurrying back into their respective holes. Those surviving the command bunker explosion were further encouraged to stay hunkered down by a loud rumbling *BBBOOOMMMM,* following a few seconds later as the Phantom's sonic drogue boom rumbled across the land. Most thought a late bomb had either been dropped or gone off delayed. Briant considered this as he once again donned the night vision starlight scope visor and made for a place eastward wherein they had determined to rendezvous. Shriver, who had been flanking Briant's blind right side during the withdrawal, paced soundlessly alongside him. Both men moved gracefully through the bush, aware of one another's presence without exchanging a word. The two of them melted back into the jungle, eventually finding Mc-Carthy, tending to Haskell.

Once back in the jungle, Gabe made for the water source they had been at the day before. It was about 300 meters from the fringe of vegetation around the camp. Because they had no night vision device, their progress was particularly slow. They both stumbled and tripped several times en route. Finally, Gabe said "Kip, close one eye," then switched on a small penlight carried in his shirt pocket. The diminutive little penlight seemed dazzling within the dark jungle. Together, they plodded on to the rendezvous point. Upon arriving, Gabe used the penlight to examine Haskell's left forearm. After untying bootlaces holding the bamboo splints in place, Gabe observed that sharp edges in the unpadded bamboo had penetrated areas of swollen skin on either side of the bulging, open fracture site. The wound already smelled badly and there was frank necrosis forming around the periphery. Haskell's fingers distal to the wound had a waxy, pernio-like appearance suggesting that circulation had been compromised, probably due to swelling within the bamboo splints. "How long ago did this break, Kip?"

"This afternoon, or I guess, yesterday afternoon now," Haskell replied through a wince.

"Well, to get this infected, this fast, means Strep. There may be some other bugs in there too, but for now, we're gonna try and get some penicillin on board."

With that, Gabe mixed a vial containing saline solute with 4.2 million units of powdered Procaine Penicillin. After shaking the resulting solution, he drew up a 5 cc syringe with 1 ½ inch 20 gauge needle, stabbing this mix into Haskell's left Latissimus muscle after raising Kip's shirt up to the armpit. Gabe then used an entire 50 cc bottle of 2% Lidocaine to irrigate the open fracture site, refilling the 5 cc syringe until it was empty. In the dark, he could not keep track of his discards, and was vaguely concerned that he must not leave behind any evidence of their presence. Afterward, Gabe secured Haskell's arm in a pneumatic splint, blowing it up to the elbow under mild pressure and thereafter securing the arm with a triangular cravat and swath. By that time, Shiver and Briant had returned. Although not recognizing Shriver, Haskell was nearly as jubilant over seeing MSG Carmen Briant as he had been upon first beholding Gabriel McCarthy back at the cage. Shriver took out a piece of dried meat, handing it to Haskell along with a canteen. "Can he travel?" Haskell nodded, hungrily taking the proffered nourishment as Gabe replied for him.

"He's likely going to develop a systemic infection over the next few hours, and we don't want to put much weight on him, but for now, he can walk."

With that, the four of them moved out, travelling southeast. Shriver led off, using his night vision visor, leading Haskell, then Briant following in their footsteps. McCarthy brought up the rear, stumbling close on the heels of Briant who wore the second visor. They moved overland, but travel was very difficult because they could not use the trails now and were constantly hindered by dense foliage. They were limited to an exfiltration LZ far enough away from the Trail to offer a decent chance of coming in without light anti-aircraft resistance. This meant twenty or more klicks distant from where they were at that moment. Until daybreak came, any chance of an exfiltration site may as well have been 400 miles away. Unable to move more than a few hundred meters, the four men finally selected a hide and hunkered down to wait for sunlight. Briant was pretty much spent. Although he had responded quite well to a steady regimen of Flagyl and Lomotil, he was still weak from resolving dehydration. Haskell was not doing well at all. Despite parentral penicillin on board, his arm was swollen and erythematous. Gabe was certain it would have to be incised and drained more thoroughly. By the time they were settled into a dense stand of bamboo for the remaining hours of darkness, it was about 0430. As Gabe tended his patients, Shriver conducted a debriefing with Haskell.

"Sergeant Haskell, I need to ask you some questions about your internment with the enemy. What you tell me is very, very important. Whether or not we can get out of here depends in large measure on how detailed you are with me now. I need to know everything they asked you and how you responded, from the time you were taken, up to and including this afternoon. Do you understand me, son?"

Haskell replied in the affirmative and for over an hour, the two of them spoke in hushed whispers as Haskell reviewed with Shriver his entire cover story and how he had divulged it during the course of interrogation. Shriver was genuinely impressed. He had known about Haskell attending SERE school. Indeed, Haskell's evaluation at that most challenging of all US military training schools was one of the things which swayed Shriver's committee to select Haskell for Operation Fisherman. Clearly, the SERE training had paid off, in major dividends. At some point, there in the inky pre dawn blackness, Shriver began rustling around with his gear and position for several minutes. Finally, he advised Haskell to don a set of black pajamas, which were placed into Kip's hands from out of the dark. At the same time, Shriver took the faded Grey, rough homespun tunic and trousers in which Haskell had been dressed since his own Fatigues were confiscated. Because of the long march back from Swordfish Lair, the communists had permitted Haskell to retain his boots, but had confiscated one of his boot laces, just the day prior, in order to tie up the bamboo arm splint. The struggle of getting out of his POW attire and into the change of clothing was about all Haskell could manage on his own. He was getting feverish and eventually lapsed off into a sound sleep, along with Briant. McCarthy and Shriver stood watch nearby their two quietly slumbering comrades.

"*Bac Si*, there is something I have to explain to you. But, before I do, I need you to answer this question. Do you understand what a direct order is?"

"Yes, of course I do sir."

"You understand that for as long as there've been armies, soldiers have had to obey direct orders as a necessary process?"

"Yes, of course, I understand this, sir. There's no need to question my loyalty here. If you give me a direct order, I'll obey it. Just put it to me straight sir."

"Very well. *Bac Si*, I know the NVA. I know how they think and what they are capable of. Largely as a result of SOG activity in Laos, the NVA have evolved, over the last decade, some very impressive hunter/trackers. Most of the best will have been pretty much inactive for the last few months since SOG has been deactivated. That means they have a lot of very good talent sitting around, itching for some action. Come sunlight, son, they'll be after us with dogs, troops, and some of the best local trackers in the world. Slowed down as we are, what with two walking wounded, we're not going to have much of a chance eluding them."

"Sir, if you want me to stay behind, maybe I can tie some of them up for a while."

"No, *Bac Si*, although I commend you for offering, it really would not accomplish anything useful at this point. Once they overran you, and they would do so in short order, believe me, it will just make them aware of the rest of our presence here and then they would come after us with a real vengeance."

"The rest of our presence? But, surely, they know about the rest of our presence here by now, sir."

"Not necessarily. Think, son. They know nothing about our Beacon technology. They probably don't even know we are here. The explosion of the command bunker back there could have been due to some after ordinance from the arc light. It could have been that Haskell was in the process of being taken to a bomb shelter when in the confusion of the detonation, he got away. Almost certainly, the only one they'll be looking for come sunrise is Haskell."

They were now both wearing the Starlight scope visors. In the dull green tint visible through the scope, Gabe examined

Shriver's head and shoulders. For the first time, he noticed that the black pajama uniform being worn by Shriver seemed to be a much poorer fit than it had been earlier in the evening.

"Sir, I can't imagine you'd send Haskell back to them. That only leaves one other possibility, but it's too crazy to even say out loud."

"Then, let me say it for us both, son. Come sunrise, I am going to lead the trackers off, dressed in Haskell's POW duds. But, there are some things you and I must attend to first.

"But, sir, to use your own logic, once they catch you, they'll realize you're not Haskell. Then, they'll be after us again."

"*Bac Si*, one of the things Westerners most often fail to realize about the oriental perspective, we look almost as much alike to them as they do to us. Haskell has debriefed me on just about everything he's done and said over the last few weeks. All they really did to him during the march back here was keep him awake and feed him slight rations. They never fingerprinted or photographed him. They didn't really start in on him until just this last week. The compound he was at is not one of their regular POW processing facilities. Most likely, that NVA field commander wanted some time to milk his prisoner before turning him over to the higher command spooks. And Haskell's done a masterful job of feeding them a cover story that could very likely keep me alive when I am recaptured."

"You! Recaptured!" Gabe started shaking his head in the dark. "What are you saying, sir?"

"That's where the direct order comes in Sergeant McCarthy. I am about to give you several direct orders here and now, and I expect them to be obeyed. Are we clear on this?"

"Sir, I can't begin to say how many ways this is *dinky dau*! For one thing, they know Haskell has a broken arm..." Shriver interrupted here;

"That's correct, *Bac Si*. That is why my first direct order to you is that you help me to break my left arm in approximately the same place as Haskell. It doesn't have to be exact, just enough to get the bones to stick out. The only one who's really examined it was an NVA medic and I watched him this afternoon while reconning the site. He didn't pay too much attention. He was more interested in unlacing Haskell's boot so that he could tie on his bamboo splint. You break my left arm in about the same place, and they'll never know the difference."

"Break you arm!" Gabe gasped and turned away, slowly shaking his head, then, while looking away he said, "Besides, Carmen Briant would never go along with this. He's only just found you out to be alive again after all this time. There's no way Briant will let you do this. Remember, we all get out of Laos or none of us do."

"Meaning *'all'* that is left of Team A-321. *Bac Si*, I am a nonentity here. I don't exist remember? For more than six years now, I've not been permitted to visit my own home state or even use my own name, the name my parents gave me when I was born. When they assigned me this new identity, they took away my past. I broke all the rules even by telling you who I really am. I have been like a living ghost within a community of spooks, very few of whom know anything about me. Staff Sergeant Shriver remains to this day listed as MIA in Laos. Look, son, this thing is going to be over someday. The South Viets are way too corrupt to hold against North Vietnam for long. When it ends, American POW's will be coming home. I could come home as a POW. It's the only way I could come home, really come home. Don't you see? This is my chance to pay the fiddler and get my life back. But that's all just a bonus. The real purpose in this is to get you all out of here. More than anyone else, I was responsible for putting Team A-321 in harm's way. I would not have done so without assurances, but I'd been around long enough that I should have known better. It was insane to trust the bureaucracy. My sin was pride, son. Like the rest of our nation, I was proud of our Democracy and of our honorable intentions to redeem Southeast Asia. I was proud to rub shoulders with elite US military and civilian power brokers. Proud that I could make them understand the plight of the

Montagnards and convince many of them that the Montagnards are worth saving. It was all pride, son, and as the Good Book says, 'Pride goeth before the fall.' In this instance, it was Swordfish Lair that fell, along with all those noble, innocent, people ..." Shriver's voice began to quiver just a bit. It was the first time Gabe had ever heard any such emotion slip from Mad Dog Shriver, who hesitated just a few moments, then continued... "So, you see, *Bac Si*, I'm ready to pay the price. A couple of years as a POW is a small price to pay, probably not nearly enough considering all I have to atone for. Now, *Bac Si*, you have to break my arm."

Gabe had been listening intently, trying to construct an argument against logic which beat him back on every front. The more he reviewed it in his mind, the more it made sense. It really was their only chance out. The only way they might all survive this.

"At least, let me anesthetize your arm, sir. You may find it easier to deal with. You'll not lead them far if you're distracted with the kind of pain a broken forearm will cause."

"Good idea, *Bac Si*, but you've already used up that particular asset."

Gabe developed a sudden panic as he thought back, realizing that he had dropped items in the dark nearby the watering place wherein he first treated Haskell, items he failed to pick up when they left. With a flush of hysteria he blurted out"

"But sir! Back there when I was treating Haskell, I failed to sterilize the area, I..." Gabe broke off as Shriver set down a plastic bag containing a small bundle of items, including the bamboo arm splints, Haskell's boot lace, and an empty bottle of Lidocaine, with a syringe.

"*Bac Si*, you were doing your job, I did mine. But, in the future, I'm not going to be around to pick up after you. You're going to have to be more careful about what may get left behind. Now, let's do the arm."

Gabe looked down at the empty Lidocaine bottle. He had used it as a sterile irrigating solution because he'd used up all the sterile fluids in rehydrating Briant. It had been a priceless irrigant. Gabe let his mind run through the variety of supplies left in his M-3 bag. He had not packed a lot of any one thing because he did not anticipate more than one single casualty. As he mentally ticked through the list, his mind settled on a particular item still in his inventory.

"Sir, there may be one other thing I can do for you."

"*Bac Si*, I can't take Morphine right now. It would hinder me too much. I'm going to need all my faculties in order to lead them as merry a chase as I can come sunrise. Come on, let's get on with it." Shriver was starting to betray an uncharacteristic impatience. Clearly, he wanted this thing over and done with and had resigned himself to whatever pain it would cost.

"No, sir, not Morphine, Benadryl."

"Bendryl?"

"Yes sir, Bendryl, Diphenhydramine Hydrochloride. It's normally a powerful anti-histaminic, used for allergic reactions. But I remember something Glickman told me. He said that I could use Benadryl in a pinch as a local anesthetic. It has the same effect but lasts a long time."

"You're sure about this, *Bac Si*? I can't carry any evidence on my person of anything beyond the break and whatever bush scratches one might expect from running blindly through the jungle at night."

"I trust Glickman sir, then and now."

"All right, *Bac Si*. I trust you. Go ahead. Let's see how this thing works, but make it quick. We have less than 30 minutes before it starts getting light."

Gabe set to work. He drew up 2/3rds of a 30 cc vial of Benadryl into a single 20 cc syringe with 25-gauge needle. Then he had Shriver lay on his back, remove his left arm from the tunic and abduct the arm out to 90° from his chest. Shriver reached up and grabbed a bamboo trunk to help steady himself. With his right arm, Shriver held the penlight for Gabriel as he performed the procedure. Gabe palpated for the axillary pulse on the inside of Shriver's left arm closest to the armpit. Upon finding it, he wiped the area with alcohol, then placed his left index and forefinger over the pulsation, using the apex of a tiny "V" created between his fingers to advance the needle. It was a difficult block to perform even under ideal circumstances. He had to advance the needle at a 30-degree angle until such time as it came in contact with a neurovascular sheath. In this area of the body, the glovelike outer sheath was quite dense and could be felt by the tip of the needle as it advanced toward the armpit. There are a number of other crucial structures in the area, which Gabe was well aware of. He focused all his concentration onto the tip of that needle, leaning his head down, close to the skin of Shriver's inner arm, closing his eyes as he felt for the subtle change in tissue consistency. "There!" Just a tiny click as the beveled tip of the needle parried off the sheath. Very gently, Gabriel advanced the needle until it began pulsating to the beat of the adjacent artery. For a moment, he let go of the syringe and watched as it pulsated in the air. Then, he aspirated to assure that he was not actually in an artery or vein. Satisfied of this, he proceeded to slowly inject the Benadryl solution. Shriver winced ever so slightly. Although Gabe had performed this procedure with Lidocaine, he had never before attempted it with Benadryl. He had no sense for how painful it might be on injection, nor for how long it would take to produce anesthesia. After injecting the entire solution, he carefully withdrew the syringe, pressing and massaging the area under Shriver's arm.

"OK, thanks *Bac Si*, now, get to it. You know what comes next."

Taking time both to let the Benadryl work as well as position things correctly, Gabe used the M-79, wedging it within some of the bamboo shoots around them. He then draped Shriver's arm over the obtund 40 mm barrel. He positioned the arm so as to nearly reproduce the fracture in the same direction as Haskell's. In the end, it only necessitated that Gabe lean the whole weight of his body against the arm in order to effect a break. He hesitated.

"C'mon, *Bac Si*, this is a direct order. Do it!"

Gabe felt short of breath and began gasping in slow, repetitive sobs. His eyes filled as he recalled something Doctor Schwartz had said, about the risk of returning to the same set of circumstances which had mentally crippled him once before. This act was so contrary to everything he believed in as a healer, against every purpose he had come to rely on as being worthy or something of value.

"Do it *Bac Si*! C'mon, do it now. Look, I can't feel my arm. You've given me all the mercy we could hope for out here. Now, come on! break it!"

Right up to the last moment, Gabriel fought the repulsion. But in the end, it was simply a matter of mathematics, all their lives against this arm. Closing his own eyes, Gabe leaned forward on Shriver's arm, which was levered over the barrel of the M-79. With a dull, "thunk!... sssnnnaaappp", he felt the two bones break, first the Ulna at mid shaft in one quick pop, then the thicker Radius on the thumb side. It did not break all at once, or perhaps Gabe could not bring himself to press down with quite as much force after recoiling from the sudden microcosmic violence of that first fracture. Both bones protruded out of the flexor side of the lower mid forearm closest the little finger side, similar to the way Haskell's arm had fractured. Shriver spoke with just a bit of edge on his voice, leaving Gabe to suspect that perhaps the sensory blockade had not been total.

"Thank you, *Bac Si*. I know how hard that was for you. Really, it's not bad. I have almost no feeling. Now, quick, bind it with the same bamboo splints used on Haskell. Tie it down tight like he had it before."

One thing the splints did accomplish was to roughly realign both bones back into the arm. As he tied the splint carefully, more concerned about alignment then tightness, he asserted: "Sir, if you are ever coming back to us as a POW, it better be with both arms. I'm giving you my last gram of Streptomycin right now and I want you to take these pills with you..."

"I'll take the shot now, but ... can't take anything with me, *Bac Si*. When they catch me, they'll know pills don't belong here in this part of the world, their world. Save your pills for Haskell."

Gabe used what sterile Benadryl solution was left in the vial to irrigate the wound as much as he could. He examined the compound fracture wound left on the arm, covering the open area despite Shriver's objections with a thin film of Betadine antibiotic ointment. The brown colored ointment seemed to mix almost invisibly with blood in the area. Gabe then checked on circulation into the arm distal to the bamboo splints by pressing on Shriver's fingernails. He observed them blanch, then pink back up in about three seconds. Shriver and Haskell were close to the same height and weight and the bamboo splints actually seemed to fit Shriver's arm better than they had fit on Haskell.

"OK, *Bac Si*, I'll ask two last things of you. First, take the lacing out of my right boot and give it to Haskell when he comes around. Second, give this to Briant for me, later." With that, Shriver pressed something into Gabe's right hand, something that he could not quite recognize under the limited glare of the starlight scope visor. Gabe deposited the object in his left shirt pocket as Shriver addressed him again, apparently unhindered from pain in the arm.

"Give me twenty minutes. By that time, the sky will be lightening up in the east. Get them up and moving. Tell Briant I have gone on ahead to scout out the area. Follow down this draw.." Shriver referred to a map, which he laid out on the ground before Gabe. "It should be wet at the bottom, probably a shallow creek or stream. Remember this from old Mad Dog Shriver. There isn't a soldier in the whole world that likes getting his boots wet. If you all wade through that stream, you should leave very little sign. The bottom will probably have a lot of dense foliage. If it's muddy, walk slowly to avoid stirring things up. Walk them down that draw all day, as far as it takes you. Make certain you are at least 20 klicks out before you call in your exfil.

This close to the trail, they have anti-aircraft installations all over. You may also risk engaging some 37 mm anti-air emplacements out to about 15 klicks. Almost any open space large enough to land a helicopter, the NVA will probably have some sort of anti-aircraft armament, most often 12.7's.

"That's about it son. Follow your nose and if you have any doubts about things, check with Briant. He'll get you all out. Take care kid. See you in a couple years, yeah?"

Gabe looked on as Shriver grinned widely at him and, with a turn into the southern fringe, he was gone.

After taking time to gather up everything in the area, checking carefully with the penlight, Gabe moved back into the hide, awakening Haskell and Briant. The brief sleep had done them both good. He explained that Shriver had gone on ahead to scout out the area for them. By the time eastern mountain ranges were pearly with newborn glare from the rising day, they were down in the draw. They continued moving east, southeast most of that day, pausing several times to rest Briant and Haskell as well as feeding them the balance of what rations were left. As the day wore on, Briant kept looking over at Haskell in his black pajamas, and back at Gabe. Briant developed a frown that had become deep seated by mid afternoon. Finally, he pulled Gabriel aside as they came out of the draw, into an open area.

"*Bac Si*, I don't think Shriver would have brought along two sets of black pajamas. He didn't expect additional survivors from *Fisherman*. *Bac Si*, you've gotta tell me straight. I've already lost him once. Is he out there ahead of us, or is he really behind us?"

Gabe looked deep into the eyes of his beloved Mormon team sergeant, old now way beyond his years. Just at that moment, a squelch came in over the radio. It was Bugeyes. Gabe made contact, arranging for pick up at an open area about half a klick from their present location. After getting a confirmation that the helicopter was en route, he looked back at Briant. Without a word, *Bac Si* reached into his left breast pocket and took out the items Shriver had asked him to give Briant. It consisted of a

Montagnard warrior's bracelet, bronze with delicate carvings all
around it. Connected to the bracelet by a small circle of pop bead
chainlet was a single dog tag:

SHRIVER, Michael D.
90031976
A Pos Mormon

Chapter 13 – Probity

1972 – 1977

By Fall of 1976, Axel Bothnerby Haskell had become the ranking military intelligence patriarch of his fledgling African homeland in Rhodesia. Over the previous decade, the land of his forefathers had transitioned through quagmires of various claims to sovereignty. Following dissolution of the so called "Federation of Rhodesia and Nyasaland" in 1964, numerous incidents similar to that which had resulted in the death of Axel's wife, Zula, inflamed the White constituency which, under British rule, had been the ruling colonial class in Southern Rhodesia. An increasingly dissatisfied Black majority also brewed up some dissidents within their own ranks. However, as it turned out, only a minority of Rhodesian blacks chose to endorse expansionist communist insurgencies fueled by Russian and, eventually, Cuban advisors. With the apparent impotency of Great Britain to act in securing the safety of both Black and White citizenry, an irrevocable movement toward sovereignty began in 1963. Southern Rhodesia took matters into its own hands in 1965 with a "Unilateral Declaration of Independence" (UDI). Initially, the UDI separatist government was not recognized by any other country on the planet (including South Africa) and the following year, 1966, Great Britain went to the UN, seeking mandatory sanctions, which were in fact imposed on the breakaway "rebel" colony. This signaled the start of a prolonged effort by Communist-supported guerrillas. Their strategy was to play on racial issues and force whites living in

Southern Rhodesia to relinquish any existing democracy in favor of a supposedly black Communist directed state that would in essence become a Marxist colonial expansion of Russian influence.

During the mid 60's, there were increasing numbers of Soviet/Cuban backed guerilla incursions into Southern Rhodesia from neighboring Zambia, with mounting atrocities committed by communist terrorists against both Blacks and Whites. Realizing the greater menace of communism, racial civil rights issues were set aside as the two-toned citizenry of Southern Rhodesia struggled to survive without formal allies against a much more ominous Communist juggernaut. Russia was seeking to recapitulate its successful exploits in Southeast Asia and Cuba. One of the reasons this part of the world was so attractive to Communist influence was the fact that Southern Africa is rich in mineral commodities, such as diamond mines. Diamonds and precious metals serve as a universal currency that knows no borders. Despite the embargo, through wit and stratagem, along with a disciplined, patriotic bi-racial military; Rhodesia armed itself, using mixed label weaponry secured from scores of different military surplus black markets around the world. From the late 60's through the mid 70's, Axel Haskell became legendary as a procurement officer for his country. He played a key role in building up the Rhodesian Air Force, replacing antiquated "crop duster" aircraft with newer, more effective air delivery systems. In 1974, he had helped to integrate the role of air power with ground troops and worked tirelessly to support training and deployment of some extraordinary military resources, including the Selous Scouts. By Fall, 1977, Rhodesian Special Forces had tracked down and eliminated most of the Communist backed Guerilla support structure within Rhodesia, thus demonstrating to the rest of the world that terrorism could indeed be defeated with elite military forces supported by a determined citizenry.

The "bush war" of Southern Rhodesia is generally considered to have started in earnest on December 21, 1972. Because of the intensity of geo-political conflicts within Rhodesia and really throughout the world at that time, Axel Haskell was unaware of his own son having been injured in Laos until summer of the same year. Correspondence between Kip Haskell and his father had been scarce as father and son were separated by multi-layered security filters, both on the U.S. side, surrounding Operation Fisherman, and by events taking place in Africa. And so it was not until Kip Jon Haskell had been an inpatient at Womack Army Hospital, Fort Bragg, for several weeks before his father was able to secure leave in order to come abide his wounded child. Kip finally recovered from a bacterial septicemia that nearly claimed his life. It cost him no less than his left arm just below the elbow. He came through the crisis on his own, opting not to inform either his father or his extended maternal family. By about the time Kip's father arrived in the States to succor his injured son, Kip was all ready to be fitted with a new arm Prosthesis. It was a hook-like apparatus, which opened and closed like a lobster claw. By that time, Kip had passed through the worst of it untended by any but his surviving teammates. It was Haskell himself, who did not want his own family to remember him in this way, should he die, that decided on this course. Fortunately, he did not die, but it cost him about 60 pounds of body weight along with the left arm. All toll, he accounted himself fortunate. The older Haskell, however, would never quite forgive himself for not being at his son's side from the beginning. Kip was discharged from active U.S. Military service in the Fall of 1972.

Over the years that followed, at the urging of his family, particularly father and maternal grandmother, Kip Haskell returned to school. He graduated from Dartmouth in 1975 with a degree in international business. The same year, Grandmother Hazel Von Hagen passed away, naming her grandson as primary beneficiary and executor of her estate. The old woman's trust was confirmed. Kip Haskell proved to be an honorable executor, effecting the disposition of his decedent grandmother's vast estate with integrity and exceptional diplomacy. He went on to apply to law school and was accepted to Yale Law with the following Fall matriculating class of 1977. Over the one-year interim, between college and law school, aside from managing affairs of the Von Hagen estate, Kip Haskell would arrange for a rather extraordinary reunion of the survivors of Team A-321. Their alumni assemblage would finally bring Operation Fisherman to closure.

Carmen Porter Briant was also discharged from active duty with the U.S. Military in the Fall of 1972. Having lost his right eye during that final saga of Operation Fisherman, the wound rendered him unsuitable for active duty service. He returned with wife and children to their familial home in Lehi, Utah. Briant subsequently used his GI Bill to enroll part time at Brigham Young University from which he would eventually obtain a masters degree in social work. Despite his handicap, Carmen Briant was accepted as a full time AST (Administrative Services Technician) for the 19th Special Forces Group of the Utah National Guard. He was based out of Camp Williams, not far from his home town of Lehi. He took to wearing a patch as the linear nature of the eye injury did not conform well to a cosmetic glass eye, which would otherwise have been provided by the Veteren's Administration Hospital in Salt Lake City. This earned him the affectionate nickname of "Top Patch" by SF National Guardsmen with whom he would serve, remaining in uniform on into the mid 80's.

Kirk Brooksly was discharged from Active Duty mid January of 1972. He had not been in contact with any male member of A-321 since his evacuation from Laos in October of 1971. He returned to his hometown in Idaho and was greeted by a near despairing mother who finally felt exonerated in receiving back her only son, sans right leg, from the same war that had claimed all of her husband. Kirk enrolled at Boise State on the GI bill, conquering his own handicap by completing a Bachelor's Degree in industrial education... on one leg. He graduated from college in June of 1976 and would eventually secure his first job as a substitute high school track coach and shop teacher, working part time until the following Fall of 1977, at which time he became a full time high school educator and athletic coach.

Ron Winkle was discharged from the service in 1973 after nearly a year of reconstructive plastic surgery. Kath remained by his side throughout the entire ordeal. Ron and Kath returned to Florida, attending Florida State University together. Kath went on to complete a Master's degree in special education. Ron would ultimately complete a Ph.D. in mechanical engineering. They both opted to remain in education. Kath went into the emerging field of special ed., teaching at the high school level. They settled in central Florida, nearby the University of South Florida at Tampa, where Ron was hired to teach collegiate level engineering. Plastic surgeons at Brooke Army Hospital in Fort Sam Houston did an exceptional job in rebuilding his face. However, no one who'd known Ron Winkle prior to Operation Fisherman could recognize him as the same young man that left South Florida to join the Army in 1969. He would never grow eyebrows again, nor could he sweat normally on his face, which had a peculiar shiny smoothness to it. There remained some scars that could not be concealed by clefts or natural curves and portions of his hairline demonstrated an unnatural recession. He would also always retain the scar on his throat wherein Bac Si had placed the cricothyroidotomy tube that saved Ron's life. Despite Ron Winkle's subtly disturbing facial features, he developed a wonderful sense of humor. He seemed to have a certain charm that empowered him as a university professor and served to enlighten those studying under him.

Gabriel McCarthy completed a four-year tour of duty and was discharged honorably from the United States Military in June, 1973. Of all the survivors from Operation Fisherman, he was the least physically wounded, on the outside. For a time, Gabe had been totally lost. He returned home to Tennessee, enrolling for an academic quarter at Austin Peay State University in Clarksville. By the end of that somewhat lost and aimless summer, Gabriel contacted Carmen Briant who invited him to come visit the Briant family in Utah. While abiding with the Briant clan, Gabriel McCarthy embraced the Mormon religion and was baptized by Carmen Briant on September 19th, 1973. The following year, in March of 1974, Gabriel entered the Missionary Training Center in Salt Lake City, thereafter serving two years in Central California as a Mormon Missionary. It was the salve he needed to quench his own personal anamnesis left over from Laos. Elder McCarthy immersed himself in work as a missionary. He learned to speak Spanish and spent considerable time laboring among migrant farm workers in the San Joaquin valley, thankful for the privilege of serving as a full time missionary on the soil of his own homeland. After completing missionary service in March, 1976, Gabriel returned to Utah where he began earnestly working toward a pre-medical degree in Zoology at Brigham Young University (BYU). SFC Gabriel McCarthy also joined Carmen Briant as a member of the 19th Special Forces Group National Guard Reserves, assigned to B Company in Provo, Utah.

That Fall of 1976, during his second semester at BYU, Gabriel McCarthy received a telephone call from Kip Jon Haskell. It was the first time they had spoken since 1972. Kip similarly contacted Kirk Brooksly, Ron Winkle and Carmen Briant. He proposed that they gather together for a reunion and offered to cover travel expenses from what Haskell referred to somewhat cryptically as "a special Fisherman's expense account." In December of 1976, just a few days after final exams for the Fall semester, Gabriel McCarthy, in company with Carmen Briant, flew from Salt Lake City to Minneapolis, Minnesota. Kip Haskell, Kirk Brooksly and Ron Winkle met them at the airport. Together again, they traveled back to the palatial estate of deceased Grandmother, Hazel Von Hagen. It was a touching, poignant reunion. There were, of course, not a few tears shed following an introductory repertoire of halting conversation about things post Laos. Kip Haskell let them re-familiarize for the rest of the day before gathering them together that evening around a huge, flat-topped rosewood dining table that had entertained many generations of Von Hagens. Kip began by passing around dossiers to each surviving member of Team A-321 present at the meeting. He gave the group some time to leaf through the 85 or so pages of material. Each packet included a classified brief on Operation Fisherman, summarizing the mission and its outcome. Several Pentagon think tanks had used the mission as a situation rep. to exemplify challenges and potential outcomes of U.S. deployment into an unconventional warfare environment. How Kip Haskell had managed to secure the very sensitive documents would be an issue that remained classified.

Also included within the file was a profile of a New England U.S. Congressional Representative named Riley Hathoway. The name was somewhat familiar from occasional evening news briefs on the aftermath of the Vietnam War as well as the Congressman's outspoken disdain over issues concerning captured U.S. servicemen in Laos. In reading the brief on Operation Fisherman, Congressman Hathoway's name was mentioned several times connected with the compromise of Swordfish Lair. Hathoway had been asked to appear before a military court of inquiry to consider the suicide of Colonel Julius Schultz. However, Hathoway exercised Congressional privilege and declined the non-binding military summons, indicating that he considered "Affairs of State" more pressing at the time.

Transitioning from ambient surprise to mounting outrage, former members of A-321 discovered for the first time the extent to which Congressman Hathoway had interfered with, and ultimately contributed to, the demise of Operation Fisherman. Everyone on the team had been aware that it must have taken powerful forces to turn awry essential mission assets without which, Operation Fisherman was doomed to its bitter terminus. No one had really understood the genesis of this interference until they gathered together now, 4 years later, around the grand table of a deceased matriarch. Records they reviewed together seemed to indicate clearly that interference on the part of this one man,

Congressman Riley Hathoway had, more than anything else, contributed to compromise of the mission. Discussion followed throughout the balance of that night and well into the next day. Initially, the group reacted with incipient anger. Those inclined to curse aloud did so, while each one expressed outrage in his own particular way. Fists pounded hardwood, eyes bloodshot with rage, old wounds throbbed, physically, emotionally. Gradually, anger gave way to introspection, then group circumspection and finally, individual resolution segueing to collective resolve. For the balance of that week, survivors of Team A-321 entered into a state of team isolation for one last mission.

Between 1962 and 1973, the United States did in fact cooperate with the Royal Laotian Government (RLG) to conduct a "secret war" in Laos against both NVA and their Pathet Lao counterparts. It is quite clear that the North Vietnamese had always considered Laos to be within their own theater of operations. Hanoi always maintained an official position that it scrupulously abided by terms of the 1962 Geneva Conference, which obliged that neither US troops nor the NVA occupy Laos. North Vietnam even went so far as to advance an absurdity of poorly fabricated maps showing the Ho Chi Minh Trail as passing through South Vietnam instead of Laos. The official position from Hanoi, following their victorious pan-occupation, was that North Vietnam never occupied Laos. To advance this position, North Vietnam insisted that any US servicemen lost in Laos were conducting illegal activities against Pathet Lao communists and as such were not POW's over whom Hanoi should have any influence. The CIA produced irreconcilable evidence of US servicemen who had actually been interned in Hanoi after being taken in Laos. However, in contravention to the so-called "Paris Peace Accords," Hanoi stubbornly refused to acknowledge that it had ever retained any POW's taken from Laos.

It became a matter of saving face. In order to assure that no US servicemen taken in Laos could lend further evidence to Hanoi's absurd historical alterations, no U.S. servicemen were ever recovered from within Laos, although two did actually manage to escape during the conflict. Most US personnel captured in Laos were in fact captured by NVA troops stationed there. For that reason, US POW's in Laos could openly testify that North Vietnam had, in fact, occupied Laos during the conflict. In complying with bilateral terms for US withdrawal between 1970 and 1973, Hanoi also negotiated clandestine terms with the Pathet Lao, asserting that Laotian communists would take sole credit for having captured any and all US servicemen in their country. In March of 1973, referring to themselves as the Lao Patriotic Front (LPF), the Pathet Lao announced that *"All US prisoners of war taken in Laos will be released by the Lao Communists in Laos and not by the Vietnamese in Hanoi."* At the time, there was a rising public furor in the US over the issue of POW/MIA's. Although the Cooper-Church Amendment had in essence rendered the US military impotent in enforcing the terms of the Paris Peace agreement, there was strong political pressure within the United States to do whatever was necessary to assure that POW/MIA's were entirely accounted for. In the meantime, returning U.S. POW's from Hanoi had asserted the identities of servicemen known to have been taken in Laos. Under scrutiny from an international press, Hanoi reluctantly admitted to nine American and one Canadian POW's actually captured in Laos and held in Hanoi. Ultimately, these were the only POW's from Laos ever to be released. They were in fact the final contingent of U.S. POW's to be returned, although here was a *"firm and unequivocal understanding that all American prisoners in Laos will be released within 60 days of the signing of the Vietnam agreement."* A cease-fire was signed between the Royal Laotian Government (RLG) and the Pathet Lao on February 21, 1973, in Vientiane, Laos. The agreement stated in writing that within 60 days after formation of a coalition government, all U.S. POW's would be released. This was a fall-back agreement the U.S. expected to reinforce the Paris Peace accords, which had involved only the signatories of North Vietnam and the United States. Henry Kissinger insisted that North Vietnam accept responsibility for Laotian U.S. POW's. But Le Duc Tho, the North Vietnamese delegate, absolutely refused, maintaining that Laos was a sovereign nation and as such would be responsible for their own POW contingent. In actuality, North Vietnam retained absolute influence over the Pathet Lao and secretly demanded that, despite Pathet Lao assurances to the contrary, US POW's in Laos be prevented from offering further testimony as to the nature of the Pathet Lao/NVA relationship.

In March of 1973, President Nixon ordered a halt to the final phase of U.S. troop withdrawal from South Vietnam because the Pathet Lao had not followed up on their promise to release Laotian US POW's. Within a day, the Four Party Joint Military Commission (FPJMC), over which Congressman Riley Hathoway had managed to acquire considerable influence, took the position that the nine acknowledged U.S. Laotian POW's would confirm the existence of others. This would mobilize considerable pressure to affect the release of all the rest. However, North Vietnam refused to release these nine (plus the one Canadian) unless the U.S. completed its total ground troop withdrawal on schedule. Nixon acquiesced.

The withdrawal of all U.S. ground troops from South Vietnam was completed on March 28, 1973. Despite the Paris Peace Accords that forbade mobilization of either NVA or U.S. troops, North Vietnam deployed 10 divisions throughout South Vietnam along with a continuous flow of supplies and troops moving through Laos along the Ho Chi Minh Trail. Unquestionably, North Vietnam violated virtually every major compliance issue of the Paris Peace Accords despite their international assurances to the contrary. Because of the Cooper-Church Amendment, there was virtually nothing the U.S. could do to enforce compliance. This suited U.S. politicos such as Congressman Hathoway just fine. Under pressure from the same U.S. political fraternity, which had advised President Lyndon Johnson into the war during the mid to late 60's, Ambassador Godley, U.S. Ambassador to Laos, reversed his position in Spring of 1973 regarding the balance of U.S. POW's in Laos. Ambassador Godley accepted the Pathet Lao position statement issued that spring that... "*All POW's captured in Laos have been released to suit the requirements of the American ambassador in Laos as well as the Paris Peace Accords.*" This became the official position of the United States government and was informally endorsed by the mainstream US press.

On March 29th, 1973, President Richard Nixon announced on national television, "*All of our POW's are on their way home*". On April 12th of the same year, Assistant Secretary of Defense Roger Shields announced that "*DOD (Department of Defense) had no specific knowledge indicating any U.S. personnel were still alive in and held prisoner in Southeast Asia.*" These two statements signaled closure to US liability in accounting for any further U.S. POW's under the Paris Peace Accords. In the end, any high-ranking U.S. military authorities retaining a contrary position about U.S. POW's in Laos were belittled and demeaned out of the service. No further reports on POW's in Laos were released before Congress and the issue became relegated to conspiracy theory. Congressman Riley Hathoway knew, of course, that it was all subterfuge. He had managed to acquire numerous intelligence papers issued under the direction of outgoing Admiral Thomas Moore, Chairman of the Joint Chiefs of Staff. Hathoway had accomplished this on the dual premise of sincerely wanting to know, while at the same time doing everything within his power to discredit Admiral Moore. To Hathoway, it was a simple confirmation of his political and personal victory in helping to "dismantle" the U.S. Vietnam era war machine as well as to punish its adherents. "*After all, every conflict requires... what was it Ambassador Williams had said? Oh yes, every conflict requires that a few 'forlorn hopes' be sacrificed for the greater good.*"

In 1975, all U.S. intelligence assets, via the CIA, were formally ordered to disengage from seeking further information on the status of U.S. POW's in Laos. This was done to avoid any embarrassing public disclosure over the startling revelations of Jerry Mooney, former Air Force/NSA analyst, who actually tracked the movements of surviving American POW's transferred from Laos to Vietnam and eventually, even in to Russia. After 1975, Congressman Riley Hathoway became the junkyard bulldog designate of Capitol Hill on issues surrounding U.S. POW/MIA's. Nonmainstream press reports continued to keep alive a simmering public interest on the issue. Highly respectable, retiring military personalities, such as Congressional Medal of Honor winner Fred "Zab" Zabitosky made compelling arguments before concerned communities within the United States. However, a powerful Washington elite public relations spin machine, in which Hathoway played a major role, quite effectively dispelled all such efforts. To the great shame of this nation, those lost in service, who lived on in captivity, were knowingly, maliciously, intentionally abandoned by culpable prelates of a profligate United States political propaganda apparatus.

Early 1977

Congressman Riley Hathoway had become a new Carter Administration spokesman for *"Washington's Official Position on the Question of American POW's in Laos."* Over the ensuing years since 1972, Congressman Hathoway was re-elected twice and by 1977, had set his sites on a Senatorial bid for the early 80's. While the rest of the world changed considerably during the previous five years, surprisingly little had changed in Washington DC. Over 90% of elected congressional seats remained occupied by the same personalities who filled them during what was now called euphemistically, "the Vietnam era." From Hathoway's perspective, Nixon had been duly punished for his recalcitrance during the conflict. Congressman Hathoway reveled over the Watergate hearings, using every opportunity to enthusiastically support the *"due process of due process"*, a quip he coined that gained popularity among some mainstream journalistic cliques. Hathoway knew, as did all the Washington elite, that Nixon's reproach during the Watergate hearings had very little to do with wire tapping or Oval Office tapes. What the term "Executive Abuse" really meant to the Washington elite was what they considered President Nixon's abuse of power in Southeast Asia, his willingness to employ measures running contrary to the terms of limited engagement dictated by the Johnson administration. To a great many of these Washington insiders, it was quite clear; Watergate was an opportunity to punish Richard Nixon for his prosecution of the Vietnam War.

After President Richard Nixon's resignation, the only thing to please Congressman Riley Hathoway even more were news clippings of the final U.S. embassy withdrawal in 1975. There was one in particular which he considered symbolic to the success of his efforts during the Vietnam era. In 1975, during the final hours, as the American military was being taught its just lessons about ambition and pride, a helicopter had been pushed over the side of an air craft carrier in order to make room for the burgeoning influx of those final, crowded heliborne refugees from Saigon. It was the type they called a "Huey Helicopter", one which had come to so symbolize the American presence in Southeast Asia. As it crashed into the sea alongside a crowded flattop carrier deck, Congressman Hathoway raised a toast to the television screen, celebrating what he considered to be a great personal victory. It was that image which sustained him as he went about various political expediencies arising out of this "Post" Vietnam era. He'd been very active in campaigning during both the Ford and Carter administrations and his efforts had not gone unrecognized by those of power and influence within the White House. Hathoway's outspoken candor on issues having to do with Southeast Asia earned him a place as subcommittee chairman on an advisory council to President Carter regarding the lingering issue of American POW's in Laos. In this position, Hathoway had access to all the old CIA files. While he would not admit it publicly, there could be little doubt about the credibility of data, which seemed to confirm that Hanoi had indeed cut a deal with the Pathet Lao regarding American POW's in Laos. Congressman Hathoway took it as his own personal charge to spin this confidential reality out of the

U.S. national conscience with official disavowal of surviving U.S. MIA's in Laos.

Monday February 21, 1977

It was another cold Monday night in Washington, DC. Congressman Riley Hathoway had just departed the Hill for his favorite unwinding place; a pub called O'Riley's just off Delaware Avenue and D Street. Prior to checking out of his office, he completed the mandatory routine of informing a member of the Secret Service where he was going and what he would be doing until returning to the Capitol the next morning. On the one hand, it rankled Hathoway that as a mere Congressman not presently holding any open chairmanship, he did not warrant a full time Secret Service agent. However, on the other hand, it did permit him the opportunity to do some discreet "socializing" without worrying about appearances before the Secret Service. For the last few weeks since Christmas holidays, Riley Hathoway had made a special effort to visit this pub on his way home from work every Monday and Wednesday. While bearing a facsimile of his namesake, it also offered him the chance to rub shoulders with generally cordial patrons. Of course, it probably also helped that he could on occasion get someone to pay for drinks all around over some issue of political prominence. The previous week, he had been extolling the issue of "...so called US POW's in Laos," when he noticed a tall, very attractive, blonde woman seated at the bar. She seemed riveted to his every word. Occasionally, as he made a particularly salient point, he would peripherally notice her nodding in silent agreement. On the previous Wednesday evening, he had been introduced to her by another regular pub-tender who could have been a lobbyist for some union. Toward the end of the evening, Hathoway had spoken with the blonde woman in semi-private conversation. Her name was Constance "Connie" Von Hagen.

She was a secretary for the new Rhodesian embassy there in Washington. Although she had some family who lived in Africa, she herself had grown up in Minneapolis. Basking in the glow of a fifth round of drinks, Connie confided to Congressman Hathoway that her own cousin had been captured in Laos. She felt that the cousin was probably dead and wished that her family could just get over the process of endless mourning and uncertainty about his fate. In his best politician's expression of concern, Riley Hathoway nodded sagely, absently realizing that all he had to do was listen as she poured out her heart to him. Their conversation ended that last Wednesday evening with his leaving the pub, just before midnight, sensing a growing chemistry between himself and the magnificent, vulnerable blonde. Over the five days that had passed since, he realized thoughts of her intruding on his musings more and more. He found himself looking forward with some trepidation, fearing that perhaps she might not be there during his next soiree at O'Riley's. However, he was not to be disappointed. As he entered the walnut accented Pub, she stood out like a dazzling light in the dim atmosphere. He went straight over to her, shaking off a couple of influence peddlers along the way. Riley Hathoway and Connie Von Hagen listed away much the rest of the evening talking and laughing and occasionally offering a polite repartee to someone seeking the Congressman's attention. Just after midnight, they mutually agreed to find a more private place in which to visit but, in the interests of public scrutiny, Riley suggested that he leave first after wishing her a very public good night all around. She should remain for another fifteen to twenty minutes, and then leave on her own. She scribbled down an address on a cocktail napkin, then wrapped it around a key and slipped it inconspicuously into his left hand. He promptly palmed it into his left trousers pocket.

After leaving the pub, Congressman Hathoway got into his automobile, a Lincoln Continental, and drove off in the direction of her address. He found it to be a townhouse located southeast of the beltway along Route 235, nearby Patuxent Navel Air Station. It was located in an upscale, middle class neighborhood of other, similar townhouses, most typical of homes for junior grade naval officers and their dependents. Riley Hathoway parked down the street at a discreet distance, not far from North Gate of the Naval Air Station. He walked back, two or three blocks, taking care to look for anyone who might be trailing him. His main concern was some zealot journalist, eager to write a yellow typeset about "Washington Insider trysts." However, there did not appear to be anyone out or about in the neighborhood at this hour. He had not seen any rearview mirror headlights for the last couple of miles into the neighborhood. Prior to leaving the city, he had telephoned home to tell his wife that he would be working late with a lobbyist who was a potential major campaigner for his future bid to the Senate. She understood. Riley had these late evening liaisons from time to time. It went with the job. She even believed some of them were legitimate.

Eventually, after walking past the townhouse and around the block, Congressman Hathoway made his way into a side alley that paralleled the side of the townhouse, again checking to assure himself that there was no evidence of a tail or journalist surveillance team. He fancied himself as being rather good at this game. It was not a particularly uncommon pastime among his Congressional colleagues. As he watched from the short distance, a small Ford Pinto pulled into the graded driveway in front of the townhouse. He observed from shadows of the adjoining alleyway as Connie Von Hagen got out of her automobile and walked somewhat guardedly to the doorstep. As she started fumbling around in her purse, evidently for a spare key, he stepped out of the shadows of the alley alongside the townhouse.

"I believe you are looking for this?" He said in his most charming come-to-the-rescue persona.

"Yes, as a matter of fact, I was just hoping I might have a spare," she replied, obviously relieved to see him.

He stepped forward, putting his hand on her shoulder as he reached around her and unlocked the door. The same key fit both doorknob and deadlock. He seemed to know this would be the case, almost as if he had opened similar doors many times. Together they walked into a darkened foyer. She turned to him and said, "I'm afraid I'm not very experienced at midnight rendezvous. I mean, I don't want you to get the idea that I do this sort of thing..."

He reached up with his hand, touching her lips and gently shaking his head. "Of course not. You come across to me as a very genuine person, I want you to know that," and with that, he kissed her full on the lips. She responded, but not with a great deal of intimacy. Clearly, she really *was* not experienced at this sort of thing. Well, that was just fine. He was experienced enough for them both. He knew very well how to play this fish. He held her with just enough tenderness to let her know that he was a respectful, caring man. He whispered in her ear, "Do you think we could have a nightcap?"

"Oh, of course! I'm so sorry. I'll get us something right away." She replied with a charming naiveté, suggesting that she was quite concerned about playing the proper hostess. She paused to put her coat in a hall closet, taking his as well and blocking it carefully on a wooden hanger before hanging it alongside her own. *"Yep,"* he thought, *"farmer's daughter for sure."*

She led him into a neat, apportioned living room, offering him a seat on the sofa. This he took as a good sign because there was also a single easy chair in the same room. She disappeared for a few minutes into the adjacent kitchen, returning with two Brandy snifters, filled to four fingers. He took the large, crystal glassware and swirled the golden brown liquor, savoring the smell of it in his most debonair way. Hathoway then sipped at it, knowing immediately that it was vintage brew, probably one she had saved up for some special occasion. Well, this was certainly a special occasion. *"After all,"* he thought, *"how often does the farmer's daughter get to make it with a Congressman?"* She also took a small sip at her own glass. In an effort to encourage her libation, he smiled at her with a look of true gusto over a fine brandy and proceeded to drink with as much aplomb as he could while still respecting the nature of a brandy snifter. This seemed to loosen her up some and she proceeded to drink more at ease. They began some light chitchat as she sat down next to him. "*All right, no need to hurry this. We have all the rest of tonight,*" he thought. He asked her about her family.

"Well," she replied, obviously warming to him, "I come from Minneapolis, Minnesota. My family is in lumber. In fact, my grandparents amassed quite a fortune in lumber and grain silos.

"Are you close to your family?" It was a standard leading question. Most often, such women had some kind of problem with a member of their family, often their father. This was a clear indication that they were searching for a father figure, and a dead certainty that they were seducible. He was, therefore just a bit surprised when she answered, "Oh, yes, we're all quite close. Living this far away from home, I miss them very much sometimes."

That made sense to Riley Hathoway. He would give her a chance to open up to him, he surmised, as he slipped his arm around her and let his own body meld into hers on the soft couch. She had been sitting quite upright and stiffly. To loosen her up, he drank more from his own glass. This encouraged a sip response from her. "So, who is your family favorite?"

"Aside from my parents, it was my grandmother," she replied without hesitation. "She died this last year and we all feel a great loss at her passing."

To this, Congressman Hathoway nodded empathetically. "I must be honest with you, Connie, I was not as close to my own grandparents as I would like to have been. It must be special to have such a warm and caring relationship. I can see why you would feel lost and alone at her passing."

"Certainly, I miss her. But there are others in the family with whom I stay in close touch. And, I must also now be honest with you Congressman…"

"Please, call me Riley."

"Very well, Riley. I feel rather badly that I have been somewhat deceptive with you."

"Really?" Hathoway replied, tickled over what this sweet innocent might possibly consider deceptive. "How so?" He was feeling much more relaxed now. This really was very good brandy. He had almost finished the snifter and would have to get her to refill them both.

"Well, for one thing, I'm not a blonde." She hung her head as she said this.

He smiled, but not too broadly. She carried a light scent of peroxide, which had tipped him off way back at the bar that she was one of a vast generation of young women vulnerable to a popular ad slogan of the time *"Is it true blonde's have more fun?"* Hmmm. He would have to convince her that indeed, blondes *did* have more fun.

"Connie, itsh not your bwonde hair that makes you so adractive to me..." He was really feeling this brandy. Maybe it would be better not to ask for a second glass.

"Actually, there is another confession I must make to you, Congressman Hathoway."

"Pleashe, my dear, call me Rileeee, uh huh, Rileee. Idsh really no so hard to shay. Let me hear you shay it shweetie pie, pucker up thosh pretty lips and shay Rileee."

"OK, Riley, my cousin, the one I told you about that was captured in Laos? Well, he actually managed to escape and make it back to the family."

"Well, thatsh wunnerful. But, Connie, Theywuz only two PeeYooW's that made it out of Laosh. Unless yur name ish Klussman or Dengler, I dun thnk...."

Gabriel McCarthy and Carmen Briant waited upstairs, in the guest bedroom of the townhouse. The place had been leased just three weeks prior in the name of Lieutenant JG R. Erickson. No one had slept there during the entire three weeks. Rather, furniture had been brought in and arranged to create the exact impression Congressman Hathoway was absorbing during his conscious moments here. The brandy from which Hathoway had partaken so willingly was laced with a stiff dose of Ketamine Hydrochloride. It would render him unconscious for about 15 minutes. Because of side effects with this particular drug, Hathoway would hallucinate about Miss Constance Von Hagen. At the same time, his twilight sleep would be carefully enhanced with a one-gram intramuscular injection of the same Ketamine, a general anesthetic agent, administered by Gabriel McCarthy. Briant and McCarthy came down upon hearing a key phrase spoken by Constance from the first floor living room below, "Are you sleeping well Congressman Hathoway?"

After administering the additional Ketamine and assuring a stable set of vital signs, Gabriel helped to gently place the grinning, somnolent Hathoway into a large trunk marked "Diplomatic Pouch" over a flag emblem of green, white and green with National Arms in the center of a white stripe. Although Rhodesia was still technically not recognized as an independent nation by many U.S. allies in 1977, it was simply considered political good manners to permit a pseudo diplomatic presence in Washington, DC. This was also done on the premise that perhaps U.S. influence might someday offer favorable advice in the ongoing dispute between the UK and its rebellious Rhodesian stepchild. For this reason, Rhodesian diplomatic aircraft were permitted access to limited US air bases, one of which being Patuxent Naval Air Station. Ron Winkle drove a Suburban station wagon around to the alleyway adjoining the townhouse. The trunk was loaded into the back and vehicle with passengers and trunk passed on into the nearby naval air base without being challenged beyond showing some diplomatic papers at North Gate, #1 entrance. This same vehicle had been passing through the same gate every early morning now for over three weeks. The Naval Security Officer on duty did not find its conveyance to be at all unusual.

Fueled and awaiting cargo delivery, an Electric Canberra T4 sat warming its engines on a runway service ramp located within Patuxent NAS. This also was rather routine, as the same aircraft had been serviced here on a regular basis since just after the first of the year. No one noticed anything unusual about the diplomatic trunk with several-screened ventilation portals constructed into the sides, concealed behind carrying handles. Once on board, the trunk would be opened and the still unconscious, grinning stowaway strapped in to a more comfortable position on canvas bench seats paralleling the side of the cargo bay. Normally, the waist of this type of aircraft is filled with racks set over bomb bay doors. However, this particular aircraft had sealed all but one of its bomb bays, converting the rest of the aircraft into a, tubular cargo area, about 20 feet in diameter. The aircraft was manifested to one Axel Bothnerby Haskell, a high ranking official of the new Rhodesian government.

There was nothing in life that Axel Bothnerby Haskell cared about more than his son. Never having remarried after the death of his beloved Zula, Axel split himself between service to country and doing what he could to advantage the life of his son. Not having been present when Kip returned from Laos was perhaps the second greatest pain that Axel had endured in his life. Over the ensuing years, Axel followed his son's recovery both close up and from a distance. He was proud that Kip Haskell was able to stand on his own in recovering and getting on with his life. The boy had pleased everyone by going back to college and doing very well academically. Needless to say, all were pleased to learn of his application and subsequent acceptance to law school. Perhaps the greatest compliment to Kip had come in the form of his being named executor by his grandmother, a move that most of the rest of the Von Hagen clan had accepted very well.

Following the reunion of A-321 that previous December, Kip came to his father with an operations plan. Axel was well aware of circumstances surrounding the failed mission to which his son had been assigned. He had long considered Congressman Riley Hathoway most directly responsible for the mutilation of his boy. When Kip proposed the mission plan, Hathoway was quite willing to comply, although with some reservations: "Why not just kill the bloody traitor and get it over with?"

"Father, that wouldn't serve our purposes. There are as yet things which we all have to inquire about concerning the whys' and wherefores' of Operation Fisherman."

"Fine, then just cut it out of him and dump his worthless carcass where it will never be found."

"In this instance, it will serve us all much better if we keep him alive."

"Well, I can hardly agree on that count, but I respect the collective resolve of your group. If this is what you have all decided, I will do what I can to help. Understand, however, that although you may use whatever Rhodesian assets I can offer under my command, if this Hathoway is to go on living, he must never know Rhodesia has played any part in this. If he should find out, even by mistake, I shall have to insist that he be terminated and good riddance."

"Father, we've gone to extraordinary measures in our operations plan to prevent any disclosure of assets during execution of the mission. That's all I can offer you."

Axel Haskell knew that would have to be enough. As he himself was a recognizable Rhodesian emissary, he could not make himself visible in any way to the Congressman. He would personally supervise certain portions of the operation to assure that when the U.S. Secret Service came sniffing around, the chain of evidence would be unlinked in several places. The rented townhouse would be sterilized under his personal supervision. Within twelve hours, the domicile would be empty, without a stick of furniture or unwiped surface. Constance Von Hagen did indeed work for the Rhodesian embassy. That was about as close as anyone could foreseeably get to a connection with Rhodesia. She would undoubtedly be questioned, probably at her home, located not far from the embassy inside the beltway of Washington DC. Her verbal recollection of the evening would indicate that she had left O'Riley's pub about 15-20 minutes after the missing Congressman departed. She then went directly home in her Chevrolet Vega. She had serviced the vehicle just the week before at a local service station and an odometer reading taken at that time would coincide with expected travel distances in and around her place of employment and home, should anyone snoop into that much detail. She lived alone, but there was a new fangled telephone security system keypad on her apartment that had been activated, approximately 30 minutes after Congressman Hathoway would be reported leaving the Pub. She would rearm the alarm the next morning in the presence of a friend on her way to work. Between setting and rearming the alarm, any part of her apartment to break seal over a door or window would have been detected at the security company during the night. In fact, she would spend the rest of the night monitoring a telephone relay should anyone call her apartment, which no one did. The next morning, she would wait on the doorstep, disarming, then rearming the keypad alarm system when her friend arrived to carpool just as they did every Tuesday morning.

U.S. mainstream press reports picked up on the story about three days later when the Secret Service issued a statement that Congressman Riley Hathoway was missing, having last been seen at a local Washington tavern. His automobile was never found and his disappearance would remain an unsolved mystery with the Secret Service who went on to investigate the matter for many years, chasing after numerous conspiracy theories. The following Fall of 1977, an interim election would be held for Hathoway's home district in New England. A candidate from the alternative party would be elected in his stead. Because missing persons can not be declared legally dead for at least seven years, Mrs. Hathoway would have to legally divorce her vacated husband the following year in order to re-marry another gentleman, a Secret Service agent, whom she would become acquainted with during the investigation. For all intents and purposes, it would seem as though New England U.S. Congressional representative, Riley Hathoway, had dropped off the face of the earth.

Mid Evening, February 22, 1977

Congressman Riley Hathoway groaned as he attempted to rise up from stiff insensibility. The first thing he became aware of was a pasty, bitter taste in his mouth. As awareness came back in degrees, he gradually took notice of his posture. He was seated upright on a hard-bottomed dais. His arms were bound to his sides by a length of flat, yellow nylon chord. As his eyes focused on the bright color, he realized that he was leaning back against a pack like structure. From the T-10 parachute pack into which he was harnessed, a static line nylon chord was led to form several wraps around his midsection before it ended at a 70 pound test string tied into the lowermost loops encircling his arms. From the string, the static line was snap linked up into an overhead fixture. As the unfamiliar posture and noisy surrounding flooded his rising consciousness, he became aware that he was dressed strangely. His Philip St. John pinstripe business suit had been replaced with a pair of slant pocket, camouflage pattern NATO issue jungle fatigues. He also became aware of the unusual feeling of Panama soled jungle boots laced up over his feet and ankles.

Riley Hathoway squinted as he looked around. Someone came forward to place on Hathoway's face a pair of glasses, which were secured around his head with an elastic strap. He normally wore hard contact lenses. Evidently, they had been removed during his sedation. Hathoway was aware of someone dressed in similar style fatigues, but colored in plain olive drab, instead of the variegated camouflage pattern. Whoever had placed the glasses on him was reaching around to secure the plastic horn rims on an elastic band extending around the back of Hathoway's head, snugly looped into the eyeglass arms just behind both ears. As the attendant finished and stepped back, Hathoway became aware that he was sitting in an aircraft cargo bay. Loud engine sounds along with a feeling of motion lent to the sense that they were airborne.

"Who are you? What do you want from me? Do you know who I am?" Several seconds passed in silence as Hathoway became slowly more cognizant. "I am a senior elected official of the United States government. My government will most certainly want to negotiate with you. What do you want?"

Standing before him, shadowed by several ambient red filtered backlights, stood five men, one of whom, now standing in the center of the group, had just put on Hathoway's glasses. As features came into focus, Riley Hathoway saw that one of the men was only standing on one leg. Another was missing part of his left arm. Abstruse facial features began to form in shadows against the reddish backlit fuselage; Hathoway saw that one of the men had an unusual, scarred, shiney facial continence with an unnaturally receded hairline, and a puckered scar on his throat. Hathoway gasped slightly as he visualized an empty right eye socket on the fourth man. They all five wore OD jungle fatigues and green berets, standing before him in a sort of semicircle encompassing the tubular bulkhead from one side to the other. The lower limb amputee leaned into the port side skin of the aircraft, facing back towards Hathoway on a single left leg. The right leg was gone from above the knee. The one armed man was leaning against his semi-armless shoulder into the starboard side of the aircraft, also facing sternward, holding on with his right hand to an overhead grip. The only man in the group who appeared to be physically intact, the one who had helped with the eyeglasses, stood center-stage with "One Eye" on his immediate right and "Scar-Face" on his immediate left.

"Who are you people? You have to identify yourselves in order for us to communicate. What do I call you?"

The man in the center spoke for the group. "You can call us MIA's if you would like, sir."

"What? MIA's? MIA's from where?"

"MIA's from Laos, sir."

"Look, if this is some kind of inquisition, I know that only two MIA's ever got out of Laos. All the rest were killed during the Vietnam conflict. I'm sorry for your lost comrades, but there's nothing I can do to bring back the dead."

"We are all certainly well aware of that, sir. Actually, this panel has been convened for the purpose of holding trial over war crimes which you are alleged to have committed against the people of Laos, Vietnam and the United States."

"War crimes? What are you saying? If you want to hold someone responsible for war crimes, look to the immediate leaders who put you in those uniforms!"

"Most of those immediate leaders are either dead or missing, sir. Dead or missing because of you."

"How can that be? I never served in the military. I've never even served on the Armed Forces Congressional Committee. I was against our involvement in Vietnam!"

"While your opposition to the Vietnam war is duly noted during the later years, sir, your record doesn't speak out much against the war back in the early to mid Sixties, it would seem."

"Well, we were all part of the Johnson era then. Everyone was pursuing Kennedy's vision of Camelot. But it became clear with the prosecution of the war that we couldn't win. I tried to make that clear to the Nixon administration. I even visited South Vietnam personally to see what I could do to help resolve the war."

"Yes, sir, we would like to discuss that more. But for now, let me ask you if you would like something to drink or eat? If you need to urinate, we have a urinal available for you. We have all used them ourselves and are quite willing to help you if you require."

"Oh, I get it. You all are part of some disenfranchised veteran's group. Well, I sympathize with your situation. My record will show that I have supported the Veteran's Administration on several occasions," Hathoway lied. A sudden realization came to him, something he had learned during one of the security briefings the Secret Service gives periodically to high-ranking officials about hostage behavior. He suddenly looked away, making an exaggerated effort not to gaze up at them.

"Look I haven't really seen any of your faces very well. Just blindfold me now, if you like. I really couldn't identify any of you later. Please, you don't need to let me see you at all."

"There is nothing to fear, sir. We are not concerned about your being able to identify us."

"Look, you don't have to kill me! We can negotiate. My government will give you anything you wish. But, if you kill me, you and your cause will never have any resolution!"

"Sir, we do not intend to kill you. While in our care, you will not be physically harmed in any way. I promise you that."

"But, you must know that if I can identify you, eventually, there is no place on this planet in which you can hide. If I'm released to civil authorities anywhere, they will return me to the U.S. federal government. I promise you that if you will not harm me, I will not identify you."

"Sir, that's a lie and we all know it. However, it doesn't matter. We actually want you to return to the U.S. Federal Government. We want you to report this abduction and when you do so, we are all willing to come forward without coercion to accept our individual responsibility for this action."

Hathoway relaxed a bit in his seat. If that was true, that they were all indeed principled lunatics, then, his chances for surviving this ordeal were very good.

"Well, then, what do you want of me? When will you release me?"

"We will ask you some questions. We expect honest answers. We will record our conversation and this recording will be placed in a safety deposit box located in Boston, Massachusetts. You may notice that a small number has been tattooed onto your inner left forearm. That number identifies the safety deposit box, which you will be able to access with that number. It will contain the entire transcript of this proceeding."

Hathoway noticed for the first time, a stinging spot on the inner fleshy portion of his left arm, which was bound to his side by the yellow, nylon static line chord. With the sensation, he knew that what they were saying was true. Somehow, it gave him courage to realize that they were indeed dedicated fanatics with some virtual commitment to being forthright with him.

"Well, then, for the record, my name is Congressman Riley Hathoway. Will you identify yourselves for the record?"

"We will identify ourselves collectively as the sole survivors of Operation Fisherman."

"Operation Fisherman? But, that cannot be. The men who were deployed on Operation Fisherman were all killed in action."

"We are in fact the only survivors out of approximately thirty five hundred men, women, and children involved with Operation Fisherman who were indeed killed in action... thanks to you, Congressman Hathoway."

Hathoway broke out into a cold sweat. Again, he knew that they were being absolutely forthright with him.

"Look, it wasn't me. It was a military appointee from my district, a Colonel Schultz. He was the one who cut off your assets. What he did was abominable. He abandoned you all up there in those mountains. I'm aware of your case, but I had nothing to do with it, really. I hardly knew Schultz. He was merely a constituent from my precinct and I offered him my congratulations on his commission, as I did with all prominent U.S. military officers from my district."

At this point, the armless man to Hathoway's far right stepped forward, reaching with his one hand down into a satchel of papers secured to a canvas bench along the side of the aircraft.

"I have here sir, affidavits of communication between yourself and Colonel Julius Schultz. In addition, there are long distance telephone billing statements between your office and the office of Colonel Shultz in Special Air Operations command headquarters, Da Nang, South Vietnam. These indicate that your office was in regular communication with Colonel Shultz. Notations from Colonel Schultz's own personal effects indicate that he briefed you regularly about Operation Fisherman and that in fact, he expected to be promoted to brigadier as a direct result of your influence with Congress."

Hathoway recognized the affidavits and had no doubt they were authentic.

"Well, all right, I may have communicated with him from time to time. But all the decisions with respect to Operation Fisherman were his alone; I did not in any way interfere with that particular mission which, as I understood, was only one of many command responsibilities supervised by Colonel Schultz. You are of course aware that he sadly took his own life as a result of letting himself become overwhelmed with the responsibilities of command."

At that point, the one armed man shook his head and moved back to his place against the starboard bulkhead. Now, the scarfaced one came forward, walking over to another satchel secured on the canvas bench. He produced a Xerox copy of a letter addressed to the attention of General Duong Anh Minh. It instructed Brigadier General Dwight Elkins to cooperate with delegates from the office of General Minh in disclosing any and all technical information regarding an electronic surveillance system referred to by the codename of "Bugeyes".

"Sir, this is a copy of a document on your own congressional letterhead, over your personal signature. It instructs General Dwight Elkins to comply with disclosure of a classified surveillance system. We have other documents which will indicate that because General Elkins refused to cooperate with you, he was summarily relieved of his command and became the subject of a congressional investigation over security breech and possible violation of the Cooper-Church Amendment. All of these documents suggest that you did everything within your power of influence to discredit General Elkins, even though he was eventually exonerated. It would appear that you took upon yourself a deep seated personal prejudice against General Elkins."

"Oh, I get it now! This whole thing, the aircraft, the military garb, it's all a vendetta for General Elkins, is that it?" Hathoway replied with sarcasm borne of rising confidence in his own longevity.

"No sir, in fact, General Elkins knows nothing about this. He is no longer on active duty. Although he cleared his name entirely over this matter, your smear campaign effectively ended his career. The significance of General Elkins in all this is that you had him removed from his post which prevented him from protecting the mission assets of Operation Fisherman, something General Elkins was uniquely qualified to do."

"Look, this is much more complicated than you all could possibly begin to understand."

"We have time, sir. Please, take as long as you wish and explain what you consider to be your purpose in compromising a critical US military mission during time of war."

"War? But it wasn't a war at all! It was a police action, remember?"

"Is that what you considered it sir? A 'police action'? Should a police action cost the lives of 57,000 Americans, not to mention many more innocent indigenous citizens of Southeast Asia? If it was a police action, as you say, then did you sanction failure on the part of your designated police force?"

Hathoway found his fear giving way to indignation as he answered, "All right then, call it a war; an immoral war if you will."

"And who was ultimately responsible for our being involved in this so called 'immoral' war?"

"Why, your military leaders were responsible."

"Really? So, did our military leaders act without authority from Congress?"

"Well, of course not. We're not a military dictatorship."

"Then, was Congress responsible for the war, sir?"

"Nixon was responsible for... well, the President of the United States; Nixon and I suppose Johnson and Kennedy before him were also responsible."

"With or without Congress, sir?"

"Look, you know very well that Congress played an integral role in funding and authorizing military intervention in Vietnam. But, Congress is the people of the United States. Therefore, it was the people of the United States, who were responsible for seating Congress and electing the Presidents who were responsible for the war."

"So, you said previously that you represent the people of the United States. You are an elected representative of the people. You speak for the people of your district. Doesn't that mean you were in large measure responsible for the Vietnam War with respect to your district, sir?"

"I tried to get us out of the Vietnam conflict. I went to Southeast Asia and spoke personally with President Thieu. I worked to cut off funding for the U.S. military to prevent our going on with a futile endeavor over there. If Johnson couldn't win the thing, Nixon certainly wasn't going to!"

"Didn't you also see to it that Operation Fisherman would be shut down?"

"Yes! Yes I did! It was an illegal operation that had no business going on in the first place! If it had been successful, we might have been dragged back into Southeast Asia over nothing more than some damn Montagnard issue. There! Is that what you wanted me to say? Yes, I did everything within my power to terminate Operation Fisherman!"

"And what of the American advisors left behind, not to mention the innocent Montagnard Laotian civilians? You know that the Cooper-Church Amendment did not forbid US advisors working with Laotian citizens. Operation Fisherman was entirely legitimate."

"Well, not by my reckoning it wasn't."

"So, you unilaterally decided to hinder prosecution of a war involving the commitment of your countrymen based on your own decision of what was right and what was not. How do you define treason, sir?"

"That's ridiculous! If you defined what I did as treason, you'd have to indict every war protestor that ever spoke out against Vietnam."

"But, speaking out against Vietnam, and interfering with US military conduct during the prosecution of the war are two different things, wouldn't you agree?"

"Look, I don't have to agree about anything here! This is not a legitimate courtroom. You people are not qualified to judge my actions during that period. I did what I deemed best as a representative of the people of the United States."

"We are not qualified? Do you see evidence of physical wounds suffered by the men standing in front of you? If we are not qualified to judge your actions, sir, who is?"

Riley Hathoway could not answer and remained without retort to this last comment.

"One last thing and we will conclude this inquiry, sir. Why do you deny the existence of surviving US Laotian POW's?"

"Because the last thing we need as a country right now is something to reopen the old wounds. It's better to sacrifice a few pawns than cause the entire nation to suffer on over some moot issue."

"Then, you acknowledge that there are surviving US POW's in Laos, Congressman?"

"I have no way of knowing that for sure, nor do the American people. My official position is that there are no surviving US POW's in Laos, and unless it can be proven beyond any doubt that there are, it's useless to pursue the issue."

"Very well, sir."

With that, the five men standing before Congressman Hathoway moved backward within the bay, toward the front of the aircraft. One of them, the one missing an arm went up into the forward cabin and spoke with the pilots, returned back and said something to the middle spokesman once again. Hathoway observed the group huddle for a moment, then turn to face him once again. Hathoway looked to the same man who had been addressing him throughout most of the verbal exchange. Hathoway spoke up.

"What do I call you? Why, why are you doing this to me?"

The tall man in the center turned to his left, making a hand motion, which resulted in a sudden mechanical change within the aircraft. To his astonishment, Congressman Hathoway became aware of two large doors that he had been sitting over as they opened in clamshell fashion below him. There was a swirl of wind and noise as the aircraft opened its belly to the outside environment. His ears popped as Hathoway suddenly realized that they must be only a couple thousand feet off the ground. It was dark below, and aside from the reddish night-light interior, the aircraft was without external lights. Hathoway was now suspended over an open bomb bay. The dais he had been seated upon was in fact a residual bomb rack framework. The sudden realization of what was about to happen flooded over him, striking terror and fear into his mind, numbing his awareness so that he only vaguely heard the shouted reply.

"Keep your feet and knees together, Congressman. When they ask you, Congressman, you may say that *Bac Si* sent you. If they ask you why, you may answer, *De Oppresso Liber!*"

With that, there was a sudden loud clanking sound, and the platform upon which Congressman Hathoway was seated dropped away beneath him. As it did so, he fell to the length of the yellow static line, being checked momentarily as the 70 pound test line strained, then snapped. Hathoway was aware of the yellow static line unraveling around him as he fell downward, into the night below. There was a terrible momentary sense of falling and spinning in the slipstream before he was jerked suddenly upright as the main parachute drogged out of its deployment bag. Then came an awareness of slowing and finally, a strange sense of freedom as his unbound arms came up without hesitation, grasping the taut risers suspended below a full, darkly silhouetted canopy above, under a quarter crescent moon. Hathoway gazed up dazedly at the full parachute above him as the noise and confusion of the aircraft wafted away. He blandly descended down, down onto the Laotian plain spread out below him with a mix of jungle and mountain to the west and a tall, flat topped mountain, crowned with a sort of dented dunces cap peak off to the east, northeast.

CPSIA information can be obtained at www.ICGtesting.com
Printed in the USA
BVOW03s1121070214

344261BV00014B/307/P